Set the Night on Fire

Also by Laura Trentham

THE FALCON FOOTBALL SERIES

Slow and Steady Rush

Caught Up in the Touch

Melting into You

THE COTTONBLOOM SERIES

Kiss Me That Way

Then He Kissed Me

Till I Kissed You

Candy Cane Christmas (novella)

Light Up the Night (novella)

Leave the Night On

When the Stars Come Out

Set the Night on Fire

LAURA TRENTHAM

St. Martin's Paperbacks

This is a work of fiction. All of the characters, organizations, and events portrayed in this novel are either products of the author's imagination or are used fictitiously.

SET THE NIGHT ON FIRE

Copyright © 2018 by Laura Trentham.

For information address St. Martin's Press, 175 Fifth Avenue, New York, NY 10010.

ISBN: 978-1-250-13130-0

Our books may be purchased in bulk for promotional, educational, or business use. Please contact your local bookseller or the Macmillan Corporate and Premium Sales Department at 1-800-221-7945, ext. 5442, or by e-mail at MacmillanSpecialMarkets@macmillan.com.

Printed in the United States of America

St. Martin's Paperbacks edition / August 2018

St. Martin's Paperbacks are published by St. Martin's Press, 175 Fifth Avenue, New York, NY 10010.

10 9 8 7 6 5 4 3 2 1

Chapter One

Ella Boudreaux drove past Abbott Brothers Garage and Restoration instead of pulling into the parking lot and marching inside like the part owner she was. She wasn't scared exactly. More like slightly nervous about her reception.

Lies. Her stomach was ready to turn itself inside out. After all, she'd unwittingly performed a hostile takeover of twenty-five percent of the garage. Ford had made it sound like buying his stake would be doing his family a favor. The three other Abbott brothers had not viewed her buyout as a favor but as an act of war.

Especially Mack Abbott, the de facto leader. The oddity of a well-off society divorcée buying into a car garage and restoration business wasn't lost on her, but the opportunity had fired some deep well of sentimentality she'd thought had been slashed and burned by her divorce.

She stopped the car on the shoulder of the narrow parish road, the Abbott Brothers sign still visible in her rearview mirror. The coward's voice in her head urged her to leave the garage in her rearview and have Andrew Tarwater negotiate a sale back to Mack Abbott. She silenced the dissenting voice with her sometimes-faked bravado. "Fake it until you make it" wasn't just a quaint saying, it was her life motto. She was going to march into the garage and prove she could be an asset.

Would they judge her on her car? She squeezed the steering wheel of the small blue convertible. It wasn't her style, but it was sexy and expensive and had annoyed her ex-husband, Trevor, which had been as good a reason as any to buy it after the divorce.

Since moving to Cottonbloom, people had assumed she was living off her divorce settlement, and she hadn't done anything to dissuade the misconception. Let them under-estimate her like her ex-husband had.

The truth was she had taken a cut of the business she had built with Trevor and formed Magnolia Investments. She was buying up promising real estate around Cotton-bloom. Her above-average instincts coupled with her methodical research meant she rarely took a loss.

She'd stayed below the radar, using a young, hungry, discreet lawyer to close deals. The last thing she needed was her ex to catch wind of her new venture and to inter-fere. Negotiating when no one knew her gender was sim-pler and faster. Dodging all the "honeys" and "sugars" and infiltrating the south Mississippi good-old-boys' network would take time and proven successes.

The garage was different. Personal. Instead of taking on a silent investor role and flipping for a profit, she wanted to get her hands dirty. Her brother had taught her that any-thing meaningful required work, and she wanted to make him proud—even if he wasn't there to see it. His passion had been cars, and the hours she'd spent shadowing him as a kid had affected her. Although at the moment, she worried her nostalgia had affected her sanity.

She whipped her car around, the tires spinning on the gravel on the shoulder, and headed back toward the garage, parking next to a big black truck that could squash her little convertible like a no-seem-um.

Her hands trembled. While hard work might not scare her off, she was a teensy, tiny bit afraid of facing Mack Abbott. Not only was he physically intimidating, but his dark eyes could cut a person to ribbons.

She slipped out of her car and smoothed her gray high-waisted pencil skirt and retucked her white blouse. The red pearl-buttoned sweater she wore did little to protect her from the bite of the March breeze.

In case anyone was watching, she pasted on a smile flavored with more than a little bit of "I don't give a damn what you think of me." It was a smile she'd perfected since leaving her childhood home in the middle of nowhere, Mississippi, and it had served her well.

She threw open the customer door and was hit by a wall of noise. Sparks arced from a corner where an Abbott grinded down a piece of metal. His coveralls and safety mask made identification impossible, although he wasn't as big as she remembered Mack being. In another corner, another brother welded, and she averted her eyes from the snapping light. He too was concealed by a mask.

That left the third Abbott on a skid tucked under a jacked-up cherry red Datsun 240Z. Ella touched her fingertips against the cement-block wall to ground herself in the here and now. She'd sat on a worktable when she was a kid and watched her brother fix up a car exactly like it, down to the same color.

Her heart rate picked up like goosing a gas pedal even though her head accepted the fact that the man underneath the car wasn't her brother. Yet, could the car be an omen?

Only the man's jeans and work boots were visible. She cleared her throat, but it sounded like a pebble falling into a raging waterfall. She stood there for several minutes without anyone noticing her. Honestly, she had expected to walk in and spark a fight, not be ignored.

The wait sent a nervous ball ricocheting around her stomach, setting world records in how high and fast it bounced. She felt physically ill.

She nudged the leg of the man under the car with the toe of her red high heel and could only hope it was one of the twins and not Mack. While they might not like the situation, they didn't seem as volatile as Mack.

The man didn't move. She dropped to a crouch and peeked under the car. The man's face was obscured by shadows and pipes. He twirled a socket wrench at his hip, not putting it to use as if he were deep in thought. His blue-and-green flannel shirt was untucked, the sleeves rolled up almost to his elbows.

It was a broad hand with calluses and visible tendons and an underlying grace highlighted by the economy of his movement. His forearm was muscular and exuded raw power. Awareness of danger tinged with something she couldn't identify streaked through her.

Her impulse trumped her common sense, and she touched his arm. Before she could register more than a sprinkling of dark hair and warm skin, the man shot out from under the car on the skid. Surprise sent her reeling back. She teetered on her heels, unable to regain her balance, and plopped on her butt.

Of course, the man under the car with the pornographic forearm was Mack Abbott. If she had to confront him first, she'd want to do it in his office, calm and cool and confident. Instead, she was on her butt in the middle of his garage with her skirt riding up and no graceful way to rise without giving him an eyeful.

He was still lying back on the skid with a direct line of sight up her legs. She pressed her knees together. Slowly, he sat up and leaned toward her. Even sitting, he loomed over her like a hawk on the hunt. Unfortunately, she was the mouse. Her muscles tensed and trembled, and she forced herself to relax before she gave away her nerves.

"What the hell are you doing on your ass in *my* garage, Ms. Boudreaux?"

She responded to his attempted intimidation the way she had since her kindergarten teacher had whispered a soul-withering question about her family in her ear while she'd traced her letters—with a knee-jerk sass that got her in trouble.

"Not entirely yours, Mr. Abbott." It was the wrong thing to say.

He stood. An anger-fueled energy threatened to burst out of him, like the Hulk. The grinding noise had ceased, leaving an eerie silence. Her attention didn't waver from Mack and the threat he presented.

She remained on her butt, unsure what he planned to do and how she would react. Men were unpredictable creatures, some more prone to violence than others and with no guessing the outcome from the way they looked or how much money they had in their bank account.

His eyes narrowed on her, his mouth in a grim frown. He raised his fisted hand, uncurled it, and held it out in offering. She stared at it for a long moment, slightly disbelieving. His palm was scored with grease.

"Too dirty for your highness?" His voice was rife with sarcasm and disgust.

Before he could pull away, she slipped her hand into his. The dirt and grease didn't bother her in the least. That Mack assumed they did bothered her more than she cared to examine at the moment.

His hand engulfed hers. A heat wave traveled up her arm and into her face as a blush. He hauled her to her feet with little effort and waited until she quit teetering on her heels before he let go. She had to berate her brain to quit clinging to him.

Standing didn't improve the situation. He still loomed over her with a stormy expression in his eyes. Eyes that weren't dark at all, but a swirl of blues and greens and browns with a golden circle outlining his pupils, highlighted by the sunbeams cutting through the windows in the bay doors.

Everything else about him was dark, though, from the heavy brows shadowing his unexpectedly lovely, complicated eyes to the dark beard covering his face. His hair was a mixture of dark browns and waved a little at his collar and over his forehead.

But, most especially, the invisible yoke around his shoulders was dark. Dark and heavy and burdensome.

"What do you want, Ms. Boudreaux?"

"I want . . . I want . . ." She blinked and forced her eyes away from his. "I want you to call me Ella. Since we're going to be working together."

He took a step back as if she'd physically shoved him, even though she was pretty sure if she'd tried it would have been like moving a two-ton boulder. His gaze roved down and back up to her face. Not in a sexual way, but in an "am I being punked?" kind of way.

"You planning to slide under a car and work a wrench in that getup?"

"Of course not. Don't be silly." Her skirt and pearl-buttoned sweater felt more ridiculous the longer she stood there. She should have worn jeans and a T-shirt, but that wasn't the professional first impression she'd wanted to make.

"Look around you. This is a garage, Ms. Boudreaux. It's grease and metal and hard work. Are you going to pull your weight?"

"Not under the hood of a car."

"Then we don't have anything to discuss. Why don't you run along to your riverside mansion and paint your nails or something." He crossed his arms and chucked his chin toward the door.

Did he intimidate her? A little, but now she was starting to get pissed. Paint her mother-flipping nails? She had a two-hundred-thousand-dollar real-estate deal to close when she got home. "I think not. Unless I'm mistaken, I own as much of this garage as you do, Mr. Abbott."

She was dimly aware that the noise of work had ceased. An old rock song played on in the background, its upbeat guitar riffs at odds with the tension ratcheting tighter like an over-torqued nut.

A door in the back of the shop opened and a person in a baseball cap stepped through. Her figure had a hint of female curves under the coveralls and brown hair curled at the edge of the cap. Ella stared over Mack's shoulder at her. An employee?

A ball of black-and-white hair streaked in her periphery, and Ella gave a little scream. A dog. Friendly or menacing? Fear was like a blanket thrown over her head, leaving her in the dark. It was all she could focus on. This dog whose intent was unknown.

It was coming at her, teeth barred. Animals could sense fear, couldn't they? She should stand her ground, yet her feet were on the retreat. Her heel hit something metal and heavy. It didn't give, but her body did. She windmilled her arms, but only managed to slow her fall not stop it. For the second time in less than five minutes, she was on her butt in front of Mack Abbott.

The dog pounced, its paws on her chest driving her backward. Would it bite her? She cringed back and closed her eyes, the nightmare of getting rabies shots or plastic surgery flashing through her addled mind.

A rough tongue went up the side of her face, accompanied

by warm, panty breaths. She cracked her eyes open. The dog gave her another lick. Ella swore it looked like it was smiling. Was it getting a taste before it took a bite?

"River! Bad dog. Get over here." The girl in coveralls tugged at the dog's collar, but it stood its ground, focused on Ella's face.

Ella swept her forearm over its legs, pushed the hairy devil off her, and scrambled backward like a crab until her back hit the cool cement wall.

"All Along the Watchtower" started playing in the background as the Abbott brothers gathered in a semicircle around her.

The girl in the hat and coveralls squatted next to the dog and held on to its collar. "I'm so sorry, Ms. Boudreaux. River is not usually so energetic with strangers. She must like you." She laughed, but it was an uncomfortable sound.

Ella smoothed her hands down her skirt and tugged at the hem. Now that she could see the dog, the threat level ramped down, but the blast of fear left her trembling. River was shaggy and harmless looking, except for her teeth. Her black-and-white face might even be cute if you were into dogs with huge canines. Which she wasn't. Obviously. She'd exposed a weakness to Mack Abbott, and the damage needed to be minimized.

She smiled when she really wanted to lock herself in her car and cry. Putting on a "face" was something she'd gotten good at through necessity. "I guess bacon-scented perfume was a poor choice this morning." If her voice was less lighthearted and quavered more than she wished, she chalked it up to being out of practice.

She rose with as much grace as she could muster under the circumstances. The dog lunged toward her with a bark and a lolling tongue. Ella pressed into the wall, wishing she was on the other side.

The girl tugged the dog by the collar, led it to a side

door, and shoved it outside. Ella took a deep breath. Not that she was comfortable facing a testosterone-hardened wall of Abbotts, but at least they wouldn't take a bite out of her. Probably. Mack's face was blank, but she could imagine he had a plan to capitalize on her epic fail.

"I'm so sorry about River. She's very friendly though. Doesn't bite; only licks you into submission." The girl whipped her hat off and ran a hand through thick chestnut hair that was at an awkward stage between short and shoulder length.

The girl shuffled closer. No, not a girl, but a woman. Younger than Ella, but only by a few years. And she was pretty. Very pretty. A woman that pretty didn't work with three men and not attract them. Ella understood from a too-young age how men manipulated and wielded power.

Mack stepped forward to stand at the woman's side. Were they involved? They looked good together and had a lot in common, no doubt. Ella's smile felt like a caved-in soufflé.

"I'll pay to have your blouse cleaned." The woman stared at Ella's chest.

Dirty dog prints dotted the front of her white blouse. Ella tried to brush them off but only managed to transfer grease from her hands to her shirt. Black streaks highlighted both breasts. She needed to retreat and regroup.

"I've got some wipes in my office. Come on in. We need to talk." Mack turned on his heel and walked away, expecting her to follow. She hesitated. The moment felt like a skirmish in their battle of wills.

The woman gave her a tight, apologetic smile. "Send me the bill. Seriously."

"Sure." Ella nodded, though she knew she wouldn't. The blouse was an expensive remnant from her failed marriage. She wouldn't replace it.

Mack had propped his shoulder against the jamb of the

door, his bulk filling the doorframe. Although a part of her wanted to stick her tongue out as she stalked past him to her car, her practical, mature side decided to concede. Just this once. She needed to establish the fact she wasn't going away.

She ambled over, making sure to swing her hips. The grease and paw prints decorating her chest dented her air of brazen defiance. He didn't immediately move to allow her inside his office, and a game of chicken commenced.

She slowed but didn't stop. He shifted like a door opening when she was inches from his chest. She sidestepped by him, so close his heat and scent enveloped her. He smelled of honest work and cars. Potent, painful memories rushed her like a flash flood and left her floundering for her footing.

Afraid to give him access to another weakness, she presented her back to him. Two deep breaths helped control her physical reaction. She rubbed at the grease stain on her hand, and like her memories, the grease didn't go away, only spread over her palm.

"Here." His voice was husky. He held out a canister with the top popped and a wipe poking out.

She ran the lemon-scented cloth over her hands, turning the white gray. Next, she dabbed it over the front of her shirt, doing nothing but wetting the cotton. Giving up, she tossed the wipe into the trash. "Thanks."

"You've got . . ." He pointed at her face.

She swiped her hand over her right cheek.

"No. The other side. Here, let me . . ." He pulled another wipe from the canister and stepped closer. Taking her chin between his thumb and forefinger, he titled her face to the right.

The cold wipe made her shiver. It had nothing to do with Mack's intimidating size and off-putting gruffness, qualities she shouldn't find attractive. Yet the surprising gentleness of his touch made her sway a little closer.

She closed her eyes and forced her quick breaths to slow down to non-sprinting levels. He continued his ministrations as the moment stretched to interminable.

"How dirty am I?" Her already husky voice entered new lows.

Dear Lord, that had sounded very naughty even to her own ears. She stopped breathing and popped her eyes open. For a split second, what looked suspiciously like amusement flickered in his hazel eyes and quivered the corners of his mouth. She blinked, and it was gone. He let go of her and stepped away.

"Your skirt is ruined too, I'm sorry to say."

She twisted to see. The back of her skirt looked like an inkblot test. She wondered what word would come to mind if she turned and presented her backside to Mack.

"Next time, I'll know what not to wear." She bypassed a leather chair and perched on the edge of a cheap vinyl one.

Mack cleared his throat and tossed the dirty wipe into the trash with a jerk. "Why did you come in the first place?"

She shifted on the seat and straightened, kicking her chin up a notch. "I own a quarter stake in the garage."

"Yeah. About that. I want to buy you out." Mack half-sat on the desk doing his hungry, looming hawk-in-search-of-a-mouse imitation once more.

"You can't afford to buy me out."

"Why do you assume that?"

"Because Ford wouldn't have offered his stake to me if you'd been able to afford it. And I expect to make a profit on my investments."

He let out a slow breath through his nose as if his control was slipping. "What happened with Ford is more complicated than money. But things between us don't have to be. Name your price."

But their situation *was* more complicated than money. Mack just didn't know it yet. "I don't want to sell."

"Why do you want a stake in a two-bit mechanic shop in the middle of Podunk, Louisiana?" He gestured to the shop floor then slammed his palm against his desk.

Was he really resentful he'd been stuck with overseeing the family business? Ford certainly had been. She rose and looked out into the shop. His twin younger brothers, Jackson and Wyatt, stood in front of the open hood of the Datsun chatting, their heads close, their bond undeniable, even at a distance.

The shop was tidy, the floors as clean as they could be, considering the work. The equipment was top of the line and looked well maintained. No. His anger didn't mask resentment, but something else. Pride. And she was stomping all over it.

The garage and his brothers were the most important things to him, and he was worried she might try to destroy it.

"My goal is to help, not hurt you." Employing an old pageant trick, she spun around on her toes.

"How the—" He caught the curse in his hand. "You're not a mechanic, Ms. Boudreaux."

"Call me Ella." At his stony stare, she shrugged and continued. "You don't need another mechanic. You have plenty of mechanics. What you need is someone to market you."

"And you know enough about cars to do that?" His skepticism hit her like a kid pulling her pigtails behind the monkey bars. Annoying.

She shouldn't rise to the bait. Unfortunately, her mouth was less mature than her mind, and she reeled off facts her brother had recited with pride.

"That Datsun 240Z you were under? It's a seventy-three with a two-point-four-liter straight-six and side-draft carburetors. It can hit sixty in eight-point-two seconds with a hundred fifty-one horsepower. Top speed is a hundred twenty-five miles per hour. Not that anyone should be driving that fast on parish roads."

He looked . . . *stunned*. She confined herself to a small self-satisfied smile. She had a feeling nothing much surprised Mack Abbott, or if it did, he made sure the world didn't realize it.

"How did you . . . How do you know all that?"

"That's not important. What is important is that I can help you."

"We don't need help." He shook his head and re-chinked the breaks in his wall of grump.

"Yes, you do."

"No, we don't." The playground-level annoyance continued with his childish denials.

"Whatever." She rolled her eyes, probably not helping to defuse the situation.

"Name your price."

"That's not how this is going to work, *Mack*."

"I say how things are run and done in this garage. Not you, Ms. Boudreaux."

"I have a quarter stake and an equal voice."

"Except, we handle things democratically around here and my brothers will have my back. Every. Single. Time."

Dangit. He had her there. Pushing against Mack was like trying to move a mountain. She glanced at the twins. If she couldn't move Mack, then she'd have to go around him. She wanted to stalk out and slam the door, but forced herself to mosey as if she wasn't bothered at all by the situation or the man. He followed her to the door. She stopped with one foot out and one in. The breeze caught her hair, and she tossed her head to get it out of her eyes.

"You might vote me down, but at least give me a chance to be heard."

"Name your price," he repeated in a growly, grizzly voice that was meant to grind down her dissension.

Where she found the gumption she didn't know, but she gave his cheek two pats and said, "You can't afford me, tough guy."

Chapter Two

Mack's cheek burned as Ella Boudreaux walked away with a sexy twitch to her grease-covered ass. He let his gaze travel down her legs and back up again. Holy hell. He'd never met a woman who exuded her kind of raw sexuality and confidence.

Was *that* what money could buy? Mack shook his head to reorder his jumbled brain. It wasn't often he suffered from a crisis of confidence, but Ella had sucked his out like a leech. He no longer felt grounded, but flailing on the edge of a precipice.

The truth was she was right. He couldn't afford her. He couldn't even afford what she'd paid Ford for the twenty-five percent stake in the garage. Not yet anyway. The upgrades to the equipment had eaten away at their capital. It had been a good investment and would pay off, just not fast enough to avoid the oncoming collision with Ella Boudreaux.

"What'd she say?" Wyatt's voice startled Mack into the doorjamb.

He had managed to come up on Mack unawares. No surprise, considering his thoughts were centered on the woman who was heading toward a tiny convertible. Its soft-top was closed in deference to the cool spring day, but he could imagine her dark, silky hair whipping through the air like an old-school movie star driving with the top down. He caught a peek of her leg as she climbed in, her skirt sliding up a few more inches.

Those legs.

The sight of her sprawled on the shop floor with her long white legs against the dirty gray floor had done something strange to his innards. He couldn't describe the feeling because he didn't understand it. All he knew was that for the sake of his sanity, he needed her gone for good.

"She's not looking to sell," Mack muttered.

"I didn't think we had the money to buy her out anyway."

"We don't. But we will. Unfortunately, it seems like she's not willing to be a silent partner after all."

"Are you worried she's going to try to change things?"

Change. He was forever worried about change.

Ella backed her car up and gave them a wave through her open window. "I'll see you boys soon!"

She hit the parish road fast and fishtailed on the gravel, correcting the skid and handling the nimble convertible like a pro. Mack stood staring at the curve where she disappeared from sight.

"She says she wants to help market the shop," he said darkly.

"Sounds like a good thing." Wyatt nudged Mack with his shoulder.

"I don't trust her. She has an ulterior motive. Why would she want to go out and hustle for the shop? Who are we to her?"

Wyatt let out a gusty sigh. "I don't know. Maybe it will all become clear if we give it some time."

Time. How much did they have? Not enough of it in the day to get all his work done, that was a certainty. Since

Ford had abandoned them and with Wyatt and Jackson spending more time with Sutton and Willa, Mack felt like Atlas trying to hold up the world by himself.

Something else bothered him. The way she'd reeled off the facts about the Datsun. Finding out which cars were being restored wouldn't be difficult, as they kept a Facebook page updated with their progress, but the Datsun had just come in, and he hadn't had a chance to post the before pictures. How had she known to memorize the details? Or was she more familiar with classic cars than he'd given her credit for? If so, a new deep worrying wrinkle complicated the issue.

"Where did you leave things?" Wyatt asked.

An unsettled feeling was in the air like a storm gathering far on the horizon. "She'll be back, but I have no clue what's next."

It cost him to admit his uncertainty.

"Might as well get back to work for now. We can have a happy hour in the back of the barn and discuss tonight," Wyatt said.

"You and Sutton don't have big plans?"

Wyatt and Sutton had gotten engaged over Christmas, and he had moved in with her. Without fail as the hands of the clock approached five every evening, he was itching like he'd been infested with fire ants to get over the river to her.

"She and her mother are talking wedding stuff. This would be a great excuse to escape. I swear if her parents wouldn't disown us both, I'd haul her to the courthouse and get it done in five minutes like Jackson and Willa."

Jackson and Willa had gotten married without fanfare and fuss the week before. Instead of heading out for a traditional honeymoon, they had been back at work the next day. Mack had pressed them to take some time off together, but Willa had smiled, shaken her head, and shared a glance with Jackson that had made Mack's chest ache.

Mack retreated to his office and stared at the numbers on his computer screen until they blurred. *You can't afford me, tough guy.*

She was a hundred percent right on that one. Her casual sophistication made him feel like Bigfoot crawling straight out of the swamps.

The rest of the day passed with him in a state of distraction. He ripped the leg of his jeans on a jagged bumper lying on the floor and dropped an air wrench on his foot. With a curse, he tossed his tools into the box with less care than usual and headed to the back of the barn thirty minutes early.

He grabbed a beer out of the refrigerator they kept for such occasions, cracked one of the wide barn doors open, and propped his shoulder against it. The sun fell toward the trees, casting deep purples and oranges over green spring growth.

How long had it been since he'd walked through the dense forest that backed up to the garage? Too long. Since before their father had died of a sudden heart attack on the shop floor a year and a half earlier. Once the forest had been his refuge. Now, he felt lost and adrift and disconnected from his past and the reasons he spent every waking and sleeping hour focused on the garage.

Failure would mean he'd failed his father, his family, himself. The last year and a half had been the hardest of his life. The ache for his father, the infighting with his older brother, Ford, for leadership of the garage, and the fear he wasn't up to the task.

Jackson and Willa made their way into the barn side by side. It's the way they'd always worked but now lived too. River trotted up and bumped Mack's hand. He gave her a rub and got a lick in return.

"I'm going to shower." Willa bussed Jackson's cheek. He caught her wrist and tugged her close enough for a kiss on the mouth.

Mack turned away to stare at the trees that stretched to the far distance and rubbed a hand over his chest. Willa sped up the stairs with River on her heels.

Jackson grabbed a beer, uncapped it, and joined him at the door. "Might frost tonight."

Mack hummed and took a swig.

"We're making spaghetti if you want to come up for dinner."

Mack took another swig but didn't answer. It used to be that Jackson and Wyatt would wander over to their old childhood home where Mack lived for dinner more often than not. He missed those evenings filled with car talk and comfortable silences that only knowing someone bone-deep could imbue.

Mack couldn't shake the feeling of being an interloper the couple of times he'd joined Willa and Jackson in the loft. Even though Willa had worked at Jackson's elbow for two years, their marriage was like a fledgling bird with all the nerves and excitement of its first flight. They needed time together to find their wings.

Jackson picked at a piece of splintering wood at the door. Their gazes met in an identical side-eye. "I take it things didn't go smoothly with Ms. Boudreaux."

"Seems like she wants to actually, I don't know, *do* something."

"Like what?"

"She mentioned marketing the shop."

"Well, hell, she can't do a worse job than Ford did and Lord knows, while Wyatt has the skills, he doesn't have the time. Why not give her a shot?"

Mack huffed and shifted to face Jackson, who did the same on the opposite side of the door. "Because this is

Abbott Brothers Garage and Restoration and she's not an Abbott."

"Dude. We all wish Ford had offered us a chance to buy him out. But he didn't."

"I can take out a second mortgage on the house or the shop and—"

"No. Only as a last resort."

"What would you suggest?"

"Wait her out. She'll get bored and move on to the next thing. Probably sell her stake for cheap."

It was a logical course of action. Any investment manager would have pegged the garage a poor return on investment. They'd never make millions. Yet something beyond a simple return on investment had driven her to buy Ford's stake. Jackson hadn't seen the light and energy brewing in her eyes and the knowledge she'd spouted like it had resided in her head for years.

Ella Boudreaux was a force of nature, and he wasn't confident they could batten down the windows and survive her.

Wyatt came through the back and provided a much-needed lightness and humor. He grabbed a beer too and the three of them took up their customary spots from oldest to youngest on the couch. Although, Wyatt was technically only a few minutes younger than Jackson.

They talked football and baseball and NASCAR, and the normalcy spackled a veneer over the unsettled feeling Ella Boudreaux had left behind. Still, Mack's worries surfaced as he lay in bed and chased sleep.

"She's back," Wyatt said on his way by the office door in a voice worthy of a horror movie trailer. He was gone before Mack could reply. The ball of anxiety in his chest tripled in size. He'd been anticipating her return, but not this soon. She hadn't even given him a day, and the beers he and his brothers had shared the night before had left a dull throb of a headache at the base of his skull.

How did he play this? If he acted like a total asshole, would that drive her away? Maybe, but that sort of behavior might also bring down the wrath of the aunts if they caught wind. Safer if he ignored her altogether and left her to flounder on the edge of things until she gave up and left. If everyone was busy and working, what could she do except sit in his office and twiddle her thumbs?

He glanced out the bay door window. She slid out of her tiny car. His black truck could roll over it like a speed bump. She was in jeans and a blue-and-pink striped button-down. More practical than the skirt and sweater of the day before, but hardly anything she'd want to get down and dirty in.

He bypassed the Datsun and headed for the welder in the far corner. He stopped Jackson as he was pulling on the welder's mask. "I'll finish up the hood. Go pull the engine on the Datsun. It's going to need an overhaul."

"You sure?" Jackson's eyes narrowed.

Mack had planned to handle most of the work on the Datsun because it was one of his favorite cars. "Yeah, I'm sure."

Jackson's gaze moved over Mack's shoulder, his mouth flipping from a frown to a smirk. He pushed the mask into Mack's hands "You're a coward, big bro."

Mack preferred calling it "strategic." The sooner she accepted he didn't need her, the better. Welding took up all his concentration, leaving no room for his worries. It was therapeutic and bordered on meditative for him.

Thirty minutes of work knitted old metal to new. He flipped his mask up and ran a glove-covered finger over the bead weld. When they got through grinding it, no one would be able to tell the difference. It would be like the two pieces of metal had always been joined.

Was she still here? He snuck a glance. She sat at his desk in front of his computer. Wyatt had propped himself in the door like he often did when chatting with Mack. Something he said made her laugh. Echoes of the throaty sound slivered through the noise to his corner.

What the hell? Mack ripped the mask off, turned off the welding equipment, and stalked toward his office.

Jackson dropped an arm in front of him like a crossing guard, forcing a stop. "You done with the weld?"

"Yeah, it's ready for grinding." Mack stared at Ella as if his gaze could punch through concrete.

Jackson patted his shoulder. "I think she genuinely wants to help."

Mack transferred his violent gaze from the office to his brother. Jackson only blinked and raised his brows.

"So we just sign over the garage to her? Is that what you want?" Mack threw a hand up.

"It's not what I want, but she owns a part and there's nothing to be done about it right now. Wyatt and I think it's best to see how things play out."

"You do, do you?"

"You would too if you weren't being so emotional about the whole thing."

"Emotional? Of course, I'm fucking emotional. Our pop built this garage up from nothing and passed it to us to nurture and grow. Ella Boudreaux is a threat."

"She'll be more of a threat if she feels backed into a corner. Wait her out, then buy her out."

Jackson's advice was sound and nothing Mack hadn't told himself. Problem was the woman unbalanced him, and he sensed an approaching disaster.

"I'll try to be charming and welcoming," Mack said through clenched teeth.

A laugh burst out of Jackson. "Don't shoot for the impossible. Aim lower. Not rude would be a good start."

"What the— I can be charming."

"Sure you can," Jackson said with the air of humoring a child.

"Get your butt back to work." There was no actual heat behind the words.

Jackson shrugged, retrieved the hood Mack had welded, and retreated to the grinder.

Mack gathered himself and paced slower to his office. Jackson was right. He should deal with Ella Boudreaux like he did with any client. Detached and professional.

Wyatt gave him a pat on his shoulder on his way back to the garage floor. Mack rounded the desk. A hope that she was surfing the internet for funny cat videos died a fiery death. She was deep into the garage's accounts. His cool detachment evaporated. "What the hell are you doing?"

Ella's blue-framed glasses did something startling to her eyes, making them appear bigger and even bluer. "I'm reviewing your spreadsheets."

"Why?"

"You could streamline your accounts payable, you know. Integrate them into a program designed to keep a real-time flow of money."

He used spreadsheets to keep track because that's what his father had begrudgingly moved to when he was forced to give up carbon copies. Mack had been meaning to look into software but with everything else going on, it kept slipping down his priority list. "I know there are better programs out there."

"Then why don't you change?" She cocked her head and raised an eyebrow in his direction. With her dark hair off her neck in an artfully messy updo she looked softer, and the blue glasses lent her a playful vibe.

"I'm not adverse to change," he said hesitantly. Actually, he was. Change was rarely for the better. Change meant growing up and complications and uncertainty.

"How about I put together an overview of the software choices and let you pick?"

The moment was loaded. If he agreed, did it mean he was giving in? Letting her in? On the other hand, giving her something menial might keep her occupied.

"Our system has worked fine for years."

"I'm sure it has." She swiveled around in his chair as if she owned it—technically he supposed she owned a wheel—crossed her legs and gestured over the piles of papers on the desk. "But I can make it work better than fine. How much time do you spend doing paperwork when you could be using your talent on the cars?"

Behind her guileless sincerity, he sensed she was buttering him up if not outright manipulating him. Before he could decide how harsh his put-down should be, River bounded into the office and scrambled up his chest to give his face a lick.

Ella gave a yelping scream and brought her legs up to her chest as if getting her feet off the floor would offer protection from a fifty-plus-pound dog. The devil on his shoulder urged him to let River sniff and lick all over her.

The expression on her face had him grabbing hold of River's dangling leash. The casual sophistication and enviable confidence had been wiped away by fear. No, more than fear. Terror. But why? River was a hairy ball of energy and good will.

Willa came around the corner, carrying a cardboard box, out of breath. "Sorry. She got away from me."

Mack sat in one of the chairs he kept for customers or for his brothers when they wanted to talk or hang out and rubbed River's head and chin. The dog put a paw on his knee and narrowed her eyes. She'd been a scrawny, mangy thing when Willa had adopted her a few months before. As if River could sense her good fortune to land with Willa and at the garage, she was sweet and loving and gentle. Unless Willa was being threatened.

Ella regained her composure bit by bit, first lowering one leg and then the other. Her hands unclenched from the armrests and, while still tense, her face shed the mask of fear for a more guarded one.

"Those the shirts?" he asked Willa so as to give Ella time to gather herself.

"Sure are, and they are awesome. Sutton did a great job on the design." Willa pulled one off the top and held it up.

They had voted to make River the official mascot of Abbott Brothers Garage and Restoration. A stylized picture of her was on the chest pocket along with their name. Willa flipped the shirt around where a larger black-and-white drawing of River was on the back, along with their logo.

"Those are cute. How are you going to sell them?" Ella's gaze moved from the dog to the shirt and back again.

"Here in the shop to customers, I guess," Mack said. "Can you put River in the barn for now, Willa?"

"Sure thing." She dropped the shirt on top of the box and took River's leash from Mack, her curiosity pinging between them much like her gaze as she backed out.

Once River was out of sight, Ella collapsed back into the chair as if a puppeteer had cut her strings.

"Are you only afraid of dogs or all animals?"

"What do you mean?" She picked up a paper on his desk detailing a fender replacement for a '72 Mustang and hid her face.

"Did you have a bad experience with a dog?"

"It's nothing." She rose and sashayed around the desk.

In the close space, she brushed his arm on her way by, and when she bent over the box of T-shirts to root around inside, her ass was eye level. Her ass had nothing to do with anything. Having a nice ass was a simple physical attribute, like being bald. Yet, he was having a hard time stopping himself from admiring the way her jeans hugged her spectacular attribute. He swallowed.

"Good quality cotton." She straightened and popped a hip to hold up a shirt, examining it.

"Sutton wouldn't allow anything but." His voice sounded like it needed to be sanded down. He cleared his throat, closed his eyes, and took a deep breath.

"I'm glad to see you didn't skimp on materials. How much are you paying per shirt?" The flap of a shirt popped his eyes open. She held it up to her body.

"Seven dollars."

"Not bad. You can easily sell them for fifteen. How about online sales?"

"Hadn't considered it."

"You should."

"Sounds complicated."

"Doesn't have to be."

"Have you done anything like that before?"

Her gaze dropped, her glasses camouflaging her eyes. "No."

"What exactly are your qualifications, by the way? You have a business or marketing degree?"

She fiddled with the hem of the shirt for a second before spinning around and shoving it back in the box. "My qualifications are a twenty-five percent stake in the business."

"So your only demonstrable skill is throwing your ex's money around?"

Any vulnerability he sensed in her vanished in a blast of anger. All directed at him. His insides churned. It felt like his first time at bat in Little League, a mixture of excitement and nerves.

"Make no mistake, I deserved every penny I got from

my divorce." Her sarcasm covered something darker. Something that had Mack on edge.

"What's that mean?"

"All that matters is that I'm invested in the garage and ready to help. If you'll let me." She stared him down.

He pushed the questions he wanted to ask away. Her ex wasn't any of his business. Maybe Jackson and Wyatt were right. A few mundane tasks would see her bored and ready to move on to a more exciting endeavor.

"Fine. Get a list of software options together, and I'll review them. And if you want to see how difficult it will be to sell T-shirts on our website, feel free to look into that as well."

A light sparkled in her blue eyes and her smile spoke of satisfaction. Even though he felt like he'd run up a white flag and given in, he couldn't hate himself for putting that look on her face.

"Now, if you don't mind, I have some estimates to send." He gestured to the computer.

"Of course. Go right ahead. I didn't mean to monopolize your computer." She stepped aside and let him scoot around his desk to plop in his chair, still warm from her aforementioned spectacular asset.

Mack turned his back and opened the first unread message in his email. The words blurred together. His senses were attuned to the woman behind him. She hadn't left yet. He snuck a glance. Ella had perched on the edge of the leather chair, a sleek steel gray laptop open on the corner of his desk.

Mack swiveled around. "What are you doing?"

"Working."

"Here?"

She made a Vanna White gesture around the room. "This is a place of business, is it not? Don't worry, you won't even know I'm here."

Mack tapped his fingers on the desk. "There's a break room you could use."

She flashed him a smile over the screen of the laptop before returning to tap on the keys. "No, thanks. I'm comfortable here. Plus, if I have questions, you're only a few feet away."

He needed a mile. Or a town. Hell, maybe even a state between them before he'd be able to concentrate. But, she had taken over his office like a squatter. A beautiful squatter whose every breath registered on the Richter scale. Retreating to the shop floor to work on the Datsun would give the impression he couldn't handle the pressure.

An hour passed in silence. Mack ticked the minutes off on the clock in the corner of his computer screen. He got the estimate sent and a few vendor emails answered, but otherwise was unusually unproductive. He'd have to work late to catch up, but it wasn't like he had any pressing social engagements.

"Okay, I have it narrowed it down to two programs." Ella rose and came around the desk with a piece of paper.

"Already?"

"The learning curve will be the worst part. It would be wise to maintain your spreadsheets throughout the transition."

She leaned over the back of his chair, put the paper down, and looked over his shoulder. A lock of her hair had come loose and fallen forward, tickling his jaw. He stared at the paper, her neat handwriting streaming together into nonsense. Her scent was light and fleeting, and like the flash of a firefly, he wanted to give chase.

His breaths grew short and shallow. She was too close and had already wormed her way into the garage in an unexpected way. The further she burrowed, the higher the risk of finding rot. A sense of claustrophobia came over him in a rush. He had to escape.

He slapped the paper facedown on his desk and spun his chair around. A Mustang he wasn't sure was worth the trouble awaited an estimate in the next parish over. He could leave now and get himself together by driving the back roads. It was a convenient excuse.

"Can it wait? I have an appointment to give an estimate."

She stepped back, her eyes narrowed as if sensing an attack coming. "Sure. There's no hurry."

He stepped to the door and surveyed the shop floor. They were busy, and guilt niggled at his selfish retreat. A Ford sedan required an oil change before they could clear the second bay, but Wyatt and Jackson and Willa were elbow deep in more important projects and it was almost lunch. He could knock it out in twenty minutes tops and clear his conscience. Or . . .

He swung his gaze to Ella. It would be a test of sorts. "You know car repair basics, right? Fluid checks. Tire changes. That sort of thing."

"I know some stuff." Suspicion laced her voice.

"I figured. Why else would you buy into a garage like this?" He gestured to the work area. "I've got to head out for that estimate, and the boys are busy on high-dollar restoration projects. We're in a pinch. You wouldn't mind helping us out, would you?"

"With what?"

"We need bay two cleared out. All the Ford needs is an oil change. Should be simple. You mind taking care of it?"

"An oil change. I'm not sure . . ." Her gaze darted around the desk as if on the hunt for an excuse.

"An oil change is the easiest thing in the world and

shouldn't be a problem for someone with your obvious knowledge. I was pretty impressed with the stats about the Datsun you reeled off yesterday."

He could almost feel her panic and hesitated, but what was the worst that would happen? Either she completed the oil change or she would learn a lesson and decide the garage wasn't the place for her. It was a win-win.

Chapter Three

Trepidation streaked through Ella, destroying the relatively calm waters the two of them had been treading. Her knowledge about the Datsun was coming back to bite her in the butt. Speaking of butts, that's where Mack was pulling this silly test from. And that's what it was—a test.

His ultimate goal was to drive her away, towing a heap of humiliation with her. She'd hoped his acquiescence to her plans for the accounting programs had signaled a turning point, but it seemed she had pushed too hard and now he was acting like a bear defending its den.

The question was what to do about it. Should she own up to the fact she had never performed an oil change or brazen it out?

Ella hadn't excelled in school, but she was scrappy and determined and didn't back down from a fight. That particular attribute had gotten her in trouble more times than not, but she had a feeling if she didn't take up the challenge, he would take the advantage and run roughshod over her like the proverbial Mack truck.

"You're going to be gone?"

"For a couple of hours, yes."

With the help of a manual and the internet, she could

surely get the job done in under two hours. Imagining the look on his face when he returned and she'd finished had her asking, "What sort of oil do you want me to use?"

She didn't wait for his answer but turned on her heel and walked out of his office to the shop floor. It was empty. She glanced to the clock and wished she hadn't. It was lunchtime, and her stomach growled on cue.

"5W-20. Oil is in the storeroom." He pointed to a door in the back of the shop. "There's a clipboard hanging to the side. Make sure to note what and how much you use, so we can reorder on time."

"Fine."

"Fine." He planted his boots, crossed his arms over his chest, and stared down at her.

"Don't you have somewhere to be?" She made a shooing motion with her hands. The last thing she needed was to have a concentration-busting wrecking ball named Mack hovering over her while she fumbled through her first oil change.

Her brother had promised to teach her after finishing his first deployment. It had never happened. But she'd watched him more than once, and it hadn't seemed complicated. Plus, she had a weapon. The internet.

He walked away, but not toward the door. Keeping her gaze on him as one did an enemy, she studied him. His movements were jerky with anger or impatience or maybe something else altogether. He opened a door, revealing a closet stuffed with blue shop towels and jackets and sundry items for the bathroom. He grabbed something off the hook on the back of the door and returned.

"Here." He shoved the gray fabric toward her. She flinched, but took it automatically, holding it to her chest as if it could protect her.

But she didn't need protection from Mack, did she? He wasn't her ex-husband. Mack met her eyes for only a second. Was that regret that flashed? Yes, he was gruff and infuriating and stubborn, but he wasn't cold and unemotional. Instead of hiding his frustration until it was too late to get out of the way, Mack wore his emotions like a placard on his chest. He banged through the door to the parking lot, leaving her alone.

She exhaled, long and slow, not even aware she'd been holding her breath. She shook out whatever Mack had given her. It was a pair of gray coveralls like she'd seen Wyatt and Jackson and even Willa wear while they worked.

She ran a thumb over the embroidered badge over the left pocket. *Mack*. The thread of the *k* was fraying a little at the top, and the material was worn and soft. She retreated to the break room to slip off her shoes and climb into the coveralls.

It felt strangely intimate to zip herself into his coveralls, his name falling on the curve of her breast. She burrowed her nose in the collar and took a deep breath. Under the oil and garage smell, she caught a hint of the man himself and shivered.

The coveralls were enormous on her, and she rolled up the pant legs and sleeves so many times it was comical. She checked the shop floor, but it was empty. Everyone was taking a lunch break. Perfect.

Pulling up the internet on her phone, she skimmed through the steps of an oil change. Her hunger turned to nerves. It looked way more complicated than she had anticipated. She would take it one step at a time and hope for the best. Could she break the sedan by screwing this up?

Why hadn't she just admitted to not knowing how? Pride. Both a blessing and a curse—too much of it ran through her veins. Her pride had gotten her out of a nightmare marriage. But, it had also gotten her into her current mess.

One step at a time, she repeated to herself. She gathered the proper oil and filter from the storeroom, making sure to make a note on the clipboard. Step one was to jack the car up. It was already on risers, thank the Lord. Draining the oil was next. The cartoon drawing accompanying the instructions showed a receptacle of some sort.

She spotted a flat, black plastic canister against the wall that niggled her memories. Peering inside, she sniffed and ran a finger around the rim. Looked and smelled like oil. She dragged it under the car with her. Now she needed to find the oil drain plug.

She looked at her phone, up at the undercarriage, and back again. It wasn't as straightforward as the picture indicated, but eventually, she located what appeared to be the oil pan and plug. She needed to use the boxy end of the wrench to remove the plug.

She lost some time searching for the correct-size wrench. The fifth one she tried slipped over the bolt snugly. "I got you now, you little bugger."

According to the website, she was only supposed to loosen the bolt with the wrench, then remove the plug by hand. After loosening the bolt, she worked at the plug. It was stuck. Or maybe she hadn't done it correctly. She repositioned herself and tugged harder.

The plug popped out and the oil flowed. On her. On the floor. Only partly in the canister. She gasped and shoved the canister opening under the gush. Her elbow slipped on the oily floor, and she banged her head against a pipe.

A string of curse words shot from her brain to her mouth. She'd heard her brother mutter choice words after busting his knuckles working under the hood of his car. What would her brother think of her right now? She could almost hear his laughter, and it made her smile.

Wait. Someone flesh and blood was laughing in the garage. She scooched from under the car.

Sutton Mize and Wyatt came to an abrupt stop. Wyatt's laughter petered out and his smile turned questioning. "What in the world are you doing, Ms. Boudreaux?"

Wyatt reminded her of her brother in so many ways. Easygoing with laughter at his fingertips. Memories of her brother added to the stress of the oil change and sent her emotions to the edge of control. Tears gathered for an exit. She ran her clean forearm over her face and took a shuddery breath. She couldn't allow herself to cry in front of any of the Abbotts.

"I'm changing the car's oil. And call me Ella, please."

"I was going to take care of that after lunch." Wyatt squatted down next to her and peered under the car, his eyebrows rising. She glanced back. It was an unholy mess compared to the rest of the garage.

"Yeah, well, Mack asked me to do it." Ella tried to smile up at Sutton. Their paths had crossed at a few Cottonbloom, Mississippi, functions. While they weren't friends, Sutton seemed nice and down-to-earth and obviously in love with Wyatt.

"This is crazy. Where's Mack?" Sutton set her hands on her hips and looked around.

"He had an estimate to handle. A Mustang, he said."

"I swear, sometimes I'm not sure what goes on in that hard head of his. Want me to finish up?" Wyatt asked.

She was tempted to say yes, but her damnable pride reared up. She wanted to be able to tell Mack she'd done the job without lying. "Maybe you could supervise me?"

"We'll take that walk later, babe." Wyatt rose and dipped Sutton back for a kiss.

When Wyatt let her go, color had flushed her face becomingly and she shuffled as if slightly off-balance.

"Don't let me interrupt your plans. The Mr. Fix-It website can guide me through the rest." Ella waggled her phone at the couple.

"Don't be silly. Looks like you need him more than I do at the moment. I'll see you at home, Wyatt." Sutton winked, then turned her smile on Ella. "Good luck, Ella. Mack needs to be shook up. I'm rooting for you."

Sutton's smile wasn't strained or fake or anything other than warm and slightly sympathetic. Ella returned it sheepishly. "I need all the support I can get."

"Wyatt better be helping you settle in." Sutton narrowed her eyes and twisted her engagement ring.

Wyatt cleared his throat, gave Sutton a double thumbs-up, and disappeared under the car.

"These boys." Sutton shook her head. "Be patient with them. Especially Mack."

Sutton was assuming Ella could act like an emotionally mature adult around Mack. If her current situation—sitting in a pool of oil and getting ready for further torture under a car was any indication—Ella was not taking the high road.

"Let's go, fancy lady," Wyatt said from under the car.

She scooched in to join him shoulder to shoulder in the pool of oil. "Not so fancy at the moment."

Wyatt turned his head to meet her eyes, his grin white against the dark metal and rubber. "Nope. Not so much. Now, where were you?"

Wyatt walked her through getting the oil plug back in place and changing the oil filter. He stayed calm and patient throughout, and with a little guidance, her confidence grew.

"That's it for under here," he said.

She didn't make a move to slide out, and neither did he. "I know you don't want me around. Thanks for helping me anyway."

"Sutton would send me to the couch tonight if I hadn't." His attempt at levity sunk. He cleared his throat and fiddled with a black rubber hose. "It's not that I think you're a bad person or anything. But this place is *ours*. The Abbotts. Ford destroyed that history."

"I'm not making a play to rename the garage Abbott and Boudreaux. And, Ford didn't destroy your history. You're all still family. Even Ford. The garage is just a place."

"Don't tell Mack that." Wyatt's laugh was dry as he slid out from under the car.

Ella would do anything to have her brother back. *Anything*. What was wrong with these Abbott men? Coming out from under the car, she let Wyatt guide her through refilling the oil and checking the level on the dipstick.

"I'll start the car. You check underneath for leaks." Wyatt cranked the engine. She got on her hands and knees and scanned the underside. No sprays or drips.

She rose and gave Wyatt a thumbs-up. Her hands were filthy, and her hair was stuck to her neck in a sweat-oil combo. She felt disgusting and probably looked even worse. Wyatt turned the engine off, his gaze darting over her shoulder, an unusual grimness coming over his face. He turned and walked away. She felt strangely betrayed and thrown to the wolves.

She tensed. Wiping her hands on the legs of the coveralls, she waited for the wolf to pounce.

"You finished it?" Suspicion laced Mack's voice.

She turned slowly and pasted a smile on her face as if wearing oil-covered coveralls was totally in her wheelhouse. "You're back early. Yep, all done and tested."

"With Wyatt's help."

"I did everything myself except crank the engine, thank you very much."

His gaze lit a fiery path down her body, and her body heated like an aluminum foil–wrapped potato in the oven. His continued silence was like a blowtorch.

"Have I proven myself adequate?" The bite in her voice

rose up from a place she thought she'd put firmly in her past. She'd spent too much of her childhood and marriage being tested and failing. Her marriage had ended with a big fat *D*.

He squatted to glance under the car. "You made a mess."

Screw him. Screw the garage. Screw her dream of finally building something for herself. She unzipped his coveralls and peeled them down her body. Anger and disappointment and the desire to pop Mack Abbott right on the mouth brought tears to her eyes. She was mostly mad at herself for thinking if she worked hard enough, Mack would eventually accept her.

She yanked the coveralls over her foot. Her shoe went flying into his crotch. He grunted and covered himself. A maniacal laugh threatened to break out of her.

She got the other leg off with minimal hopping and no shoe flinging. She stepped forward and shoved the grimy coveralls at his chest and slipped her foot in her shoe at the same time.

The Ella of a few years ago would have slinked off to lick her wounds. But, she'd made a promise to herself after the divorce. No longer would she allow anyone—but especially a man—make her feel less than again.

"I completed your pissing contest even though I'm not a trained mechanic. How about a 'good job' or 'way to go' or even a 'you did better than I expected'? Is this how you treat your brothers? Is this how you treated Ford? No wonder he sold out and left. You can be a real asshole, you know that, Mack?"

His eyes widened and his jaw unhinged. She liked him like that. Shock and awe. Performing an about-face, she grabbed her purse and laptop from his office and stalked toward her car. She swore she could feel his footsteps on the concrete behind her like little seismic shifts in her world.

"Hold up." His voice was gruff and commanding in a way that said his orders were used to being followed.

She only stopped when she reached her car and was forced to stow her things on the passenger seat. "What do you want?"

He didn't speak, and she glanced over her shoulder. His mouth opened and closed as if he was at a loss for words.

"Well? Do you want to yell at me some more? Test me? Humiliate me?" She flung her purse to the floorboard.

"I didn't— I mean, that's not—" He rubbed the back of his neck.

He couldn't finish his half-ass apology because that's exactly what it had been—a test designed to humiliate her. At least he didn't lie.

She slipped into the seat of her car and slammed the door. She reversed with a spin of her wheels. He took a ground-swallowing hop backward as if he was in danger of being hit. If she'd wanted to run over him, she would have. One thing her brother had taught her was how to handle a car, even if she hadn't legally been old enough to drive.

She left Abbott Brothers Garage in her rearview mirror never wanting to see it, or its owner, again.

Chapter Four

Ella poured another glass of wine. The ticking of the antique grandfather clock was like a hammer on her brain. She'd bought it because of a children's book she'd read when she was eight about a little girl in a mansion. A grandfather clock had been in an illustration. Something about a clock taller than her had stuck in her imagination for two decades.

By the time she had the money and wherewithal to buy one, it had lost its magic and only represented the inevitable march of time. If she had an ax handy, she might smash it to splinters and cogs.

The ring of the doorbell echoed through the two-story entryway. She could count on one hand the number of times someone had rung it since she'd moved in, and at least twice had been a Girl Scout selling cookies.

While Cottonbloom, Mississippi, was small and friendly enough, it was also insular and standoffish with new inhabitants. Especially one with a reputation as a gold digger. Even though it was dead wrong.

Barefoot, she padded to the front door and checked out the side window. Her heart stuttered. It was her ex-husband, Trevor.

She took a gulp of wine for courage, put her game face on—a hitched eyebrow and an eat-shit smile—and cracked the door open.

"Oh. I thought you were a vacuum salesman." She didn't even know if people went door-to-door selling vacuums anymore, but her slight jab had its desired effect. "A shame since I'm in the market for a new one. What do you want?"

Trevor's eyes narrowed and his hundred-watt smile dimmed to a sputtering twenty-five. "I've heard rumors."

"Regarding?"

"You bought a stake in a local car garage?"

"Garage and restoration. Glad to know the rumor mill occasionally gets close."

"What are you doing, Ella?" His sigh was one of a disappointed parent.

Her knee-jerk reaction was to tell him about Magnolia Investments and detail her successes without him. She slapped the clamoring need to please back into its dank hole like a whack-a-mole. Another weakness would pop up. Trevor was an expert in teasing out her insecurities.

"I have signed documents that explicitly state it's none of your business."

"It's my business when it's still my name that gets dragged through the muck. Can I come in?" He ran a hand through his silky dark hair. Hair she knew was thinning on top. Enough to send him running to the doctor for medicine to combat the loss of his perceived manhood.

She hesitated. Something was off with him. He looked worn down, his tie pulled askew from his collar. For a man who fought the creep of time with more effort than he'd put into their marriage, it was telling.

"Come on in." She swung the door wide, turned around, and walked into the kitchen, her favorite room in the house. The memories of cooking for her brother in their childhood home before he left were some of her most cherished ones.

Trevor dropped onto a swivel barstool, his shoulders slumped. "Can I have a drink?"

She hesitated. "All I have is wine or beer."

It was a lie, but not the first one she'd told to him. Giving him hard liquor was like spinning the roulette wheel. If her number came up, then hell would ensue.

"Wine, please." He tugged at his tie, loosening it further.

From this angle, she could see his hair loss had accelerated in the year and half since she'd sat across from him at the divorce lawyers' table. She pushed a glass of red wine over to him, keeping the island between them. How quickly her self-preservation instincts resurfaced.

"You're not here to talk about the garage, are you?" she asked.

"Not entirely." He turned the glass in his hand.

She could only think of one reason Trevor was sitting in her kitchen. "How's Megan?"

A look like tasting something bitter flashed on his face. "She's fine. I guess. I don't know."

"You're separated?"

"You could say that."

Trevor's affair with Megan had been the deepest fissure in their marriage, setting off cataclysmic aftershocks. She was several years younger than Ella—of course—but moved in the same social circles in Jackson. Unlike Ella's humble beginnings, Megan's family had old money.

The irony was that Ella had liked Megan. She was Ella's inverse—a model-thin blonde, with brown eyes. Cheery and optimistic, if not a little naïve. Apple pie personified. The girl hadn't stood a chance when Trevor turned on his charms.

Even though Trevor was fifteen years Ella's senior—

and twenty years older than Megan—he possessed a suaveness that reminded Ella of a movie star. Eighteen when they'd met, she hadn't been smart or sophisticated enough to see through the polish to the rotten core.

"She left you?" Ella asked idly.

"Yes."

"I warned her not to marry you." Of course, her earnest warning had only gotten her branded a jealous witch, and Jackson had turned its back on her.

"Dammit, Ella. I'm not a monster." Even though his words came out even, a question was on his face.

"Yes, you are," Ella whispered. He certainly haunted her nightmares.

He swept the wine glass off the counter. It smashed into her cabinets. She flinched. Bright red rivulets made their way to the floor where broken glass littered the tile. She scrunched her toes and clutched the edge of the counter.

"Get out." She hated the tremble in her voice.

"I'm sorry. I'm sorry. I'll clean up." He grabbed a dish towel and wiped over the cabinet, only managing to smear a wide reddish stain across the white.

"Why are you here, Trevor? We have no connection anymore."

He straightened and tossed the towel down. "No connection? We were married for eight years."

Eight years. It had felt like a lifetime while she was in it, but a blink of time she'd like to forget now. "We're not anymore for reasons I won't rehash."

"I'm trying to change. I want Megan back."

The knowledge he'd never tried to change for her wasn't a spike through her heart but more like a splinter digging under her fingernail. "I can't help you change. That's something that will require dedication on your part." She paused, but her mouth got the better of her. "And therapy. *Lots* of therapy."

Trevor's temper erupted like Old Faithful, right on cue. He never could countenance her acerbic sarcasm. "You are such a bitch. I'd almost forgotten why I let you go."

"Let me go? Ha! I left your sorry butt." She walked halfway to the front door and pointed, unable to control the slight shake. "Time for you to leave."

He crunched in broken glass and tracked red wine along her tile floor. "I could make things difficult for you."

"How so?" Ella had made sure he had no hold over her in any way. Instead of alimony, she'd taken half of the stock portfolio she had managed during their marriage. Even though she made a show of throwing money around, most things she'd bought, like her house, were an investment in themselves. She'd finish updating it and then bank a tidy profit on the resell.

"These people don't know what you're really like, do they? What if the fine citizens of Cottonbloom discovered that you used me and then cleaned me out in the divorce? A cold-hearted gold digger."

Given the bare facts of their marriage, she sounded like a gold digger, but she had loved him somewhere in the past. Her shame didn't originate from how things had ended from but how gullible and naïve she'd been. At eighteen she'd been like a lamb to the slaughter.

"Spread whatever poison you want. I don't care." Her defiance did a poor job hiding her lie. She hated he still held any power over her. "If Megan is smart, she'll file a restraining order against you and get a good lawyer. You won't have anything left."

"That can't happen. I want you to talk to her." He grabbed her upper arm in a punishing hold. She closed her eyes and braced herself for his reaction when she denied him what he wanted.

The doorbell chimed. Ella drew in a sharp breath and

froze. Trevor did the same, leaving them in a grotesque pose. The doorbell chimed again.

Mack kicked a pebble off the porch with the toe of his boot. Five minutes. That's all he'd promised Wyatt and Jackson. A quick apology and he was gone. The fact she had company—a black BMW 5 Series was in her driveway—only made things easier. He probably wouldn't even be invited inside and could say his peace on the porch and leave.

Except it didn't seem like she was going to answer the door. A sickening wave passed through his stomach. Did she have a boyfriend? Were they otherwise occupied? He braced a hand on the doorframe as images he couldn't scrub from his brain scrolled.

Inexplicably, he wanted to punch something. Instead he knocked on the door, harder than was polite. So what if he interrupted her and whatever pretty boy she was entertaining and killed the mood?

Two minutes ago, he'd dreaded the moment he'd have to deliver his apology; now he was pissed she didn't answer the door. He turned away and had one foot on the brick steps leading away from the dark red door when it opened. He pivoted around, bracing himself to see her half dressed or looking like she'd been making out. Or worse.

"Mack." His name croaked out of her throat.

She didn't look like he'd torn her away from a lover. In fact, if he had to name the emotion on her face it was fear tinged with relief at the sight of him. The hairs on the back of his neck stood at attention as he closed the distance between them.

He checked her from head to toe, but nothing raised alarms. She was casual in a short-sleeve button-down and tight ankle-length jeans. The toes of her bare feet were painted a bright pink.

"Everything okay?" He kept his voice low.

Her gaze darted to the side, and Mack shifted to look over her shoulder into the house. A man was outlined in the light from the kitchen.

"I appreciate you coming by to talk about the accounting programs. I even have a pros-and-cons list for each one we can discuss." Her voice had brightened, but her smile was brittle. "Come on in."

She stepped back, and he took a step into her home, never taking his eyes off the man. This man had scared Ella. Un-effing-acceptable.

Without waiting for her to perform introductions, he closed the distance and offered the man a hand. "Mack Abbott. And you are?"

"Trevor Boudreaux." The man took Mack's hand. Their shake was less about social niceties and more about a test of strength. Mack won. After breaking free from Mack's bruising grip, Trevor rubbed his hands together. "Surely you can discuss accounting matters tomorrow during working hours, Ella?"

Ella's ex-husband was in her house, and she obviously didn't want to be alone with him. Well, Mack could be an obtuse pain in the ass. In fact, according to her hurled insults earlier that afternoon, he was an expert.

"Actually, I have a car that will keep me occupied all day tomorrow. Tonight's the only free time I have." He shrugged and smiled a very non-apologetic smile. "Sorry."

"I'm sure you are." Trevor straightened his tie and smoothed it down his white shirt.

The poster child for an aging frat boy, Trevor was handsome and sophisticated, but an air of dissipation hung on him like the expensive suit he wore. He was older than Mack would have suspected, though. A good decade or more older than Ella if the lines at his eyes and mouth and neck and his thinning hair were any indication.

"I should be getting home anyway. I have an early showing in the morning." Trevor squared off with Ella at the door, and whether the intimidation was intentional or not, it was there. "We're not done. I'll be in touch."

He trotted down the front steps. Ella slammed the door and latched it. For a moment she stood facing the door. Slowly, she turned. "I guess you're wondering what that was all about."

"I'm a mite curious."

One corner of her mouth quirked up, but mostly she looked sad. "Actually, I'm not even a hundred percent sure what that was about. He hasn't bothered me since the divorce was final, and I moved to Cottonbloom. Then he turns up on my doorstep wanting help or advice about his current wife. The last woman he had an affair with while we were married, if you're keeping score. You want a drink? Beer or wine?"

"I'll take a beer. I've never been able to appreciate the finer points of wine." The kitchen was bright and airy and welcoming. He stopped short. "I guess your ex doesn't appreciate wine either, huh?"

"It was an accident. Let me get the broom." She went around the corner and came back with a broom and dustpan. Six feet from the carnage, she dropped the broom, pulled up, and hopped on one foot. "Ouch."

Mack was used to taking charge. It chafed some people, but letting a situation descend into chaos wasn't in his DNA. He picked Ella up at the waist and set her on the island countertop. She wobbled and grabbed his shoulders.

He circled her ankle and raised her foot. "A shard is stuck pretty deep. You got a first aid kit?"

"In the cabinet to the right of the microwave." She pointed over his shoulder.

He retrieved the kit, tucked it under his arms, and washed his hands. Coming back to her, he set the kit at her hip and flipped it open. The shard of glass was big enough for him to pull out with his fingers. He pressed a thick piece of gauze against the welling blood. Propping her heel up on his chest, he applied pressure with both thumbs.

The position forced her back onto her elbows, the front of her shirt taut. She was a business partner. One he disliked and wanted to get rid of as soon as possible. He shouldn't be noticing things like the way the fabric gaped enough at the button to see the color of her bra. Pink, like her toes. Was that a thing? Did women match underwear with toe polish? Or was it just this woman?

He forced his gaze to the mottled grays and blacks of the granite countertop but not before his brain registered the red marks on her arm where her sleeve had risen.

"What the—?" He kept pressure on her foot with one hand and reached to touch the marks on her arm with his other.

"It's nothing." She tugged at the sleeve. The fact she didn't meet his eye was a red flag. The woman usually couldn't help but challenge him with her eyes.

He looked toward the door. The urge to chase Trevor Boudreaux down, pull him out of his car, and beat the crap out of him was almost too much, but the man was long gone. "I get that your ex is an a-hole, but how big of one are we talking?"

"Sizable." Her lips twitched. How could she possibly find the situation amusing?

"What's so damn funny? Your ex coming in here and knocking you around?"

The ghost of her smile vanished. "He was not knocking me around." The knee-jerk defensiveness of her voice was telling.

"What would have happened if I hadn't shown up?"

"I was showing Trevor out when you arrived actually."

"You're not to allow him back in this house."

She jerked her foot out of his hands. "Excuse me? You're not my boss, Mack Abbott. Here or at the garage. Speaking of showing people out, you know where the door is."

She grabbed a Band-Aid from the kit, hopped off the counter, and did a weird heel walk out of the kitchen and into a large family room, disappearing on the other side of an overstuffed comfortable-looking couch.

Mack smoothed a hand down his beard. He had managed to piss her off again before he'd even been able to apologize for his behavior at the garage. Yet, she'd been in danger and if he hadn't turned up on her doorstep . . . it didn't bear thinking about.

Instead of showing himself the door, he took up the broom and dustpan, swept up the broken glass, and wiped up the spilled wine.

Rubbing his hands down the front of his jeans, he stepped cautiously into the family room. Built-in bookshelves flanked a massive fireplace and hearth. A flat screen TV was mounted above the mantle. Books and knick-knacks lined the shelves of the bookcases, and magazines were strewn on a coffee table. It was a cozy, lived-in room, warmer and more casual than he'd expected.

He stopped by the back of the couch and propped his hands on a cushion. Ella was lying on her back with one arm flung over her eyes and her foot propped up on her knee so she could press a tissue against the puncture.

"I'm sorry." The words emerged like the apology came from rusted-out gears in his psyche.

She moved her arm up an inch and pinned him with her eviscerating blue eyes. "You don't sound sorry; you sound like a grumpy bear whose porridge is too hot."

Had she seriously compared him to a fairytale bear? "Look, I realize I can be a little . . . high-handed."

She snort-laughed.

He rolled his eyes. "A lot high-handed when it comes to the garage. I suppose it sometimes spills over. That's why I came here in the first place. To apologize for today. For the oil change thing. I didn't mean to humiliate you or hurt your feelings."

"You didn't hurt my feelings." The faint mocking tone in her voice unsettled him.

"You weren't teary-eyed?"

"Teary?" She shot to her knees on the couch and put them face-to-face. "Your little temper tantrum this morning didn't hurt my feelings or intimidate me, Mack Abbott. You made me so mad I was ready to break something. Preferably something precious. Like your balls."

Sly humor snuck into her eyes and made him lean in. He forced his lips not to curl. "Your shoe made a pretty good start if that was your goal."

"That was actually an accident. If I wanted to bust your balls, I would have made a more concerted effort."

"Noted." He couldn't stem a small smile this time.

"If that's how you treated Ford, I get why he was so eager to quit and sell out." Her words were like a Molotov cocktail to whatever ease they were constructing.

It was true that his temper had gotten the best of him too many times since his pop had died. The expectations and stress of suddenly taking over the garage and being responsible if the restoration side of the business collapsed around their ears were overwhelming some days. His re-occurring nightmare was the bank coming to foreclose on them.

Ford was responsible for his own decisions, but had Mack had a hand in pushing him over the edge? He didn't like to think so.

"Wyatt and Jackson—"

"Put up with your BS instead of calling you out on it."

She raised her eyebrows to go along with the challenge in her voice.

He dropped his head between his arms. Why did Ella Boudreaux make him question his very purpose and existence? The mental vertigo she roused only got worse the more he was around her.

This time it was him turning on his heel and walking out the door. She didn't come after him and he didn't expect her to. He wasn't hurt or angry as much as he was confused. Part of him wished everything at the garage could return to the way it was before she smashed her way into their lives. At least then his discontent and anxiety were contained to a box he could keep taped shut.

Like a little kid studying a black widow spider, he was dimly aware of the danger she posed, but couldn't help being fascinated by her. Even after the push-pull of their confrontation tonight, he was already anticipating her arrival in the morning.

Chapter Five

Mack checked the clock. Ten o'clock. Where the hell was Ella? Had she quit the garage? Because of him? Granted they hadn't settled things the night before, but he'd interpreted the challenge in her eyes as a refusal to back down or give up.

"I thought you apologized to Ella last night?" Wyatt propped a shoulder against the jamb and slouched in the doorway, rubbing grease off his hands with a blue shop towel.

"I did." Mack shrugged. "Sort of."

Wyatt looked to the ceiling, maybe to God, and sighed before taking a seat across from the desk. "Dare I ask what 'sort of' means?"

"It means I got distracted from my initial apology when I arrived. Her ex was there."

"What's he like?"

"Older than I expected. Typical straight-laced business type. Drives a 5 Series." Mack sent Wyatt a side-eye. While he tried not to judge a book by its cover, Mack couldn't help but judge a man by his car.

Wyatt cocked his head. "Entitled jerk?"

"Even worse, I'd guess." For some reason, he didn't

share the broken wine glass or finger marks on Ella's arm with Wyatt. Those were her secrets to share. "After he left, I said some things. She said some things. My simple apology didn't go quite as planned."

Wyatt drummed his fingers on the arm of the chair. "What if she's at Tarwater's telling him to sell her share? I get that this situation isn't ideal and that you don't like her, but I do. She's nice and more down-to-earth than I would have guessed. Plus, she has some good ideas if you weren't too stubborn to hear them. We could get a part owner who's a bigger thorn in our sides than her. You get that, right?"

Mack straightened. "What makes you think I don't like her?"

Wyatt's eyes widened comically as he gestured around them. "All the yelling and assholery is a pretty big indication."

"Do you put up with my BS?" Mack slouched back in the chair.

Wyatt propped his feet up on the edge of the desk. "I feel like we're having a Dr. Freud moment here. Are you feeling the urge to lie down and describe your dreams?"

"I'm feeling the urge to put you in a headlock until you cry uncle." Mack bared his teeth.

"What's brought on the sudden self-examination?" Before Mack could locate an answer, Wyatt continued. "Ah! It's Ella. Well, well, well." He steepled his fingers like a cartoon villain. "She's gotten under your skin."

"Only insofar as she's trying to change things in the garage." Mack looked to the clock, then the door again.

"Do Jackson and I put up with your BS? The short answer is, yes."

Wyatt's gray eyes were clear and nonjudgmental, but Mack still felt like he'd let his brothers down. "Why don't you tell me to eff off?"

"We would if you got out of hand. But, you're like a pressure cooker. All the stress builds up and then *bam*." Wyatt smacked his hands together.

Mack pulled at his chin hairs. "I haven't always been a pressure cooker."

"The last couple of years have been tough. Tougher for you than anyone. We get it."

"We all miss Pop."

"Of course. But you shouldered more of the responsibility of the garage." Wyatt swung his feet off the desk. "Jackson and I could take on more, you know."

"You're already doing more by going to the trade shows and drumming up business in Mississippi. Plus, you and Sutton have a wedding to plan."

"All I have to do is show up, according to Sutton. Her mom is going a little crazy. She has mentioned a harp player and doves."

"Good Lord, one of the Abbott cousins might pull out a shotgun and shoot a dove if they're in season." Mack found a chuckle, and Wyatt joined him, his laugh lighter and closer to the surface than Mack's.

Wyatt got up and headed back to the shop floor.

"Hey, bro?" Mack called.

Wyatt turned in the door, a smile still on his face.

"You think I drove Ford to gamble and give up on the family?" The question belly-flopped in the middle of the room.

Wyatt's smile flipped into a frown. "That's a question without a simple answer."

"But did I have a part?" He'd always regarded himself as, not a hero exactly, but *worthy* of the garage while Ford was not. Ford had never put in the sweat and tears and occasionally even the blood that was required. Mack, on the other hand, had sacrificed everything.

Wyatt rubbed the back of his neck. "I think Ford *wanted* to want the garage, if that makes sense, but deep down he didn't, and it bothered him how much you did want it. Your skills outshone his, and he couldn't handle it. Of course, your attitude of rubbing his nose in it every time he came around wasn't helpful. Then again, none of us had much patience for him." What Mack saw in Wyatt's face was regret.

"You feel bad about how it went down."

"Yeah, a little. I'm not sure what we could have done differently, but Pop would hate the way it's turned out. We don't even know if Ford is okay. Who does he have to lean on in Memphis?"

A shudder went through Mack. He couldn't imagine not having his brothers there to prop him up when his doubts and worries got too heavy. Ford's plans had included starting over in Memphis where he knew no one, as far as Mack was aware. With Ford's pride smashed and the acrimony that had flourished between them, would he call home if he needed help?

"Our mother is close. He'd fall back on her if he got into trouble, don't you think?" Mack asked. "Although, I don't know how obligated she'd feel to help."

Mack hadn't come to terms with the fact the mother who had abandoned them when he was six had turned up. Or more accurately, Wyatt had tracked her down. She had made a life in north Louisiana, only a few hours' drive away. Mack was the only one who hadn't bridged the gaping chasm of years between them.

She had taken in Ford for a time and given him money out of motherly duty or guilt or maybe even love. Mack didn't trust her, not after she'd walked out and never looked back. He was older than Jackson and Wyatt, and unlike them, he possessed fuzzy but intact memories of her tucking him into bed and making him pancakes and holding his hand. Then, one morning, she was gone. He hadn't understood. He still didn't.

"Mother would help him if he asked." Wyatt gave Mack a look that settled something uncomfortable in his chest. "You should call her."

"I'm thirty-two. I've outgrown any need for a mother."

"It's not about needing someone to wipe your butt, bro. It's about family."

"I have you boys and the aunts and more cousins than we can shake a stick at. I don't need more family." He and Wyatt had had this discussion-argument multiple times, and it always ended the same.

Wyatt shook his head. "Okay, whatever. But, if anyone knows where Ford is and how he's doing, it would be her. If you're really worried about him, then call her."

As Wyatt retreated, Mack stared a hole through the back of his head. Wyatt could easily call and ask about Ford, but even if he did, he wouldn't tell Mack. This was Wyatt's way of prodding Mack into taking action. He refused to be the first to flinch in their game of chicken. He wouldn't call. Decision made.

The clock ticked off another minute. Dammit. Where was Ella?

What if her ex had been waiting for Mack to leave and returned to finish whatever Mack had interrupted? What if she was hurt and needed his help? His heart sputtered like an engine without the proper air-fuel ratio. He took a deep breath and reached for his truck keys.

The door opened and relief rushed him. Except, instead of a sassy-mouthed black-haired hellcat, his aunts strolled in. Aunt Hyacinth was in tennis shoes and a tracksuit while Hazel looked like she was headed to church. A normal Friday.

Aunt Hazel performed a right turn with military precision and entered his office while Hyacinth picked her way over to where Wyatt was working.

"Did you bring the Crown Vic in?"

"It's outside and needs some wiper fluid." She sounded slightly defensive with such a flimsy excuse. "Wanted to check on you boys before heading to sort boxes for the church rummage sale."

"You're welcome anytime, you know that. Can I get you some coffee?"

"A small cup of black would be nice. There's a chill wind outside."

Mack released his keys, and they fell onto the desk with a jangle. His death grip had carved indentations into his palm. He tamped down his impatience and worry. Returning with two cups, he handed one to Hazel and took a seat, sipping his own.

His aunt's eyes were still as sharp and calculating as ever. Age had drawn fine lines over her face and her hair was no longer dark, but a thick, fluffy white. Even so, the renowned beauty of her youth was visible.

He sipped and waited, trying not to betray the tension tightening his muscles. Hazel wanted something from him. She would speak after she had her arrows notched and was sure she could run roughshod over any excuses he might make.

"I expect you to do your daddy and your name proud, Mack Bolivar Abbott."

A youthful panic at hearing his full name had him racking his brain. Lord help him, what had he done? "I do my best for the garage every day, Aunt Hazel."

"You run a good honest business, but that's not what I'm referring to. This"—she gestured toward the shop floor— "is concrete and metal. It's not flesh and blood."

More guilt elbowed its way into his chest and settled in for a long stay. "Ford is the one who screwed up and left."

"Yes, he did." She raised one eyebrow and let the silence burrow between them. It was an old ploy of hers and one he'd never been able to withstand.

"What do you expect me to do?" He threw his hands up and knocked his coffee over. Muffling a curse that would get him yet another use of his full name, he grabbed a wad of used shop towels and sopped up the mess. Hazel sat and watched with eyes so like his pop's, it was disconcerting.

"Have you and Wyatt been talking?" He lobbed the accusation as he chunked the towels in the trash basket.

"He's my nephew, same as you, so yes, we do converse on occasion." A dry humor coated her words.

"You know what I mean."

"I know that no matter what Ford has done, he's still your brother. And whether you like him or not, you still love him."

Mack sighed and leaned his head back against the chair to stare at the ducts that lined the ceiling. She was right. He and Ford hadn't always been adversaries. Ford was a year older, and Mack had followed him around like a puppy when they were young. When had things changed?

Maybe when the twins came along? The four of them had vied for their pop's attention even when he didn't have enough to spare. The garage had been his wife and life and livelihood.

The twins hadn't seemed to mind. They had each other, after all, their bond a mystery of genetics. Mack was used to deferring to Ford and hadn't minded any attention their pop gave his older brother. Things had taken a turn when Mack had showed an interest and aptitude for mechanics at a young age and garnered their pop's admiration. Was he somehow to blame for that too?

"I'm not saying you have to convince him to move back to Cottonbloom, although that would be a welcome development, but you need to make peace for his sake and yours. Make him understand he has a soft place to land." His aunt's voice was gentle.

"I'll think about it." It was all he could give her.

The flash in Hazel's eyes was part anger and part disappointment. She stood and crossed her arms, her pocketbook dangling over her elbow. "You are the most stubborn, hardheaded Abbott that's ever been born. If I could take you over my knee—"

The door to the shop banged open on a gust of wind. Mack popped out of his chair. Pushing her hair out of face, Ella Boudreaux floated inside like Mary Poppins arriving. She shut the door with a backward kick of her foot and shook her hair over her shoulders.

Twin columns of feelings squeezed him. Relief and frustration.

"Thank God," Mack whispered. His aunt's gaze cut from Ella to him and narrowed. He cleared his throat and searched for something innocuous to say. "She's late. You know how much I hate that."

Ella stopped in the doorway of his office. He did a quick inventory. Hair that begged for his hands, check. Breasts that made his mouth water, double check. Long legs that he'd dreamed about wrapped around him last night, check. Curves like his favorite back road, checkity-check. She appeared unharmed and perfectly fine.

Worry that had built all morning tumbled out in his rough, sharp-edged voice. "Where have you been? You're late."

"Am I clocking in these days?" She gestured to the antiquated time-stamp machine. It had been a way to keep track of how much or little Ford worked. Since he'd taken off, Mack had discontinued its use.

"Maybe it's the only way to teach you a decent work ethic."

His aunt gasped and whispered his name—his full name—for the second time in less than ten minutes. A new record. "Mack Bolivar Abbott."

"Teach me . . . ?" Ella propped her tight fists on her hips. "At least that's something that can be learned. Kindness can't be taught. Too bad you got the short end of the stick where that's concerned."

He and Ella held gazes. Damn, the fire in her eyes threatened to singe him. His entire body was aware of her in the way of predator and prey. Trouble was he wasn't sure which he was. Right now, she looked like she might maim him. But something else thrummed under the surface of the antipathy. Deep and chaotic.

Lust.

He'd felt it the first time she'd sashayed into his life at Sutton's New Year's Eve party. She'd been sophisticated and uptown, yet an earthiness had upended his ability to successfully counteract her claim on the garage. He'd fallen back on intimidation by size and gruffness, which worked against men at a bar, but hadn't dented Ella's self-assured amusement that night.

The same thing was happening now. All his defense mechanisms seemed to bounce off her like rubber. What else was there to do but give her what she was owed?

"I'm . . . sorry for being an ass."

Chapter Six

If Mack had sprouted wings or horns, Ella couldn't have been more surprised. The kicker was he sounded a hundred and ten percent sincere. He even looked sincere. And tough. And altogether too attractive for her sanity.

His size and dark beard lent him a menace before he even said a word. And, when he did speak, his gruff, deep voice only added to the impression. But then there were his eyes. The seething emotions in their depths drew her like a bug to a zapper.

He was more complex than his demeanor might indicate. The previous night had confirmed her theory. He'd been alternately kind and high-handed. The weight of her accusation regarding Ford had hurt him and settled heavily around his shoulders. She'd regretted the way they'd parted, but all she'd seen were his taillights by the time she'd hobbled outside to apologize.

Now, here he was apologizing to her. Did she even deserve one?

"You *were* kind of a butthead, but I wasn't exactly sweetness and sunshine either. And I didn't thank you for cleaning up the mess last night . . . and stuff. Truce?"

She stuck out her hand because that's what one did to

seal a peace treaty, right? His hesitation sent a tremor through her, but before she could snatch her hand back and unload on him, his hand enveloped hers.

"Truce."

Time slowed and noises ceased to register. His hand was big and rough in a way that sent a tingle up her arm and electrified her body. She sensed danger like a hare approaching a snare. Her heart rate accelerated, and she needed a fan. Not a dainty Southern belle fan, but an industrial-strength one.

She tugged on her hand. He loosened his grip but didn't fully release her. Her hand kept contact with his until it was just their fingertips. When the connection broke, time stumbled over itself to catch up, and she was dimly aware of Mack's aunt speaking.

"—finally meet you. I'm Hazel Abbott." His aunt's expression wasn't unfriendly. But her eyes—a mirror image of Mack's—roiled with curiosity. This woman wasn't a warm, fuzzy relation who brought in cookies, but a matriarch who could both eviscerate and protect her nephews even though they were grown.

"I'm Ella Boudreaux. I haven't made the best first impression, I'm afraid."

"Nonsense. I admire any woman who can stand toe-to-toe with my nephew." Hazel Abbott made a shooing motion toward said nephew. "I'm sure you have work to do, Mack. Run along so Ms. Boudreaux and I can chat."

Mack's lips moved as if an argument was simmering, but he only nodded and murmured, "Yes, ma'am," before retreating.

"There now. Mack is a good boy, but too wont to control everything and everybody. Come and join me." Hazel took a chair and, not having a ready excuse, Ella did as she was told, squirming on the edge of her seat. This felt too much like a visit to the principal's office.

"What brought you to Cottonbloom, Ms. Boudreaux?"

After last night, Ella's married name grated on her nerves worse than usual. "Call me Ella, please."

"Then you're to call me Hazel or Miss Hazel, whichever you're most comfortable with."

Since she had been raised never to call her elders by their given name, Ella couldn't imagine calling her plain "Hazel." But how much to reveal to this woman with the scalpel-sharp eyes?

"I was living in Jackson, but after my divorce, I wanted a fresh start. I ran across an article in *Heart of Dixie* about the Labor Day festival competition and the tornado that damaged the downtown."

During some of her darkest days with Trevor, she'd pulled out the article and read it time and again. Imagining an alternate future in Cottonbloom had made her life with Trevor bearable, and when she'd finally broken free, her destination was not in question even though the decision to move to Cottonbloom defied logic.

Life in Cottonbloom had seemed simple and charming in black and white on the pages of *Heart of Dixie*. She shrugged. "The town seemed idyllic."

"And is that how you've found it now that you're a resident? Idyllic?"

"It's . . . quaint." It wasn't a lie, but an evasion. Cottonbloom's split over the river was complicated. Each side of Cottonbloom had its own personality—and problems. Still, she didn't regret the move. "And complicated."

Hazel's chuckle was more carefree than her appearance. "Aptly put. I was a little girl when the town split in two and I remember the pain and anger that festered—on both sides. Things are mended now, but tensions can fray at the oddest time."

"I like the duality. Part of me is drawn to both sides."

Hazel's gaze zeroed in on her, and Ella looked to the

floor. It was more than she'd admitted to anyone in Cottonbloom. More than she'd admitted to herself even. But it was true. Later she might examine the whys and wherefores, or maybe she'd lock the thought away along with all the other tangles of her life.

"Hobart, my brother, started this garage. He worked day and night to turn it into a success. He—"

"I'm not trying to destroy or change what your brother built, Miss Hazel." Ella held her hands up.

"No. I don't think you are." Miss Hazel stood and clutched the handles of her black purse in both hands, her head tilting. "My brother ignored his sons and his wife to build this place. I don't want the same thing to happen to Mack."

Ella startled. "But he's not married."

Was he divorced? Or even worse, did he have a girlfriend? Why hadn't she thought to find out before now? And why did the possibility bother her so much? Ella found him with her eyes, propped under the hood of the 240Z, his arms braced apart, his profile stoic. As if sensing her, he turned his head. She couldn't separate her gaze from his.

Hazel's voice contained more than a hint of laughter. "I need to round up my sister. No doubt she's talked Wyatt's ear off about that reality show they both watch. For the life of me, I can't understand why two strangers would want to live outside naked. Nice to meet you, Ella."

With more effort than it should have cost, Ella peeled her attention away from Mack. "Likewise, ma'am."

Hazel gathered her twin sister from the corner of the garage where Wyatt was working on the brakes of an old Camaro. Their laughter drifted over the music, good natured and open.

Hazel leaned in to whisper in Hyacinth's ear. When Hyacinth's gaze cut to where she stood in the doorway of

Mack's office, Ella tensed. It was obvious they were discussing her, but instead of coming over to introduce herself, Hyacinth gave Wyatt a hug and waved toward Ella. She raised her hand in response, fighting the urge to look over her shoulder. The sisters left together with their heads close.

As soon as the door closed behind them, Mack ambled over as only a man one hundred percent comfortable in his body could do. "Everything okay?"

"It's fine. Fine." Ella retreated to the office in search of solitude and silence, but he followed. And why shouldn't he, considering it was technically his.

Her conversation with Hazel had left her rattled. She stopped short and spun around. Mack bumped into her. It was like hitting a wall, not of concrete, but of warm, strong flesh and blood. He grabbed her upper arms, his touch firm but gentle. Heartbeats after she regained her balance, he still held her.

"Do you have an ex-wife stashed away somewhere?" The question bypassed her brain's filter.

His eyes roved her face, close enough for her to admire the gold around his irises. It reminded her of the sparks from the welding machine. "Not a single one."

"Girlfriend?"

"Why are you interested all of a sudden?" His voice held more curiosity than defensiveness.

An excellent question. She'd rather endure a hundred fire ant bites than answer. She hadn't been worried about the state of his personal life until Miss Hazel had planted the question, and now like kudzu, the worry spread until it consumed her.

His fingers moved along her arms. Not an obvious caress, but enough for her sensitized skin to drink in his touch like parched ground getting rain for the first time in forever. This was a Mack she didn't know, one whose gentleness tempered everything that was hard about him. She could fall into this man and get entirely lost.

She'd done that once before, and once was enough. She shook his hands off and put the desk between them. "I'm not interested. Not at all. Only curious how much time you spend ignoring a woman in favor of a bunch of inanimate metal parts."

He crossed his arms over his chest, all softness gone as if she'd imagined it. But she hadn't. Her skin still tingled where he'd touched her.

"Did you come in this morning to work or to quit?"

"Puh-lease. What do you think?" She met his steely stare with one of her own.

Was that lip twitch the start of a smile or did he have an itch near his unmentionables? "If you want to install the new accounting software, go ahead. I'll be on the shop floor the rest of the day."

He turned to walk out, leaving her mouth unhinged this time. She rushed around the desk. "Mack, wait."

He half-turned, an eyebrow raised.

"You didn't pick a program."

"Install what you think is best. The business credit card is in the top drawer." He disappeared into the pit under the Camaro Wyatt had been working on earlier.

She made a little sound of exasperation even though there was no one around to hear her. After everything, he didn't even care. Or else, he trusted her judgment.

No, not possible. Was it? She returned to his office and glanced over at him through her lashes while she pretended to leaf through some papers. Mack's shoulders and head were visible in the pit, his bare arms working a wrench at the underbelly of the Camaro. Had she ruined his coveralls?

Blowing out a breath, she walked behind his desk out of visible range. But as if she had special powers, she could sense him on the other side of the concrete wall, making it difficult to concentrate.

By the time she had the new program installed, she had bitten her thumbnail down to a nub—an old habit she'd thought she'd broken years ago.

Wyatt popped his head around the doorframe and, upon seeing her sitting at the computer, said, "Glad our Mack truck didn't turn you into road kill."

She snorted at the very apropos nickname for Mack. He was a giant truck running obstacles off the road with the sheer force of his personality and stubbornness. "Not a chance."

Wyatt smiled, tapped his fist on the doorjamb, and pointed. "By the way, if you're going to be around the garage most days, I'll add you into the rotation."

"The rotation for what?" Suspicion crept into her bones.

"Picking what we listen to. Today is my choice."

She cocked her head to listen to the low sounds of Patsy Cline's dulcet voice cutting through the noise of someone welding. Patsy had been a favorite of her mother's. The only emotion that surfaced was something akin to regret.

"I wouldn't have pegged you for a classic country kind of guy. You're more modern and easy."

Jackson's arm streaked around Wyatt's neck and a noogie session ensued before Wyatt elbowed him away with a laugh. He smoothed his hair down and made room for his twin. They stood with their bodies angled toward each other, and even though they weren't identical, something inexplicable linked them.

"Wyatt is redneck country to the bone," Jackson said.

"I'm not the one who risks life and limb racing around in a circle like a mouse chasing cheese. Are you ever going to hit the track again? You've lost your edge since you and Willa got together."

Ella could tell their teasing was born from love. Her

heart stung like riling up a nest of yellow-jackets. Her brother had loved to tickle her until she cried uncle through tears of laughter.

"When is my day? I'll have to really think about what to play."

"Mack is up next, then you can pick," Jackson said. "Want us to grab you some of Rufus's barbeque for lunch?"

"Okay. I've never eaten there though. Do you have a menu I can look at?"

Wyatt clutched his chest, staggered over to a chair, and plopped down. "Tell me that was a joke."

Neither he nor Jackson cracked a smile. Ella bit her bottom lip to keep from grinning and shrugged. "I keep meaning to stop in and give it a shot, but I haven't gotten around to it."

While she was invited to social functions around town, she didn't have a friend to call and invite for dinner, and she'd turned down the few men who had asked her out. As confident as her persona was, eating out alone wasn't a self-esteem climb she was ready to tackle yet.

"Today is your lucky day." Jackson rubbed his hands together.

Mack appeared out of nowhere, wiping his hands on a shop towel. "Who's getting lucky today?"

"Not you, that's for certain," Wyatt said with a cheekiness that was part of his DNA.

"Our girl Ella has never eaten at Rufus's." Jackson pointed in her direction, but his gaze remained on Mack.

Our girl. Emotion hit her like a tsunami without any warning and tumbled her in its chaos. Memories of her brother and their long-lost bond brought unwelcome tears to her eyes. She clamped her jaw shut to stop the wobble of her chin. She turned and stared at the computer monitor before the worst-case scenario occurred and Mack noticed.

"I've got to run up to Benson's Hardware. How about I take Ella so she can experience Rufus's firsthand, and I'll grab you boys and Willa a plate. What do you say, Ella?" Mack asked.

She blinked her tears away. The end goal was getting rid of her. Was this some elaborate, crazy game of good cop, bad cop? Were Wyatt and Jackson buttering her up so Mack could squeeze her out? Was this field trip another one of his tests?

"Okay. Sure. I am hungry." She narrowed her eyes at Mack, waiting for him to give his plan away.

"Meet me by the truck in five."

"I can drive." She stood up and leaned into her fists on the desk.

Mack tilted his chin up and looked down his nose at her. She wasn't short by any means, but she wished she had on heels, so she could meet him eye to eye, lip to lip. She shook the errant thought out of her head. She had to quit thinking of him like a . . . *man*.

Instead of the expected snide comment, he smiled. "Another day. The supplies I need would never fit in your car. Not sure I would, either."

"I'd like to see you try sometime." A fair amount of tease snuck into her voice without her noticing.

"Only if I lose a bet." The corner of his mouth quirked up. Contrary to their earlier battle of wills, this sparring was fun and invigorating instead of disheartening and exhausting.

"I'll hold you to that." She turned to gather her purse. "I'll be out in a minute."

She freshened up in the bathroom, running a brush through her hair before pulling it back into a ponytail and applying a soft red lipstick. This wasn't a date of any sort, yet butterflies staged a riot in her stomach.

She blew out a breath and checked herself in the mirror.

As good as it was going to get. As she pulled the door open, a body pushed and Willa staggered into her.

Willa righted herself with a little laugh. "Sorry about that."

"No worries."

"You look nice." Willa flashed her a smile and ran her hands down the front of her coveralls. In them, she was a shapeless potato.

"I'd say the same, but those coveralls aren't exactly fashion statements."

Willa stuck her hands in the pockets, cocked a hip, and fluttered her eyelashes. "You don't think?"

Ella laughed along with the other woman, an easy camaraderie settling between them. "I see Mack working in jeans. Couldn't you do that?"

"I could, but then my jeans would get gross. Once you get used to wearing them, coveralls actually make things easier." Willa washed her hands and grabbed a brown paper towel, turning to lean on the single sink.

Even with her dark hair at a ragged in-between stage of short and long and in her functional coveralls, Willa was pretty in a wholesome way. Her brown eyes were warm and sincere and Ella thought maybe, just maybe, this woman would turn out to be a friend. It would be a new experience for Ella.

"The coveralls weren't a deterrent for Jackson anyway, right?" Ella regretted the naughty tease in her voice. She and Willa weren't those kind of friends yet.

Pink flushed Willa's face, but a brilliant smile came out of hiding. "It sure didn't. In fact, I think that was part of the draw. Not many women get the Abbott boys' obsession with cars."

Ella let out a breath, relieved her teasing hadn't offended. "Sutton obviously does."

"Sewing and designing is her passion, like cars are Wyatt's. She would never ask him to give up the garage." Willa tilted her head. "Can I ask you something?"

Ella hesitated. That sort of question usually precipitated something unpleasant. "Sure."

"Why did you buy Ford's share? You don't seem a metal-and-oil kind of girl."

No one had outright asked her why. All of them, but especially Mack, had assumed and accused and insinuated reasons. "I grew up around cars."

Willa nodded. "Me too."

A knock made them both whip around. Ella cracked the door open. Jackson stood on the other side trying to peek around her. "I thought I saw Willa go in."

"You did. Sorry for monopolizing the bathroom. I'd better scoot out before Mack leaves me, and I miss out on this miraculous barbeque." She exited the bathroom with Willa on her heels.

"Tell Mack not to forget the extra sauce this time," Jackson called out.

She waved over her head and stepped outside. The cool, breezy morning had given way to a warm lovely spring day. The sun was up, the sky was blue, the birds were singing. At least she assumed they were. It was hard to tell over the rumble of Mack's truck.

She ran-walked toward the passenger door and hauled herself inside. It was cavernous compared to her convertible and surprisingly plush. He didn't speak, only side-swiped her a glance and shifted into drive. They lumbered onto the road like a battering ram.

The silence wasn't uncomfortable. Mack gave off a relaxed vibe behind the wheel, resting one arm on the console between them. His plaid shirt was rolled halfway to his elbow, and every time he tapped his finger to the beat of the country song playing on the radio, the ropey muscles jumped. Ella shifted in the leather seat, unable to take her eyes off the flagrant arm porn.

"Jackson wants extra sauce." The inane words popped out of her mouth.

From the corner of her eyes, she saw him nod once. A raised pink scar ran over the back of his hand and disappeared around the side between his index finger and thumb.

"What happened to your hand?" She reached out like she was a starving woman and his hand was a hunk of bread to touch the back.

He flipped his hand over. The scar curled halfway into his palm. "Got it caught in a claw trap out in the woods when I was ten. Would have been more serious if it wasn't for Ford. It took fifty stitches."

"That's scary. It's a wonder you didn't lose use of it." Now she was less concerned about the crazy sexiness of his arm and more with what he had omitted from the story. "How far out in the woods were you? How'd you get loose?"

He stared out the windshield and drew his hand into a fist. "Pretty far out. The boys and I spent our summers in the woods out back of the barn. Pop was busy working and expected us to take care of each other and ourselves."

"Was Ford around?"

"Back then, things were different." He opened and closed his hand as if trying to grasp the memory. "Ford managed to pull the trap apart. I was bleeding bad. He wrapped his shirt around my hand and half-carried me home. Aunt Hazel happened to be at the house. She loaded me in her car and drove me to the hospital across the river."

"I'm glad Ford was there, and you didn't bleed to death

in the forest." She didn't want to dwell on how close Mack had been to death. It could happen to the best of people and in an instant.

He stared out the windshield, and Ella didn't push him further. It was none of her business. Except whatever bad blood had formed between the brothers was the reason she was sitting in Mack's truck on the way to try Rufus's barbeque for the first time.

The pine tree–lined isolation of the parish road gave way to the occasional house, then neighborhoods as they drew closer to downtown Cottonbloom. The houses reminded her of her childhood home. Brick ranches with modest yards and the occasional swing set visible over a backyard fence. Hardly the shack Trevor had always teased her about growing up in, but starkly different than the house she lived in now.

"I guess this is slumming it for you." A familiar bite was back in his voice.

"Actually, I was thinking how much this reminds me of the house I grew up in."

"Fond memories?"

How to answer? Her memories were a mish-mash of good and bad, but weren't everyone's? Even Mack, who had brothers and aunts and a father who had loved him, bore scars from the past. So did she.

"Some were. Some weren't. My parents got divorced when I was pretty young and my stepfather was pretty terrible. I think he resented having to share my mom with us. My brother got out as soon as he graduated and turned eighteen."

"I didn't know you had a brother. Are you two close?"

She turned her head away, sudden tears blurring her vision. "I idolized him. He loved cars. I spent hours watching him tinker on his 240Z."

The truck came to a stop in a parking place along River Street, but he didn't make a move to turn the engine off. The cab took on the intimacy of a confessional.

"That's how you knew all about the Datsun."

"Yeah. He joined up right after graduation. Marines."

"What happened?" Foreboding weighted the question.

Chapter Seven

Grief reared and kicked her in the gut. Being in the garage and near the 240Z had rubbed the calluses off her brother's place in her heart, leaving a raw ache. "Chopper crashed on a training exercise. Seven men died. Grayson was killed before he even deployed."

"I'm sorry."

"Me too." A tear trickled out, and she wiped it away with the side of her hand, still staring out the window toward the river that divided the towns. Bud-tipped flower stalks burst from the ground. In another week, the river would be framed by riotous beauty and color, but for now, only the potential was there. A potential that could be struck down by something as innocuous as a late frost.

His hand covered hers, warm and strong and alive. She turned her hand so their palms lined up. Instead of pulling away, he knitted their fingers together and squeezed just enough to convey his understanding and sympathy. It was a simple gesture, but one she appreciated beyond measure.

The last years of her marriage had been devoid of any compassion and kindness. And since moving to Cottonbloom, she'd denied herself the physical and emotional closeness of a friend or lover. Her loneliness was a living breathing creature she'd nurtured for too long.

Sitting next to Mack made her want to abandon the creature, but at the end of that road lay heartache.

She pasted on a smile and disentangled their hands. "I'm starving and as much as you boys have talked up this barbeque, I'm expecting something special."

Opening the truck door shattered the sense they were the only two people in the world. The sounds of the river flowing and the clacking of cars crossing the steel-girded bridge threw a cloak of normalcy over the moment.

What was she doing making personal confessions to the man who had vowed to see her gone from the garage and his life? She'd let stupid emotions get the better of her. A mistake she could ill afford.

Before she made it off the running board, Mack was there, offering a hand. The scar along the palm took on new meaning. He had shared a memory he'd probably rather kept to himself too. It put them on even ground.

She slipped her hand in his and allowed him to help her down even though she was more than capable. He didn't keep a hold on her though, shoving his hands into the pockets of his jeans before chucking his chin toward Rufus's. She matched his long stride across the street.

A redheaded lady backed through the glass door, holding a plastic bag in one hand and a lidded drink in the other. Mack grabbed the handle and pulled it fully open for her.

"Oh. Thanks, Mack. How're you and yours doing?"

"Busy as usual."

The woman took a pull on her straw, her gaze assessing Ella. Ella assessed right back. The woman was middle-aged but with a vitality only slightly dimmed by the tired cast of her face.

"You must be Ms. Boudreaux. I'm Marigold Caldwell."

What sort of talk had the woman heard? "Ella, please. Nice to meet you."

"You too. Are you a reader?"

"Mostly business journals and stock reports these days." Ella didn't acknowledge the way Mack's head swiveled toward her, although she buried a smile. Shocking Mack was entertaining.

"I'm the librarian across the river. Come over and see me. I'll get you hooked." Her smile was impish and demanded a smile in return, so Ella let hers loose.

"How's Dave?" By contrast, Mack's voice was even grimmer than usual.

Marigold's smile dimmed. "Getting better. He's supposed to be resting but I caught him trying to clean the gutters the other day. That man will be the death of me."

"When will he be cleared for work?"

"Soon, we hope." Marigold threw her shoulders back and gave a little headshake as if it were that easy to cast off her worries. "Tell Willa I got her book in. It's waiting behind the counter."

"I'll let her know. You call if there's anything we can do to help, you hear?" Mack leaned in and gave Marigold a one-armed hug.

Marigold's smile fell and her eyes closed as she leaned into Mack's shoulder. He couldn't see her, but Ella could. Then, her smile was back. "If the Lord is willing, we'll get along fine. See y'all later."

With a wave she jogged across the street to an older sedan that had seen its best days at least a decade earlier. Even after Ella followed Mack into the bustling restaurant, she looked over her shoulder until Marigold pulled away.

Mack put in his order and three to-go orders for Wyatt, Jackson, and Willa, then raised his eyebrows at her and waved her forward. The man behind the counter had tattoos visible at the roll of his sleeves. The years re-flected in his eyes were far older than his body.

"What can I get you, ma'am?"

"She's been living over the river for a year or more and never been here, Clayton. Can you believe it?"

"That's a darn shame. Clayton Preston." The man behind the counter offered a hand, and she shook it.

"Ella Boudreaux."

She could tell by the way his eyes darted to Mack that he had heard about her. "Might I recommend the pork plate? You can pick any two sides, but the green beans and slaw are especially good today."

"Sounds perfect." She reached into her purse, but Mack stayed her hand.

"I got this." He handed over cash.

"You two eating here or heading back to the garage with it?"

"We'll eat here, but pack up the rest, would you?"

"Sure thing."

While they waited at the counter, Ella rocked back and forth, searching for something to say. "Did you remember extra sauce for Jackson?"

"Yep."

Clayton returned with two plates piled high with food. Mack took both and led the way to an empty table in the corner. It was barely big enough for the two of them.

For a few minutes, the silence was punctuated only by Ella's exclamations on how good everything was.

"Glad you like it. It's my favorite place to eat." Mack jabbed his spork into his slaw.

"Has it been here a long time?"

"All my life, which means forever for me. Pop used to bring me and Ford down here on Saturday mornings when the shop was closed. He'd meet a bunch of his friends for coffee and gossip. Ford and I would pretend our iced teas were coffee and talk about important things like which Hot Wheels cars were our favorite. The smell of smoking pork butts permeated everything. Then before we left, he'd get each of us a fresh smoked pork sandwich for the road. So good."

He shook his head, a smile on his face, and speared some pork into his mouth. It was the second time he'd mentioned Ford, and not in a disparaging way, but fondly. Had something shifted in his attitude toward his prodigal brother?

"Where is Ford? Have you talked to him lately?"

Mack moved his food around like a little kid trying to hide his vegetables. "He's in Memphis. At least I think so."

"Doing what?"

"Surviving. I hope."

The loss of Ford obviously bothered him in ways he wasn't willing to admit to her or even himself. She glanced up at him through her lashes. "Have you tried calling him?"

"He doesn't want to hear from me. Too much water under that bridge to cross."

Because Ella had lost a brother she had no chance of regaining, she had little patience for Mack's attitude. She jabbed her spork in the pork, sat back, and crossed her arms over her chest, her foot jiggling to mirror her agitation. "Bridges can always be crossed."

"Not ones burned to cinders."

"Bridges can be rebuilt with time and effort."

"Ford didn't put the effort into the garage." A hint of his frustration with the conversation flashed across his face. "What would *you* do? Would you look for him? Is he due an apology after what he did?"

He made a dismissive gesture toward her, his meaning clear. Ford had inflicted *her* onto Mack and the garage. Even though he'd not made any bones about the fact he didn't want her around, she'd hoped they were moving past the simmering animosity and into new territory. Not friendship maybe, but a mutual understanding.

"Does it have to be about who's right and who's wrong? Maybe both of you are owed an apology from each other. If my brother were alive, I wouldn't waste a single second. I would find him and bring him home."

"This is different."

"Maybe. Maybe not. But nothing's going to change the fact he's your brother."

A few minutes passed in silence as they ate, neither of them making eye contact. The barbecue had lost its flavor, and she picked at the remainder. A change in subject was the only way to salvage the lunch.

"What's the story with the woman we met outside? Marigold, was it?"

His sigh filled the space with sadness. "Her husband, Dave, has been sick. Cancer. Dave is one of the good ones, you know? Always there to lend a hand."

"What kind of work does he do?"

"Contractor. Handyman. Jack-of-all-trades sort of stuff. He helped Wyatt and Jackson renovate the loft in the barn."

"Has he been out of work for a while?"

"Too long from what I've heard."

"What do you mean?"

"He has limited health insurance and the cost of his treatments and his hospital stays have nearly crushed them. They're surviving on Marigold's salary. I'm not sure how much librarians make, but it can't be enough to put two kids through college on top of the hospital bills.

"That's terrible." Ella's issues seemed quaint in comparison. No wonder stress and sadness had shadowed Marigold's smiles.

"So you relax with business journals in the evening?" Mack's head tilted as he studied her.

"Actually, I relax with TV in the evenings. Reading business reports is part of my job."

"Which is what exactly? Besides playing mechanic at my garage."

She let a long breath go through her nose, deciding whether or not to rise to his bait. It seemed their truce was a tenuous one. "I'm an investor. In your garage, but other ventures as well. I also dabble in stocks."

Mack sat back in his seat. "Did you learn all that from Trevor?"

Resentment a decade in the making bubbled up from where it had lain dormant since she claimed her independence. "No. Not from Trevor."

In fact, if anything, Trevor had learned from her. He was a decent real estate agent, his old family name and charm offensive selling more houses than his skill. It was Ella who'd expanded their fortunes with instincts honed by a voracious appetite for business knowledge. The harder she studied and worked, the more money she made them. Except Trevor had taken all the credit, and she'd let him. But no more.

Ella raised her chin and met Mack's gaze. "I was the brains behind Trevor's business. I decided when and where and how much risk to take. I was the reason for his success." She waited for him to scoff or laugh or dismiss her.

Instead, he nodded. "That doesn't surprise me."

"It doesn't?" She voice sailed high. Mack's simple unquestioning confidence in her made her insides jostle as if realigning to a new set of natural laws.

His brows lowered, and he made a scoffing sound. "My only surprise is that you didn't leave his dumb butt and strike out on your own years ago."

Mack wouldn't understand the crippling doubt Trevor had planted and nurtured in the years of their marriage. Away from Trevor, Ella had a hard time understanding why she'd stayed as long as she had too. Would she have left if Megan hadn't wedged between them? It was a question she didn't want to examine too closely. The reality was she *had* escaped and she didn't take her freedom for granted.

"Does this mean you're welcoming my involvement with the garage?" She tensed. The plastic spork she held snapped in two.

"Hell no. I'll buy you out as soon as I'm able." Mack balled up his napkin and tossed it on his empty plate. "You ready to head to the hardware store?"

The switch from the intense to the mundane gave her whiplash. She stood. The small restaurant was packed, yet it had felt like she and Mack had been in their own world. "What are we picking up?"

"Sheet metal. Pipes. Welding supplies." Mack stacked the plates and tossed them into the trash can.

As Mack collected the to-go order, Ella stepped outside. The wind caught her ponytail and whipped her hair around her neck. She took a deep breath of clean air chilled off the river. Downtown Cottonbloom was a throwback to another time.

There was an honest-to-God quilting store on the Mississippi side called the Quilting Bee. The top of a giant sign shaped like an ice cream cone peeked from around a corner. This weekend maybe she would explore her adopted town instead of staying holed up alone in her big house reading real estate prospectuses.

Mack didn't seem to be in any hurry to get to the hardware store. He set the bag of pork plates on the hood of the truck and ambled across the street to where flower stalks waved in the wind, the buds on top closed and protected. He picked up a stone and skipped it across the water.

"Did you love the river as a kid?" she asked.

"What's not to love? It offered trouble and excitement when we were kids. Rope swings. Fishing. Wading upriver. It's a wonder none of us drowned."

"Sounds like you and your brothers got up to a bushel of fun." Nostalgia sliced through her.

She and her brother had gotten up to some no good too. Grayson had always made sure she didn't get too wild and crazy though. Other brothers would have gotten annoyed with a little sister chasing after them every free moment, but Grayson had never made her feel like she was a pest.

"We did. What about you and your brother?" Mack asked.

"He was the best. Four years older than me, but it felt like more. I guess because he looked out for me until he left." She swallowed and focused on happier memories. "He had an old red Jeep with rusted-out floorboards and no top. Taught me how to drive when I was twelve out in a fallow field across from our house. It made me feel so grown-up."

She still dreamed about bouncing through the field in a red Jeep with Grayson by her side, both of them laughing as she grinded the gears before finding the right one. Sometimes she was a twelve-year-old girl again, and sometimes she was grown. Grayson never aged though. He was forever eighteen.

"He's the reason, isn't he?" Mack's voice barely registered over the wind and water.

She didn't pretend to not understand what he meant. "Yes."

"Why didn't you tell me all this to start with?"

"Would you have listened? Would you have cared? Honestly, I questioned my sanity after the New Year's Eve party and almost reneged on the deal. If you haven't cottoned on yet, I know next to nothing about actual mechanics." She shot him a look from under her lashes.

He stroked his dark beard, his frown giving him a pensive, worried look. "According to my family, I have the tendency to overreact, and the big reveal that you'd bought Ford's stake was a shock, to say the least."

"I thought Andrew had already told you."

"Nope. He wanted to make the sale as painful as possible for us. Not all that surprising though, considering the bad blood between Wyatt and Tarwater over Sutton."

That explained Andrew Tarwater's gleefulness when she'd expressed interest in buying Ford's share last fall. It wasn't about closing a deal, but revenge. "I thought it was a straightforward business deal. I'm sorry about how it went down."

"I appreciate that. And I'm sorry I haven't been as welcoming as I could have." Alongside his begrudging tone was a fair amount of sincerity.

"Wow. You're making me feel all warm and fuzzy, Mack. What's next? A fruit basket?"

"Har-har." He hooked his thumbs in the back pockets of his jeans, putting his flexing biceps on display. She tried not to stare. "This doesn't mean I'm not working hard to gather the capital to buy you out though. Bottom line: Abbott Garage should be owned by Abbotts."

"Fair enough." A week ago—heck, even a day ago— she would have dug in and fought him, but with the new understanding between them came a tentative friendship she was unwilling to destroy with a few thoughtless words. Anyway, just because he made an offer didn't mean she had to accept it. The upper hand was hers.

They walked back to the truck. Instead of circling to the driver's side, he reached around her to open the passenger door.

"I could get used to this new and improved Mack." She swung herself into the seat. He handed over the bag of food.

"Yeah, well. Aunt Hazel would invoke my middle name if she saw me acting ungentlemanly out and about in Cottonbloom." He shut the door and made his way around the truck.

As they clacked over the bridge to Mississippi, she asked, "Do you not like your middle name? Boliver, isn't it?"

He shot her a look, half amused, half embarrassed. "It's better than Wyatt and Jackson's. Elkanah and Jedidiah respectively. But it's not so much the name as the way Aunt Hazel invokes it. When I was little, I thought she was part swamp witch."

"That's one way to keep a pack of wild and crazy boys in line. Let them think you're a witch." She laughed at the picture he painted. "Witch Hazel."

Mack joined in. The sound resonated throughout the truck and into her chest to jumpstart her heart. She had never heard him laugh before, had she? No, definitely not, because she would have remembered the smoky, whiskey flavor of the sound. It was something she could fast become addicted to.

This newfound territory they'd wandered into might prove even more dangerous to her sanity than his antipathy. Before now, a small part of her brain could admire Mack's hotness without any repercussions or temptations.

All right, so it wasn't only her brain that acknowledged the way he filled out a pair of jeans, and the way his arms stretched the sleeves of his shirts. As her inappropriate thoughts about him skid out of control, she squirmed on the leather seat.

They pulled into the hardware store lot. The building had a rustic-looking storefront a half mile from the cute, artsy section of downtown. Trucks and work vans littered the lot and acted as gathering places for men on their lunch break. Mack drove to where a loading dock jutted out with an open garage door to the inside of the shop. He backed the truck in.

"Wait here."

She ignored him and hopped out. Since she was spearheading the change over to the new software to track invoices, she needed to become familiar with what the shop regularly needed and how diligent Mack was in keeping track of purchases.

He glanced over his shoulder, his eyebrows lowering and a frown marring his features. A little thrill zipped through her. Not good. Even his irritated face registered as attractive now. It was even sexier than his laugh. She imagined him looming over her looking big and bad and doing big, bad, naughty things to her body.

She grabbed a sheet of sandpaper off the display to her right and fanned herself with it. What was wrong with her? A shift from not totally hating each other into outright lust was like going from reverse to fifth gear and caused havoc with her internals.

Instead of staying on his heels, she allowed him to continue on to the front to talk to the manager while she wandered over to a display of antique tools. She leaned over and squinted, trying to read the inscription, but her glasses were back at the garage.

"It was used to jack up buggies and wagons to fix busted wheels. I remember my daddy having one in his shed. Not that I remember horse and buggy days. I ain't quite that old." The man who'd sidled up next to her chuckled, drawing laugh lines around his eyes. "You new around here, young lady?"

"I moved down from Jackson around a year ago, but it's my first time at Benson's. My name's Ella." She stuck out her hand, which he took in a dry, boney grasp.

"I'm Delmar Fournette. Lived in Cottonbloom, the Louisiana side mind you, all my life. Suppose at this point, it's where they'll put me in the ground. Not yet though." He winked, and she couldn't help but return his smile. "Is there something I can help you with?"

"I'm sorry, I didn't realize you worked here."

"I don't. I just never pass up an opportunity to help a pretty lady." Too much tease resided in his face and voice to take him seriously.

"I'm actually waiting for my . . ." Not "friend." Certainly not "boss." What was Mack? ". . . partner to finish getting his order filled."

Delmar craned his neck to look down the aisle toward the loading dock. "Well, I'll be. You here with Mack? Are you the lady who bought Ford's share of the garage?"

"I am and I am." She failed to keep the defensiveness out of her voice.

"Hazel was telling me all about it. I heard you're shaking things up over there. Good thing, I'd say. Ever since their daddy died, those boys have been spinning their wheels, stuck in grief."

Ella shifted so she too could look down the aisle at Mack. He lifted metal sheets on top of a pyramid of pipes in the bed of his truck. He stopped to say something to a man helping him before raising the hem of his shirt to wipe his forehead. She was too far away to see the details, but even the hint of dark hair and a flat stomach was enough to quicken the flurry of her makeshift fan.

Mack bypassed the steps, hauled himself up on the loading dock like he was exiting a swimming pool, and strode toward her. His frowning intensity sent her back a step before he transferred his attention to Delmar.

"Why am I not surprised you'd corner the one pretty girl around? What would Miss Leora have to say?" The tease in Mack's voice spoke of a long, comfortable friendship with Delmar, and a true smile banished any lingering darkness.

Delmar made a scoffing sound. "She takes me as is. Plus, she knows I'm true-blue to her. How're things at the shop?" He glanced between them, his curiosity palpable.

"Fine. You should come down and play us a tune like in the old days."

"What do you play, Mr. Fournette?"

"Mr. Fournette was my daddy. Call me Delmar. Mostly the mandolin, but I'm a fair hand on the fiddle. I didn't think any of you boys inherited your daddy's love of bluegrass."

"I'm developing an appreciation."

"Glad to hear it." Delmar glanced up at the clock on the wall, two screwdrivers acting as the hands. "Lordy, is that the time? I'm overdue on the river for some fishing."

They said their good-byes, and Ella followed Mack to the loading dock. Bypassing the steps once again, he used a hand and jumped down with a grace she envied. If she attempted such a move, it would result in a busted butt.

"Delmar seems like a character," she said over the clang of the supplies in the back once they were back on the road.

"A character with a capital *C*. He's a Vietnam vet and was a confirmed bachelor until he started stepping out with Ms. Leora, a straight-laced, extremely proper spinster from the Mississippi side. Everyone is wondering if they'll make it official."

"Why mess with a good thing? Marriage isn't all it's cracked up to be." Ella estimated she was still an eon away from being able to move past the bitterness when she discussed marriage in any shape or form.

"After meeting your ex, I can understand the attitude. Honestly, I one hundred percent agree."

"Has some woman stomped all over your heart?" She shifted to stare at his profile.

"Not since Tammy Woolcott dumped me for the quarterback right before the homecoming dance my junior year." The corner of his mouth curved up. Tammy's defection hadn't resulted in true heartbreak.

She dug deeper. "You have one brother married and the other one getting ready to take the plunge. Are you seriously against marriage?"

He raised the shoulder closest to her. "I wish the best for both of them, of course, but marriage never brought any happiness to my pop. Or us kids. Only heartache."

She sputtered some inanity before saying, "Yeah, but what if—"

"Why are you arguing with me? I agreed with you."

She sat back and stared out the passenger window. Why *was* she arguing with a view that lined up with hers? Disquiet had her tapping her heel. She had her reasons to dislike marriage, but dangit, it bothered her that he was equally jaded.

Before she could examine the root of her unease, they pulled up to the garage. Wyatt met them in the parking lot to take the food, his demeanor altogether grumpy. "Geez. I thought you'd left us to starve to death."

"Sorry," Ella called.

"Ignore him. He gets hangry." Mack smiled, but it was a melancholy one. "Before he and Sutton hooked up, he would wander over to my place most nights and mooch food. Which didn't bother me, except when he complained I wasn't moving fast enough in the kitchen."

Ella guessed neither Wyatt nor Jackson had time for dinner with Mack anymore. She glanced over at the house that stood a stone's throw from the shop, wanting to tease his sadness away. "I'll bet you still sleep in your old room in a bunk bed."

It worked. She got brief chuckle out of him. "I upgraded to a king bed and knocked a wall out to make a decent-sized bedroom."

The words "king bed" and "bedroom" sent her imagination on a pleasurable jaunt down Inappropriateness Lane. She flapped the front of her shirt to dissipate the sudden heat flushing her. "I'm going to get back to work. Thanks for introducing me to Rufus's barbeque."

He nodded and turned to unload the truck. Before the part of her that wanted to pull up a chair and watch him bend over and lift heavy things gained traction, she retreated to the relative safety and solitude of the office.

Except the afternoon proved his office was far from safe. It was a danger zone. A minefield. A series of jolting sexual eruptions every time he meandered in and out of sight. She might as well have been wearing a shock collar.

She pushed away from the computer to stretch her legs and get some air as Mack walked in the office door. "I'm taking a break if you need the computer." She pointed past him.

"Thanks."

She stepped left as he stepped right. Then, they repeated the move to the other side. She smiled. "We're dancing."

"Maybe if we were in middle school." The corner of mouth ticked up enough to verify the playing field had changed drastically over the course of the day.

"I can't imagine you dancing at all."

"Why is that?"

"Because dancing implies fun."

He made a humming sound and rubbed a finger over his lower lip. "You don't think I'm fun?"

"Do *you* think you're fun?" The teasing quality of the conversation skated on something darker and more serious.

"I used to be fun. I think."

"When's the last time you went and hung out?"

He looked to the ceiling as if doing math in his head.

"I met my cousin Landrum down at The Rivershack Tavern to shoot pool."

"When?"

"Last summer maybe? And Wyatt forced me out of the house this winter."

Although she'd shed her society-maven designation after her divorce, she at least put forth an effort to social-ize, even if she faked her fun more often than not. "We should go out and cut loose."

His gaze streaked to hers, his brows scrunched. Only then did it hit her that her suggestion sounded a lot like she'd asked him out on a date.

"You, me, Wyatt, Jackson, Willa. The whole gang. Out. Having fun. And stuff." Her words came out choppy and too fast.

"I know what you meant," he said.

Did he? Because when she'd said it, a picture flashed of the two of them locked in a version of dirty dancing. "I need to stretch my legs and experience something besides fluorescent light."

"If you walk straight back in the woods behind the barn, you'll come to a path. It's a nice peaceful stroll down to the river." He turned to the side to allow her to exit.

She nodded and slipped by him. The back of her hand brushed the cotton of his shirt. Goose bumps erupted along her arm. Forcing herself not to look back at him, she pushed through the door at the back of the shop. Peace was exactly what she needed. Or maybe what she needed was a night—no, a solid twenty-four to forty-eight hours—with her vibrator.

She skirted around the barn and strolled past the half-dozen junked cars Wyatt had dubbed the Graveyard. They harvested parts for projects until eventually, they sent the shells off to the junk yard. The abandoned cars filled her with an odd melancholy. The hunks of unfeeling metal had been someone's pride and joy at some point. They had carried men and women and families through years, and here they sat, abandoned and picked apart.

She focused on the very alive trees and kept walking. What had happened to Grayson's Jeep? Did it sit in a field, decomposing and overtaken by grass and kudzu, until it was part of the landscape? A twinge of grief made her eyes misty, blurring the tree line into an impressionistic rendering of browns and greens.

A narrow path covered in brown needles and crunchy leaves cut through the pines, and she passed from sun into dappled shadows. The smell of pine and the river mingled pleasantly. She kept on the overgrown footpath, the sound of flowing water a beacon.

The bank dropped off six feet, the ripples of the water indicating a swift flow through the narrow section. She found a smooth tree trunk, leaned against it, and closed her eyes. There was peace to be found here, but it seemed intent on playing hide-and-seek.

Things were working out differently than she'd expected when she bought Ford's percentage of the garage. After the bombshell reveal at Sutton's New Year's Eve party, she hadn't expected to genuinely like the Abbotts. And she really hadn't expected the animosity between her and Mack to morph into unharnessed electricity, exciting and dangerous.

She was undeniably attracted to Mack with his dark good looks and complicated moods and rare smiles. She banged her head against the trunk, hoping to knock some sense into her brain. What she was feeling was simply a physical infatuation. The natural result of being around a virile, single man after her self-imposed celibacy. Her body would adjust. It would have to.

The slight breeze and white noise of the river worked

an alchemy and lulled her into a place between conscious thought. The rustle of leaves put her on alert. Had she summoned Mack? She opened her eyes and turned. A black-and-white animal launched itself at her head.

Chapter Eight

Mack had work to do, yet he was standing in the door of the barn staring into the trees toward the river drinking a Coke he didn't even want. She'd been gone twenty-seven minutes. He knew because he'd watched the clock since she'd walked out the back door. Had she gotten lost? Fallen in the river? It wasn't deep enough to drown in. Unless she'd hit her head or gotten her foot jammed under a log.

He straightened and debated the levels of insanity if he went to search for her. A scream echoed from the woods. He threw the can aside and sprinted toward the path the brothers had cut through the trees when they were kids.

He leapt over a fallen tree, but had to stop when his shirt got caught in a bramble. Another breathless feminine yelp was followed by a bark. It was only River. The dog wouldn't hurt her, but Ella might hurt herself in a bid to get away. Her fear manifested anytime the dog came within arm's length of her.

He yanked his shirt so hard it ripped. Finally free, he jogged toward the river and spotted her holding a stick out to keep River back. Trouble was that River's favorite game was fetch the stick, and she bounced on her paws, waiting for Ella to get with the program and toss it already.

He scooped up a stick and whistled, drawing both Ella's and River's attention. "Go get it, girl." He threw the stick behind him and River tore through the leaves on the hunt.

Ella deflated before his eyes, bending over with her hands on her knees.

"River thought you wanted to play fetch." Mack's heart was playing kick drum against his chest. "She won't hurt you."

"In my head, I know she won't, but I can't help it." Her voice was muffled, and she was breathing like she'd run a mile. She wiped at her cheeks, and Mack's stomach did a swan dive. Tears had left her eyes reddened.

Leaves stuck in her hair and along the left side of her pants leg. River trotted up with a stick hanging out of her mouth. Ella backpedaled into a tree. He threw the stick as far as he could, then approached Ella as if she was a wounded animal. And, wasn't she, in a way?

"What made you so scared of dogs?"

Ella's attention was fixed on where River had settled in to gnaw on the end of a stick. She was silent for a long moment, and when she spoke, her voice was thin. "My stepfather raised dogs."

"I'm assuming he didn't raise cute little yippy ones."

Her humorless laugh sputtered like an engine out of gas. "Not even close. They were bruisers. Mostly for protection, I guess."

"Mean dogs?" Mack asked.

"Not born mean, but trained mean. It was my stepdad's specialty." Her voice was dry with an ironic twist.

Questions popped in his head like firecrackers, each more explosive than the last. Had her stepdad been cruel to her? "Did one of his dogs attack you?"

"Since you shared your scar, I'll share mine." She untucked her shirt and lifted the right side. Puckered pink skin arced from her hip bone to her flank. A dog bite.

He traced the scar with his fingers. "That must've hurt like hell. How old were you?"

"Ten. It was a big dog. Maybe a German Shepherd or Rottweiler. I can't remember now."

"What happened?"

"The dogs roamed outside. My stepdad said they kept us safe when he was gone on trucking jobs. It happened when I walked home from school. I guess the dog pegged me for an intruder. I don't know. Grayson was home, thank God, and kicked the dog off me. He rushed me to the hospital, and they stitched me up."

Mack could picture it—the terror, the blood—and it made him want to find her stepdad. Or to do something even more foolish like hold her close and soothe her fear away. "What happened after your stepdad found out?"

"Before my stepdad made it home from his run, the animal-control people took the dog. I assume they . . ." She pressed her lips together and gave a little shake of her head. "He blamed me, of course, and accused me of provoking the dog. I realize not every dog is like that, and I do okay with small dogs. But, having one River's size come at me puts me back in my yard. It's crazy, right?"

"Sounds like a natural reaction."

"Up here"—she tapped her temple—"I know the biggest threat from River is being licked to death. It's silly."

"Not silly. Normal." He chewed the inside of his mouth and observed the way she kept her gaze on River at all times as if preparing for an attack. "But I'll bet River would be happy to help you get over your phobia."

"It's not a phobia." She sounded put out by his definition.

"Okay, not a phobia. But it's a fear that hampers your day-to-day living, especially if you stick around the garage for any length of time. River and Willa are inseparable.

You need to learn to live with her. Or at least not be terrified by her."

"And how do you suggest I overcome this?" Ella's skepticism was obvious.

How did one go about conquering fears? He'd always prided himself on meeting challenges head-on. But the last year had taught him that he wasn't as strong as he thought he was. The memory of his mother hung in the corner of his mind like a ghost. And Ford. While he thought he'd been meeting that problem head-on, what he'd really been doing was reinforcing his defenses and pushing Ford away.

He dropped to a squat and whistled for River. When Ella looked ready to bolt and jump in the river to escape the dog, he grabbed her wrist and looked up at her. "Trust me?"

She didn't pull from his grip, but her arm was stiff and the tension vibrated from her body. She stared into his eyes, unblinking. River tucked her head under his other hand, and he rubbed her ears, never looking away from Ella.

"River was dumped at Willa's trailer park. I almost called animal control on her the day she followed Willa to work. She had no one to love her and take care of her."

"Until Willa," Ella whispered without moving her lips.

"Until Willa," he said. "Now we all love on her. She's a good dog." He loosened his fingers on her wrist one by one until he was sure Ella wouldn't run. He let go, and she didn't move. River lay down in the leaves and lifted a leg to give Mack access to her belly.

"She seems to like that," Ella said tentatively.

"Do you want to give her back a scratch?"

She shuffled closer and dropped into a squat next to him angling herself to put him mostly between her and River. That was fine. He was happy to protect her.

"Right here." He demonstrated, and River's plumed tail waved like a flag in strong winds.

Ella extended a fist, only unfurling it when she got close to touching River. Mack moved his hand to rub River around the ears, hoping the dog wouldn't see a squirrel or rabbit and jump up, barking. That would negate any progress Ella was making.

Ella barely rubbed River's back with her fingertips. "She's soft."

"She was a skinny, dirty, mangy thing back when Willa adopted her."

River narrowed her eyes, slipping into a blissful state from the attention. Ella stroked once down the dog's flank then withdrew her hand and sat back on her heels. A whistle sounded from the direction of the garage. River leapt up and tore off through the trees.

Ella let out a soft yelp, plopped on her butt, and clutched his thigh.

Her touch wasn't remotely sexual, yet Mack couldn't stop the response that blazed through his body like a wildfire. His conscience tsked like Smokey Bear. A physical declaration would only muddy the already-confusing dynamic between them. While they were no longer enemies, they weren't friends either.

River was out of sight, not to return. The soothing sounds of birds and the flowing river should have calmed the fire of his attraction and her anxiety. Problem was not only hadn't she removed her hand, but it moved an inch up his inner thigh, closer to the point of detonation.

He fisted his hand in the leaves to keep from covering her hand with his and moving it even higher. Sweat broke over his forehead. He wanted to kiss her. It was wrong and inappropriate and foolish.

Slowly, as if she might spook, he turned his head. She

raised her gaze to his. Her eyes were wide and unblinking, but not from fear.

"How do you feel?" he rumbled softly.

"Proud of myself." A small smile broke through like the sun on a cloudy day.

He might never know the extent of the hardships Ella had faced and overcome, but he was damn certain they were more difficult and devastating than the ones Mack was actively avoiding. "You *should* be proud. And for more than just petting a dog."

She tilted her head, a question on her face.

Before she had a chance to ask something he wasn't ready to answer, he said, "You've got leaves in your hair."

He gave into the compulsion to touch her. As he picked leaves out of her hair, he allowed his fingertips to graze her cheek and neck. Finally, he thread his fingers into her hair at her nape and held still.

What if he leaned in and kissed her? Would she return his kiss? Would she shove him in the dirt and run? Or worse, would she laugh at him? The uncertainty roiling his stomach made him feel sixteen again.

"Am I de-leaved?" She pulled her hand off his thigh and touched her hair, her fingers glancing over his wrist.

He gave her hair a slight tug before releasing her and pushing to stand up. His thigh muscles woke and protested his long crouch. He and his brothers had spent hours huddled behind bushes and in trees waiting for rabbits or deer, but it had been years since he'd hunted. The older he got, the more sympathetic he grew to the plight of an animal trying to survive.

"Mostly de-leaved. We'd better head back before the boys send out a search party." He led them back to the path.

Every year, undergrowth swallowed more of the path he and Ford had carved. It had been their project the summer before their mother abandoned them. The twins had been too young to help. That had been the last carefree summer he could remember. After their mother left, he'd done his best for the twins, even though he'd been too young to take care of himself.

She came up beside him, their arms jostling as the creeping vegetation forced them close. "Whatcha thinking about?"

"I was thinking about how if you don't tend to something, it descends into chaos."

"Whoa. Deep thoughts from Mack Abbott. I'm assuming you're referring to the Ford situation?"

He shot her a side-eye. "Among other things."

Wyatt, Jackson, and Willa stood in the opened barn door. Spotting them, River gave a bark where she was sitting at Willa's leg.

Jackson gestured toward the woods. "We were starting to get worried."

"Everything's fine." Mack kept his voice cool and brisk, afraid he would give away how thoroughly Ella had worked her way under his skin and into his thoughts.

Willa had hold of River's collar and backed her farther into the barn.

"You don't have to take her somewhere else. It's okay. River is part of the garage too. She's the mascot for goodness' sake. I need to get over my little issue." Ella stepped within a few feet of River, but didn't make a move to pat the dog again. Still, it was a marked improvement.

Silence fell for a half second too long, summoning a dark cloud of uncomfortableness. Ella's smile was tight and polite. "I need to finish a few things up in the office and then I'm going to take off."

Mack couldn't take his eyes off her retreating figure.

Leaves clung to her backside, and he imagined helping brush those off as well.

Wyatt cleared his throat. He crossed his arms and stared Mack down like he'd eaten the last cookie. Mack ignored him and grabbed a cold drink as Jackson, Willa, and River disappeared up the loft stairs.

"Look, I'm going to have to put my foot down. Quit treating Ella like she's a pariah." With his usual easygoing tease sheared away by sharpness, Wyatt stepped between Mack and the refrigerator.

"What are you talking about? I was perfectly pleasant." If "pleasant" included fighting the urge to roll around in the dirt and leaves while he stripped her naked. As a matter of fact, that sounded positively perfect.

"Then why had she been crying? I get that she's an inconvenience to your plans for the garage, but while she's here, you could try not to be such a dick."

He opened his mouth to argue, when he got sidetracked. "Hang on. What do you by *my plans* for the garage? Don't you want her gone and her share back in our hands as much as I do?"

"Sure, that'd be best-case scenario, but don't turn into someone you'll hate later to claim a victory."

Wyatt's assessment wounded Mack. Ford had been too busy and self-centered, so Mack had taken on the role of protective big brother. He'd had Wyatt and Jackson's backs in school and at home, relishing the way they looked up to him. Their confidence in his leadership of the garage had been gratifying even as the pressure became too much to bear.

Now, though, Wyatt and Jackson had matured and gained wisdom through their committed relationships. Mack wanted to know the secret handshake to get into the club, but was too proud to ask.

Wyatt must have taken his silence for contrition. He reached into the refrigerator, pulled out a beer, and handed it over. "Take a few minutes to calm down and think things over before you confront Ella again."

Mack didn't attempt to set the record straight. What was the point? Anyway, Wyatt's assessment might not have applied to Ella, but it certainly applied to Ford. And maybe his mother. He didn't want regrets to swamp him later. Even if it all went to hell, he had to make an effort. Didn't he?

Chapter Nine

The passing scenery barely registered as Ella drove home. She assumed she wasn't breaking any traffic laws. She couldn't get her mind off Mack. His sweet understanding of her neurosis in the woods. His not entirely unsuccessful attempt to get her comfortable with River. But mostly the way his hand had wandered into her hair. Logic-destroying desire had burned through her.

She pulled into her driveway and stopped short, her seat belt catching. An unknown car was tucked up against the side of her garage. A sleek, silver Lexus. Was Trevor back?

Instead of pulling into the garage, she left her car in the driveway in case a quick getaway was in order. Clutching her cell phone in one hand and her keys in the other, she tiptoed along the stone path to her front door.

A woman popped up from the rocking chair on the porch. It took a few blinks to place Megan, Trevor's current, if estranged, wife. She was dressed to kill—Ella hoped not literally—in sky-high heels, a tight gray pencil skirt, and a silky pink pussy-bow blouse.

"What are you doing here?" Ella's voice was devoid of any warmth or welcome. The move from Jackson was meant to sever ties with her past, and Trevor's affair with Megan had been one of the most painful parts.

"I didn't know where else to go." Megan took a step forward, her hands clasped together at her waist, her fingers white against her red manicure. Was she scared? Of Ella? She supposed facing down your husband's ex would be nerve-wracking.

"Trevor stopped by a few nights ago and asked me to talk to you." Ella walked past her, unlocked her front door, and gestured Megan inside.

A flash of surprise crossed Megan's face. What did she expect? As distasteful as the situation was, Ella didn't have the heart to tell Megan to hit the road. Mostly Ella felt sorry for the other woman. Ella had been in her designer shoes and it was not a comfortable place to be.

"He's been calling me incessantly. I don't know what to do." Megan's heels tapped on the floor as Ella led her into the kitchen.

"I tried to warn you." Ella couldn't help her "I told you so" tone even though it wasn't helpful.

"Believe me, I've thought about that day more times than I can count." Regret-infused tears cracked Megan's voice. "If only I had listened."

Ella understood regret but she also understood you couldn't change the past as much as you wished you could. There were some things you had to let haunt you.

"I washed my hands of Trevor. Been there, done that, don't want to ride that merry-go-round again," Ella said briskly.

"I need somewhere to go," Megan said. "Somewhere safe."

An internal alert system blared. Ella recognized the expression and tone. It was fear, but not of her. "Has Trevor hurt you? Threatened you?"

"No. Not exactly. He's actually been . . . nice. Too nice, if that makes any sense."

Unfortunately, it did. After one of Trevor's episodes, he'd tended to act overly solicitous, showering her with presents and attention.

"What about your parents?"

"With them, he's never been anything but wonderful. They think I'm going through a phase since I married Trevor so young. A divorce would get messy. They're threatening to cut me off unless I try to work things out."

Ella understood messy divorces. Women who she'd thought were friends had walked away as if she'd ceased to exist. Still, their situations weren't the same. Megan was from a well-entrenched old Jackson family and would survive any fallout.

"Surely you have friends in Jackson who—"

"They're all friends with Trevor too. Or their husbands are. And no one believes me when I try to tell them the truth. They tell me to suck it up and enjoy the house and the trips and the clothes. They think I'm exaggerating."

Ella glanced over at the faint red wine stain on her cabinet. If she agreed to let Megan stay even a night, the drama unleashed would be epic.

Megan clutched the counter and wobbled a little. Dark circles shaded her eyes and her mouth was pinched. "Weren't we friends once?"

"I thought so until you slept with my husband." The zinger didn't contain too much zing, considering Ella was content and even flirting with happiness. She heaved a sigh. "For how long?"

Part of her wanted to stuff the offer back in her mouth. But if she'd had a safe place to land, would she have stuck it out with Trevor for as long as she had? All it took was one person reaching out a hand to change a life.

Megan's shoulders rose toward her ears, and she clasped her hands under her chin like a little child. "Not *too* long. I promise I won't be a bother."

As if she didn't have enough to worry about. The garage was starting to feel like home, and Mack was becoming more and more important to her. How long before Trevor came looking for Megan at Ella's? This would be the start of a war. A war she didn't want and couldn't win.

"Trevor will come here looking for you sooner rather than later."

"I know. I need a little bit of time to figure things out." Megan closed her eyes and tilted her head back as if praying, her hands still under her chin. "I can't leave him for good, can I? I've never had a real job. How will I support myself?"

"Divorce him. Get your fair share." Her words had a mercenary bent, but it was the way men like Trevor played and lived their lives.

"He's almost bankrupt, Ella. There's not enough to take."

Shock rippled through her. Bankrupt? Her divorce settlement had been substantial but not enough to break him. She should know, considering she'd managed their properties. "What happened?"

"Bad investments. Real estate mostly. Tried to flip some houses, but the cost overrun ate up any profit. And there was some hunting land down in Texas he invested in to turn into a resort. That went belly-up last fall."

Ella shook her head and clamped her mouth shut so hard her jaw ached. She'd told him it was a poor investment. Her last piece of advice to him before their divorce. That explained his desperation the night he confronted her. "He needs your money."

"Yes. My money, not me." Tears shimmered in Megan's eyes, and she sniffed.

His desperation to change for Megan had nothing to do with becoming a better person. Ella chuffed. She'd almost believed him. Almost. Helping Megan escape him, with her money, would be a huge F-U to Trevor.

"Do you have a bag in the car? I'll show you where you can stay."

The next morning, Megan didn't pick up any of the hints Ella dropped. It was Saturday and her plan was to head to downtown Cottonbloom and explore all the nooks and crannies of both sides of River Street and beyond. Alone. Or at least not accompanied by her ex-husband's current, albeit estranged, wife. It was too weird even for her.

"Let me grab my purse in case I see something I can't deny myself," Megan said.

"I thought you were trying to make it on your own," Ella muttered.

Megan had already hustled into the guest room. Ella threw up her hands and headed toward her car. Megan slid in with a smile, banishing the worry that had hovered over her like a black cloud the previous evening. She chattered throughout the ten-minute drive to River Street. It was relaxing in its own way.

Side by side, they wandered down an offshoot of River Street, stopping in Regan Fournette's interior design shop before moving on to Sutton's boutique, Abigail's. The bell on the door chimed, and Sutton came out from a back room, her smile welcoming.

"Hello there, Ella. Nice to see you somewhere besides the shop. How're are things going?"

"No more oil changes, thank goodness. This is Megan"— Ella balked on the last name considering they shared the same one—"a friend down from Jackson for a short— very short—visit."

"Hi, Megan. Nice to meet you." Sutton approached with an outstretched hand, and she and Megan shook.

"Can I help you find anything in particular?" Sutton turned to the nearest rack and straightened hangers.

"Just browsing." Ella moved a few feet away to flip through summer dresses.

Megan made an oohing sound and headed toward a rack of evening gowns near the back.

A sense that Sutton was studying Ella like a specimen under a microscope had Ella shifting to a rack of pants. She cleared her throat. "This is my first time checking out downtown Cottonbloom. Don't know why I waited so long."

"You make it sound so fancy. *Downtown Cottonbloom*." Sutton affected a posh accent and joined her at the rack, the contemplative look in her eyes belying her simple smile.

Ella searched for a safe topic. "How's the wedding planning coming along?"

"Mother's driving Wyatt insane. She wants something big and bold with everyone in Cottonbloom in attendance. Not exactly Wyatt's style."

Ella pinched back her smile and shook her head. Already the Abbotts had grown on her. "No, I can't see Wyatt standing at the front of the church gussied up in a tuxedo like a performing monkey."

"It's going to be a spectacle, that's for certain." Sutton laughed ruefully. "I hope you're planning to attend?"

"If you send an invitation, I'll be there."

"You can count on it." Something in Sutton's smile hinted at deeper motivations than a simple invitation, but before Ella could tease them out, the bell over the door chimed and Sutton moved away with another greeting and smile for the new customer.

Partly to support Sutton and Wyatt and partly because

the clothes were fabulous, Ella selected a silky scoop-neck T-shirt and fitted cigarette pants to try on.

A half hour later both Ella and Megan walked out with new clothes.

"Goodness me," Megan said. "I never would've thought a store like Abagail's would be in a town this tiny."

"Cottonbloom has a lot to offer." The need to defend her new home freaked her out. After leaving Dry Gulch, Mississippi, for Jackson and never looking back, she'd learned not to become sentimental over places.

They wandered farther down River Street to the Quilting Bee. Her first step over the threshold brought an array of sensations. Quilts hung along the back wall. Some new, some with the aged, frayed appearance of antiques. A selection of candles on a rack inside the door lent an aroma that was strong but pleasant.

Another wall was taken up by framed artwork, mostly landscapes, many of them of Cottonbloom. She imagined the visitors scooped up the paintings of the quaint downtown with its gazebo, footbridge, and river. The far corner was taken up by quilting supplies and swatches of fabric in color-coordinated bins.

Hand-thrown pottery of various colors covered the nearest table in an irresistible display. She picked up a bowl with swirls of blue and green and brown. It reminded her of Mack's eyes.

"That bowl was thrown by a local artist." A woman's voice at Ella's elbow made her bobble the bowl. She clutched it to her chest.

"I'm sorry, dear. I didn't mean to scare you."

"You didn't," Ella said in an obvious lie.

"My name's Ms. Effie. I haven't seen you around before. Are you from out of town?" The curiosity in the woman's eyes was something she'd gotten used to after she'd moved to Cottonbloom, and she didn't take offense.

"I'm Ella Boudreaux."

The woman's eyes widened and her mouth drew into an O.

"I take it you've heard of me?" An edge sharpened her voice even as she maintained a smile.

"Indeed, I have. Leora told me Delmar met you this week at the hardware store. With Mack Abbott no less. He said you were awfully pretty. And you certainly are." The delight and good humor in the older woman's voice set Ella back on her heels. "He went on and on about you. Leora threatened to stitch his mouth shut." Effie's laugh was big and boisterous and infectious.

"I'm working at Abbott Brothers Garage. In fact, I own part of it."

"I heard about that too." Effie straightened the pottery on the table.

"Is there anything you haven't heard that you'd like to know about me?" Ella hoped her smile tempered her sarcasm.

"I was sweet on Mack's daddy, you know."

"I . . . didn't know." The switch from inquisition to confession threw Ella.

"He only had eyes for that darn garage." Regret that could never be righted weighed on the old woman's voice. She cut a glance toward Ella. "Mack's a good man."

Ella swallowed. Did the woman have second sight? How could she know Mack had set up house in her head? He *was* a good man, even if he let his temper and stubbornness drag him down on occasion. Who was without faults? Not her, that was for certain. Not that she planned to admit anything to a woman she'd known for five minutes.

"Mack Abbott is my business partner."

"Oh really? That's not the impression Delmar got." Ms.

Effie patted Ella's arm. "Are you browsing or can I help you with something?"

"Browsing." Ella followed the lady when she wandered toward Megan, who was examining the quilts. "What gave Mr. Delmar the impression Mack and I are anything more than business partners?"

"He said Mack couldn't take his eyes off you at the hardware store. And something about the way you looked like you wanted to eat Mack up."

"I don't want to eat Mack." An evil little voice whispered in her head, *But you do want to jump him.*

Ms. Effie raised her eyebrows, her smiling knowing. Could she know what Ella was thinking about? Because now that the thought was planted, she couldn't shake the image of falling to her knees in front of Mack and *devouring* him. Heat spread like a spark in a dry forest.

"Will you tell us about your quilts?" Flapping her shirt, Ella walked past the older lady to where Megan flipped through quilts.

While Ms. Effie rattled on about the symbolism behind the placement of the squares, the possibility that Mack couldn't take his eyes off her rattled around her head. He had probably been worried she'd do something to embarrass the garage, is all.

Nevertheless, she left with the bowl that reminded her of Mack's eyes.

Mack shimmied underneath the car as carefully as possible, but rocks along the cracked pavement dug into his shoulders and along his back. Trying to fix a car on the side of the street in downtown Cottonbloom wasn't ideal, but Marigold was in tears and didn't want him to tow it back to the shop if at all possible.

The sickly sweet smell of transmission fluid pinpointed

the problem if not the root cause. It could be something simple like a loose connection or more serious like a failing part. His instincts did not leave him feeling positive about the prognosis.

He lay underneath the car debating his next move. The car needed work. Likely expensive work. Marigold and Dave were strapped for money and too proud for their own good.

A foot prodded his knee, and he raised his head. A pair of legs only too familiar were clad in tight jeans and flat shoes. A slow breath exited his lungs. She was not the wrench he needed.

She squatted and leaned down, her hair spilling over his knee. Even though he had on thick canvas work pants, he could imagine how soft her hair would feel. His grip tightened on the hose he was fiddling with to keep from wrapping his fingers in her hair like he had in the woods.

"Can I help?" Ella asked.

"How are you at breaking bad news?" He kept his voice low.

Ella glanced over her shoulder and back at him, then before he could do or say anything else, she shimmed under the car with him until they were shoulder to shoulder, face to face. It felt shockingly intimate.

"How bad? Because Marigold doesn't look like she can take more than a three on a scale of ten."

"Could be the entire transmission has failed."

Ella seemed to understand the gravitas of the diagnosis. "Do you have a loaner she can use?"

"Of course. Trouble is getting her to accept the help. I've offered before but she turned me down flat."

"Let me handle it." She scooted out.

By the time he'd hauled himself from under the car, Ella had drawn Marigold aside and was conducting a low conversation with her. Another woman, thin and blonde and looking bored stood off to the side, holding bags that bore the stamps of various businesses on the other side of the river.

Trusting that Ella had Marigold in hand, Mack called Jackson's cell and explained the situation. While he was on the phone, he stared at Ella and Marigold. Ella had a streak of dirt over and down the right butt and leg of her jeans. He got distracted with the notion of helping her brush it off.

"Ella," the woman off to the side said in a childishly high-pitched voice, "how much longer?"

Ella shot the woman an impatient look and returned her attention to Marigold.

"Do we have any loaners ready to go?" Mack asked Jackson.

"A four-door Ford sedan. Would that work?"

"Yep. Plan to take Marigold back and get her set up. Leave everything vague as to return date and cost."

"Will do. I'm ready to roll. See you in a sec."

Mack disconnected and approached Ella and Marigold. "Everything is going to be fine, Marigold."

Marigold gave him a watered-down smile. "I certainly don't mind if my car is the guinea pig."

Mack cleared his throat and side-eyed Ella. He had no clue what Marigold was talking about, but he trusted Ella to handle the situation with a deft touch. *He trusted Ella.* The thought ripped through him with the speed and ferocity of a tornado, but he didn't have the time and space to inspect the damage.

"It's good of you to offer it up for our experiment." He raised his brows, hoping Ella planned to give him some guidance.

Ella tittered a laugh that was equal parts nervous and

uncomfortable. "Mack's a stickler about me learning how to work on transmissions. I already passed the basics with flying colors, right Mack?"

"Yep. Colors flying everywhere." Right now, the color would be red like the flush on her cheeks, and blue like her wide eyes begging him to play along. "Your car will be perfect, Marigold. As long as you don't mind a novice working on it. Of course, it's only right to give you a deep discount."

"I really appreciate this." A deep breath helped draw Marigold's shoulders back and return some of her natural lightness.

The distinctive rattling sound of the shop's tow truck pulled Mack's attention away from Ella. It took less than ten minutes to hook up Marigold's car. Ella walked her to the passenger side of the tow truck, gave her a hug, and whispered something that made Marigold smile. Ella could eviscerate him with a handful of words yet seemed to possess the ability to charm and put others at ease. He teetered between resentment and admiration.

The blonde approached once the tow truck was out of sight. "I'm hungry, Ella. I thought we were going to eat."

The woman was pretty enough if you liked the type, but she didn't interest Mack beyond the fact Ella seemed reluctant to introduce them. Who was she? One easy way to find out. He stuck out his hand. "I'm Mack Abbott. Nice to meet you."

She returned his shake and gave him a glance through her lashes that he classified as flirty. Although, he might have been mistaken, considering how far out of practice he was with the concept.

"Megan Boudreaux."

He startled. A sister? Ella had only mentioned her lost brother. But, Boudreaux was her married name. Sister-in-law, then?

Ella's smile was more like gritted teeth. "Megan is Trevor's current wife."

Mack sent Ella a "what the hell" look, and she returned an "I know it's weird" shrug and shake of her head.

Megan touched his forearm. "We're headed to a restaurant Ella couldn't stop raving about. Would you like to join us?"

Ella thumbed over her shoulder. "We're headed to Rufus's."

He'd actually been headed there himself when he'd run across Marigold with car trouble. "You mind if I join you?" He directed the question toward Ella.

Megan brushed her long blonde hair over her shoulder as she leaned into him. "Not at all. In fact, I insist."

Ella rolled her eyes over Megan's head and gestured down the sidewalk, leading the way. He sidestepped away from Megan, but she aligned herself closer to him than was necessary. Every time he moved away, she closed the distance until his shoulder skimmed the brick wall.

How in the world had Ella ended up entertaining her d-bag ex's current wife? The story was sure to be a doozy. As soon as he could manage it, he'd get her alone. He found himself looking forward to it.

Megan filled the silence with chatter about the shopping she and Ella had done on the other side of the river. She showed him a dress she bought from Sutton's boutique. He glanced at it but didn't say anything. Mainly because he wasn't interested in dresses. Or Megan. His attention was on Ella.

Her long-legged stride rocked her hips on each step like she was on a catwalk. Was it natural or deliberate? Either way it was like watching a metronome. Mesmerizing and sexy as hell.

"By the way, your pants are filthy, Ella." Megan opened

the door to Rufus's and trotted inside on her heels like a temperamental racehorse.

Ella brushed over the back of her jeans then pushed her hair behind one ear and twisted to see. She'd managed to transfer some of the grime from her pants to her neck. "Better?"

"Your neck's dirty now."

She rubbed but missed the streak entirely.

"Here, let me help." He wrapped his hand around her nape and rubbed his thumb over the dirt until it was gone. She relaxed into his touch, her face tilting up. He kept stroking as if his brain had misfired. Her skin was soft and flawless.

Her tongue dabbed along her lower lip, and she drew it between her teeth before slowly letting it go, leaving her lip plumped and red. One tug would have their bodies close and her lips in striking distance. He'd suck her bottom lip between his teeth and make her moan. Make her beg. His body leapt with awareness. He dropped his hand as if she was literally too hot for him to handle.

Even though they were no longer physically touching, their gazes held. She looked away first and left him to blink himself out of the trance. It felt like an hour had transpired, but inside, Megan was still studying the menu.

"I guess you're wondering what's up." Ella gestured her head toward Megan, but didn't look in her direction.

"I can't deny I'm curious. Are you two plotting your ex's demise together?"

"Ha! I wish." Ella's still-reddened lips tipped in a small smile, but they promptly thinned into a tension-filled line. "Actually, I wish I could stay out of it. I thought I'd left Trevor behind for good."

"What does he want from you?" He stuck his clenched hands into his front pockets to hide his agitation from her. Trevor deserved to get dumped in the swamps for many reasons, but what ate at Mack was the power he still held over Ella.

"He wants me to convince Megan to take him back."

"Is that why she's here? Is that what you're doing hanging out with her?"

They both glanced inside. Megan squinted in their direction and gestured them in.

"Not exactly." Ella made a move toward the door, but Mack put a hand on the glass and pushed while Ella pulled. He won.

"I sense trouble."

"Maybe. But it's my trouble." She arched her brows. "If you don't mind, I'm hungry."

They engaged in a staring contest. This time he was the first to blink and stepped away. She entered and joined Megan at the counter.

The three of them ordered, with Megan insisting on paying with a black American Express. The only free table was in the middle of the restaurant. Mack exchanged nods with several acquaintances. This little outing would be sure to get back to his brothers.

He remained silent during the bulk of the conversation mostly because he had little to add to a discussion of shoes and interior design.

Megan leaned over the table and touched his forearm, her long blood-red nails rasping against his skin. "Tell me all about your business. Is car restoration a big money-maker?"

He pulled his arms back and crossed them over his chest. "We don't do it for the money. We do it because we love the work."

Megan's smile was bemused. "I can't imagine Ella working in a car garage. You should have seen her when she ruled Jackson society." Megan took a draw on her tea, leaving a lipstick stain on the straw.

"I didn't rule anything in Mississippi, not even my life." Ella's bitterness was like unsweetened lemonade.

Even Megan seemed affected by the change of mood. "I always admired you. Thought you were super sophisticated and together."

A huffing noise that faintly resembled a laugh erupted from Ella. "Is that why you started up something with Trevor? Because you wanted what I had?"

Megan looked stricken. "No. That's not what I meant. I'm sorry, Ella."

Ella rolled her eyes. "Actually, I should thank you for freeing me from the shackles of man and marriage. I had been looking for a way out long before you showed up."

Pain did a poor job hiding underneath her biting sarcasm. What had her ex done to her? Not just physically, but to her psyche?

"Not all guys are like him." It wasn't the first time he'd started an argument with her, but his need to change her mind was overwhelming his reserve. Her blanket dismissal of men needled him.

"Really? In my experience, they are. Ever since I was sixteen, men have been sniffing around and offering me the world if I'll let them use me. I learned that eventually you tarnish, and men like Trevor toss you over for someone shinier."

Megan made a sound that might have been a sob. She rose and quickstepped out of the restaurant. Ella closed her eyes, sighed, and ran both hands through her hair, resting her elbows on the table. "I'm a total bitch, aren't I?"

"It's part of your charm." He forced a lightness he didn't feel into his voice.

A chuckle accompanied the flash of her smile, but she didn't respond.

"Ella." He waited until she peeked up at him. "What is Megan doing here?"

"She left Trevor and needs a place to hide out until she figures things out."

"Has he threatened her?"

"I don't know. Her parents are pushing for a reconciliation. According to Megan, Trevor's made some poor real estate investments and needs her trust money."

"Does she want a divorce?"

Ella's gaze darted off to the side. "I don't know if she wants a divorce or a break."

His brief encounter with Trevor had put him on edge. The man had an unpredictable violent streak. The fact Ella had dealt with him for years and was now putting herself in danger for Megan harshened his attitude and his tone. "I don't like this. Tell Megan to go home."

"Back to him? And then what?" She turned her dark blue eyes on him, and the vehemence and strength was like a punch. "If someone doesn't help her, then she'll never get away."

"Who helped you?"

"No one. I had no one to help me." She popped to standing so fast, her chair tipped over. Ignoring it, she grabbed the shopping bags and pushed out the door.

Mack righted the chair, cleared off their table, and followed her, but Ella was already over the footbridge and across the river with Megan doing her best to keep up.

He smoothed a hand over his beard and watched them until they disappeared into her little blue convertible. Problem was he couldn't keep watch on her all the time, and troubles circled like buzzards.

Chapter Ten

Monday morning, Ella sat in her car outside the garage and stared at the door. She'd left Megan still sleeping in her spare bedroom, no closer to figuring out what to do about or for her. Trevor hadn't come calling. Yet. There was always a "yet" where Trevor was concerned.

Trevor hadn't had too much to drink, yet. Trevor hadn't lost his temper and lashed out, yet. Trevor hadn't come home stinking of another woman's perfume, yet.

Not all guys are like him. Ella hadn't been able to banish Mack's words. What was Mack like? Was he the gruff, infuriating man who could physically dominate her without breaking a sweat? Or did his eyes and touch hint at an innate kindness? And why did both sides of the man thrill her?

It was confusing and embarrassing and shame inducing. The years of emotional and physical abuse had taken a toll on her. Especially when Trevor had accused her of provoking his behavior with her sharp attitude and tongue.

As if he could sense her rumination on him, the door to the shop opened and Mack filled the doorway, wiping his hands on a shop towel. He didn't come pull her out of her car or make any sort of move to acknowledge her at all. Except with his eyes. They cut straight through metal and glass to touch her. He propped a shoulder against the jamb, one boot crossed over the other, and waited.

As if he exerted his own gravitational pull, she found herself opening the car door and walking straight up to him. "Good morning," she said softly.

"Morning. Everything okay?"

She knew what he really wanted to know. "Trevor didn't show up on my doorstep."

"He will."

His simple prediction stoked the ember of fear Megan's arrival had banked. "Yeah, I know."

"I worry about you."

"Why? If something happened, then all your problems would be solved." She kept her head down and tried to brush past him, but he blocked her, his hands on either side of the door.

"Don't say that." His fierce whisper had her looking up at him.

"Why not? It's true. You don't want me here." It was a fact, and she lifted her chin, daring him to argue with her.

"You're not an Abbott, so no, I don't want you owning part of my garage. But that doesn't mean I don't . . ." His jaw worked before words emerged in a hoarse rush. "I don't want to see you hurt."

"I can take care of myself." She poked her finger into his chest and pushed. "Now, if you'll excuse me, I have work to do."

Her puny effort to move him only worked because he chose to give way. She swept past him into his office and tensed, waiting for him to follow her for round two, but he didn't. Sidling close enough to the office door to see the shop floor, she found him talking to Jackson in the corner at the welder. Were they talking about her? She gave a little laugh at her self-centered assumption. No doubt they were discussing their favorite subject—cars.

She sat at the main computer and began the laborious process of transferring the shop's financials over to the new system. An hour passed in relative silence and boredom as she checked and double-checked her work. One mistake would wreck the foothold she'd established. She needed her work to be exemplary.

She stood and stretched, craning her neck to check the shop floor, her gaze drawn to Mack like he was her homing beacon. His hands were braced on the front of Marigold's car while Jackson and Willa flanked him. All of them stared at the engine compartment; none of them looked happy.

She chewed her lip while she debated the merits of inserting herself, but considering she was the one who had convinced Marigold to let go of her pride and allow the Abbotts to work on her car, Ella had a stake in the problem.

She weaved her way to where Mack alternately stared at the engine and paced. She sidled up to Willa. "Grim news?"

"Transmission is toast."

"How much does it cost to replace one?"

"A couple of thousand if we can find a decent rebuilt one. Upwards four K for a new one." Willa sighed. "More than Marigold can cover right now, that's for certain."

While sadness had resided in Marigold's eyes, it was the desperation that had spoken clearly to Ella. Although their circumstances were different, Ella understood the desperation of not having any options.

"I'll cover it." She whispered the words. When only Willa turned to her with wide eyes, Ella cleared her throat and raised her voice. "I'll cover the cost. That way the garage won't have to take a loss and neither will Marigold."

Mack stopped pacing and pivoted to face her. "Why would you offer to do that for a woman you barely know?"

"Because . . ." Admitting anything would reveal too much. She forced a lightness she didn't feel into a smile. "Because I have the money. Might as well put it to good use."

Mack narrowed his eyes as if he could arrow past her smile to her heart. "I appreciate that, but the garage could absorb the cost and labor. It's the fact Marigold will balk against the charity. She'd drive Dave's work truck before she lets us fix her car."

"No, she won't," Willa said. "They had to sell Dave's truck last month to cover medical bills."

Jackson muttered a curse and shook his head. Mack sighed, pulled the hair on his chin, and stared at the shop floor.

Fixing Marigold's car was only the tip of a bill-stuffed iceberg for her family. Ella remembered what it had been like after Grayson had died in the training accident. Her mom and stepdad had blown through the money from the army settlement in months. The bank had repossessed the two expensive cars they'd bought. The house would have been next if her stepdad hadn't got a new job with a long-haul tractor-trailer company.

"Marigold and her family need more help than a rebuilt transmission," Ella said.

"That's all we've got to offer. What else can we do?" Willa kicked at the tire, the slump of her shoulders despondent.

Good question. Ideas whirled around in her head. Marigold wouldn't like any of them as they skated too close to charity. But what if she could spin it somehow to make Marigold feel like she was doing the garage a favor? And if the pieces came together, her idea could benefit the garage too.

Ella steepled her hands at her chin and tapped her fingers together.

"Considering you're making the universal evil-plan hand gesture, I assume you have an idea?" The thread of amusement in Mack's voice had her gaze flying to him. The corner of his mouth was ticked up, crinkling the corresponding eye.

He was handsome when he smiled. He was handsome when he frowned too. He was, without a doubt, the sexiest man she'd ever seen. And, Delmar Fournette was right—she wanted to devour him right here on the shop floor.

"Are you planning to share with the class?" Mack took a step closer to her.

For her own sanity, she took a step back. "Not yet. Not until I have time to think it through. Anyway, it would be more of a long-term fix for Marigold's situation. The car is the immediate problem. What's the plan?"

"I say we fix it and drop it off in the middle of the night with a big bow on top," Willa said.

Mack shook his head, a resigned reluctance in his voice. "Yeah. Not sure if it will be a good surprise or bad surprise but I agree."

"How about I go talk to Dave?" Jackson asked. "He might be a little less prideful and more sensible than Marigold right now."

"Worth a shot," Mack said.

Their impromptu meeting broke up, and Ella retreated to the office where the spreadsheets and accounting program took a back seat to the seed of an idea that spread like kudzu in her head.

"You want to talk it out?" Mack's voice startled her out of her semi-meditative state. He leaned in the doorway, his arms crossed over his chest, his masculinity a wall.

"Not yet. But soon."

"Why all the effort to help Marigold?"

It was basically the same question he posed earlier. He wasn't going to give up until she gave him an answer. She met his eyes and didn't flinch. "Because I understand desperation."

His arms dropped to his side, and he looked away for a moment before meeting her eyes again. "Are you talking about your marriage?"

"Partly, but also the way I grew up."

She didn't make a habit of talking about her childhood. She and Trevor had gotten married in front of the cream of Jackson society, and her mother and stepdad had not been invited. She'd told Trevor she and her mother were estranged, and in fact, Trevor had known very little of the way she had grown up. Once she'd caught his wandering eyes, she was eager to leave her old life behind, not realizing yet that she'd only moved from one level of hell to a different one with a better view.

If anyone could understand, Mack would. Still, they weren't friends. She wasn't sure what they were. She swiveled away from him and faced the computer. "I better get my work done before the boss gives me a hard time."

Mack didn't move from the doorway, and it took all of Ella's self-control not to look over at him again. When he walked away, he left a vacuum.

The rest of the day passed in relative calm, at least on the outside. Inside she was revisiting old memories of coming home from school to an empty house where the cabinets were almost bare. Or even worse, coming home to a house occupied by her mom and stepdad.

She slipped out of the garage into her car without saying good-bye. She didn't want to answer any more of Mack's questions.

Not that her house offered respite. Megan was camped out in the spare bedroom with no immediate plans to leave.

Tonight was the night she would tell Megan that she needed to figure something out by the end of the week.

She tensed on the approach to her house, always expecting to see Trevor's BMW out front or in the driveway blocking Megan's escape. Everything was blessedly normal. Except the aroma of fresh garlic and Italian spices that greeted her at the door.

She was used to silence. In fact, she'd come to glory in her aloneness. But, the mouthwatering welcome wasn't unpleasant.

Megan skip-walked out of the kitchen wearing an apron. "I made dinner. I hope you don't mind."

Ella kicked off her shoes in the foyer. "It smells amazing. You didn't have to cook."

"It's the least I can do," Megan said. "I hope you like spaghetti."

"Who doesn't?" Ella's stomach rumbled, reminding her she skipped lunch at the garage.

As Ella headed toward the kitchen, Megan walked backward as excited as a little kid ready to show off a craft project for a grade.

Megan had set two places including wineglasses in front of the barstools. Once they were served, Megan waited for Ella to take the first taste. The uncomfortableness of being stared at made Ella take a too-big bite and all she could manage was a nodding "mmm-mmm" and a thumbs-up signaling her approval.

Megan's smile contained no artifice, and Ella was struck by how young she seemed.

"I'll bet Trevor loved that you cooked for him," Ella said between bites. "I was useless beyond the basics."

Megan's smile lost some of its brilliance, and she poked the noodles. "Not really. He preferred more-sophisticated food. All I know how to cook are casseroles and pot roast and pasta."

Ella wiped her mouth on her napkin, took a sip of the red wine, and studied Megan from the corner of her eye. What went unsaid but understood was the fact Trevor could be cutting and cruel when things weren't up to his standards. "This is absolutely delicious. You can cook for me anytime."

A portion of Megan's earlier simple happiness glowed on her face, and Ella took another sip of wine, wondering how she had acquired the role of cheerleader for her ex-husband's wife. Life was strange.

"I'd be happy to cook for you every night to make up for letting me stay here. None of my other girlfriends understand."

"Yeah, well, Trevor puts on a good show."

"Exactly." Megan swiveled in the chair, partway facing Ella. "Knowing you left him gave me the courage to do it."

Ella twirled spaghetti around her fork, not wanting to harsh the girl-power mood but needing to determine whether Megan had an exit strategy. "Have you thought about what's next?

"I was thinking about getting a job."

"Where?"

"Maybe here?"

"In Cottonbloom?"

Ella rubbed at the sudden throb at her temple and took a bigger swallow of wine. Cottonbloom was *her* refuge. She didn't want a reminder of what she'd escaped. Was it selfish to not want Megan in her new life?

"My plan is to hit downtown Cottonbloom tomorrow and put in my resume at some of the shops along River Street. The Quilting Bee and the interior design shop. Everyone told me my house in Jackson was amazing."

It had been Ella's house before it had been Megan's house. It's not like Ella wanted that life back, but she also couldn't stop the prickle of resentment. Megan had invaded her old life and was now invading her new one too.

The rest of dinner was taken up by small talk about mutual acquaintances in Jackson. Not something Ella was particularly interested in, but it was clear Megan was still entrenched in that world.

Ella set the dishes in the sink and turned to her. "You're still talking to all your old friends in Jackson, aren't you?"

"I'm texting some of them. The ones I can trust." Megan rinsed the plates and loaded them into the dishwasher. "You go on, I'll clean up."

Ella put her hand on Megan to still her. "Have you told anyone you're staying with me?"

"No one."

Ella heaved a sigh.

"Except for Courtney, but she'd never rat me out to Trevor."

Ella's relief turned to frustration. She didn't know Courtney well, but her husband and Trevor were golfing buddies. "Let's hope not."

Frustration at Megan's naïveté drove Ella to seek solitude before she said something she would regret. In her bedroom, Ella paced. She hated having to shut herself off in her own house. Maybe driving the back roads of Cottonbloom would provide some clarity.

Returning to the den, she stopped at the couch where Megan was laid out and watching a reality TV show. "I've got a couple of things to take care of. Don't answer the door after I leave."

Megan popped up on her elbow, a flash of disquiet thinning her mouth. "I won't. Promise."

Ella locked the door on the way out and stopped on her front walkway, listening. For what, she wasn't even sure. A dark harbinger? The rumble of a BMW? Only the night-time call of birds and the hum of insects accompanied the gloaming.

Without conscious thought, the roads she travelled took her over the river into Louisiana. Her destination became clear in her head, like a thick fog dissipating. She wanted to see Mack. At best, it was ill advised; at worst, it was just plain dumb.

What did he have to offer? Certainly not protection from whatever storm brewed in the north. In fact, he was more dangerous to her than Megan and Trevor and all of Jackson, Mississippi, combined.

As the garage came into sight around the bend, her heart stuttered. What if he wasn't even here? What if he was on a date? Or worse still, what if he had a woman over? The tension vibrating her body eased when his black truck came into view. Only Jackson's and Willa's cars were parked in the lot, which meant he was probably alone. Like her.

She parked and crept by the magnolia tree in his front yard. Anyone watching might assume she was there to rob the place. Before she could knock, the unmistakable sound of metal being hammered broke the quiet night. The noise came from the back of his house.

She tiptoed along the brick wall and peeked around the corner. Luckily, the banging mallet masked her not-so-whispered "Dear God in heaven."

Mack's back was to her, and he was shirtless. A standing work light threw a circle around him like he was on-stage, and whatever he was doing to the plate of metal made the muscles along his shoulders and arms ripple like he was the star of a male revue.

Ella pressed her cheek against the rough bricks of the house, but they were still warm from the heat of the sun and didn't help cool the fire raging in her body. He wiped an arm over his forehead and propped his hands on his hips, looking over his work. With supreme effort she transferred her attention from him to the twisty, graceful-looking lengths of metal in front of him. It seemed a shame to hide such beauty under the hood of a car.

When Mack shifted to the other side of the entwined metal, she caught her first glimpse of his chest. Perfection. Thick and solid with more than a dusting of dark hair, his chest was worthy of a stone carving.

Her gaze followed the trail of hair into the waistband of his well-worn jeans. Apparently, more than her gaze reached for him, because she lost her balance and took a step forward to catch herself. The movement swung his attention from his project to her.

Now that she was caught, she had better roll her tongue back into her mouth and come up with a good reason for why she had shown up at his house unannounced and was spying on him.

"Hi there. Sorry for dropping by like this." She thumbed over her shoulder as she approached him. "I went to the front door, but I heard you working back here. What kind of car is that for?"

He grabbed a black Abbott Brothers T-shirt off the rail of his deck and pulled it on, the cotton sticking in places where he'd worked up a sweat.

"It's not for a car. What are you doing here?"

When he made no move to invite her inside, she prepared to beat a hasty retreat. "I wanted to talk about . . . Marigold."

Although Marigold hadn't been on her mind as she'd driven across the river as if Mack had cast a spell on her, the woman was a better reason than the truth. The truth was a tangle of incoherent feelings.

She took a step backward. "It can wait until tomorrow. I'm interrupting."

"Wait. Stay. Come on in." The shortness of his words

made her feel a little like a dog taking commands. Yet, she padded after him up the stairs onto a recently stained wooden porch and through a sliding glass door that let into an eating nook in a retro kitchen.

"Can I get you something to drink? No wine, but I have beer and whiskey." He opened the refrigerator, and she peered around the door, wanting a hint as to what made the man tick. An enormous jar of mayonnaise was visible on the top shelf, but he and the door blocked the rest.

"A beer sounds great."

To her surprise, he pulled out two bottles of micro-brews—she'd pegged him for an old-school domestic kind of guy—uncapped them, and handed one over before taking a long pull off his. She brought the cold bottle to her lips, but instead of taking a sip, she watched his throat work with each swallow.

"You mind if I take a quick shower? I'm pretty gross from working on . . . the stuff outside." He gestured vaguely, then rubbed the back of his neck and didn't meet her eyes. If she had to guess, she would say the tinge of color in his cheeks was embarrassment.

"Sure, go for it." She spun in a slow circle and pulled out a seat at the table.

"You can hang out in the den. It'll be more comfortable." He gestured down a short hall and led the way. The room was on the small side, which fit the age of the house, but was neat and comfortable looking. A couch took up one wall and faced a flat screen TV mounted above a fireplace.

He collected a shirt tossed across the back of a recliner and straightened the magazines strewn over a beautiful rustic coffee table.

"You know . . . make yourself at home. Or whatever." He stopped in the doorway looking like more words hovered on his tongue, but only gave a brisk nod and disappeared. Two minutes later, the sound of a shower running unscrunched her shoulders and sent her on a trek around the room to investigate while drinking the hoppy, delicious beer.

A couple of nondescript watercolors hung on the wall, and Ella guessed they were left over from his childhood as nothing about them was as unique as Mack himself. Car magazines mixed with copies of *National Geographic* on the table. There were no books, but Mack didn't seem the type to sit and read. He was a doer.

Several pictures on the mantle took Ella on a trip from Mack's youth to before his father died. She was equally as fascinated by the picture of a young Mack with his arms around two squalling babies that could only be Wyatt and Jackson as she was with the picture of a teenage version of him in a baseball uniform with a bat propped on his shoulder. Unsmiling, he looked like he wanted to be somewhere else, probably under a car.

The last picture on the mantle was of all the brothers, Ford included, with their father, standing in front of the shop. They looked happy and untroubled. A deception she was only too familiar with. She'd put on a happy face for too long.

By the time the shower cut off, she'd finished her beer and had a relaxing buzz on. Until he stepped into the doorway of the den swirling a cloud of male, mouthwatering scents around her. Her buzz took on a more urgent quality.

Her breathing shallowed and picked up pace. He was in jeans and a T-shirt, nothing she hadn't seen him in before, but the vibe pulsing between them was different. Maybe it was because they weren't in the garage. Something intangible drew her to him—the same instinct had guided her across the river tonight—and it cut deeper than a sexy chest. It cut right to her heart.

He must have sensed the shifting tides, because he took a step back. "Let me grab another couple of beers."

As if she needed something else to muddle her senses and throw her off-balance. Yet, when he returned, she took the beer and drank. He slipped by her and sat in the recliner. She took the corner of the couch nearest him.

"I assume you're ready to share your evil plan regarding Marigold?" His eyebrows rose as he took a sip.

She sputtered a laugh around the rim of her beer. "Try brilliant."

"I'm intrigued. Talk to me."

She'd wanted to have something on paper before she shared with Mack, but if fumbling through her idea was the price for her spontaneous visit, then she'd gladly pay. "What about a fundraiser for Marigold and Dave?"

"Like selling stuff from the shop or on the website?"

"That could be a small part of it, but I'm thinking something bigger. Something that would get the town involved. Both sides."

Mack leaned forward and braced his forearms on his knees. "Like what though? A pancake breakfast?"

The faint memory of her school hosting a breakfast surfaced. "That's not a bad idea, but I'm thinking bigger."

"How big?"

"An entire-day event. The garage would spearhead."

"Sounds expensive. And time consuming." He rubbed and pulled at the hair on his chin. A mannerism she associated with him turning over troubles.

"Perhaps. But, along with helping Marigold, we'll get something out of it too."

"We?" He raised his gaze to hers.

"Yes, 'we' of Abbott Brothers Garage. Until you raise the money and I agree to a sale, then I'm as much part of the business as you are. And believe it or not, I want it to prosper." She refused to balk at the intensity of his stare.

"Okay, fine. What would *we* get out of it that wouldn't make it seem like we were taking advantage?"

"The event itself will be a classic car show. Pull in classic car owners from all over Louisiana and Mississippi to show off their rides. Charge an entry fee and give out prizes for different categories. Isn't that the reason they have them restored? Recognition and admiration? Some might need more work done or have another project car, and that's where Abbott Brothers will lure them in."

Mack sat back, the chair rocking with the movement. He smoothed a hand down his beard. What did it feel like? Soft or scratchy?

"That's a good idea."

"Shockingly, I do come up with them on occasion." Self-depreciating was a natural state for her, but at least since her divorce, she'd learned to inject humor.

"More often than not, I'd say. You're dragging the garage into the twenty-first century." The admiration and sincerity in his voice echoed in her head, the reverberations reaching her heart.

She'd been underestimated or, even worse, dismissed more often than not in Jackson as a trophy wife. And, she'd let it happen. She'd let everyone believe it was Trevor with the business acumen and not her, because of his pride. Mack didn't need to put her down to make himself feel big.

"Thank you," she whispered.

He sat forward and stared off into the distance. "It will be a huge undertaking. I'll need to talk to both mayors and the police departments and—"

"Let me plan it."

"What?" He returned his focus to her.

"I planned parties quite often in Jackson." She'd hated playing hostess next to Trevor. After the last guests left, she'd felt like glass ready to shatter. But this would be different. She had a cause and a job. "I'm good at organizing. Anyway, you have actual work to do in the garage. As soon the new accounting program is up and running, what will I do?"

"Are you sure you want to tackle this?"

"It's going to be awesome. I'll make sure of it."

"We need to discuss scope. And, of course, we can't pull the trigger until we have a meeting about it to make sure Jackson and Wyatt are on board."

"Tomorrow morning, then?"

He nodded and a silence filled with furtive, awkward-feeling glances at each other persisted to the point of uncomfortableness. There was no reason for her to still be sitting in his den peeling the label off her beer.

"What were you working on outside?"

He rubbed at the nape of his neck where his still-damp hair curled slightly. Was that a blush? It was hard to tell under his beard. "It's . . . private."

"Of course, I shouldn't have presumed—"

"I'll show you. If you promise not to laugh." His usual confidence had done a vanishing act, and the reason hit her like a slap upside the head. He was nervous about her opinion.

"I won't. I promise."

"Working metal is my favorite part of the restoration process." He stared at his bare feet. "After Pop died and the boys got otherwise occupied with Sutton and Willa, I got an itch to try something different."

As much as Mack was surrounded by family, he was as alone as she was. A slug of tears worked themselves up her throat, but a swig of beer helped to push them back down. Pity was not a sentiment he would welcome.

She pictured the graceful, intertwining arcs of pipe from outside, and her voice filled with wonder. "It's not for a car at all, is it? It's a work of art."

He made a scoffing sound and rolled his eyes to the ceiling. "That makes it sound pretentious as hell."

"What else have you done?"

"A few animals. Not very good ones."

"Can I see?"

"I don't want to bore you."

"To find out Mack Abbott has a hidden artistic side is the most exciting thing to happen since the discovery the earth orbits the sun." It was only a slight exaggeration.

"You're crazy." He shook his head, but a smile took up residence and his sparkling eyes did a crinkle thing that tied her stomach in knots. "I have some older stuff stored in the spare room."

She followed him down the hall. The house itself seemed to welcome her with creaks of wood under their feet. He pushed a door open. Feeling as though they were stepping through a metaphorical door as well as a physical one, she looked around and blinked.

Inside were a set of bunk beds. Posters of Nirvana and the Red Hot Chili Peppers flanked one of Cindy Crawford in a swimsuit. The corners curled around the tacks that held them up and they were faded from the sun and time.

"This was your room." She didn't bother to pose it as a question. The ghost of a younger, more-innocent Mack prowled the shadows.

"Mine and Ford's. I knocked out the wall between my pop's old room and the room the twins shared." Something in his voice drew her gaze to him. A sad nostalgia settled around him like a cape.

"You had a happy childhood, didn't you, Mack?"

"I suppose so. In the middle of it, all I could see were the defects, but looking back, it was simple and easy and good in a way I only understand now that life isn't any of those things."

She grazed his arm with her fingers. The light touch

was enough to pull him from his morose memories to fully focus on her.

"What about *your* childhood?" he asked.

"You mean besides the dogs and the stepfather and my brother dying?" Sarcasm dripped from her voice as a warning for him to give up the personal line of questioning.

"I'm sorry."

"It's okay." She'd made enough mistakes in her immediate past to quit railing at things she couldn't change as a kid.

His hand rose, and she braced for contact, but he drew it into a fist, turned to the accordion style closet, and pushed the two doors apart. He pulled out a small object but kept it hidden from her view. "You promise not to laugh?"

"I won't." Ella tried to inject sincerity.

He held out his hand, and it took her a second to recognize the object sitting on his palm was a giraffe. A Van Gogh version of a giraffe. A giggle slipped out, helped along by her second beer. Mack groaned and closed his hand around the little metal giraffe, but she pried his fingers open and took it.

"You promised not to laugh." His accusation was hampered by a good-natured smile. Maybe the two beers had had a similar effect on him.

"It's cute in an ugly sort of way." She studied it front and back.

"It was my first effort," Mack said. "I know it's terrible."

Except as a first effort, it wasn't all bad. She'd at least recognized the species. She set it on the dresser, but one leg was shorter than the others and it wobbled. "What else have you made?"

"I made something for Jackson and Willa as a surprise. I'm not sure it's good enough though."

"Let me see it." Ella made grabby hands toward the darkened maw of the closet, wondering what other treasures were hiding. Like she wondered at the depth running beneath Mack's stoicism.

He pulled out another metal sculpture and set it on the dresser next to the giraffe. Side by side, the progression in skill and talent was clear. It was two feet tall and obviously a dog on its haunches, its tongue lolling. The beads of metal and delicate welds gave the metal life. She might not like dogs, but she could appreciate the details.

"It's River." She ran her fingers along the curve of one ear.

Mack's gaze was on his feet, his toes scrunching in the carpet. "At least you recognize her."

"It looks finished. Why haven't you given it to them?"

His shrug was that of a boy unsure of himself and not the brash and confident man who strode the garage floor in charge of everyone and everything.

"I don't know. Afraid they'll laugh, I guess."

"I laughed, and you don't mind."

"Yeah, but you're different." He was studying the likeness of River.

What did he mean? That she wasn't family? That she wouldn't be around long enough for her to matter? That he didn't care what she thought? Yet, the way he said it made her think it was a compliment and not an insult.

Unable to decipher his meaning and unwilling to question him, she peeked over his shoulder. "What else are you hiding in your closet?"

He pulled out a few more projects. Mostly different types of animals but a few cars as well. They were like high-end Hot Wheels. She ran one across her hand. The metal wheels were on tiny axles. "You could sell these."

He barked a laugh. "Where? And who would buy them?"

"We could put them on the website and sell them along with the T-shirts. Or you could put them on consignment at the Quilting Bee. They take all sorts of commissioned artwork from local artisans."

"I'm the furthest thing from an artist."

She ran a finger over the dog's arched back. The precision with which he'd fashioned it was awe inspiring. "You don't have to do anything now, but think about it. It would only add to the allure of Abbott Brothers."

"Allure? There's nothing alluring about us or the garage."

"I would dare to disagree." Ella cocked her head and injected some challenge in her voice.

"You find the garage alluring?" His tone was mocking. He took a step forward and she took a step back. He was backing her into a corner in more ways than one. How much should she admit to this man?

"Not the garage." Her back hit the wall. "But the people in it."

She had bought into the garage as some sort of monument or homage to her brother. But it had turned out to mean far more to her than that. More than she wanted to admit.

"You're not what I expected. At all." His voice was low and rumbly and set off a rockslide in her stomach.

Although he stood between her and the door, she didn't feel trapped. "Good. I like to surprise people."

That much was true. From the beginning, if someone had told her she couldn't do something, it only fired her determination to see it through.

"You've been more than a surprise; you've been a revelation." His glance toward her mouth was like handing her a roadmap with a giant X on Kissytown.

A kiss was a terrible idea. The level of professionalism they maintained in the garage was shaky at best. Kissing

Mack would muddy already-murky waters. Oh, but she wanted to. She wanted to lean in, fist his T-shirt right over his heart, and pull him toward her until their lips met in a kiss that was sure to short out the electricity for miles in all directions.

Her body took up a chant of "Do it!" as if it had been taken over by a group of beer-pickled sorority girls egging on a sister in an ill-advised escapade.

"I should go check on Megan." Her voice cracked.

"Should you?"

Megan was a grown woman who could damn well take care of herself, right? She glanced toward the bunk beds. Would they fit? Before she could find out, Mack stepped away. The moment dissipated, yet the sexual tension crackled.

She walked out of the bedroom, and he lay a guiding hand on her lower back as if she needed help finding the way. His hand splayed wide. She swore each finger was leaving an indelible mark on her.

He drew the fabric of her shirt into his fist. She stopped because she had no choice in the matter. She looked over her shoulder. The hallway was dark. Only the faint light of the den diffused to them, casting his face in stark shadows.

He tugged her into his chest, her back to his front. She closed her eyes and bit her lip to keep from sighing or, worse, moaning. He felt even better than he looked. She fought the urge to snuggle into him and rest her head back on his shoulder.

"I should let you go." His mouth was close to her ear. The hairs of his beard tickled and sent vibrations through her body, crumbling her already-weak resistance.

When she didn't move, he shifted to lean against the wall, turning her and situating her between his legs. She sagged against him, her hands on his biceps, her gaze focused on his chin.

"This is not a good idea," she whispered.

"Nope."

"In fact, it qualifies as a terrible idea."

"Yep."

"If you agree with me, then why won't you let me go?" She needed him to be the strong one, because she was too weak where he was concerned.

"You're free to walk out whenever you want. But I don't think you want to, do you?"

"What I want and what's smart rarely overlap."

Smiling the smile that weakened her knees, he rumbled a laugh that muffled whatever excuses remained. She surrendered.

She inched her hand up his arm to his shoulder, stopping a moment to appreciate the bunched muscle, before proceeding to his jaw. She skimmed her fingertips along the hair of his beard. It wasn't soft, but bristly like the man himself.

"I've been wondering what your beard felt like." She couldn't keep her mouth shut.

"Have you? I've been wondering what your body would feel like against mine since the night of the New Year's Eve party at Sutton's."

"You couldn't stand me then."

"You're right. Which made my dreams that night all the more disturbing."

She tilted toward him and halved the distance to his mouth until only inches separated them. "Tell me your dreams."

"Maybe someday, but not tonight. Tonight, I want the real thing."

His lips brushed hers with an unexpected tenderness.

Tactile awareness streaked through her body. The soft cotton of his shirt offered a foil to his tickling beard. Even if this was as far as the kiss progressed, it would rank as her best.

She wrapped her arms around his neck and speared a hand through the back of his hair. He moved his hands to her hips and pulled her to her toes. An obvious erection pressed against her belly. Her answering moan would leave her mortified later, but he felt too tempting against her in the moment.

His tongue darted against her lips, and she opened for him, meeting him halfway. One of his hands moved to her buttock and squeezed. She arched and pressed into his palm. A minute or an hour passed while hands roamed and lips explored.

He gripped her butt with both hands and lifted her off the floor. She broke the kiss with a gasp and wrapped her legs around his thighs for balance. He walked into the den, flipping the light off with his elbow, and settled on the couch with her straddling his lap.

"Comfortable?"

She made a noise more from surprise than acquiescence, but before she could process the change in scenery and the fact his erection was now exactly where she wanted it—pressed between her legs—he kissed her again. This time his kiss was rougher. She answered his impatience with desperation, settling against him and rotating her hips.

She pulled her lips from his and trailed them across his cheek to his ear. "Is this what you dreamed about?"

"Getting warmer."

"Warmer? I'd say it's darn near an inferno."

His cheeks stretched into a smile, and she pulled away to observe the rare event. He was beautiful. Although he was strong and dominant, he didn't need to prove either trait like some men. He didn't scare her.

She leaned in to kiss him, fisting his hair in an attempt to curb the intensity of the moment. The opposite occurred. He roamed his hands over her lower body, slowly but surely stoking her desire until it raged out of control.

She tugged on his hair and rolled her hips against him. Being the aggressor was a new role for her, but it fit with the woman she was aiming to become—in control of all aspects of her life.

He slapped one side of her butt, the sting through her jeans not painful but shocking. And arousing. He did it again, this time on the other side. Another flare of need went off in her lower belly. But the arousal was troubling. In two moves, Mack had reasserted his power.

"Wait," she whispered against his lips. She couldn't think with their bodies melded like the metal he welded. She pulled away, her breasts cursing her selfishness at denying them the hardness of his chest.

"What is it?" His hands were on her thighs, and he squeezed.

"What are we doing?"

"Making out? Maybe more?"

"I need to go. I should go."

"If that's what you want." His voice turned cool, and he dropped his hands from her body.

She scrambled up, her limbs clumsy and disconnected from the part of her brain telling her to walk away. The space that had been filled by their need and gasps and kisses hollowed into nothing.

He didn't get up or turn a light on. She stumbled toward the front door and fumbled with the lock and handle. She was at the point of throwing herself against it in a bid for escape, when his hand covered hers. She stilled, trapped by the heat of him at her back.

It would be easy to lean into him and take what she wanted, or would she be giving him what he wanted? She'd vowed to never allow a man domination over her again. Could Mack do anything but dominate every situation and relationship?

His hand left hers to throw a bolt a foot from the top then turned the knob and released her. She stepped out, but stopped with one foot on the porch steps. She would see him at the garage and needed to normalize the situation.

"I'll see you tomorrow." She kept a false, untroubled smile in her back pocket for awkward occasions. It had gotten her through worse. This time though, her lips trembled. "We can talk about the car show then. Is that alright?"

The beats of silence between them lasted too long. Finally, he said, "That's fine. Go on and be careful driving home."

She scampered down the stairs and to her car. When was the last time she'd been this gauche and awkward with a man? Since never.

As she pulled onto the parish road, she couldn't stop herself from glancing toward his house. He stood in the doorway, a dark shadow full of mystery and temptation.

Chapter Eleven

Mack walked his thirty-second commute to work as dawn streaked light across the sky. His sleep had been light and interrupted by dreams of Ella and Ford and his pop all tangled up into a knot of emotion that bound his chest until he couldn't breathe. He'd finally given up his ghosts.

Routine had him readying the coffeemaker, the smell a small comfort after his disastrous night with Ella. Acknowledging the sexual tension between them with action had been bad enough. Her abrupt rejection had been worse.

Facing her today would be a test. His plan was to act like nothing had happened. Why relive his humiliation? He'd pretend he hadn't had his hands on the best ass either side of the Mississippi. He'd pretend her lips hadn't been on his and that she hadn't sucked his tongue inside of her mouth and pulled on his hair like she'd wanted to conquer him. He'd pretend he hadn't had to retreat to his bedroom after she'd left and take care of himself like a teenager. Twice.

He rubbed his gritty eyes and readied himself for a long, stressful day with Ella around tormenting him in ways he'd pretend didn't exist.

With a steaming cup of black coffee in hand, he settled into his office to return emails and handle some general accounting. They had three cars lined up for restorations, and various cars on the schedule for repairs of one sort or another. He stared toward Marigold's car in the second bay. He would put Willa and Jackson on it today. Working together, they could knock it out in a day and a half unless there were complications. Which there usually were. Complications were the theme of his life.

A clatter at the back of the shop signaled Jackson and Willa's arrival. Their entwined laughter reverberated against the concrete of the empty shop. A twinge in his chest had him pressing the heel of his hand against his breastbone.

He wasn't jealous. On the contrary, he was ecstatic his twin younger brothers had found partners in spite of the curse all Abbott twins were inflicted with. Maybe it was an old wives' tale or maybe the love they'd found was stronger than the curse, but Jackson and Wyatt were the first set of Abbott twins in at least five generations to settle down.

Jackson and Willa had run off to the justice of the peace and gotten married without telling anyone, which the aunts were still torn up about, but they'd have their chance to get gussied up when Wyatt and Sutton tied the knot. It was turning into the biggest shindig either side of Cottonbloom had seen in years.

Had the curse jumped to him? He hadn't come close to finding a woman he cared about more than the cars under his care.

Jackson walked into his office and plopped down in a chair with a cup of coffee. "You want me and Willa on Marigold's transmission?"

"Yep. You think you can get a salvage or a refurbished one at a good deal?"

"I would think so. Those Chevys are a dime a dozen. I'll give Jeb a call and see what he has in stock. It won't take long. When's our next restoration coming in?"

"Tomorrow. A 1973 Dodge Challenger."

Jackson whistled. "I want that assignment."

"Depends on how fast you get Marigold's car done," Mack said with a taunting smile. Injecting a competitive challenge between Wyatt and Jackson had never backfired like it had with Mack and Ford.

"I'm on it." Jackson stretched himself out of the chair and called for Willa. They met at the bumper of Marigold's car and talked in voices too quiet to carry, but Mack could tell it was about the transmission. Although the dynamic had changed after Jackson and Willa had become involved, the garage had never suffered for it.

Yawning, Wyatt walked through the door rubbing the back of his head. Mack didn't want to know what had kept Wyatt up late. It would be too depressing, considering the way his night had ended.

"What's up, bro?" Wyatt asked on his saunter to the coffeemaker.

For the first time, Mack wished the question wasn't rhetorical, and he could pour out his troubles and confusion to someone. Wyatt returned with a steaming cup of coffee to prop himself in the office doorway.

"How's the wedding planning going?" Mack asked.

"I've been tasked with getting you and Jackson fitted for tuxedos. And Sutton's mother asked me not so subtly whether or not you'd shave. I told her you'd be coming out of hibernation any day now."

Laughter lurked on the edges of Wyatt's voice and face. Sutton made him happy, and that's all Mack cared about.

Mack scratched at his neck. He hadn't had the wherewithal to clean up his beard that morning. Dreams of Ella had left him confused and exhausted. "I'll shave at Easter like normal, so she'll be pleased. The tuxedo I'm not enthusiastic about."

"It must be done. I know you'll do it for me."

It was true, of course. He would do anything for his brothers. After Wyatt left, Mack swiveled back and forth in his chair and wondered when he had excluded Ford from that circle. It was only a matter of time before guilt and responsibility and love wore him down, but he wasn't quite ready to face his mother or his brother.

Ella sidled in the door looking untroubled and well rested. Her hair was pulled into an artfully messy, sexy-as-hell updo, and she was dressed in a crisp pink-and-white striped Oxford tucked into a pair of hip-hugging jeans. Pink Chucks completed the ensemble. She was a spring breeze teasing his hibernating heart.

She bypassed the office without even a glance in his direction and headed toward the coffeemaker. A twinge that might have been hurt feelings had him abandoning his earlier declaration to ignore her. He circled the desk and followed her.

He cracked the waiting room door open. She was stirring her coffee and staring at the wall. After a good thirty seconds, he broke the silence. "Morning."

She jerked and splattered coffee across the counter. "You scared me."

He strode forward, grabbed a napkin, and swiped up the mess. "You were lost in thought."

"Was I?" Her gaze was stuck somewhere around the collar of his chambray shirt.

Now that he was closer, the circles under her eyes were visible and the blush racing up her neck was like hoisting a red flag. "Listen, about last night—"

"Let's pretend it never happened. Otherwise, this"—she gestured between them—"isn't going to work." The fact that she suggested following the same plan he'd laid out for himself didn't make a dent in his outrage.

"What do you mean 'this'?" He made the same gesture and their hands bumped. She pulled back as if he had a communicable disease.

"We need to remain professional." She turned to fiddle with her coffee before taking a sip.

"Do we?" He couldn't stop the question from popping out.

Acting on a weirdly powerful attraction to the woman who had something he desperately wanted to wrest from her was a terrible idea. He wanted her percentage of the garage back in Abbott hands. Pursuing her was counterproductive to his goal. If anything else happened between them, she could accuse him of manipulating her with sex.

The situation was complicated. But his desire for her was simple and basic and primal. He wanted to strip her down, explore every single one of her curves, and bury himself inside of her. It had nothing to do with the garage.

"Mack." Her husky whisper went straight to his groin. "Why do you even want me? Is it because of the garage?"

"Why do I want you?" It was impossible to keep the incredulity out of his voice. He spun and paced the short length of the room.

She was smart. She didn't take his crap. Her backbone was steel to survive a marriage with the biggest dillhole in Mississippi. Her sentimental love of cars, if not the expertise to fix them, was sweet. She had a heart that recognized the need of someone she'd just met, and even more amazing, the drive to do something to help. The fact she had a killer body made it a no-brainer.

"That's the dumbest question I've ever heard."

His statement woke something inside of her. If he wasn't afraid whatever he'd poked to life might burn him to ash, he would have been in awe.

"How is that a dumb question? You hated me not a week ago, you jerk. Am I supposed to think you succumbed to my charms?" She air-quoted the last word. "Men are all the same. Users until they get what they want. Then, they'll walk away for someone better. You can go to hell, Mack Abbott."

She eviscerated him with her glare on her way to throw the door open with a dramatic flourish. It bounced against the drywall and slammed shut behind her.

She was amazing. Her anger had stoked admiration in him. She embodied the beauty and energy of a thunderstorm, and he wanted to lie under the onslaught. Instead, he stayed planted and wondered if he was possessed and needed an exorcism.

The door opened. Wyatt and Jackson poked their heads through. Wyatt swept an exaggerated glance around the room. "I expected to find a smoking crater."

That about described the pit Ella had left in his stomach. "Did she leave?"

"Laid a twenty-foot strip of rubber down the road. What did you say to her?"

"Something idiotic."

"Per usual, then," Jackson said, an unusual sparkle of humor in his eyes.

"You think this is funny?" Mack backed up until his butt hit the counter. He needed the support.

Jackson had the decency to look sheepish. "A little. Is that wrong?"

"It's not very Christian of you, Jackson," Wyatt said in a voice reminiscent of Aunt Hazel. "We need to support our brother in his time of need."

"All I need is for my life to get back to normal." Even as Mack said it, he recognized the lie. His life before Hurricane Ella blew through the door had been pathetic and sad and lonely.

"Normal is safe and familiar. I get it. But you can't fight change after it's already happened." Empathy softened Jackson's words.

Mack was older. He should be wiser. Except both Wyatt and Jackson had outpaced him while he had concentrated on the garage. Just like their pop. Through the years, women had pursued their pop with casseroles and offers to mother them, but he had rebuffed them all. He'd been focused on the garage to the detriment of every other relationship in his life—even with his sons.

After their mother left, had it been easier for his pop to commit to the hunks of metal that rolled in and out of his life than attempt to traverse the dangers of a flesh-and-blood woman? Had he been afraid of being hurt again?

His pop had been a good man, but if not for the connection forged under the hood of a car, would he and Mack have been as close? Ford, with his interests outside of the garage and cars, had suffered through a no-win situation. If he'd pursued his own dreams at the outset, he would have effectively cut himself off from their pop's approval, if not his love. Yet, Ford had not been able to bury his resentment after being manipulated home to work at the garage after college.

"Pop didn't want anything to change, did he?"

The detour in topic didn't seem to faze either of his brothers. They exchanged one of their unique looks that was indecipherable to anyone else but seemed to speak volumes. Wyatt's expression was unusually grim. "He didn't. Don't make the same mistakes he did."

"The garage has to survive."

"It will, but it doesn't have to go on exactly the same as it always has. You know that or you wouldn't have pushed us into the restorations. Everyone and everything has to grow and transform or it will eventually cease to matter," Jackson said.

"Damn, you sound like Dr. Phil." When had his brothers attained a clarity and insight that he could only grasp at?

"He's paid the big bucks to be on TV, so he must be good." Wyatt's smile contained a huge helping of sympathy with a side of pity.

"I owe Ella another apology." The question was whether or not she'd accept it. Or even if he deserved to be forgiven. "When did I become such an asshole?"

"The fact you're even asking means you're not actually an asshole. Assholes aren't self-aware. You're just prone to idiocy, is all." Wyatt knuckle-punched his shoulder.

Mack barked a laugh. "I'm not sure which one is worse."

"Idiocy is fixable if you work at it hard enough. I mean, look at Wyatt." Jackson dodged a shove from his twin and barked a laugh. "I've got to run to pick up some parts for Marigold's car. You need anything while I'm out and about?"

"Can't think of anything." As Jackson opened the door, Mack said, "Actually, speaking of Marigold, we need to talk. Could you call Willa in?"

Jackson brows scrunched, but he hollered for Willa to join them. Her curious gaze landed on Mack even as she aligned herself with Jackson.

Wyatt half-sat on the table in the middle of the room. "Do you have a plan?"

"Ella had an idea on how to help Marigold and Dave. It's brilliant but it will be a lot of work and require some upfront expenditure from the garage."

"Lay it on us," Wyatt said.

"She suggested we host a classic car show in downtown Cottonbloom. We would give out prizes for Best Muscle Car or Best Convertible or whatever. Participants would pay a fee and the proceeds would go toward defraying Dave's medical bills. If we want to get ambitious, we could host events over an entire weekend. Ella had some good ideas."

"And at the same time, the garage gets an influx of advertising and hopefully work," Willa said.

"Exactly," Mack said. "Both sides of town will come out for Marigold and Dave, don't you think?"

"For sure. I'll bet the track would host an afternoon giving amateurs a chance to drive a dirt racecar," Jackson said.

"And we could sell the garage T-shirts with the proceeds going to Dave's medical funds. I bet we'd sell a ton, which means even more people walking around with our name on their back." Willa snapped. "What if we do a dog contest along with the classic car contest? That would bring out non-car enthusiasts and families with kids. You know, Cutest Dog, Smartest Dog, Ugliest Dog. We could get the mayors to judge."

"That's a great idea." Mack looked at each of them. "Do we need to vote?"

"I can't see a downside. Plus, if anyone deserves help, it's Dave and Marigold. I have the feeling people will come out of the woodwork to donate or help," Wyatt said.

"Exactly what I was thinking. Dave has done projects for a majority of both sides of Cottonbloom, and everyone loves Marigold." Jackson looked to Willa.

"You know it's a yes from me, but I'm worried Marigold will balk." Willa tucked her hair behind her ear and chewed her bottom lip. "Who is going to ask her?"

"I'll handle her," Mack said. "I have a feeling she won't argue with me if I do less asking and more telling."

"Yeah, women *love* that." Wyatt shook his head and looked heavenward.

"How are you going to plan this on top of everything else?" Jackson asked.

"Ella volunteered to be in charge." Doubts slowed his words. After his verbal bumbling earlier, would she still be willing or would she be just as happy to throw a match on the garage and watch it burn?

"Quit acting like a five-year-old who's lost his toy. She's proven herself an asset. You'd better make this right with her." Jackson's unusually firm tone reminded Mack of their pop so forcefully that he had to blink.

"I'll make it right."

A knock sounded on the door followed by a voice calling out, "You boys in here?"

"Back here, Aunt Hazel." Wyatt stuck his head out of the waiting room.

Hazel's heels tapped on the concrete floor. She stopped in the doorway. Wyatt and Jackson slipped out with murmured greetings and busses on her cheeks.

"Where's Ella?" Hazel shuffled to take a seat, smoothing her skirts over her knee and settling her pocketbook in her lap. "Did you run her off?"

"No." His knee-jerk response was so obviously a lie, he tried to cover with a polite "Can I get you a coffee?"

His aunt shook her head. "What's troubling you, son?"

Although he'd never considered Hazel his mother, she was more than his aunt. She was important to him in ways he couldn't articulate, not least of which was her ability to slice through his problems. "I think you're right."

"Of course I'm right." Hazel tapped her fingers against her pocketbook. "What am I right about this time?"

A groundswell of amusement seeped through his troubled thoughts. "I owe it to Ford to make peace."

"No. You owe it to yourself to make peace," she said with more understanding than he deserved.

"What should I do about my mother?"

"It's your decision, but it won't hurt anything or anybody to go see her. At the least, it would satisfy your curiosity. But, you might just hammer in the first plank of a bridge. Haven't you wondered what she's like?"

"Of course, but Pop—"

"Hobart was my brother and a good man, but he wasn't perfect. None of us are. All we can do in this life is make things easier for the ones we care about."

Mack wasn't sure if opening the junk drawer of his past would make things easier or harder in the long run. "Do you have Ford's address?"

Years kept at bay by the sheer force of her personality weighed on her face, deepening her wrinkles. "I don't. I pray every night he'll call, but he hasn't. I'm afraid he thinks I've taken your side."

Mack dropped his chin to his chest and closed his eyes. Another wedge he'd driven between the people he loved through his own pride. "I'll find him. Can't promise that I'll convince him to come home."

Hazel reached out and patted his knee. "Not expecting you to. But this family needs to be healed, and you're the only one to do it."

Jackson and Wyatt had already laid the foundation, it was up to Mack to finish the work. But not today. Today he had to make things right with Ella.

Chapter Twelve

Ella understood irony. In fact, she and irony were intimately acquainted, but her current situation really blew all her other experiences away. Or just plain blew.

She stared at her flat tire, the skinny spare donut on the ground beside her. The mud on the side of the road was smelly and messy. She waved a dirty hand in front of her face to banish the buzzing insects before trying her damnedest to fit the jack in the proper place. Her foot slipped, and she went to her knees, wetness seeping through her denim jeans. Lovely.

Here she was, the part owner of a car garage with four expert mechanics available to call, yet by doing so, she would also summon humiliation. She'd never hear the end of it from Mack. Not after the way she'd stormed out that morning like an immature teenager.

She'd spent her day visiting various investment properties that didn't involve Mack Abbott and his precious garage. It was a welcome break and a good reminder of her strengths. She might not be able to change a tire, but she could negotiate and close a deal like a boss.

She sat back on her heels and slapped at a bug, transferring stinky mud to her neck. She tried Megan again. No answer. She texted an SOS. After five minutes and as many mosquito bites, she heard the sound of a car coming down the road. Circling to her front bumper, she waved a hand to flag it down, but like an off-duty cab, it barreled by without an acknowledgment. Her foot stomp spattered more mud onto her shoes and only heightened her frustration.

She checked her phone. Still no response from Megan. She could leave her car and walk the two-plus miles home along the muddy, mosquito-infested shoulder or she could act like an adult and call one of the Abbotts. Not Mack though.

She dug her phone out of her pocket and punched Wyatt's number.

"Hello?"

"Wyatt. It's Ella. I've run into a problem. Actually, ran over a problem. A nail if I had to guess. I've got a flat."

"You need some help?"

"Yes, please. For some reason the jack doesn't want to stay put."

"Where are you?"

Her death clutch on the phone eased. Wyatt didn't sound put out or like he was going to lecture her or make fun of her. "On the other side of the river. About a half mile up Rambling Road."

"Be there in a jiffy."

She half-sat against her hood and fought a losing battle with the mosquitos. Once Wyatt got there, she would casually ask him not to mention her call for help to Mack.

The rumble of an approaching engine skittered foreboding down her spine. That did not sound like Wyatt's 'Cuda. Mack's big black truck rounded the curve and pulled in behind her convertible, dwarfing it. She closed her eyes and muttered a curse. Did the universe hate her?

His truck spooled to silence, and he swung himself out.

In jeans, boots, and a T-shirt that did amazing things for his chest, he was a slate of blank emotion.

Expecting him to rub salt in the wound of her situation, she went on the defense. "I called Wyatt, not you."

"I was with him when you called." His gaze meandered down to her muddy shoes and back to her face. "Why didn't you call *me*?"

Were those hurt feelings lurking behind his big, bad persona?

"Because I didn't want to hear your opinions about how dumb I am and how I don't belong in a garage if I can't even change a tire."

He invaded her space. She shrank back as far as she could on the hood without losing her balance and sprawling over it like a reject from an eighties music video.

"Let me clarify something for you." He laid his hands on the hood by her hips, looming even closer. So close in fact, he was within kissing distance. "You are not dumb. You're about the furthest thing from dumb I can imagine."

She braced her hands behind her and rubbed her lips together. "Then why did you call me dumb?"

"I said your question was dumb. Why do I want you? Let me count the ways." On the precipice of a smile, his lips twitched.

"Are you butchering Shakespeare to me?"

A slow grin spread over his face, making his eyes dance. "You mean I didn't come up with that all by my lonesome?"

She harrumphed, but couldn't control a returning smile. Yes, he could be a stubborn ass of a man, but he could also be panty-meltingly charming and sexy. And at the moment, her panties were in danger of disintegrating on the side of the road.

"How about I teach you how to change a tire? Then you'll know how."

She searched his face but only detected sincerity. "Are you serious?"

"I'm always serious. Where's the jack?"

She thumbed behind her to where she'd left it in the mud. It took him less than ten seconds to have the car levered up. Then he removed the jack and handed it to her. "Now you try."

Now that she knew exactly where to position the jack, she had no problem levering the car up in preparation to remove her flat. He was suspiciously patient with her as he walked her through how to remove the lug nuts and replace the tire. With his guidance she finished tightening the bolts of the donut she'd installed in less than fifteen minutes.

He picked up her flat tire. "I'll take this back to the shop and patch it, if I can."

"Okay." She wiped her palms over the front of her pants. "I guess I'll head home."

"You mind if I follow you? I wanted to discuss your idea. The boys and Willa thought it was great."

"Only if you don't mind hanging out while I clean up."

Another of his body-encompassing glances preceded the quirk of his lips. "You did get a mite dirty."

She returned the favor and checked him out from head to boots. Not a speck of mud was visible. It wasn't fair. "Come on then. I might have a couple of beers hanging out in the fridge."

She led the procession, glancing in her rearview mirror so often it was a safety hazard. When she pulled into her driveway, he parked at the curb in front of her house.

He hopped out and approached the house through the front yard. They met at a magnolia tree. He touched one of the glossy leaves. The one in his front yard dwarfed this one.

"You like magnolias?" she asked.

"What's not to like? They endure both summer and winter with grace, and their flowers are incomparable. The one between the house and the garage was my favorite spot as a kid."

A bud was beginning to unfurl, and she leaned in for a sniff. "They do smell amazing."

"Yep, amazing." The rough intimacy in his voice had her gaze shooting to his. The inference in his voice was unmistakable. A blush raced up her neck, and her stomach played hopscotch.

She turned and headed for the front door and hoped her internal awkwardness didn't project in her walk. Mack had a way of stripping away all her protective affectations.

She unlaced and kicked her shoes off on the porch and led the way straight to the kitchen. She didn't know if he needed a drink, but she sure did. She also needed some space. Grabbing two beers, she held them up with a questioning raise of her eyebrows.

He nodded and leaned a hip against the counter, crossing one booted foot over the other.

Megan rounded the corner in pajama shorts and a tank top, her hair damp and her cheeks reddened. "Evening, Ella. And, hello there, big guy."

Ella couldn't decide if Megan's tone was friendly or flirty. Did it matter? The reality was that Ella didn't own Mack. She killed half her beer in one go.

"Any beers left?" Megan turned toward the fridge, her hair fanning out like a bird shaking its tail feathers.

"A couple."

Megan uncapped one and scrunched her nose toward Ella. "Eww. You're gross. Why don't you hop in the shower? I think I left enough hot water. I'll keep Mack company."

Mack nudged his chin toward the door. "That mud's

going to start to itch like the devil soon. You go on. I can wait."

The mud on top of the mosquito bites was already uncomfortable. She retreated, but not before giving Megan a keep-your-hands-to-yourself look. When she glanced back before turning down the hall, Megan was leaning back on her elbows and laughing at something Mack had said.

Megan might turn out to be a friend, but she would always bear the label of the friend who'd slept with her husband. It made for an uncomfortable dynamic. But if Mack wanted Megan and not her, then she would just . . . curl up on her bed and cry. Instead of marching back to call dibs, she forced herself on to her room.

Mack propped his hip against the counter and masked his side-eye glance toward Megan by taking a sip from his bottle. He didn't know Megan well and what he did know about her didn't inspire trust. Ella had been hurt and talked tough, but her actions revealed a soft heart. Between Marigold and Megan, Ella wanted to help those in need who crossed her path. A woman like Megan might take advantage.

"What brings you over the river?" Megan asked.

"Ella had a flat. I helped her change it." He scraped at the label for something to look at instead of Megan.

"I'd love to learn some basic car maintenance. Do you run a class at the garage?"

He choked on the swallow of beer and stepped to the sink in case she rushed to perform the Heimlich. "Garage keeps me busy. No time for lessons."

"You should look into it. Women are more independent these days and should know how to take care of basic car repairs." She crossed her arms over her chest, her gaze cutting. "What's the deal with you and Ella?"

"Wc work together." As if it was that simple.

"I want to make sure you aren't taking advantage of my friend."

Nonplussed, he opened his mouth but closed it when nothing sensible presented itself.

Megan filled the gap, her voice dropping to threatening levels. "Ella is a good person, and a better friend than I deserve. I don't know all the reasons, but being part of your garage is important to her, and if you try to screw her over, you'll have me to deal with."

Megan propped her hands on her hips, took a step closer, and tilted her head back to glare at him. One of his hands instinctively dropped to protect his crotch. The woman looked ready to de-nut him.

"Look, you've got the wrong idea here," he said.

"Do I? You're not trying to use your masculine wiles to manipulate her into giving up or selling out?"

Masculine wiles? He wasn't sure what they consisted of but was positive he didn't keep any tucked away. Still, her accusation poked a sensitive area. His undeniable attraction toward Ella had nothing to do with the garage, yet he still wanted her share back in his hands. His dilemma was he wanted her in his hands too. Could the two warring wants stay separate?

"I'm not even sure it's possible to manipulate Ella. She's her own woman and makes her own decisions."

"Yeah, but—" She bit off her words and shuffled backward.

Now Mack was the one advancing on Megan. "But what?"

"Nothing." Megan wagged her finger in Mack's face. "Just know that I'm watching you and if you hurt her, I know people."

While her insinuation was clear, Mack wasn't intimidated as much as impressed by Megan's protectiveness. And uncomfortable at the rocks she'd turned over, revealing the dark underside of his situation. "Ella is taking forever, isn't she? I need to conclude our business. I have things back at the garage to take care of."

He walked away but didn't miss her mumbled, "Business, my butt," along with a harrumphing laugh.

Now he was in a quandary. Did he check the rooms along the hall until he stumbled on Ella's? If there was a protocol in this situation, he'd never learned it. Only one door was closed. Logic had him knocking.

"Come in." Her voice called from deep within the room.

He slipped in and shut the door behind him. A canopied king-sized bed straight from a fairytale stood against the far wall, looking small in the enormous room. A sitting area with a loveseat and chaise was situated in front of floor-to-ceiling bay windows in the corner.

Ella was accustomed to an upscale lifestyle. Her bedroom drove home the fact they lived vastly different lives. Yet, he couldn't imagine rattling around in such a huge space alone. It would be depressing.

Ella emerged on a puff of steam from a bathroom that appeared to be as big as his bedroom. Wearing a white terrycloth robe sashed around her waist, she toweled her hair dry.

"Oh. I thought you were Megan." She stutter-stepped to a stop.

"Sorry. I needed to escape."

A grimness drew her mouth into a frown. "What'd she do?"

As if he planned to mention masculine wiles and manipulation. "Nothing."

She pulled her bottom lip between her teeth and maintained eye contact as if contemplating more questions. Finally, she gestured to the sitting area by the windows. "I need to dry my hair or it'll go crazy. Make yourself comfortable."

He didn't move. Couldn't move.

She positioned herself in front of the mirror. Dryer noise drowned out any need to make conversation. His gaze met hers in her reflection. He tried to impart everything he wanted to say through that connection. An apology for certain. Also a need. Maybe it was his imagination, but the awkwardness and misunderstanding between them eased the longer they stared at each other.

Watching the intimate, domestic activity was like a slowly tightening clamp around his heart. Her robe loosened with the rise and fall of her arms and split the fabric apart. She was naked from the waist up underneath. The clamp moved south and his jeans grew tight and uncomfortable. He pulled in a ragged breath.

The dryer shut off and left a heavy silence. Still, she didn't break eye contact in the mirror. As if she'd cast a spell on him, he was drawn closer. Her hands came to the counter as if her balance was iffy.

He stopped behind her, his bulk framing her in the reflection. "I'm sorry."

"For what?" A tremble hid poorly in the bravado behind her words.

"For not making it one hundred percent clear that I think you're amazing."

"You mean, you think my body is amazing." A slight lilt to her words landed between a statement and a question and betrayed her own uncertainty with whatever had exploded between them.

"Your body is my dream come true, but that's not what I mean. I mean, *you're* amazing." He wasn't sure he could adequately summarize what he meant without sounding like he'd lost his mind.

But, it seemed he didn't need to. She swallowed and her mouth opened, then closed, her chin wobbling. She spun around and looked straight into his eyes. Nothing, not even a reflection, remained between them.

"I'm bossy," she said.

"So am I."

"I have a temper that gets the best of me sometimes."

"Me too."

"I'm opinionated."

"Ditto."

"I lived too long in a relationship where I was made to feel inferior. I won't do it again."

Fury like he'd never known streaked through his body. He fisted his hands and shoved them—and his rage—into his pockets. She didn't need him to play a white knight. She'd already saved herself. Like the magnolia tree outside her window, Ella possessed a delicate beauty but would weather all of life's seasons with grace because of her indomitable strength of spirit.

Trevor was her past. Mack was more concerned about the here and now. The future was too disorienting to think about. He reached for the tie on her robe and tugged her closer. "I'm nothing like your ex."

"I know."

"Why did you run out on me last night? Did I scare you?"

"*I* scared me."

"How?"

"When you . . . spanked me." She whispered the last two words.

A kink twisted his throat like a water hose in summer. He had no idea what kind of abuse she'd suffered under her ex-husband. Was it physical or emotional or both? At any rate, his actions had spooked her. She needed to be handled gently.

"I'm sorry. It won't happen again." He stuffed his hands

back in his pockets, not confident in his ability to keep that promise.

"The problem isn't that you spanked me. The problem is that it felt good and I sort of enjoyed it."

"Okay." He drew the word out, confused once more. "How is something that feels good a problem?"

"Because I liked it and that's not"—she waved her hand around as if grasping for words—"healthy, right?"

"What do you mean? I didn't actually hurt you, did I?"

"No." Her gaze dropped before rising to meet his once more. "But you could."

Finally, he caught a glimmer of understanding. The question that had haunted him finally escaped. "Did Trevor hit you?"

"Once. Only once." She turned away and meandered to the windows. "He was drunk and beyond using insults to put me in my place."

"What did you do?"

"It was the most humiliating moment of my life. Mostly, because my first instinct was to apologize for setting him off like that. How messed up is that?"

"He's the one messed up, not you." His palms itched to touch her, but he didn't, sensing she needed to excise the poison.

"He made me feel like I had a problem, not him." She chafed her arms even though the room was comfortable. "Do you know how I met him?"

"I don't." He would guard all her secrets, but he wouldn't demand them.

"A high school beauty pageant. He was one of the judges."

"You were in high school? What a creep." He couldn't keep the shock from his voice.

"Not how I saw it at the time. He was mature and sophisticated and my ticket out of Dry Gulch. He was my savior, and I loved him. I wasn't a gold digger."

The declaration was hard to hear, but she'd been no more than eighteen. "You were too young."

She glanced at him. "Of course I was, but that's how he likes his women. Once I hit twenty-three, I was too old, never mind the birthdays he continues to rack up."

"Too old or too bold?" Mack asked with a sudden clarity into Trevor's mind now that the mysteries of Ella were unfolding.

She turned to face him. "What do you mean?"

"You're beautiful. His preferences had nothing to do with your physical age. My guess is around that time, you became less malleable. We've established that you're bossy and stubborn and smart with a mind of your own. *That's* not how he likes his women."

Her eyes widened and she chuffed out a breath, the glimmer of a smile at her lips. "You're right. Oh my God, it had nothing to do with the way I looked."

"You were—and still are—too much woman for him to handle."

"What about you?"

"What about me?"

"Am I too much woman for you to handle?"

The sudden pivot made him feel like he was on a roller coaster in the dark. "I wouldn't be here right now if I thought that."

The sunset cast a multitude of colors across the darkening sky. A line of trees stood sentinel. Beyond them, the river flowed as it had for hundreds of years, linking this place to the garage. They weren't so far apart, were they?

"Why don't we pick up where we left off last night?" Mack grabbed the ties of her robe and backed up to the loveseat, sitting in the middle of the long cushion and guiding her into a straddle on his lap.

"Let me lower the shades." Her voice was shaky with what he hoped was excitement and not fear.

He tightened his grip on her thighs, holding her in place. "Nope. I want to be able to see you. That okay?"

"I guess so." Her nerves were apparent in the way she fiddled with the collar of her robe.

He couldn't do anything about the shadows of the night that skulked closer every minute, but he would do his best to banish the shadows of the past in her eyes. He wrapped a hand around her nape and pulled her lips within inches of his, but didn't initiate a kiss. She needed to take the lead.

A slight smile flashed before she closed the distance and kissed him. Any hint of timidness vanished. Her natural sensuality drove the kiss into new territory. Her tongue and lips explored and dominated his senses.

He had always been the aggressor in his relationships. Maybe it was his personality or size or profession, but women seemed to expect him to drive in all aspects of his relationships. Giving over to Ella's desires was a new experience. She wrapped her arms around his shoulders, pressed her breasts against his chest, and settled fully onto his erection.

He slipped a hand between them and untied her terry-cloth robe. She sat back on his lap. A stripe of skin was visible from her neck to the black waistband of her underwear. He clenched his hands and waited to see if she was going to reveal herself or hide. Did she trust him?

Chapter Thirteen

Ella swallowed and grabbed hold of the lapels of her robe, waffling in the importance of the decision she faced. She could cover herself and end this recklessness. Or she could take a chance for the first time in years. Did she trust herself?

For as much grief as Mack had given her for buying a stake in his garage, he'd given her something else as well. A confidence she'd misplaced somewhere along the way. He had let her choose the new software and handle the website updates and seemed to think she was more than capable of planning the classic car show and fundraiser.

She peeled the robe apart and let it slip to her elbows. He stared at her breasts, and under his gaze, they grew heavy and sensitive. She fought the urge to cover herself under the intensity. She could either own the moment or be crushed by it.

She'd accepted challenges all her life, and this one was more important to conquer than any. She shook her hair over her shoulders and covered his fisted hands with her own.

"Will you say something?" Her too-high voice didn't contain any of the sultriness she attempted to inject.

"I'm speechless." In contrast, Mack's voice was deeper and rougher than usual.

He brought his hands to her waist, gently tracing the long scar from the dog bite. Slowly, he inched his fingers up her sensitive skin and encircled her rib cage. His thumbs brushed the underside of her breasts. Tingles zipped through her body, tightening her nipples until they were almost painful.

"You're amazing." The harshness of his tone offset the sentiment, yet his lack of discipline was a turn-on.

She reached for him, but her arms were caught in the robe as surely as if she was tied. He took advantage, tilting her forward. Even though she was experienced enough to know where his mouth was headed, the first contact between his lips and her nipple wrung a moan from her. She didn't have time to be embarrassed when his tongue did something equally as knee weakening. He alternately flicked the nub and sucked it deep. While he worked back and forth, his beard rasped against her skin, piling pleasure upon pleasure.

"That feels . . ." She hesitated a moment, searching for a word to adequately describe the effect he was having on her body. One wouldn't do. "Incredible. Magnificent. *Magical.* Do you have special powers or something?"

His soft laugh while her nipple was still in his mouth sent a different sort of weakness through her. This one had a warm quality, like a quilt being stitched between them with every shared experience.

He transferred his mouth to her other nipple but covered her abandoned breast with his hand. She squirmed and arched her back, driving herself onto his erection. Dear Lord, she couldn't wait to get her hands and mouth on him.

Why did she have wait to take what she wanted? She fought her robe off her arms and let it puddle around his feet. She was left in a pair of black lace underwear she'd spent too much money on at Abigail's Boutique. Their purpose hadn't been seduction, but a way to bolster her confidence.

He plucked at the two strings across her hip connecting the front scrap of lace to the back. Thank goodness she wasn't in white granny panties.

She shifted enough to cover his erection with her hand. He bucked, one hand squeezing her breast while the other pulled at her panties, the constriction doing crazy good things to her already slick body.

"Going in for the kill, are you?" he asked.

She liked knowing she was the cause of the desperate edge to his teasing words. "I want to touch you."

She leaned over him for another kiss. The soft cotton of his shirt caressed her nipples and his jeans roughed the inside of her thighs. The fact that he was still clothed while she writhed nearly naked on his lap was exotic in a way she'd never experienced.

But she was ready for less clothes on him. Way less. Without breaking the kiss, she worked the hem of his T-shirt up until her breasts rubbed against his hair-covered chest.

"If you get to see mine, I should get to see yours," she said with her lips against his, teasing out a smile from him.

"No one said this was going to be fair." His voice held the hint of an erotic threat. Yet, he didn't prolong her wait. He pulled his T-shirt off and tossed it over her shoulder.

She explored him with her eyes and hands, her bottom lip caught between her teeth. He was masculinity encapsulated in flesh and blood, so unlike the groomed, fastidiousness of her ex-husband. She shook her head, trying to force Trevor out of her thoughts. He had no right to invade and dominate her life anymore.

Mack smoothed his hands over her hips and around her

buttocks. The warmth from his big palms scored through the lace to her flesh. "What's wrong?"

She tensed. "Nothing. Why?"

"I lost you for a second."

The epicenter of the tremble was in her chest, but it flowed outward until her hand shook on his erection. He grabbed her wrist, pulled her hand away, and gathered her close, swinging her legs around until she was cradled in his lap.

He didn't ask questions or demand answers. Instead, he stroked her hair and down her arm in a gesture that was meant to comfort her, but took a U-turn when his hand continued down her hip to tug at her underwear once more.

"It's been awhile. A long while. The last time was with Trevor and he made me feel . . ." The mathematical symbol $<$ jumped into her head. With Trevor, she was always on the "less than" side of the equation. Squeezed to zero compared to everything Trevor wanted and was. Not as smart or well bred or attractive. "He made me feel less than."

"That's bullshit he shoveled to keep you down. He needed you to feel less than so he could feel big, but you proved him wrong."

Mack had a way of blustering past her insecurities to rip the curtain away. His confidence in her strength, as misplaced as it might be, gave her courage. She turned in his embrace to kiss him and draw his hand between her legs. He caressed up her inner thigh. Her legs fell apart and her pelvis tilted.

By the time his fingers made contact, she hovered on the brink of something special. Maybe even momentous. He teased her over the thin, damp lace.

"Mack, please." Her voice was husky and embarrassingly begging.

He stood and cradled her to his chest as if she was a

featherweight. "Not so fast. My job is to make sure you understand you're not less than. You're . . . *everything.*"

Her breath caught. Darkness had fallen while they'd been testing each other on the couch, but even with the shadows darkening his eyes, she sensed his earnestness.

He laid her on the edge of the bed, pushed her knees apart, and stepped in between. Laid out for his viewing pleasure, she felt both shy and powerful. The woman she aspired to be clung to the power, and she raised her arms above her head, hoping the arch of her back and slight shimmy would spur him into action.

It did. But it wasn't the action she expected. He squatted, his shoulders forcing her legs farther apart. Had he dropped something? She came up in her elbows and only had time to open her mouth to ask before he grabbed the hip strings of her underwear and ripped them.

The sudden strength of the move shocked her. He tossed the tattered lace over his shoulder.

"Those were expensive." She huffed.

"They were in my way."

He wrapped his hands around her thighs and pulled her closer to the edge. She fell back. Was she dreaming? His beard tickled her inner thighs and a giggle slipped out as she squirmed.

"What's so funny?" His breath was warm on her most intimate of places, squashing her giggles.

"Your beard tickles."

He rubbed his cheek against her inner thigh, this time the feeling not at all tickly, but rough and arousing. Without warning, he made contact with his tongue. She squeezed her eyes shut and bit the inside of her mouth.

She tried to relax. Trevor had been totally into receiving but not giving. At her age and with a multi-year-long marriage behind her, her inexperience was embarrassing.

Her legs had locked at his shoulders. He pulled away,

and she was relieved but painfully aware she was a disappointment.

"Relax," he whispered.

"I'm not sure I can."

"Why not?" He kissed the inside of her thigh as his hand kneaded one side of her butt.

It felt so delicious, she lost the train of her worries. "Because . . . because . . ."

He wiggled his tongue straight through her to suck at her most sensitive spot.

How could she not give him a measure of her truth, considering she was naked and his head was between her legs? "No one's ever . . . you know . . . done this before. To me, I mean. I'm sure lots of men—women too—have done it plenty." She sealed her mouth shut to stop her babbling.

His pause seemed loaded. "Then I'd better make it unforgettable."

He pressed his lips against her and hummed, the vibrations setting off a tsunami in her belly. His tongue was gentle and thorough, exploring every square inch before making its way back to where she ached for him.

He hadn't seemed disappointed or put off by her confession. If anything, his determination to please her had kicked into overdrive. The least she could do was let him, right? She closed her eyes and focused on the spiraling pleasure. Spearing her hands through his hair, she set her heels on the edge of the bed and let instinct guide her.

She rotated her hips, chasing the combination of pressure and speed that would get her over the edge, but unable to find it. A mewl of want and desperation and frustration escaped.

His hand joined the undertaking, his touch gentle. Which is why, when he roughly plunged a finger inside of her, she launched into a climax so intense, the space-time continuum ceased to exist.

Mack pumped his finger and circled his tongue to give her more and more and more. She didn't feel less than with Mack.

Her legs flopped open, her body lax and sated in a way she'd never experienced. He rose, his hands trailing from her knees to her waist, leaned down, and touched his lips to hers. He was undemanding, only asking for a kiss in return. A kiss that tasted erotically foreign.

But *she* wanted more. She wanted *everything*. With a franticness she couldn't put into words, she sat up, pushed him to standing, and yanked at his belt. She brushed over his erection and licked her lips. If anything, it was even more prominent than it had been on the couch.

He put his hands over hers and stilled her fumbling. "Are you sure?"

The simple fact he didn't assume he could take whatever he wanted only added to her determination.

"I've never been more sure about anything." The declaration sounded melodramatic to her ears, but it was the truth.

She got his belt unbuckled and his zipper halfway down when the chime of the doorbell froze them. Ignoring it, she went back to work on his pants. She didn't want whatever they were selling. She only wanted Mack between her legs.

Megan's voice echoed in the two-story foyer and down the hall to her room, muffled but agitated. "Why are you here? It's over. I told you that already."

"Dammit all to hell and back," she muttered.

Why did Trevor have to insert himself at the worst possible moment? It was like her ex had sensed she was ready and willing to give herself over completely to Mack. Maybe Megan could handle Trevor, and she and Mack could get down to business. But Mack buckled his belt and left her on the bed, grabbing his T-shirt and pulling it over his head.

She flopped back and felt like throwing a tantrum that would make any two-year-old proud. Mack was right though. Ella couldn't in good conscience leave Megan to face Trevor on her own. Ella rolled off the bed and pulled on shorts and a T-shirt, forgoing a bra out of expediency.

"What's he doing here?" Mack asked.

"Trying to convince Megan to take him back."

"Will she?"

Ella stopped with her hand on the doorknob and blew out a breath. "I honestly don't know. She's talked about moving to Cottonbloom for good and getting a job."

The sound of Trevor's voice reverberated, the anger apparent but the words indistinct. They had moved farther into the house. She opened the door and led the way. Mack maneuvered himself ahead of her, and she got the feeling he was trying to protect her.

Megan and Trevor had moved into the living room, a formal, stark space that generally went unused. In fact, most of her house went unused, except for the kitchen, den, and master bedroom. The second-floor balconies and wraparound porch had drawn her to the house and given it a storybook look, but she'd never spent significant time on either. She'd bought the house to fulfill a childish daydream, but found it impossible to replicate the magic.

Trevor had cornered Megan between a couch and a side table. His unintelligible whisper was snakelike with venom.

Mack stopped halfway in the room and took up more space than his physical presence would suggest. His hair was mussed, and his T-shirt was half-tucked and inside out. He was an angry bear woken from hibernation. A super-sexy angry bear.

"Trevor. I would appreciate a call before you show up at my house." Ella put a hand on Mack's arm and scooted around him. Although she appreciated having backup, Trevor was her problem.

"I shouldn't have to call to visit my wife." He imbued the word with a possessiveness only too familiar to Ella. Once upon a time, he'd spoken about her like that.

"This is my house, and I made it clear last time you are not welcome. Now get out." She crossed her arms under her breasts.

Trevor's gaze darted down, and she cursed herself for not spending five extra seconds to put a bra on. The urge to cover her chest came with a decent amount of shame. If he pulled from his well-used playbook, he would accuse her of betrayal or worse, even though they were long past that point in their history.

But why should she feel any shame? Her decisions regarding Mack didn't concern Trevor. Not anymore. She forced her arms to her side and her shoulders back, daring him to comment.

With a glance over her shoulder at Mack, he seemed to realize he was in the weaker position and took a different stance, one of honey. "I want to work things out, but I need a chance."

"Your chances are used up with me. This is Megan's decision."

Just say no. Ella attempted to send the chant telepathically to Megan.

"I don't know. It would be easier for everyone." The resolve and confidence Megan had accrued since arriving in Cottonbloom had been squandered, and the uncertainty in her voice was like a red flag to Trevor's bully personality.

Ella exchanged a glance with Mack. It would be all around easier for her if Megan left. Ella didn't need or want a roommate, especially one with such complicated ties to

her old life. But, one thing Ella understood intimately—
what was easier wasn't always right. She'd tolerated too
much because the alternative of choosing what was best
for her seemed too difficult.

"Come with me tonight." Trevor circled closer for the
kill. "Your parents would be thrilled to see us together at
their barbeque this weekend."

"You talk to them?"

"Every day."

Megan gnawed on her bottom lip and looked from
Trevor to Ella. If she stayed silent, Megan would leave tonight, and Ella could drag Mack back to her bedroom to
take what she wanted so bad it hurt.

"You've got a job interview tomorrow, Megan. It's too
late to cancel without ruining your chances." Ella stepped
up to stand next to Trevor in an attempt to neutralize his
influence.

"A job?" Trevor made a scoffing sound. "That's ridiculous. You don't need to work. We'll have your inheritance."

Megan met Ella's gaze and slowly her chin lifted and
her eyes narrowed. Somewhere deep inside, she had located some gumption. "Not if I divorce you. I need to be
able to take care of myself like Ella does."

Trevor snorted. "Yeah, right. It's my money that bought
this place and everything in it. Money she had no right to."

Ella balled her hands into fists and visualized punching Trevor right in the face. Or raising a knee to his balls.
"I deserved every penny, and you know it. I only wish I'd
done it sooner."

Trevor's darting gaze settled on Mack. "You'd better
watch this one. Once she gets you in her web, she'll bleed
you dry for the privilege of sharing her bed." His tone was
conspiratorial and teasing as if engaging in so-called
locker room guy talk, but with his typical marked cruelty.

Before she could form a harsh enough insult, Mack

grabbed the front of Trevor's shirt and raised him to his toes. "You want to say that again?"

"Let me go." Trevor grabbed Mack's wrist with both hands, but Mack, the bigger man in every way, didn't budge.

Ella was unchristian enough to revel in the thread of fear in Trevor's voice. It wasn't often he'd crossed paths with anyone willing to stand up to him. His money and status kept him insulated in Jackson. But Cottonbloom wasn't Jackson, and Mack wasn't like any other man Ella had ever met.

"Let me summarize the conversation that just took place for you." An impressive calm left Mack's expression stony even as Trevor squirmed in his hold. "Megan has a job interview tomorrow and will be staying here. She will contact you if she so desires. You're not to call or text her. Ella doesn't want you at her house anymore, so don't come back. Now, I'm going to walk you out, and I'd advise you to make for Jackson immediately before I lose my temper."

Mack released Trevor and pointed toward the front door. Trevor smoothed the crumple left by Mack's fist and shot a heated glance over his shoulder at her and Megan. Ella managed not to stick her tongue out at him, but nothing could stem her good riddance smirk. His gait stiff, he stalked out of the living room, and Mack followed.

The front door opened and shut, and the chain and deadbolt rattled. The finality of the sound triggered tears in Megan. Not delicate, manipulative tears, but a good ugly cry. Ella put an arm around Megan's shoulders and rocked her back and forth uttering nonsense like "He's an utter bastard" and "There, there."

"I still love him and part of me wanted to go back to him. A big part." Megan wiped her running nose on her sleeve like a little kid. In fact, she *was* young in both years and trials. Until now, her life had been blessed. Ella hoped she'd emerge from this situation stronger and wiser.

"Why didn't you?" Ella asked.

"I've gotten a glimpse of what my life could be like without him. Without my parents hovering and controlling me. And without the expectations that are tied to their acceptance. You're happy, right? With him." Megan tilted her head toward the hallway where Mack could very well be standing outside listening to them.

Was she happy? She wasn't sure. She was confused. Fascinated. Excited. But happy? She wasn't sure she understood the concept. It was too simple. "I'm content with where I am right now."

"You have Trevor's money though."

Although Megan had not meant it unkindly, the assessment stung. It was what everyone thought. She was a gold digger living off her divorce settlement. Except, *she* had been the investor with the magic touch, not Trevor. She'd made him rich beyond what he'd thought possible, but he'd never given her the credit. She'd never asked for it—a mistake she refused to make again.

"My road is different than yours. I can't tell you how to travel it, but I don't mind if you stay here to figure it out."

"Thanks, Ella. It means a lot." Megan hugged her. Not a polite pat-on-the-back-and-break-apart hug, but a tight hug that lasted longer than Ella was comfortable with.

Mack poked his head around the doorjamb and raised his eyebrows. She sent her regrets with a shake of her head. Even if he stayed, rekindling the magic after the emotionally wrenching confrontation with Trevor would result in something less than satisfying. She didn't want her ex haunting her while she was with Mack. Was that asking for the impossible?

He cleared his throat, and Megan stepped away, wiping at her eyes and casting a wet, swollen smile in Mack's direction. "Thanks for taking out the trash."

The unexpected sass from Megan sent a wave of relief through Ella. "Why don't you go pour a couple of glasses of wine, Megan, and we'll binge on a TV show? I'll be there in a minute."

Once Megan was gone, Ella joined Mack in the foyer.

"I should go," he said with the slight lilt of a question.

"Megan needs a friend right now."

"I get it." He worked the locks of the front door and stepped onto the wraparound porch.

She followed, closing the door behind her. "By the way, your shirt is on inside out."

He held the front out and chuckled. "I guess it's no secret what your ex interrupted."

"I guess not." When he turned to go, she laid her hand on his arm. "Thanks for everything tonight."

"*Everything*?" The sexy innuendo was mistakable.

She was an expert at superficially flirting with men. The blush heating her cheeks proved Mack was a different beast. A very sexy different beast.

"I'm only sorry I didn't get to return the favor." Her lips were rubbery with nerves. She and Trevor had never teased and flirted and bantered. The sex had been mechanical at best and boring toward the end. Based on tonight's sampling, nothing about Mack in bed would be either.

"Another time, hopefully soon. If the anticipation doesn't kill me first." He leaned back on the column at the top of the porch stairs, his hands caught in the small of his back.

She tightened her hold on him, popped to her toes, and kissed him. She swept her tongue over his bottom lip, but put space between them before it could go any deeper. Feeling naughty and brave in the near darkness, she walked her fingers down the front of his jeans. He was still semi-erect.

Before she could fall to her knees and do something even riskier, he grasped both her arms, brushed a kiss over her forehead, and clomped down the stairs, as if she'd transformed from lover to relative. A distant one at that. He turned at the bottom. "I'll see you in the morning."

"Yes. In the morning." The words emerged on a croak.

His truck rumbled off and disappeared. Megan toed the front door open and offered a glass of red wine. Ella sipped, still staring where the road was swallowed by hundred-year-old water oaks.

"I'm sorry," Megan said softly.

"You can't help the way Trevor acts."

"Not that. I sort of warned Mack off you. I worried he might be using you to get to your portion of the garage. I didn't realize how serious the two of you were."

"We're not serious."

"Oh really?" Megan arched one eyebrow as if she were mapping an attack plan. "So you wouldn't mind if I tried to hit that?"

Something visceral and green stretched its wings in Ella's chest. "Keep your hands off him. He's mine."

Megan smiled, her tear-swollen eyes scrunching into slits. "That's what I thought."

Chapter Fourteen

Ella rubbed at her gritty eyes and headed straight into the break room for a cup of coffee. Last one out of the garage was tasked to set the maker up to brew on an automatic timer. She swirled the dark mass in her cup and sniffed. The smell alone offered a pick-me-up. She took a sip, the concoction so strong, it was almost chewy. Copious packets of sugar and creamer made it palatable.

Closing her eyes, she leaned against the counter and sipped until the caffeine lubricated the cogs of her brain. She and Megan had split a bottle of wine and stayed up late discussing the situation with Trevor. When she'd managed to drift to sleep, Mack had bulldozed his way into her dreams.

"How's the coffee?" Jackson rubbed a hand over his face, poured a cup, and took a sip of the black brew.

"It has the consistency of motor oil." Ella's voice was rough from overuse. Her evenings since moving to Cottonbloom had been mostly quiet and solitary mixed in with the occasional party or fundraiser. The last time she'd stayed up talking half the night had been a middle-school sleepover.

"It'll wake you up, that's for sure." A companionable silence fell as they sipped. Finally, Jackson asked, "I assume Mack made nice last night?"

The image of Mack's mouth making nice between her legs flashed. As if Jackson could see her thoughts, a jolt of adrenaline, super heated by the coffee, blazed through her. Boy howdy, she was awake now. "He made nice, yes."

"Good, because sometimes he can be stubborn. And intractable. And closed off."

"And lonely." The assessment slipped around her better judgment.

Jackson's gaze sharpened on her, his eyes freakily similar to Mack's. "Maybe so."

"I'd better get to work." Her quickstep out of the break room matched her heartbeat.

Settling herself behind the desk, she did a double-check on the new program. Everything was processing smoothly. It was time to get Mack up to speed and hand it over to him to manage. It would be a relief. She could concentrate on planning the car show, which would keep her out of Mack's hair and away from other parts of his anatomy while they were working.

Twenty minutes after eight, Mack backed through the front door, tucking a thick tan work shirt into black pants. His hair was still mussed from bed. He stopped in the doorway of the office and finger-combed it, making the sexy chaos even sexier.

"Your face!" Ella shot up from behind the desk. Her heart traipsed along like she'd injected coffee straight into an artery.

He'd shaved his beard off, revealing a strong jawline and chin—not that she'd thought he was hiding a weak anything underneath the facial hair. He looked younger and slightly less intimidating. Although, there was still a fire in his eyes and a stubbornness in his jutting chin.

"It was past time to lose the winter beard." He rubbed a hand over his jaw. "Sorry I'm late."

"No need to apologize to me. You run the joint."

"Last time I was late, I had stayed out late drinking at the Tavern. Pop put me on the grinder all day. It was miserable." He shuffled farther into the office.

The nostalgia in his voice made her smile before a different worry settled. "You're not nursing a hangover this morning, are you?"

"Not of the alcoholic variety, no." A grumbly awareness in his voice had her sitting up straighter and squirming. Modulated to professional levels, he continued. "What's your plan for the day?"

"The new software is ready to roll out. I need to train you."

He checked the wall-mounted clock. "How long will it take? I have a car coming in for an estimate soon."

"We can do it after." *Do it.* Why did the adolescent words have to go on repeat in her head?

"Sounds good." The way his gaze flicked over her made her body temperature rise another degree. Thankfully, he stepped onto the shop floor to talk to his brothers, and she was out of his pheromone range. She grabbed a handful of papers and fanned herself. Mack with a beard had been devastating to her concentration; Mack without a beard was the iceberg to her *Titanic*.

Ella had never been obsessed with sex. In fact, just the opposite. She'd learned early on that sex was used too often to hurt people. Trevor had manipulated her with it, and she had avoided being drawn into the web of complications sex weaved. Which is why her sudden obsession with Mack was so disconcerting.

By midafternoon, Mack had wrapped up his work and was ready to spend time learning the new program. He pulled up a chair, situating himself a little behind her and to the side. "Got your tire patched and back on your car. You should be good for another ten thousand miles or so."

She had forgotten about her tire, but Mack hadn't. Taking care of cars was his job, but in this, it felt like he was taking care of *her*. "Thank you."

"No problem." He rubbed his hands together. "Let's get this party started."

"Party? Your expectations are high, but I'm confident the program will save you time and streamline orders and payments."

Her tutorial started well enough. She pointed out what each column meant and went through one order, walking him through the process.

"So here . . ." He draped an arm over the back of the chair and leaned in, his hand on the mouse. It felt like a mock embrace. "This is a recurring order. How do I trigger the reorder when inventory gets low?"

"This column." She put her hand over his on the mouse, guided it to the correct place, and right-clicked to bring up a side menu.

"Nice. That will definitely save me time."

Was it weird she hadn't moved her hand off his? It felt weird but good at the same time.

"And what about this?" He moved their hands on the mouse in tandem to another column.

"That's—" She cleared her throat when the word came out broken. "That's for bulk items. Nuts, bolts, washers."

Finally, she removed her hand and picked up a piece of paper she'd tucked under the keyboard. "Scroll to the bottom, and we'll enter this order together."

He leaned even closer, his breath tickling the side of her ear. She only had to turn her head and her lips would be touching his smooth jaw.

It wasn't fair that the first time in her life she'd been

stupidly, undeniably, unbearably on fire for a man, it was for one who complicated her life immeasurably.

"This is crazy," she whispered.

"Seems pretty straightforward to me." He moved his hand to the keyboard to enter the numbers, his biceps brushing her breast.

"I'm not talking about this." She waved her hand over the monitor. "I'm talking about this." She pointed back and forth from her to him.

"Why is *this* crazy?" He mimicked her actions.

"I have something you're desperate for. Twenty-five percent of the garage."

"That's not all I'm desperate for." His lips quirked.

God, his lips were lovely. So was his now-undisguised smile. She blinked and forced her gaze onto the computer monitor. "The question of ownership—"

"Doesn't enter into the equation when it comes to me and you."

She harrumphed. "Of course it does."

"Why can't we separate business and pleasure?"

"This doesn't feel separate to me. Does it to you?" Their faces were inches apart, and she wondered what he would do if she leaned in and kissed him with his brothers on the shop floor and with the office door wide open.

"I don't know, Ella, but I can't leave you alone. Not yet."

Was she something to work out of his system? Or maybe would she eventually work him out of *her* system.

"Speaking of business, let's finish up here." He nodded toward the computer

She took a breath and concentrated on the screen. The heat emanating from Mack was distracting and intoxicating, but she got through the training without doing anything inappropriate.

He hit return to finalize the last order, and she pushed

at the desk, sending her office chair rolling to a safe more-than-arm's-length distance. "That's it then. Simple, right?"

"Simple." He rose and put the desk between them. "I'm not sure I would have had the gumption to make the change. Thanks."

"You're welcome." It was still a shock to hear words of thanks come out of his mouth when it came to the garage.

He looked like he wanted to say something else for a minute, but retreated to the shop floor. She worked on the last details of the program and wrote up basic instructions. By the time she stretched herself out of the chair, the garage floor was quiet.

Mack sauntered in, his hands stuffed into his front pockets. She plopped back in the seat as he came around to her side of the desk and half-sat on the edge.

"Almost done?"

"I guess you're ready to lock up." She gathered her purse.

He reached forward and tapped her glasses. "I like you in these."

She'd only recently broken down and gotten a pair of glasses for reading and computer work. She yanked them off and fiddled with her hair. "I know. Real cute, right?"

"Actually, more like sexy as hell. It's why 'Hot for Teacher' was a monster hit."

"Oh." Would putting them back on be too obvious a ploy?

"You interested in having dinner with me tonight?"

Her heart did a funny jig in her chest. Was this a date or a continuation of work? Where did business end and pleasure begin? "Sure. A girl's got to eat. Where do you want to go?"

"A fancy little place I like to call Chez Abbott."

"You're going to cook for me?"

"You like ramen noodles, right? How about fried Spam,

then?" At her grimace, a slow smile spread across his face. "Kidding. I can do a better than that."

She could care less what they ate. They'd be alone at his house with a king-sized bed to finish what they'd started without interruption from her ex or her ex's ex. "I'd love to join you for dinner."

She gathered her things while he waited. He flipped the lights off as they walked to the main door. Darkness enveloped them. Her hand was on the door, yet she didn't turn the knob. He wrapped an arm around her waist and brought their bodies together.

His was hot and hard and tempting. She reached around, put her hand on his butt, and pulled him even tighter against her. Dinner? She was hungry, but not for food.

The smoothness of his cheek brushed her neck a heartbeat before his lips made contact. Sensation streaked through her body. She felt like a grenade with the pin hanging on for dear life.

She turned, put her back against the door, and yanked him forward by two fistfuls of shirt. Her lips slammed into his with more enthusiasm and less finesse. He eased the pressure and took control, his hand encircling her nape.

She let go of his shirt, stood on tiptoes, and wrapped an arm around his shoulders, bringing her breasts into full contact with his chest. She wished she'd worn heels today. And a skirt. With no panties. What did that say about her? That she embraced her sexuality and this new phase of her life? Or that she was desperate for this man's touch? Maybe both.

He framed her face with his hands, his thumbs caressing her cheeks in a way that made her chest tighten. The kiss was slower and gentler and held more emotion than she could handle.

She hitched her leg up and curled it around his thigh, canting her hips and putting just enough space between them to slip her hand to the front of his pants. He was rock solid in every way.

Yes. The word echoed in her head, and she was pretty sure she'd said it aloud.

"I promised you dinner." His lips moved against hers.

"I promised you something last night before we were so rudely interrupted." Courage flared in the darkness. Or was it recklessness? There was a fine line between the two, and she couldn't distinguish which swept her along.

She fumbled with his belt and button and zipper, finally succeeding in peeling his pants open to run her fingers over the ridge concealed by his cotton underwear. He sucked in a breath and rested his forearms on either side of her head.

"This is crazy," he said in a mimic of her earlier declaration.

It was crazy, but she blamed him. He made her crazy.

She slipped to her knees, pulling his underwear down with her until it gathered, along with his pants, mid-thigh. His erection bobbed mere millimeters from her lips. The concrete was cold and hard under her knees. The glowing exit sign cast an eerie reddish light over them.

She cast a glance up through her lashes and ran her tongue along her lips in preparation. He was looking down at her, but in the shadows his mood was a mystery. He didn't touch her or force himself into her mouth. He waited for her move.

With her eyes still upturned, she opened her mouth and pulled him inside. His head dropped to rest against the door between his arms as if he'd collapse without the support. She wrapped one hand around the base of his erection and one around his thigh.

It felt dirty and a little seedy to be on her knees in the garage doing what she was doing to a man she thought she'd hated a few short weeks ago. Yet, it was a turn-on for all the same reasons. Even though she was the one on her knees, power and confidence emboldened her.

With every stroke of her mouth, she took him deeper. His hips started a counterthrust, and she moaned around him.

"I'm going to lose it, babe." His voice was low and growly and bordered on animalistic.

His warning made her suck harder and faster. With a roar, he pushed her off of him and leaned more fully onto the door, shuddering. He banged his head once against the door. "Damn."

Was that a *Damn, what have I done?* or a *Damn, that was awesome!* She rotated her jaw and wiggled out from between his hips and the door. The awkwardness of the aftermath rushed through her. Escape was not an option, considering he was still face-planted against the door.

"That was . . . that was . . ." His voice rumbled then stalled.

"Can we go with 'incredible'?"

"Not even close."

"Obviously, you enjoyed yourself." She forced an indifference she couldn't find locate into her voice and gestured to the stark evidence on the door.

"Massive understatement." He pushed himself upright, blew out a relieved-sounding breath, and used the nearest shop towel to clean up the mess.

"I would have "—she gestured toward his crotch—"you know, *finished* you."

"Would you have?" His voice had evened from the raw, sexual heat of his climax. He pulled up his pants and re-fastened them.

Was he disgusted by her aggressiveness? Was dinner a no-go now she'd given him what he was after? She shifted on her feet, the ebb of her confidence leaving her stomach in knots.

He opened the door, and she stumbled outside ahead of him. Purple clouds snuffed out the sunset. An electric feel in the air and the smell of rain portended a spring storm. A burst of wind whipped her hair out of the messy bun and around her face.

"I should go." She stared at the horizon, wishing the onslaught would get here already. Maybe a strike of lightning would put her out of her misery.

"What about dinner?"

"I thought . . ." She made a vague motion toward the garage and hoped he wasn't cruel enough to make her explain.

He tipped her face to his, forcing her to either look at him or close her eyes. She wasn't a total coward and met his gaze, even though her knees trembled.

"You thought I wouldn't want to have dinner with you because I *got mine*?" He one-hand air-quoted the last words.

"Something like that."

He shook his head. "I've acted like an asshole in many ways, but I would never treat any woman—especially you—like that. What kind of men have you been dating?"

Especially you. What did he mean by that? Because they had to keep the business aspect of their relationship intact?

"Date? What's a date?" She attempted to joke her way out of the awkwardness. Her advantage in most situations hinged on the fact that men and women found her to be experienced and intimidating. It had been an important defense as part of her life in Jackson, and had served her well negotiating deals in Cottonbloom.

"You're telling me that the men in Cottonbloom haven't been beating on your door?"

Yes, men had come onto her. Single men. Married men. Divorced men. But none of them had asked her out on a date. Instead they had made assumptions about her. Wrong assumptions. She shrugged in what she hoped conveyed nonchalance. "I swore off men after my divorce."

Thunder rumbled in the distance and a raindrop hit her cheek. She shifted, not sure where to seek shelter—the garage, her car, his arms. Mack caught her hand and tugged her back around. More raindrops fell. One hit his temple and trailed down his jaw. Before she could stop herself, she followed its path with her fingertip.

"What makes me so special?" The way he asked gave her pause. He wasn't fishing for compliments or teasing her. If anything, he sounded a little hesitant and unsure of the answer. But for goodness' sake, she couldn't tell him what made him special. It would hand him too much power.

"I've never been with anyone like you." That much at least was true. She'd never been with a man who was as hard working, loyal, and stubborn as Mack Abbott.

"What? You've never been with a blue-collar grease monkey?" His voice was half teasing and half combative.

Her heart quickened, sensing the danger, but she wasn't sure if it emanated from the coming storm or from the man. The raindrops were coming faster now, and she finger-combed her hair off her forehead.

A crossroads approached, one answer led to safety and the other to a ROAD CLOSED sign. She could laugh and agree that all she wanted was a good time. Or she could admit that she was in over her head and terrified of how he made her feel.

She did neither. Without letting go of his hand, she wrapped her arm around his neck and pulled him to her, settling her lips against his.

It was a kiss like none other they'd shared. An exploration. An explanation. An apology.

The sky opened up with a flash of lightning and a crack

of thunder. She pulled away with a yelp. Hand in hand they made a run for his front porch, stopping to drip over his front mat. Mack laughed and shook his head, water droplets flying from his hair. His shirt molded across his broad chest. She was breathless from more than the scamper across his yard.

The sound of the rain was deafening on his roof. It poured over the side of his porch like a curtain, concealing them from the world. A shiver passed through her as her wet clothes chilled.

Somehow he noticed, like he seemed to notice everything, big and small. "Come on in. Let's get you dry."

His door was unlocked, and he led the way, turning on lights as he went. She followed him to his bedroom. Trying not to let her curiosity shine too bright, she swept a glance around the room.

Rain pelted the windows lining the back wall from floor to ceiling with no blinds or drapes. The dark, solid wood of his bed frame took up one wall. The covers on one side of the bed were tossed aside, but the other side was still made up, a quilt tucked under the pillow. A few items of clothes were scattered around the room, but otherwise it was neat.

He opened the drawer and pulled out a flannel shirt, then rummaged through a different drawer and pulled out a pair of athletic shorts. He held them up. "This is the best I've got unfortunately."

She took his offerings. He grabbed a T-shirt and pair of jeans for himself and backed out the door. "Bathroom is through that door."

"Thanks."

He raised his chin in acknowledgment and left her alone. She shuffled to the bathroom, stopping by his dresser to pick up a picture. A thirtysomething-year-old man stood in front of a smaller-looking Abbott Garage, one hand propped on the cement corner and the other on his hip. A smile crested his face. It was obviously Hobart Abbott, the family patriarch. Mack favored him more than any of the other brothers.

She caught a glimpse of herself in the mirror and stopped short. Mascara smudged under both eyes, giving her a morning-after party-girl look. And her shirt—she would have at least placed in a wet T-shirt contest. Yet, Mack hadn't made even a teasing comment. He was more a gentleman than any of the old-money, high-society men in Jackson.

She stripped off her wet clothes, including her soaked bra. His shirt fit her like a dress, and she didn't bother with the athletic shorts. The flannel was soft and well worn. One of his favorites? She buried her nose in the collar and took a deep breath. Heady.

When had the smell of detergent on old flannel become intoxicating? Since Mack. All her senses had sharpened and become sensitized since the night she'd met him at Judge Mize's New Year's Eve party.

She remembered every second of their blistering encounter from his aggressive handshake to the moment he'd advanced on her like an angry bear before sweeping out the door. She'd been rattled, true. But, the encounter had acted like a life-saving shock to her heart. She'd felt alive for the first time in too long.

It was a big reason she'd stayed away from the garage at first. While she'd been worried for a repeat reaction, deep inside, she'd been even more worried that she'd imagined the entire episode. Turns out she'd underestimated her reaction to Mack.

She washed her face clean and used her brush to get the tangles out of her hair, leaving it damp and loose around her shoulders. She examined herself in the mirror and before she could second-guess herself, she popped an extra button open on his shirt. After laying out her wet things to dry, she made her way barefoot toward the delicious smells emanating from his kitchen.

Unlike the spaciousness of his bedroom, the kitchen was an old-fashioned narrow, galley-type with a small breakfast nook. He was barefoot and wearing an Abbott Brothers Garage T-shirt and jeans. No apron. He hadn't noticed her, and she let her gaze wander over every inch of his body. She should be embarrassed knowing what she'd done to him in the darkness of the garage, but her overriding thought was that she wanted a repeat performance in the light.

"No 'Kiss the Cook' apron?" She propped her shoulder against the door and put a hand on her hip, going for casual and sexy.

He smiled and glanced toward her, then took a second, longer look. His smile faded as his gaze streaked up and down and back again. "Would you have taken advantage of the message?"

"I've proved my lack of self-control where you're concerned." She wandered farther into the kitchen. "Can I help?"

"You want to throw the salad together? Unless you're high maintenance and want the dressing on the side." He lifted a brow.

"I'm not sure I qualify as low maintenance, but I love lots of dressing. What are you making?" She sidled closer and peeked over his arm. A box of pasta sat next to a boiling pot of water ready, to go in, while he sautéed peppers and onions and chicken strips. The spices were strong.

"Cajun pasta. Easy but tasty. Hope it's not too simple for you."

"Simple? This is a treat." She leaned closer and took a deep breath, her stomach already performing a celebratory dance. "I can't cook worth a darn. I'm usually eating salads or frozen stuff or takeout."

"I'm shocked. I didn't think there was anything you weren't good at."

The compliment left her nonplussed. The only person in her life who'd ever built her up instead of tearing her down had been her brother, Grayson. And compliments from people—men especially—were always received with a healthy skepticism. Usually the giver was after money, connections, or sex. While no doubt Mack wanted sex, his compliment didn't seem calculated to get it. He'd sounded earnest.

"Believe me, there's plenty I'm not good at." Right now, she was struggling to maintain the illusion she was a healthy, mature adult.

His side-eye glance was filled with curiosity, but he didn't pursue the line of questioning. Instead, he poured the box of twirly pasta into the water and set the timer. "ETA of ten minutes. Do you want a drink?"

He picked up a tumbler filled with ice and whiskey and took a sip. She tensed, her mind calculating how much was in the glass and wondering if it was his first.

"No, thank you." She needed to keep a clear head in case it became necessary to bolt.

The tumbler hit the counter with a bang, and her gaze followed it the whole way.

"What's the matter?"

"Nothing." She forced herself to look in his face.

"I call bullshit. I offer you a drink and all of a sudden you— Hang on, it's my drink, isn't it? Trevor is a drinker. Whiskey?"

She dabbed her tongue along her bone-dry bottom lip. "Yes."

"Your stepdad too?"

"Yes." It was an evil irony that she'd escaped her

alcoholic stepdad to marry another alcoholic. The liquor had brought out the worst in them both. Did the devil lurk in all men, waiting to be unleashed?

He picked up the glass, and she took a step back as if the whiskey itself could hurt her. Instead of reacting in anger or making fun of her deep-rooted fear, he turned to the sink and poured the contents down the drain.

"Better?" He set the empty glass down.

The gesture may have been small, but it was meaningful. She relaxed against the counter. "Thank you."

"You're welcome. How about setting the table while I finish up. Everything is in that drawer." He pointed with a wooden spoon.

She pulled out silverware and headed into a small dining room off to the side. It had an unused feel to it, but the table was riddled with scratches and missing a few chips around the edges. She imagined a group of rambunctious boys eating here every night and rolling their Hot Wheels across the top.

Place mats and napkins were stacked in the middle, and she set two places side by side. He brought out two plates, each loaded with the Cajun pasta and a mound of salad.

"Water or sweet tea?"

"Tea would be great."

He nodded and disappeared, but only for a minute, returning with two glasses. After setting them down, he pulled out a chair and gestured.

She pulled at the hem of his borrowed flannel shirt and sat, pulling it as far to her knees as possible. He joined her, and they dug in without preamble.

"This is really good," she said between bites. She wasn't being polite. The chicken was loaded with spices and paired with the creamy sauce well.

"You don't have to sound so surprised." His lips quirked

before settling into a more-somber curve. "Around here, it was either cook or starve."

She tilted her head to study him. He didn't seem to be hiding any angst. "Because your mother left?"

"Yeah. The aunts brought food by at least once a week, but you can imagine how long that lasted with four—five, if you counted Pop—males in the house. Leftovers were a foreign concept."

"Did your aunts teach you to cook?"

"A little. Mostly though, I watched cooking shows on TV."

"You enjoy cooking." Yet another new facet to appreciate in him.

"I do. Wyatt and Jackson used to wander up from the barn a few nights a week to mooch. Not so much anymore. They're busy with their own lives now. I'm happy for them." Even though his declaration rang true, he couldn't mask the bite of loneliness in his voice. It was a too-familiar demon.

"Where do you find your recipes now?" Had his mother left old cookbooks or notes behind?

He stabbed at his lettuce, his face averted, but now he was clean-shaven, the red on his cheeks signaled his embarrassment. "Pinterest," he mumbled.

"I'm sorry, I thought you said 'Pinterest.'" She did her best to stifle a spate of giggles.

"It's good for recipes, okay?"

Her giggles escaped as very unlady-like guffaws at the image of rough-and-ready Mack Abbott cruising Pinterest for recipes. He joined in, shaking his head. "Don't tell my brothers or I'll make you pay."

And in a blink, her laughter dried up. "How?"

"How, what?"

"How will you make me pay?" Too many naughty possibilities flashed for her to settle on one.

"A spanking perhaps?" All his sheepish embarrassment had been burned away by an intensity that made her squirm. "I like you in my shirt, but I'm going to like you even better out of it."

She ran her fingers from the collar to where the first button was fastened between her breasts. A singular awareness of her near nakedness underneath squashed her appetite for pasta. She was ready to head straight to dessert.

"Quit looking at me like that." The warning in his voice only amped up her arousal.

Chapter Fifteen

"Like what?" She attempted to project innocence, but it was impossible, considering she'd been on her knees for him an hour earlier. She would do again, right here, right now, if he asked her to.

An animalistic sound rumbled out of his chest. He stood up so fast his chair tipped over and banged into the wall. Her breath caught in her throat as she waited for his move. He grabbed her wrist and pulled her into his body, clamping his arm around her. He speared his hand into her hair and kissed her with a ferociousness that arched her over his arm.

"I've been thinking about this for a long time." Mack walked her backward, one hand on her hip and the other wandering over and under the flannel shirt to skim over her bottom. He squeezed, and she moaned against his neck.

She wished she'd grabbed something lacey and seductive that morning, but she was wearing a pair of plain pink cotton panties. He didn't stop until they were in his bedroom, a bedside lamp casting a soft light around the room. The heart of the storm had passed, leaving a steady patter of rain against the windows. The illusion of privacy and solitude relaxed her.

He stopped at the foot of his bed and leaned against the tall bedpost, spreading his legs and pulling her in between. He cupped her bottom, teasing his fingers under the edges of her underwear.

"This ass has been tormenting me for too long."

His stance put them close to eye level, and she rubbed her palm against his smooth cheek. Would she ever get enough of him? His multi-hued eyes were as complicated as their situation.

"If we do this—"

"*If*? This is happening, babe." He worked a hand into the top band of her panties and fully cupped one buttock.

The heat and roughness of his palm spiraled her into a fugue state of arousal where nothing mattered but her satisfaction. Tomorrow didn't exist.

"I want you." It seemed important for her to state the obvious even though the direction his hand was headed would provide undeniable evidence.

His finger slid through her core. She sagged into him and popped her butt up to give him better access.

"I love how wet you are for me."

"I've been like this since the garage."

"You liked going down on me?"

She tensed, but when he forced her face up to his, no disgust or need to shame her was discernable. His eyes were bright and his color high.

"How could I not like it? Next time though, I want you to let me finish you."

"Eff me," he muttered.

He was off-balance, and for a man as self-contained and confident and intimidating as Mack, she reveled in the fact. "That's the plan."

Her confidence bloomed and instead of letting him retain control, she spun away from him and crawled onto his bed, sitting in the middle on her knees. He paced alongside like a panther ready to pounce.

She shook her hair over her shoulders and touched the top button of his shirt. Did she dare strip for him? While her mind waffled in horrified indecision, her body was totally on board with the new and improved Ella. She popped the top button and let the fabric pull apart. He stopped and stared, his gaze glued to her chest, his hand pressed against the bulge in his pants.

Her breathing increased as she moved to the next button. She released it and the next and the next until the shirt was unbuttoned and the inside curves of her breasts and a strip of skin was revealed. She spread her knees wider on the bed and let the shirt fall open another inch, enjoying the tease.

"Drop it, woman."

"Or what? Are you ever going to follow through on any of your threats?"

"You're getting me riled up." He jerked his T-shirt off and tossed it over his shoulder. Next up were his jeans. He unbuttoned and unzipped them. No underwear blocked her view of his erection, looking way bigger than it had felt earlier. She couldn't tear her gaze away and rubbed her suddenly dry lips together.

A sound halfway between a laugh and a groan came from his throat. He moved fast, taking her off guard, landing in front of her on his knees. She tightened her hands on hem of her shirt, holding it in place over her breasts.

He ran his fingers down the edges, his touch skating along the sensitive skin of her inner breasts. "I'm naked, Ella."

Her gaze dipped to admire said nakedness. "I can see that."

"It's your turn."

She hesitated. He'd already seen her naked, but that's not what this undressing was about. It wasn't a physical baring she was worried about, but an emotional one.

"Are we making a mistake?" Her voice was barely a whisper. She forced her gaze up to meet his.

"If this is a mistake, it's a pretty damn sweet one."

She a million percent agreed. They were at least on the same page with their uncertainty, which for some reason settled her nerves. She shrugged the shirt off, leaving her in her panties.

He ran his hands from her hips, through the curve of her waist, to cup her breasts. His work-rough, tan hands on her white skin had her reaching between his legs.

He squatted lower to tease her nipple with his lips and wrapped an arm as support under her butt. She held on to his hair, fisting her hands and tugging as she walked a dizzying tightrope of pleasure.

He flipped her to her back in a move that highlighted his strength. Her laughter petered into a whimper when he came over her, his mouth continuing to torment her breasts. His ability to dominate her should have had her running scared, but she wasn't moving unless there was a five-alarm fire. And maybe not even then. She'd just go up in flames.

His thigh settled between her legs, the barrier of her underwear unwelcome. As much as she was enjoying his attention to her nipples, she'd been aroused since the night before. Twenty-four hours of unrelieved desperation. She squirmed and yanked his head up by his hair.

"Why does that feel so damn good?" His question came out with a groan.

"You like a little hair pulling?" She did it again, and his answer was a gasp.

"Apparently, I love it. Or at least my dick does."

Satisfaction rolled through her like a slow wave and

made her hips undulate against his thigh. He took the hint without her having to beg and slipped his hand inside her panties. His hum was an echo of her own satisfaction.

"I've been thinking about this since last night." She grabbed his wrist and tried to force more contact, but instead he worked her panties off until she was naked.

"Even sitting at the computer teaching me the new software?" His fingers went back to work, stroking and rubbing her in all the right places, but never filling her.

"It was torture when all I wanted to do was throw you across the desk and climb on top of you." Why did sexual confessions pour out of her with him? He sank a finger inside of her. That's why. A reward.

"I thought about laying you over my desk and going down on you like last night. In fact, it's all I've thought about since." He moved as if he was going to slip down for a repeat of the night before, but she yanked on his hair.

"Later. Right now, I want this." She let go of his hair to circle his erection, running her thumb over the slick evidence of his need on the tip. They'd had twenty-four hours of foreplay. The main event was long overdue. "And you want it too."

He shifted off her to grab a condom packet from the nightstand. He knelt between her knees, grabbed her thighs, and pushed inside of her, achingly slowly but relentless until he was seated deep.

"'S'okay?" He slurred the question.

Even the semblance of words was beyond her abilities, and she hoped whatever whimpering moan came out counted as an affirmative. She twisted her hips closer in case he was confused. He wasn't.

He pulled almost all the way out before driving forward. She closed her eyes, close to tears and not sure why. It felt incredible. In fact, she'd never expected to find herself in this situation with anyone ever again, much less the man who'd once declared himself her enemy. But here she was, each thrust of his hips spiraling her closer to a mind-shattering climax.

Would she ever be the same after tonight?

He slipped his fingers where they were joined, the slight pressure enough to detonate her. She chanted his name and pulled at his shoulders, needing his weight to anchor her. He dropped to his elbows for a rough, breathless kiss.

He buried himself and held still and silent, his head back, the tendons along his neck taut. A long, slow breath signaled his return to the world, and he tilted his head to look down at her.

The intensity of the moment was in stark contrast to their earlier playfulness. Did he sense the shift in their world's axis as well? Would sex stabilize them or spin their relationship out of control?

A tear slipped out of her eye and ran down her temple. She turned her head, hoping to hide her irrationally emotional response, but it was hard when he was still . . . well, *hard* inside of her.

It was sex. Sex that had been building like the night's thunderstorm. But, the onslaught had passed, the storm's energy dissipated. One time with her might be all he wanted.

He rolled to her side, disposed of the condom, and came back to face her on his elbow, his head propped on his hand. She rubbed the evidence of her tears in the quilt and forced the sunny smile that had earned her Miss Congeniality.

Instead of returning her smile, he narrowed his eyes as if suspicious of such happiness. "What's wrong?"

"Nothing at all." She even managed to work a lilt into her voice.

"Bullshit." The word came out with the force of a punch. Her smile wavered until it disappeared. Part of her hated the way Mack cut through her tried-and-true methods of avoidance. It was uncomfortable. Could she be her messy, awkward self with him or would he ridicule her and make her feel small?

She had a choice. Keep her mouth shut and a smile on her face and let uncertainty rule her life, or woman up and take charge.

"Was this a one-time thing?" She tensed, preparing herself for his answer. If it was yes, she'd be okay. She'd survived worse humiliations, after all. It might take a few days under her covers and a more than a few pints of ice cream, but she'd hold her head up high.

"Do you want it to be?" He ran a hand into her hair and twisted strands around his fingers; the tug on her scalp was like raising the bat signal to her body.

Not only didn't she want it to be a one-time thing, but she'd be ready for it to be a two-time thing in sixty seconds flat. She cut her legs against each other. "No. I want more."

Although her body meant physically, her mind was operating on a higher plane. One where sex wasn't just sex, but meant something. She had no clue whether Mack was aware such a plane even existed.

"I'll give you as much as you can handle, babe." The tease in his voice signified the physical implications of his thoughts.

She hid her disappointment. If all he was offering was amazing, incredible sex, then she wasn't going to kick him out of bed. He dipped his head to take her lips in a kiss sweeter than any they'd shared. The calm after the storm.

He flopped on his back, his arm over his head and yawned. Not sure if that was a cue for her to leave, she scooted off the bed and darted to the bathroom to clean up. Looking in the mirror, she finger-combed her tangled hair and stared at herself.

She looked shell-shocked instead of satisfied, even though her body was sated and slightly sore. What now? Did she tiptoe back in the bedroom, gather her things, and head out? And did they pretend nothing had happened at the garage from eight to five?

As quietly as possible, she opened the bathroom door and stepped out. He'd turned the lamp off, and she was night blind. She stood in the middle of the room, waiting for her eyes to adjust enough to locate clothes. Any clothes. Or maybe she'd drive home naked. She'd make sure to obey all traffic laws.

"Come here." His voice rumbled in the dark.

"I can't see."

"Walk straight ahead and get your butt back in bed."

She shuffled forward until she bumped into the mattress. His dark shape was on the far side of the bed and she crawled over. He'd thrown the covers back, and when she got close, he maneuvered her to his side and pulled the quilt over them.

"I wasn't sure if you wanted me to hang out or not."

"Stay all night." His yawn was drawn out and noisy.

"I can't roll into work tomorrow in the same clothes I wore yesterday. Anyway, they'll be a wrinkled mess after getting caught in the rain. What would your brothers think?"

"Probably something along the lines of 'Thank the Lord, our big brother finally got laid.'"

His teasing tone wiped some of her tension away. "Have they been worried about your sex life?"

"Wyatt dragged me to the Tavern right after New Year's and threw every available woman from twenty to eighty in my path."

She popped up on her elbow and stared down at him even though the shadows were too deep to make out his expression. "Did you bring anyone home?"

"I didn't."

She sank back onto his shoulder, her hand making circles on his chest, her relief acute. Which was crazy considering their interaction up to that point had been confined to dirty looks. And not the fun kind of dirty looks. "Even though I barely knew you two months ago and what I did know about you, I didn't like, I'm glad."

He rumbled a laugh and played in her hair. Not the panty-melting tugs of earlier but a soothing, affectionate touch. "I didn't like you either, but that didn't stop me from imagining having sex with you."

She propped her hand and chin on his chest. "Let me get this straight: You didn't like me, but still wanted to do me?"

"The way you didn't back down was a major turn-on." A smile lightened his voice. "Plus, do you own a mirror?"

She turned that information over in her head. From their first encounter to every fight since, the sexual awareness hovering on the edges had coalesced into a living, breathing entity. "Will your brothers be shocked?"

"Maybe. They still think I don't like you."

"But you do like me, right? A little?"

"Are you seriously asking me that after we had sex?"

"You admitted that you imagined having sex with me after New Year's Eve even though you didn't like me."

He crunched up enough to kiss her forehead. "I like you." He let a few beats of silence pass before adding, "Mostly."

She jabbed him in the side, and he laughed in a way she'd never heard from him. Not that he laughed often, but this laugh made her think that hadn't always been the case. This laugh had her picturing him as a kid playing out in the woods with his brothers when life was simpler and his responsibilities were lighter.

Silence settled over them, but it was a comfortable sort.

"Tell me something that happened to you as a kid. Something no one else knows about."

He hummed. "This really isn't a secret, but there's this reoccurring dream I've had since I was a kid."

"A nightmare?"

"No, it's a good dream. I'm holding a woman's hand, and we're walking through the woods toward the river. I'm kind of skipping along, not more than three or four, I'd guess. I felt really happy. Safe. For years, in my dream, the woman was Aunt Hazel."

"But something has changed?"

"Now it's a different woman. Younger and with dark hair like Wyatt's. She would laugh and swing me in her arms. I think . . . I think it's a memory and not a dream."

"Your mother."

His shoulder moved under her. "Pop got rid of any pictures of her after she left."

Ella had to bite the inside of her mouth to keep from expressing anger at his father's selfishness. Cutting his wife from his life might have made things easier on him, but his sons deserved more.

"When did your mother replace Ms. Hazel in the dream?"

"Last fall when everything with Ford blew up and there was talk about tracking down our mom."

"Is it a sign?"

"A sign of what? The end of times?" He baited his words with humor, but she didn't bite.

"The end of a two-decade-long estrangement."

"She left us and never looked back."

"That's what your father told you. Maybe you should ask her."

The rise and fall of his chest tracked time. She didn't push him further. Familial harmony wasn't exactly her wheelhouse, considering she hadn't spoken to her mother in over a year.

Finally, he said, "Your turn. Tell me something you don't share with most people."

She let her mind wander into her memories. Most of her good memories involved Grayson, but they held a bitter-sweetness she didn't want to invite into the moment. "I was voted Miss Congeniality during my senior year pageant."

"What was your talent? Playing water glasses?"

She laughed. "I did an interpretive dance to Nelly's 'Hot in Here.'"

"You didn't." His laugh was rife with shock.

"No, I didn't, but I wish I'd had the nerve so I could see everyone's faces. I did an interpretive dance to Pachelbel's Canon. It was a horrible mess, but as I can't sing or play an instrument, it's all I could think of that didn't cost any money to pull off. I was pageant-ing on a budget."

"What about your mom? I thought pageants were prime mother-daughter bonding."

She made a pishing sound. "Not in my house. My mom didn't care what I was doing at that point. Almost every girl in our class signed up, except for me. This girl who thought she was all that and a bag of chips started making fun of me. Telling me I was smart to sit it out because I'd come in last anyway. I got mad and told her not only was I going to sign up, but I was going to beat her."

"So what you're saying is you couldn't resist a challenge even then?"

A small laugh escaped. "Nope, but I had gotten myself in a pickle. I couldn't afford a new gown and professional hair and makeup."

"Any fairy godmothers around?" Equal parts humor and understanding were in his voice.

"Not a single one. I taught myself how to put on makeup

and do my hair from YouTube videos, and used my baby-sitting money to buy a gown from a secondhand store. Only it turned out, one of the girls had worn it the year before in the same pageant. One of the snotty, popular girls."

"Oh man. Did she skewer you?"

"Announced to everyone that I was wearing castoffs. They all had a good laugh. And, so did I. I played it off as best I could, threw a few insults masquerading as compliments their way, and somewhere along the way, I became the champion for all the other girls. The ones who weren't popular or particularly pretty but dreamed of winning."

Ella had learned a valuable lesson in that moment. Even as she cowered on the inside, she could fool people as long as she held her head high and projected confidence, no matter how false. It had served her well walking into the garage to face Mack.

"Did winning Miss Congeniality shut those bitches up?"

A slice of evil satisfaction made her smile. "Nope. But winning the crown sure did."

"That must have been a great feeling."

"It was the most exciting night of my life up to that point." Her smile faded. The pageant had been a triumph, but her fairytale ending was more worthy of the Grimm brothers than Disney.

Trevor had been one of the judges and had pursued her afterward, casually at first and then with relentless determination after she'd graduated. At the time, it had seemed romantic.

"I'm not surprised you won the crown or Miss Congeniality. Not only do you have killer looks, but you have a way with people."

She blinked in the darkness. "I do?"

"We were all determined to be as unwelcoming as possible when you showed up at the garage. Wyatt and Jackson like you and look where I ended up."

"Asking me perform an oil change was low."

"You could have owned up to the fact you didn't know how."

"Then you would have won. I couldn't let you see how intimidated by you I was."

His hand in her hair tightened, and he rolled to the side, leaving them facing off. "You're not afraid of me now, are you?"

The question rumbled with an importance emphasized by his tense body. Was she afraid he'd physically hurt her? No. But her heart was tender and unprotected where he was concerned. She didn't trust him not to trample it. No way was she brave enough to lay those truths between them.

"I was never afraid of you. Just a teensy bit intimidated at first. But then I realized instead of a raging grizzly bear, you're more of a cuddly teddy bear."

"A teddy bear?" He rolled them until he was on top of her and ground his hips against her. "Cuddly?"

He was hard between her legs. Her body shut down any attempt to stay nonchalant. Her back arched and her nipples tightened with the friction against his chest. "Okay, a teddy bear who carries a big stick."

Her ringtone cut through his laughter. They both looked out in the darkness, still and waiting.

Chapter Sixteen

Her phone rang again, and she cursed herself for not muting it.

"You want to get that?" he asked before dropping to nuzzle her ear. Her toes curled with an onslaught of a shiver.

"No. I'm sure it's nothing. Keep going with the demonstration of your non-cuddliness."

The call went to voice mail and only the sound of their mingled, quickened breathing filled the silence. The tip of his erection brushed her entrance. She should insist on a condom. Except she was on the pill, and he felt so damn good. She lifted her hips, seeking more.

Her phone rang again.

She rarely got calls unless they involved her investments, and those came during normal business hours. Was it an emergency? Her mother had her number although she hadn't used it in a long time. It could be Megan. Had Trevor returned to cause trouble?

She would never be able to relax and enjoy the havoc Mack was ready to unleash on her body until she checked who was calling and why. She dropped her hips and put her hand on his chest. With the slightest of pressure, he sighed and fell over on his back.

The bedside light flicked on. Squinting, she scrambled off the bed, grabbed her purse, and fished her phone out of a side pocket. Between her lack of glasses and the bright light, she could barely make out the name on the screen—*Megan.*

She'd gotten several texts from her over the last hour. Not wasting time reading them, she hit Megan's name. Mack was propped up in bed watching her, and she became aware of her total nakedness with a wave of self-consciousness. His flannel shirt was next to the bed, and she scooped it up, sticking her arms in the sleeves as Megan's phone rang.

It went to voice mail. She tried again with the same result. Her worry grew. Putting on her glasses, she sat on the side of the bed and scrolled through Megan's texts. Mostly they consisted of *Where RU?* and *When will you be home?* They could be innocuous questions or they could have been sent in a panic. What if Trevor had forced her back to Jackson with him? Or worse. She stared at her phone, waffling.

"Problem?" Mack had propped himself up on his elbow, the sheet riding low on his hips.

She held the shirt together and shifted toward him on the bed. All she wanted was to crawl back to him and finish what they'd started. "I'm not sure. It was Megan. She sent a few ambiguous texts, but didn't answer my call."

Her phone rang, and she bobbled it in her haste to answer. "Hello? Megan, what's wrong?"

"Who's this?" A male voice was on the other end. Not Trevor's cultivated, old-money accent but one as country as cornbread.

"This is Ella. Who's this?"

"Name's Butch. I got your girl down at the Tavern. Y'all need to come get her."

"Is she okay?" Ella continued to stare into Mack's concerned eyes.

"She puked all over the pool table then tried to crawl into her car to drive home. Told her I was either calling a friend to pick her up or the police."

"I'll be there in—" She hesitated, unsure of where the Tavern was even located. She lowered the phone and whispered, "How far is the Tavern from here?"

"Less than ten minutes," Mack said.

"I'll be there in ten minutes. Can you keep her from drinking anything else?"

The man on the other end made a disgusted-sounding snort. "You'd better bring a barf bag." He ended the call.

She sat on the edge of the bed with the phone in her lap for a moment. The worry she felt for Megan was half sisterly and half exasperated.

"Who was that?" Neither his voice nor face reflected the frustration and anger he must be feeling.

"Some guy named Butch, and he did not sound happy. Apparently, Megan is blitzed out of her mind, and she threw up on a pool table."

"Butch is kind of a d-bag so don't worry about it." Mack threw off the covers and walked around the bed, grabbing his jeans on the way.

She was struck still and mute as he pulled them up. Next, he slipped his shirt on. Only when his body was covered did she snap out of her Mack-induced trance. She grabbed her mostly dry but wrinkled clothes from the bathroom. Hopping, she pulled her pants on, haste making her clumsy. "Could you give me directions to the Tavern?"

"I'll do you one better and drive you."

"Are you serious?"

"If she's as drunk as you say, you'll need help getting her home." His voice was so even it might qualify as easygoing.

"But . . . but . . ." She fiddled with a button on his shirt. "Why aren't you mad?"

"Why would I be mad?" He paused with his T-shirt half tucked, his face serious but not reflecting a hint of anger.

"Because our plans got shot? Because we were interrupted before . . . you know? Because you don't even know Megan, and this is a major inconvenience?"

He smoothed a hand over his chin and jaw in a beard-smoothing gesture she'd become familiar with, except he no longer had a beard. He seemed to realize the same and turned the movement into a neck scratch where dark stubble was showing. What would that feel like on her inner thighs?

He stood in front of her. She stared at the Abbott Brothers emblem with River's face on it over his heart. When he squeezed her upper arms, she looked up. His head was tilted, his gaze wary but curious.

"As we already decided tonight is only the beginning, not the end, of whatever this is, and bearing in mind I'm not sixteen or an asshole, then I can deal with a little interruption without throwing a hissy fit." He squeezed her arms tighter for emphasis. "But, let's be clear. I'm not doing this for Megan; I'm doing this for you."

She fought the warm gooey rush his words released in her body. Mack would be easy to lean on. Too easy. He exuded confidence and competence. She'd given up her independence once at great personal cost. Being beholden to any man meant sacrificing part of herself.

She fought the desire to accept his help. "I can handle Megan on my own."

"I know you can, but that doesn't mean you have to, okay?" When it was clear she was still waffling, he sighed.

"Look, you're being a good friend to Megan by picking her up and taking care of her, right? Let me be a friend to you."

"Is that what we are? Friends with benefits?" Hurt feelings niggled where there should be none. Sex and love might not be mutually exclusive, but it was rare they co-existed in her experience. Anyway, she wasn't looking for love. No way. Not a chance. Panicked heat wavered through her.

"I don't know what we are, but we're closer to friends than enemies, aren't we?"

"I suppose."

"Then I'm coming." He walked out, not giving her a chance to argue.

She didn't really want to argue with him. She buried her nose in the collar of his shirt and inhaled. God, he smelled good. And solid, if such a smell existed. Would he notice if she kept his shirt so she could roll around in it later?

She slipped his shirt off and dressed, the stiffness of her clothes abrading after the soft flannel. The sound of a truck revving drew her outside. The headlights blinded her like the flash of camera, and she fumbled for the door handle.

The cavernous feel of the interior squashed any remaining intimacy from his bed. She tucked her hands under her legs. The pine tree–lined parish road gave way to houses and a few shops. The next side street he took opened into a parking lot. "The Rivershack Tavern" was on the sign and strings of white lights decorated the front of the bar. It possessed a ramshackle charm.

Mack drove past the rows of cars and trucks to idle at the front. There was no sign of Megan. He rolled down the passenger side window as a man built like a two-hundred-and-fifty-pound keg of beer sauntered up.

"Mack Abbott. What can I do for you?" Although the

man directed the question at Mack, his gaze and a slight smirk were aimed at Ella.

"Yo, Butch." Mack tipped his chin up.

"You called about picking up my friend, Megan. Where is she? She'd better be safe." Ella shifted in the seat so Butch would have to deal with her and not Mack.

"She's inside at the bar."

Ella pushed the truck door open, hopped out, and advanced on Butch, her finger in his face. "At the bar? You were supposed to keep her safe."

Her aggression de-smirked his face, and he took a step back. "I have better things to do than babysit a shit-faced woman."

"Actually, as a bouncer of this establishment, handling drunk customers should be the main part of your job. I wonder what the owner would have to say about your job priorities. Should I give them a call?" She pulled out her phone and pretended to scroll through her contacts. It was a bluff. She had no idea who actually owned the place.

"Hang on. Geez. Clint is watching out for her."

"Who is Clint?"

"The bartender."

She harrumphed and rolled her eyes. That was like letting a wolf protect the sheep. During her confrontation with Butch, Mack had turned off the truck and joined her.

"Let's round her up," she said over her shoulder, leading the way.

She stopped inside the door and scanned the floor. Pool tables took up a section on her left, all of them occupied but one. A wet stain marred the green felt. She grimaced, but secretly hoped Butch had been the one to clean it up.

Conversation muffled the country music. An equal mix of men and women milled around the tables on the right side of the room. The bar ran along the back and was two-people deep trying to get drinks. It seemed crowded for a weeknight, but from what Ella had gathered, social outlets in Cottonbloom were few and far between—unless church activities counted.

So this was the place Wyatt had brought Mack to find a hookup. A goodly number of the women were pretty and around Mack's age. One in particular, a blonde in a V-neck to showcase a set of amazing boobs, yelled out a greeting along with a flirty little wave. "Hey, Mack!"

Ella's gaze shot to Mack. He tipped his chin up, a smile on his face, but didn't call out in return. Without stopping to consider the ramifications, she wrapped herself around Mack's waist and sent a "hands off, he's mine" glare her way.

The woman turned away to continue her conversation with the group she was standing with. Mack laid an arm over her shoulder and leaned in so she could hear him. "Megan is holding down a seat at the end of the bar by the restrooms."

He guided her in the right direction, cutting through the crowd with a series of handshakes and "How've you beens?" It seemed like Mack knew everyone, and everyone liked him. When one man asked a car question, Mack clapped him on the shoulder and said, "Got something to take care of right now, Rick, but bring her by the shop anytime."

Mack parted the crowd at the bar. Megan was slumped on a stool at the end with a coffee mug, her chin propped in her palm as she talked to the man behind the bar handing out beers and mixed drinks. Although the bartender wasn't watching Megan, he smiled at something she said.

Mack said, "Yo, Clint. We're here to get Megan out of your hair."

Clint uncapped a bottle of beer and thumped it on the bar where it disappeared into the crowd. He wiped his hands on a towel thrown over his shoulder and came to prop his arms on the bar in front of Megan. "No bother. She's a happy drunk."

"You're cute, even if you are kind of scruffy. Isn't he cute, Ella?" Megan reached out and tugged Clint's dark beard. Clint laughed and shook his head. His beard was longer and thicker than Mack's had been but well groomed. It was hard to get a read on his age, but his dark eyes were kind and crinkled when he smiled.

"Sure, he's real cute." Ella had learned early on that to disagree with an alcoholic stoked unwelcome drama. "You ready to go home and sleep it off?"

Megan spun around on the swivel barstool and slid to the side like a toddler thrown off a merry-go-round. Mack caught her under the arms, and she tipped her head back and grinned. "Hello, there. You're pretty cute too but Ella has called dibs."

"Dibs?" Mack asked.

"Yep. She said, 'Mack is mine so quit shaking your ass in his face.'"

"I did not!" Ella caught Mack's amused gaze. "I didn't say that."

"I'm paraphrasing." Megan stepped away from Mack and swayed.

Ella notched herself against Megan, a steadying arm around her waist. "Clear a path for us, would you, Mack?"

Ella guided Megan in Mack's wake until they were outside. He lifted Megan into the back seat of his truck and had them heading over the bridge into Mississippi within a few minutes.

"I don't feel so good." Megan's voice wavered from the back.

Mack lowered her window, and Ella turned to monitor her. Megan leaned her head against the door and closed her eyes, the cool wind whipping her hair around her face.

Mack pulled into Ella's driveway. The two of them managed to get Megan into the house and to the bathroom off the guest room. She fell to her knees in front of the toilet and threw up.

"I'll wait out here." Mack thumbed over his shoulder and retreated.

Ella wished she could do the same. Instead, she sat on the edge of the tub and rubbed Megan's back until her heaves faded into a moan.

"I made a fool out of myself." With her head still down, her voice echoed off the porcelain.

"It's not the first time someone has gotten drunk there. It is a bar, after all."

"Not that. The job thing. Why did I think I was qualified to do anything?"

"No offers?"

"The pizza place offered me a waitressing job alongside a bunch of high-schoolers."

"What about Regan Fournette's interior design shop?"

"She didn't come right out and say I wasn't qualified, but she did not act enthused at my resume. She said something about being in touch, but I know a blow-off when I hear one." Megan plopped on her butt next to the toilet, her arm across the seat.

"It was one day, Megan. Are you going to give up already?"

"I don't know. Maybe. It would be easier to just pretend everything is okay."

"Would it? It's not easy to watch the days of your life waste away without any purpose or happiness."

Megan lifted her head and focused bleary eyes on Ella. "I should keep trying?"

"You should take two aspirin, drink a glass of water, and go to sleep. We can talk tomorrow."

Megan nodded and Ella helped her to her feet. Squirting some toothpaste on a toothbrush, she handed it to Megan while she went to the kitchen for water and medicine.

"Everything okay?" Mack's voice from the darkness prodded her heart into a quickened rhythm. He was almost lost in the shadows of the couch in her den.

Ella shuffled halfway to him, wanting nothing more than to cuddle into him and feel his arms around her. Craving comfort didn't mean she was weak, did it? She'd never felt equal to Trevor. He'd never let her feel equal to him. With Mack, the dynamic was different. Had she changed or was Mack unique?

"I figured you'd hightailed it home," she said.

"I figured I'd stick around in case you needed help picking her up off the bathroom floor."

"She's up. Or at least she was. Let me get some aspirin in her. I'll be right back." By the time she returned to the bedroom, Megan had changed into a T-shirt and was curled on her side in bed, snoring softly. Ella set the water and pills on the nightstand and pulled the door shut.

"How is she?" Mack asked. He lounged into the corner of her couch, his legs stretched out and crossed at the ankles, his hands linked behind his head. A stance that spoke of total comfort with his surroundings. No, it was more than that. He was comfortable in his own skin, which in turn lent him an aura of confidence anywhere he landed. His attractiveness quotient rose even higher.

A tiny voice in her head fought to put some distance between them. They'd gone from enemies to lovers fast enough to give her emotional whiplash. She took two slow steps toward him, but before she could stop herself, she quickened her pace and crashed into him on the couch. Heaving a huge sigh, she notched her face in his neck and wrapped her arm around his thick chest.

"She's going to feel like crap in the morning. She was talking about going back to Trevor. It's the path of least resistance, but I wish she could see it's a dead end." The smoothness of his face was still a revelation. She walked her fingers up his chest to stroke his jaw.

"The job hunt didn't go well?"

"No, it didn't." She chewed on her lip. "I wonder if I could talk Regan Fournette into hiring her on a trial basis."

"I would imagine she needs the help, considering how much time she spends up at the statehouse. Although, Fournette Designs is doing well for Sawyer and Cade, so I doubt she needs the money."

"Do you know the Fournettes well?"

"The twins are around the same age as Sawyer, so I knew him better than Cade. The Fournettes had a rough childhood. Lost both their parents young, but they're nice guys. Honest. Loyal. They always use us for any car repairs."

"What about Regan? How well do you know her?" Maybe he could put in a good word for Megan. Not that she'd done much to earn it.

"Not well at all. She was a 'Sip."

"A 'Sip?"

Mack chuckled and played in her hair. "If you live on the Mississippi side of Cottonbloom, you're a 'Sip. Louisiana is full of swamp rats. The two sides have coexisted like warring countries for decades."

"Is it still bad?"

"Lots of Louisiana folks invited to your fancy parties?"

She blinked as her mind whirled, unable to identify a single one. Although, there were plenty of successful business owners on the Louisiana side of the river. Why weren't they invited? "Prejudice against swamp rats? That's so old fashioned."

"Don't worry, it goes both ways. Swamp rats think the folks on the Mississippi side are stuck up and too big for their britches."

"Am I a 'Sip?"

"You could be. But you're down-to-earth enough to be a swamp rat."

"What about Wyatt and Sutton?"

"Sutton caught some heat for slumming it with my brother."

"That's terrible." Ella sat up, her hand braced on Mack's chest. "I remember the fight Wyatt had with Andrew Tarwater at the gala last fall. That was the first overture Ford made in terms of selling his share. If I'd known . . ." What would she have done? Walked away? Considering how everything had played out thus far, saying she would have passed on the deal would be a lie.

"But you didn't." Although his statement could be construed as judgment, he circled his arm around her shoulders and pulled her closer. "Anyway, eventually I'll be able to buy you out."

It was safer not to discuss the what-ifs and wherefores of the murky situation they found themselves in. At least he was honest. He wouldn't quit until he'd wrested her portion of the garage back into Abbott hands, of that she had no doubt. Part of her even admired him for it. It was his family legacy, and family was the most important thing to him.

"Ella?" Megan's weak-sounding voice carried to them.

"I should—" She gestured down the hall.

"Yeah. I'm going to take off, but I'll be by to pick you up in the morning. Is eight too early?" He rose and made his way toward the front door.

"Why?"

"Your car is still at the garage, and Megan's is at the Tavern. You're carless. Unless you have a hot rod stashed in the garage I'm unaware of?"

"I totally forgot. Nothing hidden away in the garage unfortunately. Hang on for a second." She popped into the guest room.

Megan was spread-eagle on the bed with the covers kicked off, her arm over her eyes. "The room is spinning."

"Not much to do except sleep it off." After making Megan take the aspirin and drink most of the water, Ella backed out of the room and joined Mack on the porch. "Thanks again for tonight. You made things easier."

"That's what friends are for. To make troubles easier to bear."

While she still took issue with his classification of their relationship, the sentiment was appreciated. "I guess that's my job with Megan."

"Maybe, but don't let her take advantage of your big heart."

Big heart? She felt emotionally stunted at eighteen, her heart contracting a little more each year of her marriage. Not sure how to respond, she said simply, "I'll see you in the morning, then?"

"Soon, we're going to watch the sun rise over the trees from my bed." He wrapped his hand around her nape, his thumb brushing her cheek.

She closed her eyes and shifted enough to lay a kiss on the edge of his palm. "Is that a guarantee?"

"It's a promise."

"Promises can be broken." The air around them thickened with currents that couldn't be explained by meteorologists. They weren't discussing a simple sunrise anymore.

"I keep my promises."

She wanted to believe he was different—an outlier—but her life had provided too much evidence to the contrary. For now, she'd ride this wave with Mack as long as it lasted.

"I can't wait." Her tone was overly perky. His eyes narrowed, and before he could question her, she said, "I'll see you in the morning."

He kissed her. The press of his lips was brief and hard as if he wanted to make a point. He sidestepped down the stairs, never taking his eyes off her. As he climbed behind the wheel of his truck, he called out, "Dream about me tonight."

"I will." She had no doubt that was a promise she would keep.

Chapter Seventeen

Jackson and Willa showed up at her door bright and early. Her disappointment had been sharp. Fantasies of pulling Mack straight to her bedroom had had her pacing the floor since seven. It wasn't just her body acting like it was being denied food and water, but she had been looking forward to sitting next to him and talking about mundane things on the way to work together.

Why had he sent his brother? Was she becoming a bother? Or could it be that she was overreacting instead of trusting him and herself? Since she wasn't going to put voice to her insecurities in front of Jackson and Willa, she accepted her keys with a smile and thanks.

Instead of the garage, Ella headed for downtown Cottonbloom and parallel parked across the street from Regan Fournette's design studio. Was she actually doing this? She checked her hair and gave herself a galvanizing smile in the makeup mirror before crossing the street and stepping inside. A bell tinkled overhead.

Regan popped her head around the doorjamb of a room in the back, a phone pressed to her ear and a welcoming smile on her face. "I'll be with you in a sec, Ella."

Ella and Regan had crossed paths at several Cottonbloom events, but they were acquainted on only the most superficial level. Certainly not the sort of connection that invited favors.

Ella wandered farther into the room, running her fingers along upholstery swatches hung onto rods. A bin of throw pillows was in the middle of the room, and she sifted through them, more to occupy her hands than out of a true interest in buying one.

She planted herself at the counter and flipped through the pages of a book full of Regan's previous designs. Her design style was warm and welcoming but with a sophisticated edge. The woman was talented.

"Sorry about that. No rest for the wicked politician." Regan walked to the back side of the counter and slid onto a stool.

"Are you keeping them straight up in the state house?" Ella asked.

Not only did Regan own a successful interior design studio, but she was also the Mississippi state representative for their district. Juggling two successful jobs had to be stressful and time consuming. Surely she could use help in the studio.

"They've taken to calling me the Dragon behind my back." Regan winked and waggled her eyebrows. "Which I secretly love, of course. What can I do for you? Are you looking to update your house?"

"Actually, I'm here about Megan Boudreaux. She inquired about a job yesterday. Do you remember her?"

"Of course I do. Although, I didn't put two and two together. Are you two cousins or something?"

"Not exactly." How much should she tell Regan? Too little, and she wouldn't generate enough empathy for Megan. Too much, and they would end up being the talk of Cottonbloom.

"She's married to my ex-husband."

Regan's eyes widened, but other than that she showed no response. "Are you here to warn me off hiring her?"

A laugh sputtered out of Ella. The situation was ridiculous and borderline crazy. "The opposite, actually. We've become sort-of friends, and I'm here to put in a good word for her, if it means anything."

"I guess you two have got something in common." Regan's smile hinted at an impish sense of humor.

"True. Although, it's like being bonded by war."

"That's why he's your ex, huh?"

"Exactly. Maybe soon to be Megan's ex too. She's looking to start over in Cottonbloom."

Regan leaned back on the stool and set her hands on the counter. "I see. That's why she needs a job."

"It is. I know you took her resume and said you call if something opened up, but you were being polite, weren't you?"

"I was. Honestly, I could use the help, but she doesn't have the experience."

"She's got a great eye, though. After Trevor and I divorced, she redid my old house from top to bottom. It looked fabulous."

"It's more than having a good eye though. It's about being responsible, trustworthy, and good with people."

"Do you have anyone else in the running for the job?"

Regan sighed and looked to the ceiling. "Unfortunately, experienced applicants aren't running amuck around Cottonbloom.

"Why not give her a trial run? Two weeks. If it's not working out then let her go, no harm, no foul."

"Will she agree to that?"

"I'm sure she will, but you have to be the one to offer her the job. I don't want her to know that I came here. She's already struggling with her confidence."

Regan chewed her bottom lip and fiddled with the

strawberry blonde hair at her nape. "A two-week trial. If we don't get along or I can't count on her, then it's done."

Ella grinned. "Would you call her today?"

"Right now, if you want."

Ella's smile morphed into a grimace. "Could you wait until this afternoon? She wasn't feeling great when I left this morning." An understatement if her green complexion and dark under-eye circles were evidence.

"I hope she appreciates you. I sure don't know where I'd be without my best friend." Regan came around the counter to offer her hand. They shook as if making a pact.

"I wouldn't call us best friends." Although, considering Ella couldn't name another female friend, she supposed by default Megan qualified.

As Ella reached the door, Regan said, "Sawyer told me you're planning a car show in downtown Cottonbloom."

"I am. Abbott Brothers Garage is sponsoring, but I'm hoping other businesses will take part and the show will attract people from all over to compete."

"It's a great idea. Anything to draw tourists to downtown and get them to spend their money. Lots of good advertising and profit for the garage too."

"We want to get the word out about our restoration business, but any profits will go toward Dave Dunlap's medical expenses."

"Poor Dave. I've used him quite often on projects. No one can build a set of bookcases like him." A fire entered Regan's eyes, and with the red in her hair, Ella could see why she'd earned her nickname at the statehouse. "How can I help?"

Ella was smart enough to recognize an asset and humble enough to accept help. "Any vendor contacts you have would be great. I'll need to book food and drink carts."

"I'd be happy to pass that info along. I still have a file

on my computer from when I was mayor of Cottonbloom. I'll email you."

Ella rattled off her number and email, and Regan entered the information into her phone.

"Hang on a second. I want to give you something now." Regan disappeared through the door in the back. Ella didn't have long to wait. Regan emerged holding a piece of paper. "Here."

It was a check for a thousand dollars made out to Abbott Brothers Garage. Ella shook her head. "What's this for?"

"A donation for Marigold and Dave's medical fund."

Ella bit the inside of her cheek to distract from the stinging tears in her eyes. Past experiences had dulled her optimism and lowered her expectations. Slowly but surely, Cottonbloom and the people in it were dusting them off and raising the bar. "This is so generous, Regan. Thank you so much."

"Marigold and Dave are good people." Regan gestured toward her front door. "If you ask, most of the businesses will donate something. Never be afraid to ask for what you want."

"I'll keep that in mind." Ella folded the check and tucked it into her pocket.

"I'll be in touch with both you and Megan soon."

Ella stepped outside and took a deep breath of spring air. Energized by her victory, she bypassed her car and visited the local businesses up and down the street. Not only did she book the pizza place and ice cream shop for the car show, but they too offered donations. Before she could second-guess herself, she wrote another check from her Magnolia Investments account for two thousand dollars. Even if the car show didn't make the kind of money they were hoping, Marigold and Dave would still be better off.

She stopped on the footbridge connecting the two sides

of Cottonbloom and stared into the water. It rippled over grasses and reeds that had sprung up with the warming weather. Yellow and orange buttercups bloomed on the Louisiana side with dozens of buds from other types of flowers reaching for the sun.

A sense of calm flowed over her like she was one of the bending reeds in the river. No, not calm. Happiness. She was happy. It had been too long since she'd felt this way. Since before Grayson had died. Her happiness wasn't entirely of her own making though. It was Mack related, and the realization niggled.

She tossed her head back and closed her eyes. Pinpricks of light from the bright sun danced on her eyelids. Putting her trust and happiness in someone else's hands was dangerous. Especially a man who did nothing to hide his ultimate goal. He wanted something she possessed, but it wasn't her heart.

Mack wrote a note on the ledger he used for work orders and glanced down the road. He'd sent Jackson in the tow truck on a call with Willa trailing behind in Ella's car. They'd delivered her car and picked up the stranded vehicle on their way home. Except Willa and Jackson had returned two hours earlier and there was still no sign of Ella.

After finishing the estimate on the disabled car, he weaved his way around full bays.

Jackson looked up while continuing to torque a bolt on the underside of a Ford sedan up on the lift. "What's up?"

"What exactly did Ella say when you dropped her car off?"

"She said, 'Thanks, Jackson. Appreciate you.'"

"What then?"

"Then, I told I'd see her later, waved, and left. What kind of information are you digging for?"

"I don't know. Did she look mad or disappointed or whatever to see you and Willa?"

"Who was she expecting? You?" Jackson raised his eyebrows, the twitch of his lips slight enough to masquerade as bland if Mack didn't know better.

"I told her I'd bring it by, but the Corvette showed up."

A man from Baton Rouge had rolled up in a beautiful but neglected 1970 Corvette LT-1. Her paint job was cracked and faded and the panels were rusted in places, but the engine still had the power to vibrate his internal organs. Or maybe that was his excitement at the potential project. His cousin Landrum Abbott had steered the man in their direction. Next time Landrum was in Cottonbloom visiting his parents, Mack would be sure to buy him a bottle of Jack.

Mack had spent over an hour with the man detailing what needed to be done and his estimates for the work. It was a fair price. The man had left with a handshake and a promise to bring her back at the end of the week to get started.

"That's going to be a jacked ride when we get done," Jackson said. "I've got to button up the Ford and test for leaks, and then I'll get started on the car we towed in."

"Sounds good." Mack drummed his fingers on the ledger. "She didn't say anything else?"

Jackson dropped the socket wrench into the bottom drawer of a red toolbox on wheels and emerged from the dim underside of the car. "What's going on? Did you want her to be upset it wasn't you? You said you helped her get her drunk friend home. Is there something else going on? Because, I've got to tell you, Willa thinks you're sweet on Ella."

Mack made a scoffing noise. "Sweet on her?"

The truth was he was more than sweet on Ella Boudreaux. He was addicted. She was all he thought about and dreamed about and worried about.

"You usually don't shave until Easter. That's still two weeks away."

"Blame global warming." Mack concentrated on his nails and the grease that had worked its way under. He'd shaved for Ella. Beard rash on her inner thighs did not sound comfortable. The way she'd kept touching his face last night made his early shave well worth it.

Jackson threw a blue shop towel at their feet. "Foul on the play."

"What's going on?" Wyatt joined them, a grin on his face. Of course, he was always grinning these days. It was nauseating.

"Mack lied right to my face." Jackson crossed his arms over his chest, but didn't look the least bit upset. In fact, a hint of dimples showed on his cheeks. "Mack is sweet on Ella Boudreaux."

Mack looked around and shushed Jackson. It would be his luck Ella had snuck in and could hear everything.

"Holy shit. Goldilocks has tamed the bear." Wyatt snickered.

"Or did Little Red Riding Hood vanquish the wolf?" Jackson stroked his chin as if seriously considering it.

"Shut up." Little ire made it into Mack's voice.

Honestly, he was happy to be able to discuss his confusion with his brothers, if they'd stop making fun of him long enough to get serious. It was strange to think his little brothers had a leg up on him in terms of experience with women.

"How long has this been brewing?" Wyatt asked.

Before Mack could answer, Jackson did. "Since the New Year's Eve party. She got under your skin that night, didn't she?"

Was he ready to be honest? "She got under my skin, but more because she was confident and—" *Sexy.* He bit off the admission. That veered into brutal honesty territory, and he wasn't ready for that. Yet.

"So all the fighting has actually been foreplay. Nice." Wyatt held up a hand for a high-five.

Mack batted it down. "This is not funny. She still owns a quarter of the garage, and I want it back."

Jackson scratched the back of his head and sent a glance through his lashes toward Mack. "I understand getting Ford's part back into our hands would be ideal, but is it that big a deal? Ella has proved an asset, and you like more than her office skills. Why not let the arrangement ride as is?"

Mack paced in the small space and jammed a hand through his hair. "Because it's all my fault. Pop would be disappointed in me."

Wyatt grabbed Mack's arm, forcing him to a stop. "Whoa. That's a lot to unpack. How is this remotely your fault? Ford's the one who got himself in trouble gambling and was forced to sell."

"But, I should have . . . I don't know, done more. Been the bigger man. Instead, I rubbed it in. Made everything worse. You two know I did."

The twins exchanged a glance that encompassed a conversation he would never be privy to. It was part of their powers.

"As much as you like to take responsibility for everything, we can't let you take all the blame for Ford. We played a part and so did Pop." Wyatt gave his arm a squeeze before letting go. "And Ford has to live with his decisions."

"You think he feels bad about selling out?" Mack looked back and forth at Jackson and Wyatt. They didn't look alike, but something in their different-colored eyes reflected the same regrets and worries Mack carried for their oldest brother.

"Don't know." Jackson stuffed his hands into the pockets of his coveralls. "But he's not dead. You can ask him. Make peace. Invite him down for the car show. The aunts miss him."

In a strange way, so did Mack. "I'll think about it."

Jackson and Wyatt nodded in synchronicity.

A clatter from the back broke them up. Willa and River moved through the garage. Jackson met her halfway, wrapped an arm around her waist, and pulled her into a hug. Mack turned away.

River gave a yippy, happy-sounding bark and streaked across the garage. Ella stood frozen inside the door, both hands around her throat as if genuinely scared River might go for her jugular.

Willa scooted around Mack to corral her dog, but Mack caught her arm. "I'll handle River. And Ella."

Willa nodded, but twisted a shop towel in her hands. "I don't know why River goes crazy around her."

Mack could say the same thing about himself. He strode across the floor and tugged River back by her collar. Her lolling tongue and expressive eyes held a joy only dogs possessed.

"Why does that beast love me?" Ella asked in a creaky voice.

"Bacon-scented soap?" Mack leaned in to sniff her. It was meant to be a joke to set her at ease, but he had to quell an impulse to gently bite her neck. Her hair was windblown and her cheeks were pink, and she smelled like a spring day.

She gave a little laugh, her eyes rolling. "Why did I dab bacon-grease behind my ears?"

"Sorry I had to send Jackson and Willa this morning. A potential project rolled in looking for an estimate."

"It's fine."

"I thought maybe you'd be upset."

She arched her eyebrows, one corner of her mouth hitching up in a way that made him feel both gauche and turned on. "I don't expect your undivided attention."

"Did it take all morning to get Megan feeling human again?"

"She'll live. I left her with a bagel and ginger ale this morning and headed downtown to work on the car show."

"Any success?"

"Some. I have the pizza place, the ice cream shop, and Rufus's on board to sell food. Plus, Regan Fournette is going to send me a list of vendors she used for block parties when she was mayor."

"That's fantastic."

"And not only that, but we have a nice start on a fund for Dave and Marigold." She presented a fold of paper from her back pocket.

Mack thumbed through the checks. "Good grief. This was kind of everyone." He stopped at a business he didn't recognize. "What is Magnolia Investments?"

She plucked the checks out of his hand. "They prefer to stay anonymous. I'll open a new account and get these deposited."

His curiosity about the anonymous donor faded. As long as the checks cleared and the money helped his friends, he didn't care who signed along the dotted line. The car show felt real for the first time, and a shot of nerves had his stomach flip-flopping. "What's next?"

"I'm going to work up fliers for you boys to approve and line up advertising. Let me know if there are any websites or magazines you recommend I target."

"You've made an incredible amount of progress." When she went to step around him, he blocked her. "Thank you. I would have never been able to pull this off."

Her smile was sweet and made her eyes sparkle. "I know."

A laugh burst out of him, startling River who barked and jumped around their legs. Ella gave a surprised yelp and shifted away. River calmed down with some well-placed rubs behind her ears, and she looked at Ella with her tongue out and adoration in her eyes.

"Why don't you try giving her a pat on the head?" Mack asked.

"Isn't that a little close to her mouth?" Ella held her fisted hands against her chest.

"Give me your hand."

"No, thank you."

"You don't trust me?" The question reverberated around his head.

"It's not you I don't trust."

"She won't hurt you." Mack rubbed down River's nose, and the dog gave his wrist a little lick. River's puppy-dog eyes begged for her attention. He hoped to God he didn't look that pathetic.

Ella took a step backward. "Okay. I get it, dog. You like me and aren't going to eat my face, but I'm still not petting you." She retreated to his office and pulled out her laptop.

Mack was too agitated to sit behind a desk and enter numbers. What he really wanted was to hammer and shape metal until he couldn't feel his arms. Couldn't feel anything.

He whistled for River and headed outside to play fetch. The magnolia tree in the front had certainly grown since he was a kid, yet it seemed smaller to his adult eyes. What was it about youth that distorted memories and made people and places seem bigger than life? But his pop had only been a man—as confused and fallible as Mack.

A fundamental shift occurred like a dislocated joint popping into place. It was time to act.

He strode back into the garage and stared at his brothers hard at work. While they meant everything to Mack, he needed to finish this alone. He glanced toward his office. Or did he?

Ella was wearing her glasses as she twirled a pen between her fingers like a mini-drumstick. Maybe a spot in his truck was waiting for a smart, sassy-mouthed woman who'd stormed into his life like a hurricane.

As if caught in her vortex, he moved closer. "Will you come with me?"

Chapter Eighteen

Ella looked up. If Mack's roughened voice wasn't clue enough that something was amiss, the stark emotion writ large on his face was. She stood and followed him to his truck without asking where they were going. The truth was she would go anywhere with him. Which scared the hell out of her.

He steered them onto parish back roads, bypassing downtown Cottonbloom entirely. At first, she assumed they were headed south, but when the sun peeked out from the clouds she realized they were actually headed north.

North toward Jackson?

The atmosphere in the cab felt full of portent, and she was loathe to break the spell with the trivialness of words. Wherever they were headed, she trusted Mack had his reasons, and good ones too. The truck ate up the miles. She'd never known a comfortable silence with a man. She'd been taught her job was to fill the silence and make things easier. Smoother.

But she wasn't a smoother by nature, she was an agitator. That's one thing she learned the hard way with Trevor.

When they crossed the wide, muddy Mississippi, her

curiosity got the better of her. "I'm all for a sightseeing trip, but may I ask if you have a destination in mind?"

Mack sighed. It was a sad sound and she reached her hand out to touch his arm. A light touch before she pulled away, not sure if she was overstepping whatever bridge was under construction between them.

"I'm sorry. I should've asked before dragging you off."

"Are you kidnapping me? Are you taking me out in the boonies to dispose of me after you get me to sign papers selling you back the garage?" She kept her voice light and teasing because despite everything—their rocky beginning, her rocky past—she trusted him.

"When I got up this morning, this was the last thing I expected to be doing."

"Where are we headed, Mack?"

"Oak Grove to see my mother. I need to find Ford."

Ella swallowed past a lump. She'd interrupted enough discussions between the brothers to know what this meant. Was he ready to forgive Ford? Or did the plan call for a physical reckoning?

"Are you sure you don't want Jackson and Wyatt with you? This should be a family affair."

"I don't want them with me. I want—"

You. The unspoken word hung in the cab and stole her breath.

"Do you want me to take you home?" Mack let off the gas, his hands tightening on the steering wheel, his gaze on the road stretching out between the pines.

A turning point was upon them, the signposts indistinct.

If she had any hope of protecting her heart, she should insist upon returning to Cottonbloom. Except all she had waiting was a bottle of wine and a cold house. She wanted to stay right where she was—by his side.

"No," she said. "I'll gladly go with you if that's what you want."

"I want." The two words seemed to embody more than her accompanying him on a road trip to see his estranged mother and brother.

Now that they were in agreement and barreling closer to Oak Grove by the minute, she filled the space with small talk. Although, it didn't feel small. From his favorite movie (*Braveheart*) to his favorite food (chicken and dumplings) to his favorite color (green like the forest that backed up to the garage), every new thing she learned about him fascinated her.

As they drew closer to Oak Grove, his body lost its relaxed state behind the wheel. He sat up straighter and clutched the wheel.

"How much farther?"

"Another half hour, I think."

"What are you expecting to find? Answers?"

His laugh contained no humor. "I'm not even sure what the questions are."

"Is this all about Ford?"

He laid his head back, his shoulders hunching. "I don't know anymore. I mean, that's how it started. But once Jackson met with our mother I couldn't help but be curious."

She didn't sense anger in him, but something potent simmered below the surface of his stoic attitude. Frustration perhaps. Resentment certainly.

"You want to know why she left." She didn't pose it as a question.

"How could a mother walk off and leave her kids without looking back?"

"How do you know she didn't look back? How do you know she didn't want to come home but couldn't?"

"You sound like Jackson. He said she wanted to come back but Pop wouldn't let her." He ran a hand through his hair, leaving it as messy as his mood. "I don't know. Maybe it's better not to know. Maybe the past needs to stay there. This is crazy." His foot eased off the accelerator.

"It's not crazy to want to reconnect with your mother, Mack."

"She doesn't know I'm coming. I wasn't sure I'd make it before turning around."

"If I were in her shoes, it wouldn't matter. She'll be happy to see you."

Ella ran her hand down his arm and linked their fingers. She didn't know what they were to each other or what they might become, but in the moment, he'd chosen her to have his back, and she refused to let him down.

"I'm not sure I'll ever be able to forgive her." While vitriol clung to his words, it was losing its grip.

"Give her a chance to look into your eyes and explain before you decide if she's worthy of your forgiveness. Either way, I'll be here."

The tension in his body dissipated, his hand loosening around hers, but he didn't pull away. Sitting next to him holding his hand felt scarily natural.

"And if she's not worthy?"

"You move on, and she becomes a footnote to your life." If it were only so simple. Ella shifted to watch the trees streak green past the passenger window.

"Is that what your mom is? A footnote?" he asked.

"Actually, she takes up an entire appendix." She tried to laugh, but failed. Although, he didn't press her, she could sense his curiosity. Considering their mission, did she owe him a piece of her past? "I tried to reconcile with my mom after the divorce."

"It didn't go well."

"It did at first. My stepdad had left the year before on a trucking job out west and never came back." She'd had to bite back a relieved "Good riddance" when her mom had shared the news. "I hoped, with him out of the picture, Mom and I could rediscover a mythical mother-daughter bond where we went shopping and watched movies together. Instead, all she wanted was money. And lots of it."

"Did you give it to her?"

"Some. Even when I was writing the checks, I recognized money was our only bond. Once I quit bankrolling her, she got snippy and tried to guilt me into taking care of her. I'd had it by then and told her to come find me when she actually wanted to be my mom and not a leech. That was over a year ago."

"Where is she now?"

"She tracked down my stepdad out west and joined him. I guess he got tired of whatever sidepiece he had followed. We have no contact."

"And you're good with that?"

"I have to be. It was the family I was dealt. And I hit the jackpot with Grayson. I only wish I'd had him for longer. He was the best brother anyone could ask for." A lump in her throat choked off the words. "I don't have a family anymore."

It was a strange thing to be without family. Her divorce from Trevor, as necessary as it had been, had been yet another tether snapped. Being around the Abbotts reminded her how wonderful and stabilizing a family could be while highlighting her own loneliness.

Mack lifted their joined hands and pressed a kiss on the back of hers. The gesture was sweet and left her unable to speak for entirely different reasons. They travelled the roads together in silence, but a new level of understanding had been unlocked.

Mack straightened and pulled away, gripping the steering wheel in both hands. "We're coming into Oak Grove."

Using the truck's navigation system, she guided him to

his mother's house. Mack pulled the truck up to the curb across from a normal-looking middle-class one-story brick house similar to the one she'd grown up in.

She pushed her car door open and was halfway out when she realized Mack hadn't moved. "Do you want to do this?"

He made a noise that might have been a bark of laughter. "Of course I don't want to do this. I feel like I'm checking into the hospital for open-heart surgery."

"Then turn the truck around and let's go home. It's as easy as that."

Mack rested his forehead on the steering wheel. "Nothing's been easy since Pop died," he said softly.

Ella wanted to curl herself around his back and lay her head on his hunched shoulders. But that's not what he needed. He needed someone to give him a kick in the pants. "Get out of the truck, Mack. Let's do this. Sitting here dreading it is worse than facing up to it."

At a loss for a quick response, Mack blinked at Ella. Any empathy in her voice had been hacked away and replaced by determination and fire. She was right, of course. The longer he sat in the truck, the harder it would be to break the laws of inertia. Might as well get the painful process rolling even if it was like pulling a truck with his teeth.

Best-case scenario, he got Ford's address and was back in the truck in five minutes. Worst-case, he didn't get Ford's address, his mother turned out to be as selfish and hateful as his pop charged time and again, and he was back in the truck in five minutes.

He forced himself out of the truck, gravity working double-time on his limbs. Ella met him at the bumper and threaded her fingers in his, giving them a slight squeeze.

The hours he'd spent imagining his mother's return had included hugs and apologies and promises to never leave.

As he grew older, the bitterness that had infected his pop found a new host in Mack. "I can't do this."

"Yes, you can."

Her statement shouldn't mean anything to him, but it meant everything and lent him the strength he needed to walk across the street on legs that threatened collapse.

Rosebushes lined the brick path to her front door. A memory surfaced. Multi-hued roses in a mason jar on the kitchen table, dropping petals onto the dark wood. He remembered taking a fallen petal and rubbing it against his lips, marveling at the softness with a new awareness of the amazingness of nature.

From the budding rosebushes to the green ferns on the porch to the dark red bricks, the house exhibited a warm welcome. When she'd crossed his mind in recent years, he alternately pictured her in a cold, decrepit trailer or remarried with new kids to replace him.

"I should've called," he croaked out.

"She'll be happy to see you no matter what."

An Easter-themed welcome sign hung on the door. It was such a homey, motherly thing to have. A hot knife of emotion sliced through his chest. He was torn between resentment and a longing for something and someone lost forever.

When he didn't move, Ella held his gaze and pushed the doorbell. He balanced on a point of no return.

Slightly discordant notes chimed, and the longer he waited, the more lightheaded he became. The door chain rattled and the door creaked open. His mother was revealed as if time had lost any relation to Einstein's theories.

The first thing he noticed was her hair. Once dark like Wyatt's, it was shot through with gray, and hung to her shoulders in a thick mass. Her eyes belong to Wyatt too, but something about the set of her mouth, determined and a little cynical, was reminiscent of what stared back at him in the mirror every morning.

She was a stranger yet eerily familiar from his dreams and memories.

"Mack." She breathed his name as if any sudden movement might scare him away.

Actually, that wasn't too far off the mark. He considered hightailing it back to his truck and hiding like the time she caught him eating all of the cookies she'd made for dessert. He couldn't have been more than four. Instead of spanking him, she had made him sit at the table and read to her while she made another batch.

"Hi," he said inanely.

His mother's gaze ricocheted between him and Ella, but he was too far lost to attempt an introduction.

Ella smiled and held out her hand. "I'm Ella Boudreaux."

"Nice to make your acquaintance. Come in. Please." She stepped back and gestured them inside, never taking her eyes off Mack.

Entering her house felt like a betrayal of his pop. His head and heart tried to reconcile his feelings as he slid one foot across the threshold. When nothing momentous happened—like getting struck by lightning—he stepped fully inside.

The smell of fresh-baked goods cast him back almost thirty years, and he was a little kid again. A timer beeped, and his mother started as if coming out of a dream.

"I need to check the cookies. Come in and make yourselves at home." She hustled through a doorway to their left.

Mack followed one slow step at a time. Ella gave him a push from behind, and he entered a wood-paneled den that opened into a remodeled kitchen. His mother was fanning a baking sheet of what appeared to be oatmeal raisin cookies—his favorite.

The mantel was lined with photographs. They were a

march through their family history from when they were babies to the final picture of the brothers in suits from their pop's funeral. Hazel had taken the somber shot.

He returned to the first picture. Ford and Mack stood on either side of a rocking chair grinning like fools. His mother was perched on the seat of the rocker, juggling two squalling newborns. Although she was young and pretty, her smile was so slight as to be missed and a desperation was aimed at the camera or perhaps at the man taking the picture, his pop presumably.

"Those were hard days." His mother's voice came from behind him.

Picking up the picture, he turned. She'd set a plate of cookies on the coffee table. The rocking chair from the picture was behind her. Ella sat on the couch, a silent observer. She gave him a single, bracing nod when he caught her eye.

Instead of allowing the bitterness his pop had cultivated overtake him, he asked, "Why was it hard?"

"You and Ford were still so young when I found out I was pregnant with twins. Your father was ecstatic, of course, even more so when we found out there would be two more boys."

"You weren't happy?"

"Sometimes I was. It's taken me a long time to understand it."

"Understand what?"

"I suffered from severe postpartum depression. It started after Ford and got worse with each pregnancy and birth. After the twins were born, I thought about killing myself. That was bad enough, but when I almost—" She covered her mouth, turned, and sat in the rocking chair, the slight squeak of the motion sparking memories.

He joined Ella on the couch. "Almost what?"

"Jackson wet his bed, and I almost hurt him. At the

time, leaving was the only way I could protect you boys from . . . me." She rocked and fiddled with the floral ruffle of the cushioned seat.

"Why not get help? There are medicines for that sort of thing, aren't there?"

"I was young and didn't understand what was happening to me. I thought I might be going insane. Your father was busy with the garage. It's not that he didn't care; it's that he wasn't able to understand, if that makes sense."

It did make sense. His pop had been old school. His mother's distress would have been viewed as a weakness or might have been ignored altogether. His pop wasn't a sensitive, demonstrative guy. He hadn't been a hugger and rarely had expressed his love in straightforward words. More precious than any declarations had been knowing he'd made his pop proud. A "good job" meant the world to Mack and to all the boys.

"Why didn't you get straightened out and come back? We missed you."

"I tried, but your father wasn't interested in repairing our marriage. He refused to let me see you boys."

"Why didn't you fight for us?"

A small, sad smile ghosted across her lips. "Your father convinced me you were better off without me. And after the way I'd screwed up and was still struggling, I believed him."

He wanted to deny and rail against the truths his mother dropped like mini-grenades, leaving his memories in rubble.

She continued. "Once I was back on my feet and stable, I reached out to Hazel. Your aunts were more forgiving and understanding than I deserved. Through them, I've at least been able to follow your lives from a distance. It wasn't what I ever wanted, but it was better than nothing."

Mack swept his gaze over the pictures on the mantle.

How different would their lives have been if his pop had been able to let go of his hurt and welcome her back into their lives? He'd made them all suffer because of his broken heart and smashed pride.

"We could have been a family. A real family again." Anger welled up, and as hard as it was to admit, it was mostly directed at his pop. His stubbornness and inability to understand that not every problem could be fixed like replacing a part in a car engine. Sometimes you had to make it work with the parts you'd been given.

His mother sat forward and touched his hand. "Don't blame Hobart. He was a good man, but meant for a different time. Or maybe a different kind of wife."

The conversation took on a surreal cast with his mother defending his pop while Mack reassigned blame. "That's no excuse."

"We both made mistakes, but the reality is I left and he raised you and did a damn fine job. My regrets are plentiful, but the last few months have given me hope that maybe it's not too late?"

"Maybe it's not."

Her eyes glimmered with tears, and she pressed her fingertips to the bridge of her nose to stem them.

If her existence had been sprung on him, he'd probably be reacting differently, but Wyatt and Jackson's softening toward her had in turn primed him to accept the possibilities. Whether those possibilities would flourish into a relationship, he couldn't say, but he was no longer barring the door against one.

"Can I have a cookie?" he asked partly to break the emotional tension and partly because suddenly he was hungry and no cookie in his lifetime had ever lived up to his mother's.

She laughed through her tears. "Of course. I make them for you."

He stilled with a warm cookie halfway to his mouth.

"How did you know we were coming?" Ella piped up for the first time.

"I didn't."

"But the cookies . . ." Mack gestured.

"I make them all the time. I try to always have some on hand. Just in case."

The implication of her confession tumbled his emotions. How many batches of cookies had gone uneaten and unappreciated on the off chance one of them turned up on her doorstep? He took a bite. The cookie was even better than he remembered.

"Good?" his mother asked, dimples cut into her smiling cheeks.

"Better than good." Mack could see pieces of her in all of them. He'd thought himself as one hundred percent Abbott, but he wasn't. "Oatmeal raison is my favorite."

"I know. I remember every minute with you boys. Even the times I wished I could forget." She didn't sound bitter, only resigned and accepting of the years lost.

He picked up another cookie and hoped it would fill the hollow place in his chest where his heart resided. "There's another reason we're here."

"Ford," she said.

"Yes. Any idea where he is?"

"In general or an address?" The wariness and protectiveness in her voice surprised him.

"An address. I need to talk to him face-to-face."

"To make peace or to lay more blame on his shoulders?" The motherly disapproval in her voice felt oddly natural.

"Depends on my welcome."

His mother sighed. Her rocking picked up speed and reflected her agitation. "He's not blameless, but he's hurting, Mack. Like I was hurting when I left."

"Depression?"

"Depression. Anxiety. I made him go see my doctor here in Oak Grove. I have a feeling he wants to make things right with you and your brothers, but doesn't know how. Has he burned all his bridges with you or is there a way back?"

Mack swallowed, almost choking on the remnants of the cookie in his dry throat. It was like history repeating itself. Her question seemed to encompass more than Ford. They could never go back to the way things were, but could forgiveness reveal a path forward for Ford and his mother?

Could he be a bigger, better man than his pop? The thought hurt. He'd idolized his pop. And he wasn't a bad man, just one who'd nurtured his hurt for too long. It was easy to hang onto resentment; scarier to let go and hope for the best.

Mack stole a glance at Ella. Concern but also an unshakable steadfastness to back him up was written on her face. She had forgiven Megan and become a true friend to her. Couldn't he do the same for his flesh and blood?

While he teased out the universe's lessons for him, his mother transferred her attention to Ella. "Ford told me about you, Ms. Boudreaux. You bought his stake in the garage."

"I did. Please call me Ella."

"But you're more than a business partner now, aren't you?" His mother glanced between the two of them, her eyebrows up.

He stuffed another cookie in his mouth. It was childish and cowardly but there was no way he was answering that question.

"Yes. We are more than business partners." A slight lilt at the end revealed her uncertainty.

He could tell his mother had more questions, but the tenuous connection they had forged didn't support a heart-to-heart about his love life. Not yet anyway. "Will you give me Ford's address if I promise my intentions are good? How's he doing?"

"He calls once a week to check in." His mother frowned, the tiny lines radiating from her mouth betraying her age. "He's got a job at an insurance agency and is studying for an exam to expand into financial planning."

"Isn't financial planning a fancy way to gamble with other people's money?"

"He's excited about this, Mack. Don't shame him." His mother rose and pulled out an index card from a drawer in the kitchen. Mack held out his hand, but she only tapped the card on her chin. "I expect you to approach him as his brother, not a scorned business partner. Can you do that?"

"I want to make things right, I promise you that." Mack held his mother's unblinking gaze for what felt like minutes, but was probably only a few heartbeats. She nodded and held the card out. He ran his finger over his mother's loopy, strong handwriting. Each new discovery about her, no matter how mundane, rocked his foundations.

The address was a suburb of Memphis. He snapped a picture with his phone, stood, and handed her back the card. "We should hit the road."

"Are you driving to Memphis tonight? You could stay here and leave in the morning."

"I appreciate the offer, but I'm determined to see this through and if I wait I might talk myself out of it." Neither was he ready for a sleepover at his mother's. He needed to separate himself from the push-pull and regain his balance.

"I understand. Let me pack up some cookies for your trip." His mother took the plate of cookies and retreated to the kitchen.

Mack turned to Ella. "I'll take you back to Cottonbloom. I never meant for this to turn into an odyssey."

"Don't be ridiculous. We're more than halfway to Memphis already."

"You sure?"

She ran her hand down his forearm to link their fingers. "I'm sure."

His mother returned with a plastic baggie filled with cookies. Mack made his way to the front door. Ella leaned in to give his mother a half hug. "So nice to meet you, Ms. Abbott."

Ella sent a side-eye look his direction that dripped with meaning. Unfortunately, he didn't have a dictionary handy. She brushed by him and headed toward his truck.

"I'm so glad you came by, son." His mother held out the baggie of cookies.

He took it as if accepting a packed lunch before school. Another memory surfaced. She used to leave little notes in his lunches. Words of encouragement or a simple "I love you." He'd forgotten until this moment.

He fiddled with the bag. "You should come down to Cottonbloom soon."

"I should?" Tears battled with the smile breaking over her face.

"Wyatt and Jackson would like that. So would the aunts."

"What about you? Would *you* like that?"

He swallowed. He wished Ella had stayed at his side, but he could feel her behind him, giving him courage. "Yeah, I would like that. It might be hard at first though."

"I'm used to hard." She covered his hand on the bag. "This will be the best kind of hard there is."

"Okay." He took a step back, feeling overwhelmed and unsure. Two foreign emotions for him. "I'll be in touch."

She crossed her arms and leaned in the doorway. "Let me know how things go with Ford, will you?"

He nodded, turned, and focused on getting himself into the safety of his truck. Ella didn't speak until they were on the road, headed north to continue his tour of atonement.

"Your mom seems really nice."

"Yeah."

"How did you leave things?"

"I invited her down to Cottonbloom. A homecoming of sorts, I suppose."

She shifted to face him, tucking her leg up on the seat. "That's a big step."

"Too big? Should I have waited?" He drummed his thumbs on the steering wheel, an agitated energy seeking release.

"No, it's good. I'm proud of you."

He shot her a look, the smile on her face and her words of praise soothing his nerves. "I wasn't sure I had it in me."

"Had what in you?"

"The ability to forgive. Pop never had it." A smidgen of resentment snuck into his voice. "I think that's why Ford stuck around the garage even though it wasn't his passion. Pop wouldn't have forgiven him for leaving the business, just like he couldn't forgive our mother for leaving."

"I didn't know your father, but sounds to me like he was human with strengths and frailties. You need to forgive him too. He loved her. And I can only imagine what it was like being left with four young, rambunctious boys to look after by himself. He did a good job raising all of you."

"We're so dysfunctional we could be a case study for a psychology class up at Cottonbloom College."

"If that were true, we wouldn't be on our way to see Ford." The simplicity of her evaluation settled over him.

"I'm not sure I would have had the nerve to make this trip if it wasn't for you." His confession rushed out into the darkness of the cab. He tightened his hands on the steering wheel, hoping she wouldn't press him further. His emotions were raw and needed time to scab over before facing Ford.

She was silent, but her hand slipped to his leg for a squeeze and stayed there. He was grateful for the contact. For too long, he'd borne the crushing weight and responsibilities of the garage and the family alone, doing his best to shield his younger brothers. He didn't have to shield Ella. She was strong enough for them both.

Although the coming showdown was sure to test him, he relaxed and let the rhythm of the road lull him into a state of peace.

He pulled into Ford's apartment complex. Road noise from the nearby interstate permeated the night, so different from Cottonbloom and their sleepy parish road.

"This is it." He made no move to open the door and neither did she.

"I should wait in the car," Ella said.

"No. I want you with me."

"Mack." The way she said his name contained both comfort and exasperation. "I'm not family and will only complicate things. You and Ford need to hash this out brother to brother. But no matter what happens, I'll be waiting."

Although she was referring to the single moment in time they occupied, a warmth settled in his chest. He wanted her with him *always*.

He got out of the truck, climbed the steps to the second floor, and stared at a door with Ford's apartment number. It was nine at night. He fought the urge to retreat. Ford could be out partying or gambling on a riverboat or sleeping. Or he could be behind the flimsy piece of wood and metal.

With one last look at the truck, he faced the door, squared his shoulders, and knocked. The sound of a chain rattling had his heart pounding. The door cracked open and revealed Ford, looking healthier than Mack had seen him in a long time. He'd put on much-needed weight, his hair was neatly trimmed, and his eyes had lost their shadows.

"Hey, Ford. How's it going?" Mack asked as if they were seeing each other across the dinner table after a day apart and not after the gulf of months that had separated them.

If Ford was surprised, he hid it well. Although, their mother might have warned him of Mack's arrival. She had been protective of Ford.

"You're a long way from home." Ford made no move to invite him inside.

"Are you busy? Can we talk?"

"Is that all you want to do? Figured you'd want to rearrange my face."

"Not gonna lie. I did want to take you behind the barn for a while. Especially after the stunt Tarwater pulled on New Year's Eve."

"That was Tarwater's game. He was looking to humiliate Wyatt. Believe me, I didn't plan it."

"His unnatural glee in the situation clued me in on that." Mack hesitated on the threshold. "Can I come in?"

Ford stepped back and gestured, shutting the door behind Mack.

The apartment wasn't anything special, but Ford had furnished it in new, comfortable-looking furniture. A flat screen was mounted above a gas fireplace.

"Can I get you something to drink?" Ford moved toward a small kitchen.

"Tea or a Coke would be good. Something with caffeine."

"How about a coffee?" Ford pointed to a fancy one-cup brewer.

"Perfect. Thanks. I take it black."

Ford shot him a small smile. "I remember how you take your coffee."

It had been a long time since Mack had seen his older brother smile. Maybe even since before their pop had died. They were silent as the coffee brewed, the aroma bracing. Ford held out a mug, the dark brew swirling against white.

"They're engaged. Wyatt and Sutton, I mean," Mack said to try to deflate the rising tension.

Another smile from Ford, this one bigger and containing real happiness. "I heard. That's great. How did Tarwater handle the glad tidings?"

"Madder than a wet hen, as you can imagine."

They chuckled and sipped at their coffees, the silence less tense and more expectant. Mack set his coffee mug down. With his words hitching slightly, he asked, "Are you good? I mean, any more trouble with . . . stuff? You know I'll help you, right?"

Ford gave an audible swallow, his gaze fixed on the window like he was considering escape, even though the curtains were drawn. "I'm better. I haven't gambled since I moved up here. It's been a battle though. Winning gave me a high, if that makes any sense."

Gambling was an addiction like any other. "I want you to know if something changes, all you have to do is pick up the phone."

Ford nodded. "I appreciate that, but I'm working things out on my own."

As Ford didn't mention any struggles with depression and anxiety, neither did Mack. Maybe one day, they could talk freely, but for now, they were still feeling each other out. "I'm glad."

"How is Ms. Boudreaux working out?" Ford didn't take a seat or invite Mack to sit, but leaned against an island that separated the kitchen from the living area.

"Surprisingly well."

"So you don't hate me? Because sometimes I hate myself."

Mack rubbed his forehead. "I thought I hated you for a while. But I don't. How could I, when half the problem is me?"

Ford's eyes widened. "That's not true. I'm the one who gambled. I'm the one who didn't know how to tell Pop and you guys that I wanted out. I felt trapped."

"Don't get me wrong, you bear plenty of the blame too." A brotherly tease snuck into Mack's voice when he was least expecting it. "But I didn't make it easy on you. None of us did. I should have offered you an out. I'm sorry I didn't understand how much you hated the garage and your life in Cottonbloom."

Ford knitted his fingers together at his nape and tilted his face down, his eyes hidden. "I didn't *hate* it. At least, not at first. But Pop pitted us against one another, and I always came out the loser."

Mack rubbed the heel of his hand over his chest. "I was jealous of you."

Ford's head popped up. "What?"

"You went to college and made Pop proud. I felt like I had to play catch-up in Pop's eyes, so I threw myself into the garage and the cars."

"That's what you wanted though." Confusion crept over Ford's face. "Right?"

"Yes. It's what I wanted, but your success at school fired a desperate kind of competitiveness I couldn't control. Things got ugly, and I'm sorry for that."

"I'm sorry too. For more things than I can list at the moment."

Mack believed him. He took a sip of his cooling coffee and looked around. "Not a bad place. You like Memphis?"

"It's alright. Big enough for a man to get lost in. I like that after Cottonbloom."

"You got enough money?" Mack chewed the inside of his lip, hoping he wasn't overstepping. He didn't want to squash their burgeoning reconnection.

"I got a job. Insurance and investments. Finally putting my degree to good use. Lowest rung, but if I can pass my standards test, I'll be up for a promotion. I'll get it. I'm good." The Abbott confidence hadn't skipped over Ford after all.

Mack smiled. "I'm glad. And happy for you."

"You're not here to talk me into coming home? Because I'm not leaving."

The fact Ford still referred to Cottonbloom as home was telling, but Mack shrugged. "You'd be welcome, but I understand why you need a fresh start. I hope you won't be a stranger though. The aunts miss you something fierce."

"I miss them too." Ford looked away and rubbed his nose as if trying to quell his emotions. "Aunt Hy hit anything lately?"

"A curb jumped out in front of her the other day, but nothing living. Aunt Hazel's been pushing me to contact you for a while. And our mother too."

"Is that how you got my address?"

"Just came from her house. She made cookies and sent them along with me. I left them in the truck though." Along with Ella. She was probably getting cold and bored. He needed to make a move.

"What are you going to do about her?" Ford asked.

For a heartbeat, Mack thought he was referring to Ella. And the question reverberated in his head. It would need an answer. And soon. But then, reality settled. Ford had been asking about their mother, not Ella. "I invited her down to Cottonbloom. Maybe you two could come together?"

"Yeah, maybe." Although, it wasn't a commitment, his smile lent Mack hope everything would be okay. Not tomorrow or next week. Maybe not even for years, but eventually. "She's been really great to me the last few months. Like a real—" Ford's mouth thinned and clamped shut.

"Like a real mother."

Mack and Ford let out two identical sighs, and then shared a soft laugh.

"I started remembering things when I was around her." Ford's voice was soft, as if imparting a secret.

"When she gave me the bag of cookies tonight, it's like I was six and standing on our porch while she handed us our sack lunches. You remember the notes she would put in?"

Ford smiled and shook his head. "I used to act embarrassed if one of my friends saw, but I loved those notes."

"I did too."

The silence that fell between them wasn't quite companionable, but Mack could foresee a time when it might be. He ran his hands down the front of his jeans. "I don't want to wear out my welcome."

"You can stay. The couch is comfortable."

"I appreciate the offer, but Ella is in the truck, and I need to get her home."

"Ella Boudreaux rode all the way up here with you? You didn't kidnap her, did you?"

"Nope." Mack couldn't stifle his smile.

"Holy crap. You and Ella Boudreaux?"

"Me and Ella."

"She's so sophisticated and gorgeous. How the hell did that happen?"

A laugh burst out of Mack, and he knuckle-punched Ford on the arm. "You don't have to sound quite so shocked. I have my charming moments, or so I've been told on occasion."

"Wow. How serious is it?"

"Not sure. The garage complicates matters. I still want her portion back in Abbott hands." Mack moved toward the door and stepped outside.

Ford leaned in the doorjamb, his hand braced on top of the door. "Don't be as obsessed as Pop was and put the garage above your happiness."

Mack let the advice sink in a moment before nodding and sticking his hand out. Ford took it and, before Mack could react, pulled him into a brief hug.

Ford's voice was a near whisper. "Thanks for making the first move. Not sure I would have ever found the courage."

Mack tapped his fist on Ford's back and pulled away. "Sure thing, bro. Come home to see us, okay? We'll kill the fatted lamb and everything."

Ford smiled at Mack's reference to the prodigal son. The aunts would be proud they'd retained something from their forced march to Sunday school every week as kids.

The door closed. He turned away in time to see his truck door open and Ella slide out. The frayed threads of his past had been smoothed and knitted into something new tonight.

She met him halfway across the parking lot. Before he could question himself, he pulled her close and wrapped his arms tight around her. She understood his inner workings like she had read a manual.

"Did it go well?" Her voice was muffled in his neck.

He curved himself around her and took a deep breath. "Better than I expected. Better than I deserved."

"What now? Do you want to get a hotel or something?"

Part of him did, but a bigger part of him longed for home. Home with her. "I know it's a haul, but I want to drive back tonight. Ford made me some coffee."

"Are you sure?"

"I'm sure."

They loaded back into his truck and headed south. Knowing every minute and every mile brought him closer to home regulated the chaos raging in his head. They stopped for food and talked about inconsequential things, but it felt natural and comfortable.

Finally, at four in the morning, the sign designating the Cottonbloom, Mississippi, city limits flashed.

"You want me to drop you at your house?"

"My car's at the garage." She yawned.

"Let's crash at my place then. We both need sleep."

She listed over and laid her head on his arm. "Okay. You did promise me a sunrise, but this is not how I envisioned it."

He pressed a kiss on the top of her head. He envisioned weeks, months, years of sunrises on the horizon. He parked in front of his house. Everything was quiet and peaceful, and he heaved in the dewy air. The birds were waking and calling out greetings.

Like a sleepwalker, Ella made her way straight into his bathroom. He followed with a towel and a T-shirt in case she wanted to shower. He perched on the edge of his bed waiting for her to finish. His body was exhausted but his mind was punch-drunk with lack of sleep and bounced around, ignoring all logic.

She emerged with damp hair, his T-shirt hanging to mid-thigh, and made her way to the bed like a robot. He stood and flipped the covers back. With a groan, she fell to the mattress and snuggled under the covers.

He took his turn in the bathroom, taking a five-minute shower before pulling on a pair of boxer briefs and padding to the bed. She was asleep, curled up on her side facing his pillow with her arm extended as if waiting for him. He slipped under her arm and repositioned her with her head on his shoulder. She slipped her leg between his and lay half on top of him.

Sleep remained elusive. Luckily, the next day was Saturday, and they could sleep in. Although, no doubt one or both of the boys would be by with questions as soon as they spotted his truck out front. He'd ignored their texts, unwilling to lie.

"I used your toothbrush." Her admission was mumbled, and at first he thought she might be dreaming.

"What's that?"

"I used your toothbrush. Was that overstepping?"

"No. I don't mind." Which was weird because with any other woman, he was pretty sure he would mind. The intimacy of her confession settled his mind enough to drift into a deep sleep.

Chapter Nineteen

He woke to bright sunshine and a hand in his underwear. And not his hand. He kept his eyes closed and his body relaxed as much as possible considering what was happening in his pants.

God, it felt fantastic.

"I know you're awake." Ella's voice was husky from sleep but melodious with laughter. "You're not snoring anymore."

He cracked his eyes open, squinting in the light. Ella was up on an elbow, her head propped in her hand, staring down at him with the sexiest bedhead he'd ever seen.

"I don't snore."

"Don't worry, it was a cute snore and not a snorting kind." Her hand continued to perform magic under the covers. "There's no one to interrupt us. Megan is at my place. Trevor doesn't know where you live. My phone is dead. It's Saturday. We missed the sunrise, but we could stay in bed all day and catch the sunset."

He'd never been with a woman he'd wanted to loll around in bed with all day. Until now.

"Sounds like a plan." He tugged at the hem of the shirt she wore. "I like you in my T-shirt."

"Would you like me better out of it?" Her voice was sultry and her eyes half closed.

"Yes. Take it off. Now." His voice had taken on a growly edge at her teasing.

Her hand on him stilled, and her breath caught. She sat up, jerked the shirt off, and went after the sheet to pull it over her breasts. He caught the edge and whipped it away from her body. She was naked.

"Mack." Embarrassment drew his name out of her mouth and caused a flush to bloom over her chest.

"That's pretty."

"What is?"

Instead of answering with words, he let his hands and mouth show her what he thought was pretty. Which was everything. The next time she said his name, it emerged on a moan.

Her hands tore at his underwear, and his were equally as frantic to get free of them. He kicked them off and rolled to his back, maneuvering her into a straddle across his hips. She covered her breasts with her arm.

Where did the woman who had been teasing him about rolling around in the sheets all day go? It was becoming clear, she was all talk and little experience. Well, he could expand her experience right quick.

He lifted his head. "This doesn't seem right, does it?"

A look of relief flashed over her face. He scooted up on the pillows so he was half-sitting with her still in a straddle.

"Much better." He skimmed his hands up her sides to cup her breasts. Her hands fell to his chest, her nails digging into his skin in pleasure-pain.

"It's too bright," she whispered as if someone might overhear and be scandalized. "And the windows."

"No. It's perfect. You're perfect." His words must have had some effect, because she rotated her hips on him and her gaze met his.

"Can I . . ." She pulled her lip between her teeth and slowly released it, leaving it plump and red. Was she trying to torture him?

"You can do whatever you want, babe. But, if you're taking suggestions, I would love to be inside of you." He grabbed a condom from the nightstand and handed it to her.

She ripped the package open and pulled the circle of latex out. "I just roll it on, right?"

"You act like it's your first time?"

"Putting a condom on a man? It is. I've been on the pill—"

"You're on the pill?"

"Yeah. Have been since I was eighteen." She glanced away and back to him. "Do you want to skip the condom?"

"That's like asking a man if he wants to drive a Shelby Cobra. Ninety-nine point nine percent will say 'Hell yes.' And I'm clean."

"Me too. In that case . . ." She tossed the condom over her shoulder, lifted her hips, and lowered herself excruciatingly slowly.

He could feel every inch of her wet heat around him. Closing his eyes, he took two deep breaths and tried not to embarrass himself. She rolled her hips and ground against him, propping both her hands on his chest.

He let her ride him however she needed to as he concentrated on her breasts. One of her hands fluttered across his stomach but stopped before reaching the point where they joined.

"Go on. Touch yourself."

She did, and Ella taking charge of her pleasure and using him as the instrument was the sexiest thing he'd ever seen. He wanted it to last forever, but too soon, her head fell back and she moaned her orgasm. Employing all his self-control, he kept himself from seeking the same quick end.

Only when her body turned boneless did he move. He shifted her off him and onto her hands and knees, facing the headboard. Kneeling behind her, he tilted her hips and drove inside of her. Their bodies were both slick from her orgasm.

He took a dozen hard thrusts. She met every one. A wildness built then threatened to break free. He wrapped a hand in her hair and tugged, her back dipping. The new angle invited him even deeper inside.

If it was all about him, he would finish this way, but he wanted more for her. He let go of her hair, scooped his hands under her arms, and pulled her up until her back was against his chest. Her head fell back against his shoulder.

"That's better," he murmured while nuzzling past her hair to her ear.

The connection, both physical and emotional, was tangible. She reached behind her and took hold of his hips, urging him back into a rhythm. This time he took her slow and deep. He slid a finger between her legs and cupped a breast with his other hand.

She squirmed against him. "A little harder."

He worked her harder from all directions. The ripple of her second orgasm sent him careening toward his own. He bit the side of her throat and groaned, burying himself inside of her until his spasms ceased.

He pushed her down to the mattress with his weight, still on top and still inside. Once his toes uncurled, he forced himself to roll off her. She continued to lie there with her face in the covers.

"I'm dead. I think I'm dead. Am I dead?" Her voice was muffled.

"Sorry. I didn't mean to crush you."

"Not that." She waved a hand over her bare butt. "All of *that*."

He grinned at the ceiling. A rap on his front door wiped his smile away.

"Knock, knock!" Wyatt's voice carried to the bedroom and grew closer. "Are you okay?"

He cursed, rolled off the bed, and yanked his jeans on.

"He wouldn't just walk in, would he?" Ella scrambled under the covers.

Considering Wyatt had never had to worry about walking in on him and a woman before and the fact Mack had taken off the day before with little explanation and without returning any texts, the answer was yes. Wyatt would barge straight in and embarrass everyone.

Mack quickstepped out of the bedroom and pulled the door shut. He was fastening his jeans when Wyatt turned the corner from the den to the hall. He stopped short. "There you are. Is everything okay?"

"Fine. It's fine." Mack spun Wyatt around and herded him into the kitchen. The endorphin rush from sex had been overtaken from the adrenaline rush of Wyatt's arrival.

"You didn't return any of my texts. You could have been in a ditch for all we knew." Wyatt propped his hands on his hips in a fair mimic of Aunt Hazel. Except he was dead serious.

"I'm sorry, man. Took a road trip to Oak Grove."

Wyatt's hands dropped. "To see Mom."

Even though he had posed it as a statement, Mack nodded. "I saw Ford too."

"Are you ready to discuss it?"

He wasn't. He was ready to loll around the bed all day with Ella, but apparently those plans were shot to hell. "Jackson around?" At Wyatt's affirmative, Mack continued. "How about we powwow in the barn in ten."

"Sounds good." Wyatt stopped with a foot out the door. "Do we need to get Ella's car back to her place?"

"Uh, no." Mack rubbed his nape. "She's here."

Wyatt's mouth drew into a circle the same time he fought a smile. His smile morphed into a grimace. "Oh crap, I almost pulled a coitus interruptus, didn't I?"

Mack shushed him. "I'll meet you in the barn. Brew some coffee, would you? I pulled an all-nighter."

"You dog! I'm impressed a man of your advanced years can still do that."

"*Driving*. I was driving. Mostly. Now get out." Mack threw a pillow from the sofa at Wyatt, but he escaped and it bounced against the screen door.

Mack padded back to his bedroom. Ella was huddled under the covers with a pillow over her head.

"He's gone," Mack said.

"I'll never be able to look him in the eyes again." The pillow remained in place.

He sat on the edge of the bed, his lips twitching. He didn't want her to think he was laughing at her. "At least it wasn't Aunt Hazel. She might have dragged you out to the reading of Bible verses on sins of the flesh."

"Does everyone make a habit of letting themselves into your house?" She pulled the pillow off her face and tucked it under her arms, her shoulders bare.

He wanted to run his fingers along her curves and strip all her physical and emotional defenses away. A deep breath quelled his primal urge to pounce. "Up to now, it hasn't been an issue, to be honest."

"Really?" She cast him a look under her lashes as color flushed her cheeks. "No sunrise watching lately?"

"Not for quite some time."

A small smile played peekaboo.

As tempted as he was to climb back in bed with her, he couldn't ignore his family situation. "I need to talk to

Wyatt and Jackson about yesterday . . . our mother, Ford. They need to know everything. Do you mind if I head over to the barn for a bit?"

"I'll leave." A slightly uncertain look was aimed in his direction.

"I want you to stay, but I understand if you have other things to take care of."

"I really do need to change clothes and check on Megan, but I can come back later. By sunset." She waggled her eyebrows.

"Sounds good." His disappointment was fierce, but a laugh simmered at the easy tease between them.

He leaned in, and she met him halfway for a simple kiss but with a promise of later. He grabbed the same T-shirt she'd slept in and pulled it over his head on his way out the door. It held her scent, and he nearly turned back around, his obligation to his brothers be damned. But he didn't.

He weaved his way around the punching bag, the aroma of fresh-brewed coffee drawing him in like a cartoon mouse to cheese. Whatever small talk the twins had been engaged in ceased when he got close. Wyatt lounged on the couch and Jackson leaned against the open door of the barn. Spring had sprung and even though the morning was cool, the breeze snaking through held a sunny warmth.

Two sets of eyes bore into him as he poured a mug of coffee and took a bracing sip. The stressful day and sleepless night was catching up to him. His brain was rusty. He took the end of the couch opposite Wyatt. "Morning, boys."

"It's almost eleven." Jackson's sly smile showcased his dimples.

"Still morning, by my reckoning. Anyway, it's Saturday. Can't a man sleep in?"

"According to Wyatt, you weren't sleeping." Jackson's grin was infectious.

Mack tried to summon a hint of indignation, but couldn't locate any. He hadn't realized how dour and serious Jackson had become until Willa had turned his frown upside down. Mack had lost sleep worried about the fallout from a Jackson-Willa workplace romance, but it had turned out fine. Better than fine. His brother was happy, and that's all Mack had ever wanted for him.

"Ella and I are together. I think." Mack covered his discomfiture with a sip of coffee.

"That was said with resounding confidence." Wyatt made an "I don't know" shrugging gesture.

"It's complicated. You two wouldn't understand."

Wyatt and Jackson exchanged a look and burst into laughter.

"That was dumb. You two would probably understand better than anyone, but I'm not here to talk about my feelings. Or her feelings. Or whatever." Mack waved a hand in the air.

"You saw our mother," Wyatt said. "What did you think?"

"She had cookies waiting on the off chance one of us showed up. And they were good, dammit. Just like I remembered."

Jackson looked out at the trees, and Wyatt smiled a sad smile. "It's crazy how the memories rewrite themselves, isn't it?"

Wyatt had put into words what had been bothering him. "Yeah. All of sudden stuff came rushing back. Good stuff."

"How did you leave things?"

"I invited her down here sometime soon. Maybe for the car show."

Wyatt popped up to the edge of the couch, and Jackson abandoned his slouch and closed the distance to Mack.

"Are you serious?" Jackson's voice was rougher than usual.

"It's time to mend things, don't you think?"

Wyatt smoothed a hand over his chin. "I think so, but I never expected you to agree."

"Pop was a good man. A good father. But he had a blind spot when it came to our mother," Mack said. As hard as it was to admit, it was the truth. "And I've had a blind spot when it came to Ford."

Jackson cocked a knee and hooked his thumbs into his front pockets. "Did aliens abduct you?"

Wyatt held up a hand. "I don't want to hear about any anal probes."

Laughter skittered out of all three of them. There was nothing like having brothers—which only increased Mack's determination not to cut Ford out of their family.

"Ford had his reasons for selling out and leaving. Like our mother did all those years ago."

"The gambling," Jackson said.

"The gambling was a symptom of deeper problems. Ford felt trapped, and has for years. He was depressed and battling anxiety. The gambling was a way to escape all of that, until it turned into its own problem. Mom forced him to get help." It was the first time Mack had called her "Mom," and although it hadn't rolled off his tongue, the word expanded and filled the space she'd always occupied in his heart.

"Can you forgive and forget so easily?" Wyatt leaned back into the couch, but a new tension scrunched his shoulders.

"After leaving Mom's house, Ella and I drove to Memphis. Ford and I spent some time hashing things out."

"And?" Wyatt prompted. "No broken bones?"

"None. I'm not sure things are mended, but we're talking again. I invited him home too. He looks better. Healthier. Happier." Mack didn't feel the need to go into the specifics of their talk. Wyatt and Jackson would have to find their own peace with Ford, but with Mack's tacit approval, it would happen.

Wyatt and Jackson exchanged one of their twin looks. A clatter swung everyone's attention to the back of the barn. Wyatt and Mack stood up and Jackson moved between them.

Landrum Abbott, their distant cousin, worked his way toward them, giving the punching bag a flurry of hits on the way by. His good nature shone through his grin.

"Morning, boys. I drove my buddy up to drop his Corvette off. He's a go on all the restorations." He nudged his chin back toward the garage.

"Sweet," Wyatt said. "Let's check it out."

The three of them met Landrum at the punching bag and exchanged handshakes and hugs. Mack led them out and around the garage to the parking lot where the Corvette was parked in a ray of sunlight like the Second Coming. She was a beauty.

Speaking of a beauty, Ella's car was still parked in the lot. He glanced at the house, wondering if he could manage a detour to give her another kiss. He sidestepped toward the magnolia. Landrum grabbed Mack's arm, and Mack did his best to hide a grimace.

"You boys go on. I wanted to talk to Mack for a second," Landrum said.

"I appreciate you recommending us to your buddy." Mack nudged his chin toward the Corvette and her owner. "Getting steady business from Baton Rouge would be a huge boon for the garage."

Landrum was the same age as the twins and had been a star on the Cottonbloom, Louisiana, high school football team. LSU had come calling with a scholarship offer, and Landrum had become a local legend. Although they shared a great-great-great-grandfather, Landrum's darker skin pointed at a scandal no one liked to discuss but everyone was aware of. After LSU and a brief stint in the NFL, Landrum returned to Louisiana and opened a string of successful car dealerships in Baton Rouge.

"Happy to help. In fact, that's what I want to talk to you about."

Mack stifled a yawn, his one cup of Wyatt's weak-ass coffee doing little to combat his fatigue. "What's on your mind?"

"Let's head inside for some privacy."

The unusual shot of seriousness from Landrum had Mack perking up. He led the way inside the garage. The lights were off and the bay doors closed. Mack blinked and stopped in a shaft of weak light from one of the narrow windows.

"What's up?"

"I know the fact Ford sold his quarter away has been chapping your hide. What if I put up the money to buy Ms. Boudreaux out?"

The offer stunned Mack into silence for a few beats. "Are you talking a loan or a partnership?"

"I love cars, I'm in the business, and I wouldn't mind having a piece of the garage. I think you boys are onto something. Plus, Wyatt mentioned your obsession about keeping the garage in Abbott hands." Landrum held up his hands as if surrendering. "I'm an Abbott. Even if our great-great-great-granddaddy didn't want to claim my ancestor."

Mack ran a hand through his hair, trying to order his thoughts. A few weeks ago Landrum's offer would have been heaven sent. But in the moment, he searched for reasons to turn Landrum down. Even though he'd been upfront with Ella about wanting to buy her out, he'd assumed that day would be well into the future. Far enough down the road for him to figure out how to untangle the emotional knot he'd gotten himself in where she was concerned.

"I feel like we would be taking advantage," he finally said.

"No, I want to do this. For you and for me. I see a moneymaker in the restoration business. My contacts would benefit you. If you really want, you can buy me out when you have the cash. But this way, the garage would be in Abbott hands until then. I know that's your ultimate goal. What do you say?"

It *was* his goal. Wasn't it? He didn't know whether it was lack of sleep or the realigning of his life and priorities after finding his mother, settling old debts with Ford, and building a relationship with Ella, but he didn't know what he wanted anymore. "It sounds too good to be true."

"You worried I'll be too much of a pain in the ass?" Landrum grinned.

"That's a given. I wouldn't expect you to get a personality transplant." Mack grinned back. Landrum would be a seamless addition to the garage. He was an Abbott and even better, he was a savvy businessman with contacts and ideas galore. Mack should take the offer. Yet, the words that came out of his mouth were noncommittal. "Can I get back to you after I talk to the boys?"

"Sure, but don't wait too long. I might go spend the money on some other garage." Landrum cocked his head and winked, taking any threat out of his words.

Mack clapped him on the back of his shoulder. "Let's go see if the Corvette is everything I remember it being."

Chapter Twenty

Ella didn't move even after the garage door banged shut. She performed an inventory of her emotions. Did she even have a right to the anger and hurt sucking all the air out of her body?

Mack had never lied to her about wanting Ford's old share of the garage back in family hands. The offer Landrum Abbott had made to Mack made logical sense. Why wouldn't Mack take it?

Eavesdroppers were never rewarded, even if she hadn't meant to listen in. She'd slipped into Mack's office to grab her laptop in case she had emails to return after falling off the grid for a day and night.

She'd been ready to step out and introduce herself until Landrum Abbott's offer hit her ears. Shock had frozen her with her laptop hugged to her chest as her hopes fizzled like a firework dud. An ache spread from her heart to every inch of her body, like she really had been hit by a Mack truck.

Now that the offer was on the table, Mack would take it to his brothers for a vote. It would be unanimous, of that she had no doubt. What he wanted from the beginning was within his grasp—the garage in Abbott hands and her out of his hair.

She didn't need a crystal ball to foresee the future. Without the garage to bind them, they might sleep together a few more times, but his interest would wane and they would drift apart until she would be a speed bump in his memories. A story to tell at holidays. *Remember that time Ford sold his share to Ella Boudreaux. Glad that whole situation is over and done.*

She wouldn't fight him. In fact, she could preempt him. Draw up the papers and drop them off signed. Cauterize the wound. A deep shuddery breath forewarned a rising tide of tears. She had to get home. A threesome in bed with Ben and Jerry was all she craved.

But she still had to escape without running into Mack or his brothers. She squeezed her eyes shut, but teleportation hadn't suddenly been gifted to her. She tiptoed out of Mack's office and peered through the window of the bay door, squinting at the brightness.

The Corvette's owner, Landrum, Jackson, and Wyatt were gathered around the open hood of the car. No sign of Mack. She took a deep breath and made a break for her car. She heard Wyatt call her name, but she only waved over her head in acknowledgment. The inside of her convertible seemed minuscule compared to Mack's truck. Her life would shrink without him in it as well. Banishing the morose thoughts, she glanced around as she started the car. Mack wasn't there. Had he returned to the house to break the news?

She wasn't sticking around to find out. Her tires spun on loose gravel before catching and sending her hurtling down the parish road. Only when the garage was out of sight did she relax into the seat.

Her only goal was to get home and crash in her bed. She

turned onto her street, let her foot off the accelerator, and released a string of curses. Trevor's car was parked in *her* spot on the driveway.

Her hurt and sense of betrayal evaporated in a blast of anger. She was over her ex shouldering his way back into her life. By the time she parked and stalked into her house, she was in a snit. Or more accurately, she was ready to burn shit down, preferably with Trevor in it.

Megan and Trevor were in the den and both stood when she appeared. Megan's eyes were puffy and red, and Trevor's smile was full of smug self-satisfaction. How had she ever thought he was handsome and sophisticated? He was a nasty little bug, and she wore the shoes to smush him.

"I told you not to come here again, Trevor."

"I have business with my *wife*." Although he came around the couch with his hands up in a placating gesture, the edge of a threat was in his voice. "And since you're brainwashing her, I had little choice but to come here."

Ella closed the distance between them and poked him in the chest with her finger. "If brainwashing consists of giving Megan the room to breathe and make her own decisions, then I'm guilty and proud of it. I only wish I'd had the courage to leave you sooner."

"It's best if she comes home with me."

"Best for whom?"

"Megan and I are a family and plan to stay that way. I'm ready to have kids and Megan will be the best mother, don't you agree?"

Ella took a sharp breath. Trevor was treading over an old battleground. He'd pressured Ella to get pregnant, but she'd gone on the pill before their marriage and as time went by, she'd been thankful nothing more than bad memories held them together. A child would have made things harder to bear.

"She will be, but not to your children."

"That's her decision to make." His face made her fist itch to make contact with it.

If Mack had been there, he could have thrown him out the door without breaking a sweat, but she couldn't physically win a fight with Trevor. Ella swallowed. She couldn't think about Mack right now. He was her weakness.

What was Trevor's weakness? His desperation to hold onto youth was a big one.

"Goodness, can you even father children at your age? Have you had your swimmers checked?" She raised her eyebrows and pointed at his crotch.

"I'm fine."

"Oh, I'm sure you are." She marinated her words in sarcasm. "No trouble getting it up yet?"

His face reddened. "That's none of your damn business."

She'd hit a nerve and, like any good scorned ex-wife, she exacerbated the wound. "It's okay, Trevor, I hear it happens to all men at some time or another, especially the older they get."

"Shut. Up."

"I don't have to. This is my house, and you're trespassing." She turned her back on him and faced Megan. "Do you want to go back with him?"

Megan shook her head and bent over, her arms wrapped around her torso, her shoulders scrunched. Ella recognized the desire to make oneself so small as to not be noticed. The fear Trevor had once instilled in Ella was alive and thriving in Megan.

"I'll help you get on your feet. You won't have to do this alone," Ella said.

Megan straightened, her expression firming. Ella's promise hadn't erased Megan's fear, but hopefully it made a dent big enough to house some courage.

"You can't support yourself." Trevor stood next to Ella,

as if the two of them were battling for Megan's soul. "Ella is only keeping you around to spite me. She doesn't give a damn about you."

Megan stood. "I have a job now. I don't need your or my parents' money."

Ella gave her a bracing smile before turning to Trevor. "I'm helping Megan because she's my friend."

Trevor ran a hand through his hair. The disarray gave him a frazzled look. "You don't understand."

"I think I do. You've squandered the business I built for you." Ella kept all emotion out of her voice. Trevor would use any pity against her.

"Who all did you tell?" He directed the question toward Megan, but the fact he didn't launch into a denial was telling.

"Just Ella."

"Jesus." Trevor paced. "I'll bounce back. All I need is one good deal."

His attitude belied his words. Going bankrupt meant losing status in Jackson. It would destroy Trevor.

"I told you that recreational opportunity in Texas was not a good investment. It went belly-up?"

"It was a cluster from the beginning. Poor planning, mismanagement. By the time I tried to sell, it was a sinking ship and no one wanted on." Defeat marked Trevor one feature at a time. First his shoulders fell from bullish to defeated, then his gaze dropped, and a frown exposed age lines she hadn't noticed until now.

"I'm sorry." Ella did feel sorry for him in so many ways. "But you can get back on your feet with hard work."

"Not without your advice, Ella. I didn't realize . . ." He shook his head.

"How totally awesome I am?" She tried to inject some lightness into the moment. She was used to the domineering Trevor or even the obnoxiously confident Trevor, not the contrite, apologetic Trevor. It was disconcerting.

"You're a brilliant businesswoman, and I took you for granted. Or maybe I convinced myself all those deals and great ideas were mostly mine. I don't know."

She'd craved his praise for the long years of their marriage and had never received it. While his words were gratifying, she didn't need them anymore. "Thank you for admitting that."

Trevor licked his lips and gave her a look from under his lashes. "I don't suppose you'd be willing to loan me—"

"Way to ruin a warm, fuzzy moment. It's time for you to go." Ella pointed toward the door.

"Megan?" Trevor faced her.

"It's over, Trevor. I'll be contacting a lawyer to start divorce proceedings."

He blinked back tears and nodded. "I deserve it."

Ella didn't voice her agreement. Kicking a low-down dirty dog while it was injured wasn't fair. She followed him to the door. "You'll get through this."

"Things won't be the same."

"Nope. Can I give you some advice?"

"On real estate?" He perked up.

"No. On life, you moron." She shook her head, feeling confident her words would be lost on him. "Spend some time alone and figure out what you really want."

"Like you?" His voice was mocking. "Are you and the mechanic done?"

As she didn't know how to answer, she went with a classic comeback. "That's none of your business. I wish you all the best." It was *almost* the truth too.

She stood on the front porch until his car disappeared. The moment had the feeling of finality. A least for her. Megan would have to bear the legalities and emotional baggage that came with the divorce.

Holding herself, Megan stood in the hallway looking younger than her years or experience. "I almost went back with him. He actually started to make sense right before you showed up."

"Why didn't you call or text me?"

"I did. But my calls went straight to voice mail."

"My phone died last night." Ella chewed the inside of her mouth. "Megan, this is what you want, right? A divorce?"

"I never thought I'd be divorced at twenty-five. It . . . well, it sucks, but I don't want to be married to him either." Megan stood up a little straighter. "Regan Fournette offered me a job."

"Are you serious?" Ella played dumb, but didn't have to fake her enthusiastic support. "That's fantastic. You're going to kill it."

Optimism brightened Megan like a sunrise. "I'll start with a two-week trial run, but I can do it. I know I can."

"Let's celebrate with ice cream." Ella made straight for the freezer.

"But it's lunchtime."

"I need to drown my sorrows, and ice cream is less troubling than hitting the bottle before happy hour."

"What happened? Something with Mack?"

"Yes, Mack Abbott has rolled over me like a semi."

"I assume you don't mean that in a sexy way?" Megan took a stool at the island.

"In a sexy and a non-sexy way. Basically, every which way you can imagine, I've been flattened." Ella plonked two bowls of ice cream down and slid onto the stool next to Megan. "He's going to borrow money from his cousin to buy me out."

"You don't have to sell. Tell him no." Megan licked her spoon and half-shrugged.

A month ago saying no would have been easy, satisfying even, but no longer. "If he doesn't want me, then I'm not going to force myself on him."

"But you've fought so hard to get them to accept you."

"Things have changed. I want Mack to want me around, and I don't think he does. Not at the garage anyway." She stuck a spoonful of ice cream in her mouth, the resulting brain freeze minor compared to the stabbing pains of her heart.

"What's the plan? Because you always have one." Megan swiveled to face her.

Ella licked her spoon and raised her eyebrows at Megan. She was right, a plan had been formulating since her dash from the garage and Mack. "If you're up for it, you and I are going to go see a lawyer. This afternoon if I can pull some strings. We're going to take our lives back."

Chapter Twenty-One

Mack paced beside his truck, itching to get behind the wheel and tear through the parish to find Ella. Except, he had no idea where she was. He'd called and texted and went to her house to find her car gone and no one there to answer his knocking.

He didn't know whether he had something to worry about or was acting like an idiot. They weren't attached at the hip or even committed to each other. A few hours of radio silence meant nothing. But they'd shared something important the day before and had an amazing morning. His instincts might be rusty, but a discordant feeling had him fretting.

"What's got your panties in a wad?" Wyatt stood in the open bay door, wiping his hands on a towel. They'd pulled the Corvette into the bay and already started work on her.

"Ella isn't returning my calls."

Wyatt sighed a put-upon sigh. "What did you do?"

Mack stopped and pointed at himself. "What did I do? Why do you assume it was me?"

"Because it obviously wasn't Ella. She's too smart."

"That is the most ridiculous—"

A car coming down the parish road cut him off. He

quickstepped to the edge of the parking lot, but it wasn't Ella. Disappointment coursed through him.

The silver Lexus slowed, turned on its blinker, and pulled into the parking lot. Mack didn't recognize the man who got out of the car. He was tall and dark-skinned. His black-rimmed glasses and rumpled suit gave him a teacher vibe.

The man glanced around, his gaze landing squarely on Mack. He straightened the ends of his LSU yellow-and-purple tie and approached.

"Mr. Mack Abbott?"

"That's me. What can I do for you? Problem with the car?"

The man glanced over his shoulder toward his car with a surprised expression. "No, I'm not here about my car. My name's Victor Halstead."

Mack exchanged a handshake with the man.

Victor cleared his throat. "I'm actually here to present you with these." He held out a sheaf of papers.

Mack glanced from the papers to Victor's earnest-looking expression back to the papers. Incredulity crept into his voice. "Are you serving me?"

"Nothing of the sort. I'm a lawyer, not an officer of the court. This is a contract detailing the sale of my client's portion of your business back to you. At a very favorable—ridiculous, actually—price."

Mack stared at the stark-white papers. His head swam, and his heart kicked at his ribs. This is exactly what he'd wanted and hoped for and dreamed about. He was going to be sick all over the man's shiny brown loafers.

"Give me the CliffsNotes version." Mack's voice came out like gravel.

"Basically, you transfer the money into the account listed, sign the papers, and the transaction will be final. If you want to take care of this right now, one of your brothers can witness, and I can notarize the contract." Victor moved the papers closer to Mack, forcing him to take them. It felt like a surrender.

"I need to talk to Ella before I sign anything."

"In that case, I'll leave the contract with you and head home, Mr. Abbott." Victor checked his watch. "I don't usually work on Saturdays."

"Doing a favor for Ella, are you?" Mack's hand tightened, wrinkling the papers.

"A favor she's paying me well for." The man's grin was boyish. Ella would chew him up and spit him out. "My number is listed on the cover page. Call me and we can make it legal at your convenience.

"Make it legal," Mack muttered as the man drove away. The words went on repeat, and a shot of adrenaline had him feeling queasy. *Make it legal.* Was that the answer?

"This is a good thing, right?" Wyatt sounded as unsure as Mack felt.

"I guess so."

"You can buy her out, but still date her. It doesn't have to change things."

But it *would* change things. Mack wasn't naïve enough to think that his and Ella's relationship wouldn't be affected by something so monumental. He rolled the papers up and tucked them into his back pocket. "I need a drink. Care to join me?"

"Watching you get plastered and rail on the world sounds delightful compared to what I have to do tonight. Sutton has strong-armed me into working on seating arrangements for the rehearsal dinner. Isn't a chair a chair?" Wyatt's half smile was indulgent.

"I do not envy you." Even as Mack said the words, he recognized the lie.

"Jackson's already gone up to the loft with Willa. You want me to holler at him?"

"I don't need a babysitter. You head out. I'll close up the shop. I don't have anything better to do apparently."

Wyatt waved out the window and tapped the horn twice as he drove off. Mack went through the motions of locking up the garage. The contract was like an anchor in his back pocket. For what seemed like too often recently, his decision-making process was stymied.

Part of him wanted to take Wyatt's advice. Sign on the dotted line and get Ford's percentage back into his hands. It had been his goal from the outset, after all, and would remove the garage as a sticking point between him and Ella. On the surface, it was a win-win. Or was it?

She had thrown herself head and heart first into planning the car show. She wanted to help Marigold and Dave in their time of need as much as she wanted to see the garage succeed.

By signing the contract, he would be taking that away from her. And he had a feeling, before coming to work at the garage, she had lacked direction and purpose and passion. He could only imagine how he'd feel if the garage was taken away from him.

Two choices bubbled up through the mire. He could leave the situation to fester or he could confront her. His experience with Ford taught him festering led to fractures and encouraged doubts and resentments. The thought of whatever was going on with Ella ending with such rancor made him feel ill. If it actually happened, he might not survive.

He stuffed his hands into his front pockets and meandered toward his house. Halfway across the yard, his aunts' Crown Vic came into view around the curve. He met them in the parking lot. Hyacinth rolled the driver's side window down and cocked her elbow on the sill. "Hi-ya there, Mack."

"Hey, Aunt Hy." He ducked slightly to catch his aunt Hazel's eyes. "What can I do for you?"

"We were on our way to our bridge group and thought we'd perform a little drive-by. How are you?" Hazel asked.

Her question wasn't born out of mere politeness, but a knowing of what had transpired between him and his mother and Ford. Unless his aunt Hazel really was a witch, she couldn't know about the papers in his back pocket.

"Life is moving right along."

Hazel leaned over the console to see him better. "Things with your mother and Ford are worked out?"

"Worked out? Let's not go crazy. But we left things better than they've been in years. You'll be happy to know I invited both of them down to Cottonbloom."

"Will Ford come home?" Hyacinth's voice reflected a rare somberness.

"I don't know if Cottonbloom will ever be his home again, but I'll get him back down here for a visit. He seems to be getting his life straightened out up there."

Hyacinth squeezed his arm with a thin, bony hand, the one part of her that reflected her years. "A visit would be most welcome. Hazel and I have been thinking we should have done more."

As he waved the aunts off, the "more" bothered Mack as well. But how much more, and exactly what he could have done for Ford was a mystery. His regrets were a burden he would bear until their family life reached a new equilibrium.

Ella was the here and now, and he vowed to do anything and everything to make it right with her. He would leave no room for regrets. If she rejected him, he'd live at least knowing he went down fighting.

Around the fifth call that went unanswered and unreturned, he accepted she didn't want to talk to him much less see him. What had happened between the time he'd left her in his bed and now? Not bothering to turn on the TV, he threw the contract on the coffee table, sat in his armchair, and stared at the innocuous paper spelling his possible doom.

In the silence, his thoughts veered toward chaos. He'd go crazy if he sat here all night thinking about her and wondering what she was thinking about him. His choices included getting drunk by himself or being productive. Decision made, he made his way out back to his metal working station.

None of his current projects grabbed his interest so he picked up a sheet of metal and began cutting and working it. Curves emerged. Without conscious thought he'd fashioned the first petal of a magnolia flower. He continued until he'd completed a magnolia bloom made from metal. More than anything, what he'd created represented Ella. A delicate beauty with indomitable strength.

What he wanted—needed—was the real thing. The real woman.

He showered and dressed in jeans and a T-shirt. Laying the contract in the passenger seat, he set out across the river. He had no plan and no idea what had driven her to such drastic measures. In fact, he couldn't even put a finger on how he was feeling. Anger. Desperation. Disappointment.

Her car was in the driveway, and he blew out a slow breath, preparing himself for what might be an epic fail.

He rang the doorbell. Megan answered, her gaze darting to the papers in his hand then to his eyes. She didn't greet or question him, only opened the door and made a sweeping gesture with her hand.

He skipped any polite preamble. "Where is she?"

"She's taking a walk out back."

He nodded once and made his way to the sliding doors between the kitchen and den. A large deck jutted from the back of the house with stairs leading down to a field. A magnolia tree stood halfway between the house and river and injected a sense of fate.

Full night was upon them, the call of insects growing louder. He stopped where the light from the house petered into darkness. No sign of her, but he could feel her close. The magnolia tree was his beacon in the half moon.

When he was a dozen feet away, she stepped out of the glossy green leaves. She was in jeans and a thin white T-shirt that glowed in the moonlight like one of the magnolia flowers at her shoulder.

"What are you doing here so late?" Instead of the expected animosity, there was only curiosity.

"Your buddy Victor dropped the contract off."

"Hours ago. Why didn't you sign it?"

"I needed to talk to you first."

"It's a dream come true, isn't it? It's what you've wanted since I started."

"It's what I wanted *when* you started." He moved closer.

"That's what I said."

"Not exactly. Yes, when you started, I wanted to buy you out, but things have changed."

"Have they?"

"I sure thought so this morning."

"I thought so too, before I heard you and your cousin."

His head whirled, and his reaction was knee-jerk as he unspooled his conversation with Landrum. "You were eavesdropping?"

"No." The adamant denial lost its punch with the way her gaze dropped from his. "Not on purpose anyway. I was in the office grabbing my laptop when you two came in. I was going to step out, but I heard his offer."

"Then, you also heard I didn't accept it."

"You didn't turn it down either."

"He caught me off guard.

"You want the garage in Abbott hands. I get that. In fact, I've been selfish for hanging on. I told myself when you had the money, I would bow out like the lady I pretend to be. So, it's yours. All you have to do is sign."

He crumbled the papers in his fist. "Drawing up a sales contract and having your pretty-boy lawyer deliver it was pretty low."

"I thought it would be less messy this way." She crossed her arms over her chest and popped a hip. "Sign those, and I'll be out of your hair and the garage for good. This is your dream come true."

His dream come true. Why did she keep saying that? He let the statement roll around his head and heart until the truth crystallized. "Nope."

It wasn't enough to wad the papers into a ball. He had to destroy the contract. He ripped the pages down the middle, then ripped them again and again, until the breeze caught some pieces and sent them whirling into the air.

"I'll have Victor print another copy and drop it off Monday morning." She crossed her arms over her chest.

"I'll rip it up too. And if you send me another copy, I'll run over it and leave rubber marks. Or dip it in oil. Or take a blowtorch to it. Whatever it takes."

She shook her head and gave an exasperated little sigh that she somehow made sexy. "What is wrong with you? I'm giving you everything you wanted."

"What about what you want? I thought the garage was important to you. What about your brother? The car show? Marigold and Dave?"

"The garage is—*was*—important to me." She ran a hand through her hair.

He took a step closer. "Am I important to you?"

The silence was unnerving. Finally, her voice thick, she said, "What do you want from me?"

"I want anything and everything you're willing to give me." He stuffed the pieces of the contract into his pockets and ran his hands down the legs of his jeans. Nerves set off tremors in his body.

"I'm basically giving you the garage. What could be more important than that?"

"*You*. You are more important to me than the garage."

"I don't understand."

"It's simple," he said. "I want you more than I want the garage."

"Simple? You want me to keep my share of the garage?"

"I want to see you every day at work. Hell, I want to see you every night in my bed. What I don't want is for the garage to come between us."

"There's an 'us'?" She obviously wasn't a believer. Yet. And could he blame her?

"I sure thought there was an 'us' this morning." He stepped closer. "I love you, woman. Don't you know that?"

She took a step back as if his words had packed a physical punch. Then, as if he'd applied jumper cables to her, she sprang into life, crashing into him. He wrapped his arms around her and would have been content to never let her go again.

"I didn't know that," she whispered in his ear.

"You do now."

"I love you too. It scares me how much."

"I'm scared too, Ella. After talking to Wyatt and Jackson, I think it's supposed to be scary. And exciting."

"Your brothers." Dread weighed her voice. "Won't they be upset if you don't take Landrum's offer?"

"They don't know about Landrum's offer."

She pulled back enough to put them nose-to-nose. "I thought you boys voted on everything."

"This is between you and me and no one else. But I'm not too worried. They like you. More than they like me most days." His attempt at teasing her didn't lighten her expression.

"What happens now?"

It was a good question. And one that could have many answers. He stuck with an easy one. "How about we take things day by day?"

She buried her face in his neck and nodded. His answer felt a little like a cop-out, but she didn't want to delve any further into the future than he did. The ground they'd already covered was immense and left her reeling. He loved her. Not only did he love her, but he loved her more than his precious garage.

"How about we start with tonight?" she asked with a naughty lilt.

His breath shuddered out. "You read my mind."

The softness of the night gathered around them. The scent of the magnolia sweetened the loamy air coming off the river in the distance. Contentment washed over her.

"Will you come home with me?" he whispered.

"My bed is closer." She looped her arms around his neck and leaned back.

"Yeah, but . . ." He shot a look toward her massive back deck.

When she'd bought the house, she'd planned to buy a grill and decorate with potted flowers and plants. The deck was still bare.

"Are you worried about Megan? I have a lock on my bedroom door."

"It's not that. It's just your house is so . . . so . . . big."

The truth hit her like a slap upside the head. "You hate my house."

"I don't *hate* it."

"But you don't like it."

"It's cold. Impersonal. Nothing like you."

She took his meaning, and it had nothing to do with the thermostat. Her house had no personality, and she hadn't done her part to bring life and memories to the wood and brick.

He continued. "I know my house isn't up to your standards. It's too small. There's plenty of land though. We could add on. A sunroom in the back. An extra bedroom. Whatever you want. Although, it might take a while to save up the money."

She slipped a hand to his chest and grabbed a fistful of cotton. "Are you asking me to move in with you?"

"Yeah, I guess I am." He sounded as surprised as she felt.

Knocking down walls together negated the inherent casualness of taking things day by day. She should tear off in the opposite direction in terror. Instead, she tightened her hold on his shirt. "Okay. Although you might regret asking once you see how much closet space I'll need."

"You can have it all. I don't care."

"Mack, there's something you should know."

He tensed against her as if expecting a blow. "What?"

"I'm kind of rich."

"I don't want to use the money you got in your divorce."

"I started Magnolia Investments after my divorce, and I've doubled my money. Even this house"—she gestured to the stately mansion—"was bought because I'll make a profit when I sell it. I didn't buy it because I thought it would be a home. It was an investment."

He chuckled and tightened his hold. "So you're the mysterious donor. I should have guessed. I don't give a damn about your money, by the way. I want you because you're stubborn and passionate and aren't afraid to put me in my place." In his voice was a truth she'd been searching for all her life.

When men handed compliments her way, they landed in the charming and beautiful categories. Not Mack. He saw a different woman when he looked at her. The real one. Messy and sometimes unsure but fierce. And fiercely in love with him.

"You really do love me." Her laugh scared a roosting bird out of the branches of the magnolia. As if finally on the same wavelength, they fit themselves together and strolled toward her too-big, cold house. "What am I going to tell Megan?"

"She's not moving in with us." An edge of warning was in his voice.

"Of course not." It was premature to think about selling the house anyway. Too many what-ifs circulated in her head. Having a safe place to retreat if things went south would be smart. "Let me throw some essentials in a bag, and we can head over the river."

"We're going to lock the doors, pull the drapes, and ignore everyone. I promised you a sunrise."

Before they left the moonlight for the artificial light shining through her windows, she stopped him and pulled him down for a kiss. Even though they'd been together that morning, she was starved for his touch. The events of the day had ripped them apart, and she'd experienced the start of a life without him, hating every moment.

But he'd come to her and laid everything on the line for her—the garage, his heart—and she would never take that for granted. A thrumming urgency had her pulling away, taking his hand, and quickstepping toward the house.

She left him waiting in the den while she threw an assortment of clothes in a suitcase. As she was packing up her toiletries, a soft knock sounded.

"Come in."

Megan shuffled in. "Are you leaving for good?"

Ella paused and propped her shoulder in the bathroom doorway. "I'm going over the river with Mack."

"Is this because of me? I can get my own place."

"Of course not. I might eventually sell this place, but

you're welcome to stay until then. In fact, you'd be doing me a favor. Right now though, I want to be with Mack. I love him."

"I'm happy for you." Megan glanced away, but not before Ella noticed the tears in her eyes.

Ella hesitated a moment before pulling Megan in for a hug. "It's going to be okay. Not tomorrow, or the next day, but eventually."

"I know." A laugh skittered out of Megan. "If you survived and even thrived after leaving Trevor, I can too."

Ella pulled away. The smile on Megan's face was strained, but hope flickered. "You certainly can."

"I'll lock up after you guys leave and keep an eye on the house until you decide what to do. If you want, I can work on staging it for the market." Megan was quieter and more circumspect than the woman who had landed on her doorstep. Hard times either broke a person or applied a maturing lacquer. Ella was gratified to see Megan fell in the latter category.

"That would be fabulous." Ella looked around her bedroom. It already felt like it belonged to someone else. She walked out without a second's hesitation.

"Ready?" Mack took the suitcase out of her hand.

She nodded and closed the front door behind them. She'd be back to get the rest of her things, but a chapter of her life was ending. An important chapter. She followed Mack in her car, the trip spanning only a few miles, but crisscrossing years of her memories.

She loved Mack and followed him not because she was deferential or meek, but because she knew what she wanted and was ready to grab hold as his equal. They would disagree and fight, but Mack would never belittle her or intimidate her into submission.

By the time they reached his house by the garage, her

past had realigned itself in the background. The future was what mattered now.

They didn't speak. Didn't have to speak. As soon as the door was shut and locked, she pushed his T-shirt up and off. He fumbled the zipper of her jeans down while shuffling backward toward the bedroom. Grabbing the open flaps of her waistband, he forced her to walk with him.

Not that she fought him or the destination. Her shirt floated to the floor of the hallway. Her bra was left hanging on the doorknob. It was a race to see who could get their jeans off faster. He won and was waiting on his back in the bed, his grin barely discernible in the dim room.

She crawled over him and lowered herself until they were welded as close as the metal he loved so much. It was a moment she would always remember. "I love you."

"Love you too." He slapped her butt, and she squealed with surprised laughter.

Their lovemaking was wild and a little rough, as if he too realized how close they'd come to screwing things up. The night passed in long talks, fits of sleep, and bouts of sex until the sun rose, casting an orange glow around the room.

She was reeling from the roller coaster of emotions, her mind jumping from path to path with no grounding logic. "I wonder if Grayson knows."

"Knows what?" His hand played in her hair.

"Knows all of this happened because of him."

He stilled before hugging her close. "I'd like to think the people who've gone before are looking down with pride."

"Your dad?"

"Yeah. Not sure how Pop would have reacted to us reconciling with Mom, but I hope he knows it doesn't make us love him any less."

"Of course, you don't. It's not like we have a finite amount of love to go around. The room gets bigger. You've made room for Willa and Sutton, right?"

"You're right." He kissed the top of her head.

Her eyes fluttered close on a wave of contentment. She tried to open them to watch the sunrise, but they refused to obey. "I like the sound of that."

He murmured more words, but she drifted away, safe in his arms and knowing that they had time to share everything. Maybe even a lifetime.

Epilogue

The next weeks passed in a blur for Ella. While Mack was elbows deep in car restorations, she was neck deep in planning the car show fundraiser for Marigold and Dave. They'd scaled back from a weekend to a full day's worth of activities, with thoughts to expand in future years.

It had taken time for Marigold to come around to accepting the idea of a fundraiser. Ella cajoled and Mack ordered, but finally, it was the common sense voice of Dave who swung the tide. They couldn't afford to not take the helping hand.

Still, Marigold insisted on working with Ella as much as her schedule allowed. Ella was grateful not just for the extra pair of hands, but also for the burgeoning friendship. Through Mack, Ella had met another layer of Cottonbloom—one that threw backyard cookouts, not wine-and-cheese mixers.

She moved in both worlds, the only constant being Mack. He was at her side during social events in Cottonbloom, Mississippi. Well, if not by her side exactly, then holding up a wall while she greased wheels and solicited donations.

Jackson, Willa, Wyatt, and Mack were gathered in the office while Ella ticked off items from her to-do list.

"T-shirts?"

"They made me sweat, but I got the order in yesterday," Willa said. River gave a little bark from her side as if she knew she was somehow involved.

"Hazel and Hy have the bake sale coordinated through their church group." Wyatt rocked back on two legs of the chair, his foot on the side of the desk. "And I took care of getting permits with Gloria and her counterpart on the Mississippi side. We have a hundred cars registered to take part in the judging, but my guess is more will show up to be seen and to see what else is out there."

"I have booths lined up to advertise our services, with brochures and postcards and magnets to take home." Jackson was propped against the back wall, his arms and feet crossed.

"I have the food and drink carts booked and ready. They've all agreed to give ten percent of profits back to the Dave Dunlap Fund. Mack, did you finish making out the judging forms?" Ella looked up from her list.

"I did. The four of us will judge and confer as needed. What time do you want to present the awards?" Mack paced in the open space behind her chair.

He had gotten progressively more agitated as the days ticked down to the car show, but Ella couldn't pinpoint his nerves to the actual show or the fact his mother and Ford were expected down.

"I'm thinking right before dinner on Saturday. Hopefully, that will encourage people to stay to eat and enjoy the music," Ella said.

Delmar Fournette had volunteered the services of his bluegrass band for Saturday night, and Ella had jumped at the offer.

"I'll get the numbered tags for the car entries printed

this week and triple-check everything, but I think we're in good shape. Anyone have issues to discuss?" Ella tilted the clipboard into her chest and tapped her fingers on the back.

After a unanimous shake of their heads, everyone got back to work. The pressure was on to complete the Corvette for Landrum's friend in time for the show. For the rest of the week, last-minute details kept Ella busy from morning to night. Still, she and Mack found time to talk in bed after making love.

"I can't believe the show is tomorrow. You nervous?" Mack ran his fingers up and down her spine.

Ella was face down on the bed where she'd collapsed. She turned to the side and pulled the sheet up under her arms. "Yes, but I've thrown enough parties that I'm expecting to have to put out unexpected fires. You can't anticipate everything that could go wrong. What about you?"

He flopped back on the pillow and covered his eyes. "I'm keyed up."

"Is it because of your mom and Ford?"

"No. Partly," he qualified with a sigh. "What if things go to hell?"

She snuggled into his side. "They won't."

"How do you know that?"

"You're too stubborn to let it."

Mack chuckled, but an electric energy manifested itself during the night, driving him out of bed before the sun rose. Which was saying something, considering Ella was naked under his covers. His mother's and Ford's return to Cottonbloom did worry him, but the decision he'd made regarding Ella and the garage struck him with even more anxiety.

Mack didn't slow down until after the award for Best in Show was given out to a father-son duo and their '64

Corvette Stingray. By Mack's reckoning, they not only raised twenty thousand dollars for Marigold and Dave, but if even a fraction of the people who'd expressed interest in using the garage for their restorations followed through, they would be booked for the rest of the year, not counting their usual work.

While the official part of the car show was over, Delmar's bluegrass band kept the energy humming. If anything, the crowd swelled with locals interspersed among the out-of-towners. Mack stepped back and surveyed the scene. It was incredible what Ella had organized. A rousing success by anyone's estimation.

"You should be proud of yourself, Mack." His mother had come up without him noticing.

"It was Ella. I would have never come up with this idea or been able to execute it." He snuck a look at his mom.

She had been nervous on her arrival that morning, but the aunts had welcomed her home and Mack had found himself hugging her before considering the ramifications. It had felt good though. Like the universe was righted. "I'm glad you decided to come."

"Thank you for inviting me." While a formality remained, a warmth he remembered as a child drew him to her.

"I'm sorry I haven't been able to spend much time with you today."

"I understand. We have tomorrow and beyond."

The aunts had planned a lunch the next day for his mother and Ford, and Mack was both excited and nervous to have his family back under the same roof after so long.

She patted his arm. "I'm going to have some of Rufus's barbeque before he runs out. I've never found any better." He watched her weave through the crowd, an achiness in his chest.

"She's a good person." Ford had taken their mother's spot at his side. He too was watching her.

"She is. I wish . . ." Mack shook his head.

"I know. Me too. But wishes aren't worth a fairy's fart. All we can do is accept our mistakes, forgive ourselves, and move on."

Mack shifted to face Ford. "Since when did you become so wise?"

A grin flashed. "Since therapy."

Mack laughed and threw an arm around Ford's shoulders. His laugh petered into an awkward silence. "I'm sorry I was—"

"Can we stop apologizing? Because if you keep going, then I'll have to take a turn, and we'll be here all night." Ford sent a half smile in Mack's direction.

Mack gestured at the bag in Ford's hand bearing the Quilting Bee's name and logo. "Are you going all Zen and taking up knitting or something?"

"No. I got something to decorate my new place." Ford reached into the bag a pulled out one of Mack's metal magnolia blossoms.

Heat suffused his face. Ella had talked him into selling his creations on consignment in the Quilting Bee. Jackson and Wyatt had been surprised to hear about his hobby but had kept their ribbing to a minimum. Still, he wasn't exactly comfortable revealing this side of himself. He mumbled, "I do it as a stress reliever."

"It's cool, bro." Ford ran his thumb along one of the petals, his voice dropping as if he too was confessing something uncomfortable. "It reminds me of home. And you guys. It'll have a place of honor on my desk at work."

Mack cleared the emotion from his throat. "You're staying for lunch tomorrow, right?"

"Wouldn't miss it. I'm looking forward to fatted lamb." Ford strolled off, his laughter trailing. Mack smiled.

His pop's death had spun his life into chaos and uncertainty. Now, almost two years later, he was a better son and brother and lover because of the changes. Urgency had him scanning the crowd. It was now or never.

He spotted Ella close to the raised platform where the bluegrass band played. He made his way toward her, pasting on a smile and shaking hands, but inwardly cursing the delay. Finally, he reached out and touched her shoulder. She swung around. The smile that came to her face lit her from within. And it was for him.

He leaned in so she could hear him over the music. "Can we talk?"

She nodded and took his hand, leading him behind the platform and along the grassy bank of the river until they left the crowd behind. The sun was setting, turning the sky brilliant colors. The wildflowers along the bank swayed in the slight breeze.

"It went even better than I expected," Ella said. "Once I get totals in from the food vendors, I'll have a better idea how much money we collected for Marigold and Dave."

"You did an amazing job."

"It was a team effort. I was thinking—"

"There's something I need to say." He cleared his throat and shifted on his feet. This moment had been percolating for weeks. Ever since the day the lawyer had dropped off the contract he'd ripped up.

"You know having the garage in Abbott hands has been an important goal for me."

Trepidation tempered the joy on her face. "I assumed you were past that."

"I'm not. It's still something I want."

"I'll sell you my part, Mack, if it's that damn important to you." She propped her hands on her hips. "I thought I was just as important though."

He wanted to smile at the ignition of passion, but he was

too nervous. "I don't want to buy you out. I want to make you an Abbott." He cleared his throat. "In my bumbling way, I'm asking you to marry me."

"Marry you?" All the fire in her eyes had been replaced by shock.

"I want to make it legal. I love you and want us to be partners in everything for forever. If you'll take me." He fished out the ring box that had been burning a hole in his pocket all day and dropped to one knee.

She grasped her throat and her mouth opened and closed, but nothing came out.

"Geez, woman, put me out of my misery one way or another."

"Yes. Of course, yes. Oh my God." She held out a trembling hand, and his was none too steady as he slipped the ring on her finger. "I love you, too, but I thought you were against marriage."

He recalled the conversation they'd had in his truck on the way to Rufus's. It seemed a long time ago. "I had a change of opinion. What about you? I thought your experience ruined you on marriage forever."

She grinned. "I had a change of heart."

His heart swelled and his head grew swimmy. He stood and leaned in to kiss her. A kiss full of promises and endless sunsets and sunrises.

Turn the page for a bonus epilogue!

A Cottonbloom Wedding: Wyatt and Sutton

Wyatt opened his eyes to the sound of rain on the roof of the barn. Through the skylights, the rain turned the world gray, masking time. His internal clock told him it was midmorning. Later than he usually rose, but plenty of time considering the wedding wasn't until three in the afternoon.

The wedding.

His stomach flopped like a frog trying to escape a gigging. He was excited, but nervous. Even though he and Sutton had been living together for months, marriage was a commitment he'd never thought he'd make. Not because he didn't believe in the institution, but because as an Abbott twin, he hadn't expected to escape the curse. None of many sets of Abbott twins through the years, his aunts Hazel and Hyacinth included, had married.

Movement at the door to his old room drew his head up. Rubbing his eyes, Jackson shuffled in, lay down next to Wyatt, and pulled the quilt to his chin. It felt like the old days when they'd shared a room and bunk beds. Having his twin brother close was his security blanket—a comfort beyond measure.

"Morning, sunshine," Jackson said in a scratchy voice. "How's your head?"

Wyatt, Jackson, Mack, and Ford had stayed up late drinking beer and talking. They'd tried to take Wyatt out for a bachelor party but all he'd really wanted was to hang with his brothers. Having Ford back in the fold was like finally getting their family engine running smooth.

Ford had crashed with Mack, Ella had stayed at her old house with Megan, and Willa had stayed with Sutton, which left Wyatt and Jackson back where they had started so many years ago.

"Now that you mention it, my head hurts, but I've been in worse shape," Wyatt said.

"You remember that time we snuck out into the woods with a bottle of Jack?"

Just the memory made him feel queasy. "I couldn't sit down for a week after Pop got hold of us."

Their laughter joined before petering out, leaving the sound of the rain. Besides his brother, the feeling of being close to nature was the one thing he missed about living in the loft with the skylights overhead.

"Rain is supposed to be good luck for a wedding," Jackson said.

"Says who? Seems more like a bad omen to me." Although his voice was light, he was only half-teasing.

"You worried about the curse striking you like a bolt of lightning? Relax. I already broke it for you." Jackson knuckle-punched Wyatt's arm, but it lacked any force from their prone positions.

Jackson and Willa had run off to the justice of the peace and gotten hitched months before without telling anyone or making a big hullaballoo about it. In fact, they were back to work the next day as if nothing momentous had happened. Yet, Wyatt could sense a change in Jackson like a river carving a new path through bedrock.

"I wish I could have talked Sutton into eloping like you and Willa."

"This wedding is important to Sutton and her mama. All you have to do is stand up there in your monkey suit and do what they tell you to do."

Jackson was right, of course. Sutton had designed and sewed her own wedding dress and her mama had invited half the parish to witness the vows. He would endure as long as Sutton was happy. At least he wouldn't be alone—his brothers would be standing up front with him in identical monkey suits.

A snicker born of a long history of brotherly torture snuck out of Wyatt. "Getting Mack into a tux might be my life's greatest accomplishment."

"He acted like a disgruntled toddler at the fitting until Ella whispered something in his ear that made him blush. After that, he was the definition of compliant."

A grin spread over Wyatt's face. "I wish I could have seen him. I'll have to admit the garage is a more pleasant workplace since Ella tamed the beast."

Jackson's laugh faded into his characteristic seriousness. "I'm glad he's happy. Ella's a good woman."

"Good? She's a saint for dealing with Mack's grumpy ass." Wyatt sat up. "Speaking of asses, we should move ours. Sutton's mama will string us all up if we throw off her schedule. I swear she has it down to the minute."

Jackson grabbed Wyatt's arm before he could rise. "Hey, bro. I'm glad you're happy too."

Wyatt stared for a moment into Jackson's eyes. Wyatt's breath squeezed out of his lungs. Their shared family history—good and bad—was written in Jackson's eyes and, no doubt, reflected back from Wyatt's. The fact all of the brothers, including Ford in his roundabout way, had found their places in the world was a near miracle.

No more needed to be said. Jackson let go and the solemnity of moment passed into a kind of excited peace as they got ready. They laughed through tying each other's bow tie. After smoothing the lapels of his black jacket, Wyatt gave a twirl.

"How do I look?"

"Not as god-awful ugly as usual." Jackson smiled, his eyes twinkling.

Coming from one of his brothers, it was a compliment. Wyatt was ready to get hitched.

He took one more look around the loft. Although he hadn't lived there in months, and Willa's touch could be seen from the matching dishes in the kitchen to the built-in bookcases flanking the TV and filled with books, a sense of melancholy finality overcame him.

But he was ready to move on to the next phase of his life with Sutton. He jogged down the stairs and didn't look back. The back barn doors were open a couple of feet, the rain obscuring the woods and puddling in the entry.

Ford and Mack milled around the couch. They too were in their rented tuxes. Ford's bow tie was neatly tied and his jacket was on while Mack's tie hung loose and his jacket was thrown over the back of the couch.

"There's the man." Mack pulled him into a big bear hug, lifting his feet off the ground like he used to when they were kids. Mack was still the biggest and strongest of all of them. Once released, Wyatt exchanged a fist bump with Ford, then the four of them stood in a quiet semicircle.

"Pop would happy to see us all together," Wyatt said gruffly.

"All of us settled and happy and the garage thriving," Ford added.

Mack clapped him on the back. "He'd be proud. Of all of us."

Age-old rivalries and tensions had been finally vanquished. Having all his brothers there to stand next to him while he took the biggest leap of his life was more important than he could put into words. Yet, he had to try.

"Guys, I don't want to get too sappy, but—"

A crack of thunder had them all jumping. The rain outside turned from a downpour into a deluge.

"That was close. Lightning must have hit a tree." Jackson peered out the back door careful to stay out of the spray of rain. "Should we wait until it dies down?"

A niggle of unease had the hairs on Wyatt's neck standing on end. Or maybe it was the electricity vibrating the air. He checked his watch. They had plenty of time, yet an urgency to get to the church had Wyatt pacing.

Fifteen minutes later, the rain had eased up enough to see the tree line in the distance. Sure enough, a pine tree looked as if God had taken an axe and split the trunk down the middle. Wyatt swallowed and turned to his brothers. "Not sure it's going to get any better for a while. Let's hit it."

They filed out of the barn and made a run for Mack's black truck, shaking the rain out of their hair and brushing their jackets once they were safe and dry inside. Mack cranked the engine, flipped the wipers to their fastest speed, and eased them onto the road where water sluiced across the pavement in mini-waves.

Mack gripped the steering wheel with both hands and sat forward in his seat, his concentration focused on the rain-camouflaged road. Wyatt pulled out his phone and pulled up his weather app.

A yell came from Ford in the front seat. A heartbeat later, the truck jerked to the left and hydroplaned. They came to an abrupt stop. Wyatt's head knocked into the door, and he blinked to clear the ringing in his ears. Tilted into a shallow gully, the front end of the truck was against a tree. Luckily, Mack hadn't been going fast enough to do major damage.

"Everyone okay?" Mack turned in his seat, his brows low.

"What happened?" Jackson asked.

"Looked like a white-tailed deer to me. Jumped right out in front of us." Ford unclipped his seat belt and turned too.

"I hit the brakes and managed to miss him but skid out." Mack blew out a breath. "How you doing back there, Wyatt?"

"Fine." The ringing in his ears had abated but the side of his face throbbed. He shifted to check himself in the rearview mirror.

"Ah, shit. Your face." Mack looked horrified. Which in turn freaked Wyatt out.

Wyatt touched his cheek. It was wet. He looked at his fingers. They were red. Spatters dotted the front of his formerly pristine white shirt. "I'm bleeding."

Jackson turned him around and grimaced. "You busted your eyebrow open and your eye is already swelling. Damn."

"Sutton is going to kill me," Mack muttered.

Ford handed a napkin back to Wyatt. He pressed it against his eyebrow. "No one's going to die today. I'll slap a Band-Aid on it and one of you will change shirts with me. No one will be looking at me anyway. Let's see how good the four-wheel drive is in this monster."

Mack cranked the truck. The engine clicked but didn't turn over.

"On the other hand, Sutton may indeed kill you if you can't get me to the church on time." Wyatt tried to inject a tease, but the anxious knot in his stomach elbowed out his sense of humor.

Mack ran a hand through his hair. "It could be something simple like the battery cable coming loose. Let me check."

He popped the hood and slipped out into the pelting rain. Two minutes later, he dropped the hood and Wyatt expelled a sigh of relief. That had been fast. Mack climbed back in accompanied by a litany of curses.

"Radiator is busted. We're stuck." He punched the steering wheel.

Jackson said, "Alright, not a tragedy. Is Landrum in town yet? He'd be happy to help out."

"He had a deal to close and wasn't coming up until today." Wyatt leaned his head back and closed his eyes. "The aunts should be able to squeeze us into the Crown Vic."

"I was going to pick them up later so they wouldn't have to drive in this mess. What about Ella or Willa?"

"Ella'd have to make four trips with her tiny convertible. Plus, I'd rather Sutton didn't hear about this so she won't stress. I'll call the aunts." Wyatt grabbed his phone from where it had fallen on the floorboard. The screen was covered in tiny cracks and remained dark. "My phone is busted worse than my face."

Mack picked up his phone and punched a contact. Wyatt met his gaze in the mirror.

"Aunt Hy. The boys and I need a favor."

While Mack gave her a brief rundown, Wyatt asked, "Does anyone else appreciate the irony?"

"What? The fact three and a half—sorry, Ford—mechanics are sitting in a broken-down truck on the side of the road waiting for a lift?" Jackson settled back in his seat and propped his foot up on the middle console.

"That, but mostly because we're waiting for Hy and Hazel to roll up in their Crown Vic. A car that's been in our shop more than any car ever." Wyatt checked the napkin. His face seemed to have stopped bleeding.

"Considering the number of times we've changed the

oil and air filter and given it a once-over, it's the most reliable car in the parish," Jackson said.

"As long as Aunt Hy doesn't hit anything on the way over." Mack elbowed Jackson's foot off the console.

"What? Like you did?" Jackson shot back.

"Touché."

"What? You can't be serious." Sutton's stomach took a flying leap to flail on the floor. "How did it happen?"

Clutching her robe together with her hair coiffed and shellacked into place, Sutton's mother paced in front of the twin bed Sutton had slept in as a child. Her teenage posters still decorated the walls, giving the room a time-warp feel. Sitting on the bed, Willa looked like Sutton felt—horrified.

"Bad oysters. You didn't have any, did you?"

"I was too nervous to eat much, but no. Obviously, neither of you ate them either." She glanced back and forth at the two of them

"No. *I* didn't." Her mother covered her mouth.

"What? Spit it out, Mother."

"You know how much your father loves shellfish."

Sutton sank to the edge of the bed. Nausea rose but it was due entirely to nerves and not tainted oysters. "Wyatt had the steak last night, so he should be fine."

"So did Jackson," Willa said.

"Who else is sick?" Sutton looked up at her mother who still had her mouth covered.

"Reverend Mitchell. The organist. The florist. Several others too."

Sutton fell backward and pulled a pillow over her head, not caring if her hair was squished at this point. The pouring rain had been unwelcome but not a surprise after keeping an eye on the front moving through. Finding out half the wedding party had been poisoned at the rehearsal dinner might not qualify as a tragedy, but it was a shock.

"Could I have a minute alone?" She didn't raise the pillow until the door snicked closed.

Without rising, she reached for her phone and called Wyatt. Even though he couldn't fix things, she needed to hear his voice. Straight to voicemail. She tried again. No answer.

No need to panic. He was with Jackson, and no one was more levelheaded than Jackson. Except when he got a wild hair and raced hell-bent for leather around a racetrack. Oh God. She punched his name with a trembling finger.

"Sutton. Great to hear from you." Jackson's voice had an artificial cheeriness.

"Are you with Wyatt? He's not answering his phone."

"Yeah, he's right here. Hang on a second."

Confined, muffled conversation overlay the noise of rain. Even though she wasn't going to see him before walking down the aisle, knowing he was on the way to her beat back the tears that threatened.

"Hey, babe." Wyatt's warm voice was like an enveloping hug.

"God, I'm glad you're okay."

"We're fine. How did you hear?"

"Mother told me."

"Wow. News travels fast."

"So none of you are sick?"

"Sick?" There was a pause on his end. "Let's back up. What are you talking about?"

"The food poisoning."

"Aw, hell. From what?"

"The oysters last night. My dad, the minister, the organist, and no telling who else." Her brain whirred, and she sat up. "Hang on. What were *you* talking about?"

"Dang it, Aunt Hy, slow down. It's not a race." His voice

came over as if he'd dropped the phone from his mouth. Then, he was back. "Sorry, Aunt Hy thinks she can drive the parish roads like Jackson."

"Why is Miss Hyacinth driving you and not Mack? Is he sick?"

"Not sick. We're all fine and crammed into the Crown Vic with Hy and Hazel. I'm getting a sharp elbow from Aunt Hazel right now. Hang on." A pause. "She wants me to tell you how much she's looking forward to the wedding."

"There's not going to be a wedding if we don't have a preacher. And I'm not sure if my father will be well enough to walk me down the aisle." Her tears were back at the thought of canceling.

"Babe. It's Cottonbloom. We have more preachers per capita than any town east of the Mississippi. I'll scare one up even if I have to offer free oil changes for a year. Leave it to me."

As usual, his confidence encompassed her. She couldn't imagine facing life's travails with anyone else. "I love you."

"I love you too."

"Are you going straight to the church?" she asked.

"Yep. Listen. Before I see you, I need to tell you something."

"What? You don't have another wife stored in the attic, do you?" She gave a halfhearted laugh. Willa had insisted she read *Jane Eyre,* and Sutton had since used gothic romances as an escape from the unrelenting details of planning the wedding. A wedding that was falling apart.

When Wyatt didn't join her laughter, she clutched the phone tighter. "You're scaring me, Wyatt. You are coming, aren't you?"

"*Babe.* Of course, I'll be there. It's just I don't want you to freak out when you see me."

"Oh my God, did you wake up with a face tattoo or something? I'm going to kill Mack."

His laughter throttled her panic down to second gear. "No. But the reason we're all stuffed in the Crown Vic with the aunts is because we had a little bit of an accident in Mack's truck. Everyone is fine, but my eye is a little swollen."

"Oh, sweetie. I'm so sorry. I don't care what you look like as long as you're waiting for me at the altar."

"I'll be there. Don't worry. We have time to get it all figured out."

She let out a breath. He was right. They'd figure it out together. "See you soon."

"You know it."

They disconnected. Sutton sat up and readjusted her thinking. Her wedding wasn't going to be perfect, but that wasn't what was important anyway. All that mattered is that at the end of the day, she and Wyatt were together. That's what she'd focus on.

She opened the door and found Willa leaning against the wall while her mother paced the hall. "Wyatt and the boys are on the way to the church. He's going to find a replacement preacher."

"You're not going to cancel?"

"I don't want to cancel, Mother. I don't care if everything isn't perfect, I just want to get married to Wyatt."

Her mother's lips compressed and she nodded. "Then we'll make it happen."

Sutton gave her mother a hug, resting her forehead on her shoulder. Yes, she was a grown woman with her own business and a burgeoning design studio, but having her mother's support and strength behind her meant more than she could put into words.

"Where's Maggie?"

"She's steaming your dress," her mother said.

Sutton headed toward the spare bedroom they were using as a dressing room. Her sensible sister was kneeling and steaming the wrinkles out of the hem of the wedding dress. Her brown hair was in loose curls instead of her usual ponytail. She looked up as Sutton walked in.

Something must have shown on Sutton's face, because Maggie rose and propped her hands on her hips. "I know things seem dire, but we're going to have a good laugh about this someday."

Sutton garbled out a tear-filled laugh. "You think?"

"For sure. You wanted a memorable wedding. This will talked about for decades to come, so *score*. Are you ready to put this gorgeous concoction on your body?"

Sutton and Maggie had grown closer over the last months. Maybe Sutton had softened because of Wyatt or maybe it was a progression of growing up, but doors that had once been closed due to natural sibling rivalry opened, and Sutton couldn't be more grateful to have Maggie in her corner.

Sutton had designed and made her wedding dress and the bridesmaid dresses Maggie and Willa would wear. Her wedding dress had a full skirt and tight bodice with a sweetheart neckline and cap sleeves. It was straight out of a Disney movie.

The bridesmaids' dresses were less traditional and more like cocktail dresses. Willa and Maggie both made excellent models and Sutton designed something they actually could wear again—midnight blue, knee length, and sexy.

The next half hour was spent getting dressed, and their laughter returned a sense of normalcy, even though the rain continued to pound the roof. Sutton kept a picture of Wyatt waiting for her at the front of the church in her mind's eye and her optimism crept out of the cellar.

The ringing of the doorbell and a commotion echoed from the marble entry of the Mize family home and stilled all three of them. A premonition sent Sutton running for the stairs.

All four Abbott brothers in tuxedos and two Abbott aunts in their Sunday best milled around. Wyatt, his back to Sutton, had his head close to her mother in conversation. What else could have possibly gone wrong?

She fisted her skirts and tackled the steps. Her mother saw her first. "Sutton, no! It's bad luck to be seen before the wedding."

"We've already had all the bad luck we can handle, haven't we?"

Everyone quieted and with everyone's gaze upon her, she dropped her skirts and slowed. Wyatt stepped forward.

She gasped and stopped two steps up. All she could manage was a whispered, "Your poor face."

His grin was off-kilter because of the swelling. "I think it gives me a roguish charm, no?"

It looked painful. She brushed her fingertips lightly across his forehead above the cut on along his eyebrow. Her chin wobbled and the tears she'd been holding back all morning finally broke free.

His smile disappeared. He lifted her off the step and carried her into her father's office. "I'm sorry our wedding day hasn't turned out perfect. Because you deserve perfect."

She buried her face in his neck. "I'm not crying because of the rain or the food poisoning. You're hurt."

His arms tightened around her, and she could feel his smile. Sure enough, when she looked up, his smile was so tender, she found herself smiling back.

"This is only one day out of thousands we'll have together. You know that, right?" He wrapped his hand around her nape, and she didn't even care if he messed up her hair. Their photographer was sick anyway.

"I know and I'm grateful I get to spend thousands of more days with you." She leaned in to lay the gentlest of kisses on his mouth. "Not that I'm not glad to see you, but why aren't you at the church?"

A grimace replaced his smile and his gaze streaked off to the side. "Yeah, about the church."

She stepped back. "Did lightning strike it down? Did an earthquake swallow it up? Is this an omen from God?"

"Nothing so dramatic. Apparently, the wind knocked out power sometime last night. They're working on getting it restored, but it might take a couple of hours or more and with no air-conditioning, it's miserable inside."

"That doesn't sound good."

"It gets worse. The food."

The plan had been to move into the church's main hall for the buffet reception. The caterer had the food ready and stored in the industrial-sized fridges in the church kitchen. But, no power meant spoiled food.

"This is like a farce. What are we going to do, Wyatt?"

"I hung a sign on the church."

"What did it say?"

"That the wedding was cancelled."

"It's the only logical thing we can do, right?"

He nodded. He took her hand in his. The wedding was only a formality after all. She was already bound to this man with or without a piece of paper to make it legal. The chatter in the entry hall had gained momentum with Willa and Maggie joining the Abbotts.

Everyone fell silent as Wyatt and Sutton walked up. Wyatt brought theirs hands up and kissed the back of hers before turning to address the group. "Based on everything that's happened, I don't think we have a choice but to cancel."

Hazel exchanged a pointed look with her twin sister and stepped forward. "We've been talking about that and came up with an alternative. If you're interested."

Without letting go of Wyatt, Sutton shuffled forward.

"We're interested, but we don't have a church, a preacher, music, or food."

Hazel adjusted her black patent leather pocketbook on her arm and linked her hands. "I took a few online divinity courses and got ordained along the way."

"Are you telling me you can legally marry us?" Incredulity sailed Wyatt's voice high.

"I can," Hazel said in her usual understated yet indomitable way.

"I can play a rousing wedding march on the piano," Hyacinth said over her sister's shoulder. "Looks like you have one in your living room."

Mack put his arm around Hyacinth's shoulders. "I called Rufus to put him on standby for barbeque with all the fixings."

Jackson looked up from where he was texting. "Landrum can swing by the church and grab the flower arrangements."

Sutton's mother took one of her hands. "What do you want, Sutton? Do you want to get married here today or cancel until the church is available?"

There was no question in her mind. She hadn't wanted a big society wedding anyway. As the daughter of a prominent judge, she'd gone along with her mother's plan because it had made her parents happy. She turned to Wyatt and smiled. "I want to get married here. Today."

"You sure?" As if they were the only two people in the entry, he waited, his fingertips gliding down her cheek.

"More sure than I've ever been. This is all I ever wanted or needed. Us surrounded by our family and friends." She wrapped her hand around his wrist and kissed his palm.

He drew his hand into a fist as if he could catch her kiss and turned to the others. "You heard the lady, the wedding is on!"

The next hour was a whirlwind of activity. Her mother

fielded calls from townspeople. Most people she put off with regrets, but a few Sutton wanted there. Like Bree, her childhood best friend. The healing from her betrayal wasn't complete and their friendship would never be the same, yet Bree would always hold a special place in her memories. Anyway, it was hard to be upset when Bree's actions had led Sutton to Wyatt.

Wyatt's mother and Ella arrived, and Sutton only had time to exchange hugs before Maggie whisked her back upstairs to finish getting ready. A half hour later, a knock sounded and the door cracked open.

"Everyone decent?" Her father's voice was a mere echo of his booming, courtroom tone. Sutton swept the door open. Looking pale but determined, her father smiled and took her hands. "You look beautiful, dear. Then again, you always do."

"Are you sure you're up to walking me down the aisle? You can sit at the front with Mother."

"I wouldn't miss it."

"Are they ready?"

"Ready whenever you ladies are. Maggie, you and Willa look spectacular."

"Thanks, Daddy." Maggie gave her father a kiss on the cheek on her way out the door.

"Thank you, Judge Mize." Willa ducked her head, a blush on her cheeks as she followed Maggie.

"Shall we?" Her father crooked his elbow and Sutton slipped her hand through. At the top of the stairs, the familiar notes of the wedding march started. Much like she approached life, Hyacinth played with gusto and enthusiasm with only a few sour notes.

As they reached the bottom and paused at the entrance of their family living room, her father whispered, "I'm sorry everything wasn't perfect."

A riot of colorful wildflowers filled the room. Someone

had commandeered folding chairs, which were filled with all the most important people in her life, both new and old. Others stood along the sides. Most important, Wyatt waited, his brothers lined up beside him.

She smiled and everyone except Wyatt blurred as tears pricked her eyes. "No. This *is* perfect. Absolutely perfect."

Her father handed her to Wyatt and as if Hazel had performed a marriage ceremony before, she hit every note, her command of the ceremony impressive. The only hiccup came when Hazel recited the traditional vows— love, honor, and obey.

Sutton hesitated, but as usual, Wyatt saved the day. "How about love, honor, and talk out our disagreements until I admit Sutton is always right?"

A few titters and laughs rang out from the crowd. Sutton joined in and said with a smile in her voice, "I promise to love, honor, and talk out disagreements as long as we both shall live."

Hazel smiled and had Wyatt repeat the same. They slipped rings on each other's fingers, hers a simple gold band, his made from trendier black rubber since rings were banned from the shop floor.

Breaking with tradition once their vows were spoken, Hazel leaned in to give them both a kiss on the cheek, tears sparkling in her eyes. "I'm so glad you and Jackson broke the twin curse and with such wonderful women. I'm proud of the men you've become." She glanced toward the wall of Abbotts behind Wyatt. "All of you. Now, you may kiss your bride, Wyatt."

Sutton closed her eyes when their lips met and the world fell away for a few shining moments. Even though she didn't think getting married would make her feel any different, somehow the ritual strengthened their bonds in a tangible way.

Hyacinth played them out to a rousing rendition of

"When the Saints Go Marching In." The next hours were a whirlwind, and Wyatt and Sutton didn't have a chance for a private moment.

Rufus had sent Clayton Preston with enough barbeque and fixings to feed them all. As he set up folding tables to form a makeshift buffet line in the entry way, Sutton's mother sidled next to Sutton.

"Who is that?"

"It's Thaddeus Preston's brother, Clayton," Sutton said. Thaddeus was the Cottonbloom, Mississippi, chief of police and well known to everyone.

"I heard the brother was a convict."

"Clayton did some time, but as far as I know, he's been a model citizen. He's very nice, by the way." And he was, but Sutton could also sense an edge of darkness in him and wondered if he still flirted with danger.

At the moment though, he was in a long-sleeved button-down that covered the tattoos on his arms and a pair of khakis covered by a white apron.

Her mother made a slightly disapproving humming sound but said no more. Sutton turned away, looking for Wyatt. From the corner of her eye, she caught sight of Maggie. Her sister had never looked better with her contacts in and her hair loose and her killer body outlined by her dress.

Yet, she was half-hidden in the shadows of the hall, intently focused on something—or someone. Sutton followed Maggie's stare to Clayton. If there was a list of men Sutton would pair with her sister, Clayton wouldn't even make the top hundred.

Maggie had never had a serious boyfriend, and Clayton was . . . well, a man who projected a life lived beyond his years. Was her sister crushing on the bad boy across the river?

Interrupting her musing, Wyatt grabbed her hand, held

a finger to his lips and guided her up the stairs. Giggling, she pulled him into her room and leaned against the closed door.

"Finally alone, Mrs. Abbott." He advanced on her, any sentimentality stamped out by the distinctly sexual tease in his voice and face.

"Why, Mr. Abbott, whatever are you planning?" She fluttered her hand over her collarbone in faked outrage.

"Something dastardly that will no doubt wrinkle the gorgeous concoction of your wedding dress."

She slipped by him and flopped backward on her twin bed, laughing her head off.